Now all he had for company was the sound of his panting. He told himself he was mad and tried to recall the mental exercises he had been taught to cope with his fear. He began with the multiplication table. At two times thirteen he couldn't go on. The fears were swarming. The sound of mortars filled the air. And the mad faces began to cluster around his head, screaming.

The Trade

WILLIAM H. HALLAHAN

SPHERE BOOKS LIMITED
30-32 Gray's Inn Road, London WC1X 8JL

First published in Great Britain by
Victor Gollancz Ltd 1981
Copyright © by William H. Hallahan 1981
Published by Sphere Books Ltd 1982

Set in Linotron Baskerville

Printed and bound in Great Britain by
Collins, Glasgow

For Janet

PROLOGUE

In April 1945, American and British forces, sweeping across the Rhineland of Germany, reached the Elbe River and waited there while Russian troops, driving from the east, overran and sacked Berlin.

The place of the Allied halt was profoundly significant, for the Elbe River became a principal part of the boundary line between East and West Germany. It was the line of permanent dismemberment of the Third Reich. Today few people believe that the reunification of the German nation will occur in the lifetimes of those now alive. For already the barrier has existed for nearly forty years.

But there are those who dream of removing it forcibly.

1

The heat in the streets was malevolent.

All the military advisers had told Colin Thomas that here in Central America, neither the government troops nor the revolutionists ever commenced shooting before four in the afternoon.

It was only noon, far too early, yet Thomas had ordered all the troops in place, where they crouched in misery, for the sun was directly overhead, and it was difficult to find any cover. The very sidewalks and the street pavings, the walls and the stones of the buildings that the troops hugged were radiating heat like ovens, and the sun was making them hotter every minute.

Thomas stood on the rooftop and felt the sweat run down his face and down his back. A heat breeze, panting, stirred the scaly, scraping leaves of the palms while high in the sky, the vultures circled expectantly. Not a civilian was in sight; no traffic moved: the noncombatants had cleared out. The town pigeons hid in the coolness of the belfries. It was 105 degrees in the shade.

The leader of the government troops, Colonel Mendez – part Spanish, part Indian, part black – looked at the thermometer and then, with doubt, at Thomas.

'Are all the units in position?' Thomas asked.

'Yes.'

'Then it's your show, Colonel Mendez.'

The two of them, from the rooftop of the office building, studied the terrain with their field glasses.

The objective was a collection of half-finished high-rise apartments being built for Galápago's swarming poor. During the night, the rebel Sindicalistas had slipped into

3

the city and occupied the buildings, where they now waited in the cool shade.

The colonel didn't move. 'The sun has made our rifles too hot. My men cannot hold them. And they have no water.'

'That will give them the incentive they need to fight their way into the buildings. There's plenty of water and shade inside.'

'We will wait until four.' Colonel Mendez folded his plump arms and looked exactly like a bountiful Buddha.

'Go,' Thomas said. 'Now.'

Colonel Mendez's flat brown eyes looked into Colin Thomas's pale-blue gringo eyes and attentively read their message. He glanced down once at the pistol in Thomas's hip holster, then turned and made a signal with raised hands showing huge sweat stains at both armpits of his tunic. The signal was received. The attack would begin.

It was ironic that the rebel Sindicalistas had occupied the apartment complex. The Benevolent Leader himself had a great financial interest in those buildings, and he was having an unpleasant task in explaining the huge cracks that had appeared in the walls.

It was murmured in the cafés that the cement had far too much sand, and many doubted that the buildings would stand long enough to be finished. The government leaders had stolen too much cement money for their secret bank accounts; they were behaving like grasping men who expected soon to be out of office – exiled or executed. They waited with their families in the Jockey Club near the airport with their private aircraft for the outcome of the battle.

At fifteen minutes past noon the government troops started the battle with a mortar shell that blew a hole in the side of an apartment three stories up. The boom roared inside the hollow building like a drum, and a great cloud of cement dust roiled across the compound. Government snipers on the burning rooftops and government troops in the side alleys began to pour a thundering hail of fire into the buildings. Other units hurried into the streets and ran toward the complex, shouting wildly. The government's two tanks crawled forward, so sun-hot the tank commanders risked their own safety rather than shut their ports and vents. Behind the tanks crouched parts of several platoons.

All the weeks of Thomas's training program in the jungle north of Galápagos City were now put to the test.

Sixth Platoon quickly cut off Avenue May First at the rear to prevent rebel reinforcements from entering, and, once in position, the Sixth commenced firing a heavy, pounding barrage at the complex. More mortar shells blew holes in the walls, and the hollow buildings reechoed with booms that carried for miles. The concussions made the ground tremble, and cement dust rose in a cloud over the complex.

Seventh and Eighth Platoons reached the walls of the apartment buildings before the first rebel shots were fired. When the rebels began firing back, Thomas detected the sound of Russian Kalashnikov automatic rifles and some old American M-1s. The rebels were also firing rifle grenades down at the doorways and along walls to create blizzards of stone fragments amid the charging troops.

The fire fight increased in ferocity and now the afternoon was filled with screams and cries, shouted orders and earth-shaking noise.

Government snipers on the rooftops kept up a raking fire at the windows of the buildings while the other platoons at street level maintained a covering fire. More government units hurried out of the side streets toward the complex.

The attacking platoons were now mounting the scaffolding outside the buildings in order to clean out the rebels from the top floors down. Many, hit by rifle fire, fell screaming into the streets. Smoke began to flow from a number of fires inside the buildings.

Thomas felt he had only four or five hours to clean out the rebel Sindicalistas, for with darkness the rebels could regroup to plan new strategies. He would then have to bring up enough artillery to pound the buildings to rubble and that could take days or weeks.

The ferocity of the government troops surprised even Thomas, for within two hours it was clear that the rebels were in a bad position and that the midday surprise attack had caught them unprepared. They had occupied the buildings as a staging area – a place to wait out the day's heat. Their laxness had let the government troops get control of the upper floors and of the streets around the buildings. And now outnumbered, outgunned, with no reserves of ammunition, the rebels were cut off from both supplies and reinforcements.

By four o'clock it was all over. The government soldiers draped flags from many windows. Their comrades in the streets waved flags back, cheering.

The water tankers drove into the complex, followed by ambulances and trucks, while the troops were openly shooting prisoners through the head with their pistols. There would be few captives.

The last shots were fired at five.

Thomas found Colonel Mendez and his staff standing in the long shadows of the apartment buildings, smiling and chattering. They awaited the Benevolent Leader. The thought of promotions and decorations and bonuses danced in their eyes.

Thomas and four of his drill instructors walked quietly past them and into the complex. One of the instructors, Masters, had gone to the rear with Sixth Platoon and was now missing. Thomas spoke sharply to a government soldier looting a body, and soon guards were posted in the area.

The walls were badly damaged, full of large holes, covered with pockmarks and streaked by smoke and fire. Several large bloodstains had leaked down the outside walls from windows. No one had been detailed to put out the smoldering fires, and no one paid any attention to them. Everywhere, scattered through the streets, among cement

6

mixers, wheelbarrows and construction tools, lay dead rebels.

On the other side of the complex, behind a burned-out truck on Avenue May First, they found Drill Instructor Masters, shot through the temple. The back of his head had been blown out.

Nearby two sandaled feet stuck out of a doorway and the five men stared at them. Thomas stooped and picked up the rifle – an M-1. The safety had never been taken off. The soldier who had carried it and died without firing it was about eleven years old. As they walked back, the daily five-o'clock breeze began to cool the streets, announcing that it was time for the cantinas and cafés to open. At the Jockey Club by the airport, jubilant government figures and their families could return to their luxurious homes, safe for another six months or a year. The city would return to normal.

A long black limousine approached, its official banner fluttering. The Benevolent Leader emerged in his cream-white uniform and dark sunglasses and hugged his colonel and patted the others. He put his arms around them and made smiling remarks that caused them all to giggle.

'Too bad about these splendid buildings for our suffering poor,' said the Benevolent Leader. 'They are ruined, completely ruined. They will have to be torn down and rebuilt.' His eyes clearly wished for more holes.

He spoke to Thomas softly, away from the others. 'You are truly a great teacher, Mr Thomas. And a great patriot of human freedom. I can hardly believe these are the same troops I turned over to you for training. They are tigers! I am convinced that Excalibur Ltd is the finest arms company in the world and I am preparing testimonials for you and your partner Mr – ah – Gorman. Did you make a body count?' The official newspaper was holding its press run for that tangible evidence of the Leader's invincibility.

'A few more minutes. There are about sixty percent communist Sindicalistas.'

'Good.'

'And about thirty percent Centralistas.'

'Good.'

'And about ten percent children.'

The general removed his sunglasses and gazed intently into Thomas's eyes, seeking even a trace of insolence.

'It is as you say,' Thomas said. 'Your people adore you.'

In Amsterdam, Colin Thomas's business partner, Frank Gorman, sat in a small café and watched the traffic crossing the Blue Bridge in a downpour. The first autumn gale off the North Sea had swept the streets and bridge of pedestrians with a pelting rain, and in the canal the boats all bobbed and reared on their mooring lines. Gorman ordered another cup of coffee and waited patiently

A taxicab crossed the bridge and turned into the square, then drove in a diagonal directly to the coffee shop. The passenger dashed through the rain into the shop.

'Well,' he said, 'what's a little rain when fair-weather friends get together?' He spoke with a Russian accent and he smiled merrily as he shook hands with Gorman.

'How is the travel business, Uri?'

'Marvelous. I am booking groups from all over Europe to visit the socialist paradise of Mother Russia. I am going to get a People's Medal of Achievement if this keeps up. More group tours to Moscow were booked out of my office than in any three other offices in Western Europe.'

Gorman smiled skeptically at him. 'I'm glad for you, Uri. How much repeat business do you get?'

Uri Gregov smiled yet again. 'You are my best repeat business, Frank.'

'How is Dudorov?'

'Ah, you know about that? Everyone knows about that. He's well.'

'I hear he's still weak as a kitten.'

'Well, you know what major surgery is like. He'll coast

for a while. Even asleep in bed, he's the shrewdest agent in the business. Why do you ask about Dudorov?'

'He's your arms specialist.'

'I see. We talk weapons, then? Good. How can I help you?'

Gorman leaned forward and said in a low voice, 'I want the RPG-8.'

'Oh. I see.' Gregov lit a cigarette. 'Hmmmm.'

'Two boxcars.'

'Two!' Gregov sighed. 'You like our little antitank gun, then? Marvelous weapon. One man can carry the whole thing in a small case.' He smiled again. 'You see, we did learn something from the Arab-Israeli war of seventy-three. Two boxcars?'

'Two.'

'The price will be high.'

'How high?'

'The new American assault rifle.'

'Oh, come on, Uri.'

'It's the only thing I'm allowed to accept. What did you have in mind? You must have known I would have to get something exceptional in exchange for the RPG-8. What are you authorized to offer?'

'Any standard items from the US arsenal.'

'Thank you, but there's nothing we need. We are still dining on the loot we got from Vietnam.'

'That stuff is moldy by now, Uri. We have lots of new toys. If we could go back to Vietnam with our new stuff, the outcome would be a lot different. Ask for something.'

'No, I think I'll stick with the new rifle.'

Gorman rubbed his face thoughtfully and looked out at the rain. 'How's the coffee?'

'Excellent. I shall have another.' Gregov waited patiently as he watched Gorman's face.

'Okay, Uri. You've got the rifle.'

'Excellent. It's a pleasure doing business with you. How many can I have?'

'How many do you need, Uri?'

9

'The cash equivalent of the antitank guns.'

'Bullshit We're not scrap iron dealers.'

'Shhhh. I am just a Soviet travel agent.' Uri Gregov smoked and studied Gorman's face, trying to find the price. 'You must want the RPG-8 very badly to put your new toy up for it. I think I'll ask a stiff price. One hundred cases.'

'Are you out of your mind, Uri?'

'I'll throw in a free ten-day all-expense tour of Moscow just for you.'

'And a one-way Aeroflot ticket.'

'Russia is a paradise, Frank. You'll never want to leave it. Do we have a deal?'

'Sixty cases.'

Gregov considered that. He sighed a cloud of cigarette smoke and drank half his coffee. 'Good. I accept. See how nice I can play? Same arrangements? Same signals? Two jet transports each – and only two. Same pickup point in the South Atlantic.'

'Agreed. Will yours be from Interpol?'

'Yes. Best quality.' The Russian looked thoughtfully at Gorman's face. 'I have one more piece of business, something very small.'

'Oh?'

'Yes. Are you ready, Frank? I want to defect to the United States.' He waited while Frank Gorman took a long measuring look at him. He stood up. 'Think about it, Frank.'

Gregov dropped his cigarette in the half cup of coffee and walked away buttoning up his raincoat. In three quick steps he was back in his waiting cab.

Gorman watched the cab diminish in the rain as it hurried back across the Blue Bridge and up Amstelstraat.

He often wondered at the wisdom of these direct swaps. In effect, the United States had just told Moscow that it had a new steel alloy for tanks that take direct shots from the RPG-8 missile. At least that's what tests were expected to show. In a few days, on a secret ordnance range in Texas,

American military ballistics men would be firing RPG-8 missiles at test stand models of a new American tank.

And Moscow had just told the United States that it was very worried about the new US assault rifle. In fact, it was admitting for the first time that it had not yet mastered the technology of turning out machine-stamped barrels like the new assault rifle.

He stood up. He would have to call General Wynet in Washington. Then he smiled: he'd been authorized to give up to 150 cases of the new rifle.

As he skipped and jumped over the puddles to his car, he wondered what the United States would do about Gregov's request to defect. Everyone in Washington would be drafting a dream list of secret information that Gregov would be expected to bring with him. It would take two boxcars to carry all the documents. It was none of his business, of course, a matter for the counterintelligence people in Washington. But it was a shame: he would miss playing at 'I Spy' with Uri Gregov.

In Paris, Bernie Parker stepped in haste from the train onto the Métro platform of the Madeleine station. He couldn't have been mistaken. With just one glimpse he had recognized the man, the boyish innocent face, the curly blond hair and the cherubic blue eyes.

It wasn't just the identifiable features; it was the mocking smirk that he had fixed on Parker. There could be no doubt. It was the same one he had eluded in Cologne. Parker glanced back; he still had three blocks to go before he could escape his homicidal pursuer.

Parker hurried down the platform amid the late-afternoon crowd, along the tiled walls of the Métro and up the stairs through the exit. Flight wasn't his style. Parker was a big, physical man, a brawler and a trained combat veteran. He wanted to turn and slap the insolent smirk off the man's face. But he had a more important errand. He hefted his attaché case and promised himself he would deal with his pursuer on another day.

He quickly started up the stairs to street level, toward streaming sunlight. A glorious autumn day waited at the top of the stairs.

A premonition made Parker turn his head. The man was not ten feet behind him, closing the gap and smirking as though he knew a terrible secret. Parker began to mount the steps two at a time, knocking people aside. He had nearly reached street level when the muffled shot hit him in the middle of the back. As he fell, his attaché case was pulled from his hand. His assailant stepped quickly past him, up the stairs and into a waiting automobile.

He was known as Quist. Just Quist. His smirk had slipped somewhat when he got out of the car still holding Bernie Parker's attaché case. He entered the phone booth by the Paris American Express office near the Printemps department store and placed a call to Cologne. Perplexed, he tugged his lower lip while he waited.

When Quist was a small child, people said he was an angel. He had golden hair, golden skin and a cherubic baby's mouth set between two full pink cheeks surmounted by two singularly beautiful blue eyes. People often stopped his mother on the streets of Stockholm to admire her baby and to congratulate her. All the world loved to pet him. What made him seem particularly angelic was an irresistibly lovely smile he turned on everyone. He was never any bother, his mother said.

But like the sardonic grin nature had given to the fox, Quist's smile was not a mark of affability. It was full of mockery and cunning and as he matured, the smile often turned downward into a cruel smirk as though nature was trying to correct her error. Yet although he was a seasoned enforcer of thirty-two now, his face remained unalterably angelic. It still looked boyish and loving. It inspired immediate trust, which made it exceedingly easy for him to get close to his victims. It also made him irresistible to women. One of his early bedroom conquests said he used his face like a Venus's-flytrap.

12

The connection to Cologne was made and Fritzsche came on the phone at last.

'It's not in his case,' Quist told him.

'Double back,' said Fritzsche. 'Retrace his steps. He was in Paris only a few hours.'

'Maybe he mailed it.'

'No, no. He might have given it to someone but he wouldn't have mailed it. Double back, Quist. I'll send you more people if you need them.'

'That won't be necessary, Mr Fritzsche.' Quist's grin was back when he stepped out of the phone booth. He had realized where Parker had put it. He told the driver, 'Take me to the Pan European Messenger Service over by the Trocadero.'

When Thomas's plane reached Miami from Galápagos late that night, he had already decided to catch the 2 a.m. flight to New York for a morning interconnection to London. In his attaché case was the largest arms order Excalibur Ltd had ever received.

He settled in his seat, removed his shoes and lay back. He was weary: stunned was probably a better word.

In Galápagos as the sun had set, he'd made himself stand in the square amid the rubble of the ruined apartment buildings under the hastily erected lights. And there he watched the stunned couples – husbands and wives – walk along the double row of dead boys, searching the beardless faces, fearful of finding their own. They walked clutching each other, their mouths open in terrible dread, in mute prayer. Then came the sudden stiffening and the shriek of recognition and the collapse. The square was filled with their cries and weeping.

Afterward, during the ride to the Galápagos airport, during the flight to Miami, through the uneaten meal and the too-many scotches, he had been trying to compose a speech that would go with the arms order when he handed it to his partner, Frank Gorman. He wanted to tell Gorman that this time he really meant to leave the arms business.

13

As his mind rehearsed yet again the words he would say to Gorman, he fell into an exhausted sleep.

Several hours later the pilot announced an unscheduled stop at Washington, DC. Thomas shrugged at the news and tried to go back to sleep. Shortly the jet landed at Dulles.

When the door opened up front, three men got on board and stepped down the aisle, watched grumpily by the sleepy passengers. The three stopped by Thomas's seat.

'Mr Thomas?' one asked.

'Yes.'

The man held forth a wallet with his ID. 'May we see you outside?'

Thomas stood and gathered his things and followed the three men off the plane. He glanced unhappily behind him as he heard the door shut.

'Your bags will be held for you in Kennedy,' the man said.

This was going to be more than a brief conversation. He walked with the three men around the edge of the terminal to a parked car. The night was clear and chilly, a shock after the tropical heat of Galápagos.

He heard the jet plane moving back to the flight line as the four of them got into the car. The driver drove very fast toward Washington. It was after 4 a.m. and there was little traffic. Abruptly, before they reached the Leesburg Pike, the driver turned off the dual highway and drove on an undulating, high-crowned back road. Thomas glanced back several times and saw another black limousine driving closely behind.

They were in an evasive pattern, switching from one road to another, moving always and obliquely toward Washington. They made a last left turn, drove under an interstate turnpike and entered a vast parking lot. Before them stood the world's largest office building – the Pentagon – and beyond it, across the glittering Potomac River, stood the Washington Monument, brightly lit.

The limousine drove around to the main entrance on the

14

east side. At the reception desk, the four signed the register for their plastic lapel badges, walked in a tight group down a long corridor to an elevator, rode up several floors, walked along another corridor and stopped at an unmarked door.

Thomas was ushered into the room alone and the door was shut behind him.

It was a secretary's office and reception room, empty, dimly lit, and beyond it was another doorway. Thomas crossed the room to stand on the threshold and looked into a large executive office.

Looking back at him, with his stocking feet up on the desk, was General Claude Wynet. His tie and collar were open, his face showed a day's stubble of beard and he looked tired. Idly, he stretched a rubber band with his two hands.

'Hello, Thomas. Come on in.' He watched Thomas cross to the desk. 'Sit down. I have a frightening tale to tell.'

Thomas shook his head. 'I don't think I want to hear it.'

'That's right. You don't.'

'Let me tell my story first,' Thomas answered.

General Wynet dropped his rubber band with a soured expression on his face. He'd heard this before.

'It wasn't a year ago,' Thomas said, 'that you dropped by for a friendly poker game in London with a frightening tale and conned Frank and me into shipping a load of contraband Russian arms to Africa.'

General Wynet agreed with a nod.

'We're the only people that can pull that off for you, General,' Thomas said. 'So we're big Pentagon heroes for all of maybe two days. But a week after delivery one of our men is down in the Arabian peninsula, and who does he meet but the Pentagon's own arm bender, Wolfe. And what's Wolfe doing? He's telling all the Arabs who will stand still long enough to listen that the Excalibur people are back-alley hucksters who fail to deliver the goods. Liars and cheats he called us.'

General Wynet held up a protesting hand.

'Wait,' Thomas said. 'There's more.'

'I know. You're going to tell me about the Czechoslovakian Interpol arms shipment from Poland to South America and then about your report on the new Russian smart bomb–'

'I was going to tell you about my partner in Amsterdam yesterday sniffing out two carloads of Russian ordnance for you.'

'I know,' General Wynet said. 'I owe you both some big ones. And I promise to put a muzzle on Wolfe. Sit. What I have to tell you makes all this sound very unimportant.'

Thomas began to protest again and Wynet put a finger to his lips. 'Shhhhh.'

Impatiently, Thomas sat down.

Wynet's eyes rested briefly on the scar on Thomas's deeply tanned face that ran from the corner of his eye down his cheek and neck into his shirt collar. After all these years, the redness was gone. The scar was looking old and debonair. Also gone was the callow expression that Wynet remembered from Thomas's early days. In its place Thomas wore another expression: shrewdness. And something beyond shrewdness. It was animal cunning. Thomas had learned how to operate in the half-world of international skulduggery: he had become a dangerous man.

'I just read the decoded report from Galápagos,' Wynet said. 'You did an outstanding job.'

'You could have told me that in a letter.'

Wynet stretched the rubber band in his hands and sighed. For a moment the silence unnerved him. Then he said: 'Bernie Parker's dead.'

Thomas never blinked. Wynet might as well have said that rain is expected.

'It happened in Paris,' Wynet went on. 'He was shot in the back on the Métro steps. One of our people got to him and rode on the ambulance with him but Parker never made it to the hospital.' Wynet ceased talking and watched Thomas's face. There was only a hint of a reaction: the

16

touch of insolence in his gaze had faded. There was also a slight tightness around the mouth.

'Parker said two words before he died, Thomas. Does this mean anything to you?' Wynet held out a foolscap pad. In felt pen was written 'Doomsday Book.' Around the two words, General Wynet had drawn circles, rosettes, geometric figures, daggers and bombs. He had written the word 'Métro' over and over.

Thomas glanced at the pad and handed it back. He shook his head once.

Wynet was clearly disappointed. 'I thought you might know. You were his best friend.'

Thomas shook his head again.

Wynet sighed his frustration. 'Look, Thomas. I've been staring at those words for hours. An old Sunday-school boy like me breaks out in a sweat when he hears the word "Doomsday."'

It was evident, since Thomas and Gorman and Parker had first served in his unit, that Wynet's face had aged. The cheeks had sunken, the furrows on the brow had deepened and the eyes had acquired the staring look of a border guard who'd been too long gazing at the horizon.

Wynet said: 'The West German Defense Department is conducting a large surplus arms auction in Cologne. Am I right?'

Thomas nodded. 'We have a staff attending it.'

'Are you going?'

'I wasn't planning to.'

'Bernie Parker was in Cologne yesterday. He was interviewing people who were flying in for the arms auction, picking up information for his newsletter. Then suddenly, he's a man on the run, all the way to Paris, where he's shot in the back. He has an airline ticket to Washington in his pocket. And his attaché case is missing. We have to know what happened that made him run. We have to know who shot him in the back and why. We have to know about the Doomsday Book. And we have to know all that fast.'

17

'Come on, Claude. I'm a gun seller. Use your own people.'

'I am. All of them. Around the clock.' He spun a finger in the air. It conjured up the frantic world behind closed doors long familiar to Thomas: offices in the Pentagon and elsewhere around the globe crowded with tired men, bells ringing, half-empty mugs of cold coffee, smoldering ash-trays, strained overly controlled voices, endless telephone calls, probing everywhere for a hint, a clue, something to go on. Baffled faces staring at other baffled faces.

'We've done everything short of calling the Russians on the hot line and asking point-blank, "What's a Doomsday Book?"' Wynet dug his knuckles into his red eyes. 'If those bastards are going to pull anything, I want to know it. We want to hit them first!' His brandished fist hung in midair and seemed to embarrass him. He lowered it and lowered his voice. 'Look. It all comes down to Cologne and the arms auction. The answer has to be there. It's our only clue. If this were anyone but Parker I would ignore it.'

'What do you want me to do?'

'Jesus, Thomas, do I have to draw pictures? You were one of the best men I ever had – you and Gorman and Parker. You were a sweetheart team. Look. I can't slip any of our intelligence people in to Cologne. The Germans would raise hell. And the Russians will notice immediately; so will the French and all the others. It would draw a crowd. But I can send you. You're a perfect choice. What's more, you've got some of the best intelligence men in Europe on your sales staff. You could fill that town with your people and no one would notice. It's the biggest arms auction of the year and you're there by invitation of the German Government. Not only that. You knew Parker – you knew his habits, his friends, his hangouts, so you can check out his movements faster than anyone else. And if you make inquiries about him, you're just doing it as his best friend.'

Thomas picked up the foolscap pad and studied the

words again. Doomsday Book. 'What are the Russians doing?'

'Nothing. They haven't moved so much as an extra bullet from point A to point B in months. The border's quiet. Our satellite monitoring shows nothing. There's no troop movements, no talk, no gossip, no rumors.'

Wynet tugged anxiously at his rubber band again. 'Look, Thomas. We've covered everything else. I just want you to investigate that auction. Forget the regular intelligence channels and the diplomatic apparatus. Even the assassin has to be an outsider: he wasn't from the usual ghouls' parade over there. We've checked them all out. The answer's in Cologne and it's in that arms auction.'

Thomas pondered the pad again.

Wynet said: 'Parker was no fool. He was an excellent intelligence man in his day. Hell, you worked with him. And he was damned good at that newsletter. A very calm, gutsy guy – never hysterical. So I have to get really serious when a man like that dies saying words like "Doomsday Book." And so should you.' Wynet shoved a key ring across the desk. 'Those were his. Go find the locks. Find out what he found out. Fast. Okay?'

On the flight to London, Thomas held Parker's key ring in his hand and felt the ache. He knew very well what each key was for. This was for his apartment; he could shut his eyes and picture every detail of it. This was his office key in Cologne, another familiar setting; this his car key (where, he wondered, was the car?); this his mailbox key; and this? This was probably the key to the missing attaché case. Five keys: the remains of a friendship.

For the first time in many months, he felt his dormant claustrophobia stir. Fingers of dread danced up his spine, following the channel of a deep battle scar. The inside of the jet plane became too small, too confining. The walls threatened to smother him. He calmed himself, and the phobia slithered away, back into a dark corner of his mind, to wait. For the claustrophobia was part of his friendship with Parker.

People had called them Wynet's dream team or the whiz kids or the brats, depending on the speaker's viewpoint: Thomas and Parker and Frank Gorman, who later became Thomas's business partner – and one night the three of them went on a patrol together in Vietnam.

There had been a rumor that Chinese troops were secretly mingling with the North Vietnamese and were carrying a new lightweight rifle of enormous firepower. Military intelligence in Saigon had set up a hit-and-run party to investigate and if possible to get one of the new lightweight rifles. Thomas and Gorman and Parker, three lieutenants, each with more than two years' experience in Vietnam, were selected. They were given two interpreters and an army platoon for an escort.

Thomas remembered the lurid sunset. It had turned a small stream into shimmering copper as they walked in the descending dusk. They emerged from a grove of trees to walk along a savannah of tall grass by the edge of the trees. Beside them was a high bank of grass-grown earth.

No one ever figured out how many mortars were involved in the attack. It could have been only a small enemy unit. Two mortar shells went off near Thomas. He felt himself lifted off his feet like a child, the earthen bank burst open and before it closed and collapsed on itself, he was deposited inside the momentary pocket. He was deeply buried, in total darkness, smothering, his mouth and throat filled with mud, his outstretched arms pinioned, his legs immobile. He was unable to shout, unable to expel air or inhale it. The earth was warm and fetid and he knew he was going to die in it and he was terrified, suffocating, every square millimeter of his body packed tightly in the great weight of damp earth. And after that he remembered nothing.

The mortar attack was sharp and short. The troops located the source and began returning fire into a clump of trees. No one else was hurt and, as the platoon moved out after the mortars, the others watched and waited.

Finally, Parker said, 'Tommy? Where the hell did he get to?' Like someone taken by a sudden madness, he seized a piece of broken tree or root, and began to dig furiously into the bank. The rest stood curiously by as he dug. He shouted, 'He's in here, for Christ's sake! He's buried!' And still they stood until he scraped away a great mound of dirt and exposed Thomas's combat boot. Quickly they all set to with branches and gun butts and hands. But the earth seemed determined to claim Thomas, for as they freed him a new fall of dirt collapsed on top of him, burying his rescuers up to their knees.

Parker was like a madman. He shouted curses at them and dug heedlessly, tearing the flesh on his hands and flinging yards of dirt in the air. The second time, after a great tug-of-war, the earth surrendered and they had him out. Parker plucked some of the dirt out of Thomas's mouth with his fingers, then upended him and gave him a great jerking hug. The plug of mud burst from his mouth and Parker spun him around to blow air into his lungs.

Thomas began to breathe at last and they sat him up. One of the interpreters pointed at his back. It was split open from his shoulder to his belt. Parker seized him, hoisted him on his shoulders and carried him two miles at a dogtrot to a medical station. But they had no plasma there and the corpsmen went checking dog tags by flashlight. Parker was found to have the same blood type as Thomas – A negative.

'Lie down, Lieutenant,' said a corpsman. 'You're going to give him some of your blood.'

And for the fourth time within the hour, Bernie Parker had saved Thomas's life.

After the back operation, Thomas was able to lie only on his belly or partially on his left side, his mind drugged, floating above the pain that distantly called to him. The shell fragment had grazed his face, tracing a shallow gash that ran down the right side of his temple and cheek and down his right shoulder. Then like a plough, it opened a deep furrow all the way to his waist. It cut through all the major back muscles and stopped just short of severing his spine. He was micromillimeters away from paralysis and a permanent half-life in a hospital bed.

Three nights later Thomas was struck by his first attack of claustrophobia. He had floated off in a fitful sleep, the ward was in darkness, save for the night lights. As he writhed in discomfort, a pillow moved and softly fell down over his face. He woke, unable to breathe, his mouth and throat filled with mud, suffocating, his limbs pinned again under the great weight of dirt. He had torn the needle from his arm, ripped several stitches in his shoulder and soaked the bed with sweat and blood. His shouting woke the whole ward. A nurse sat with him for hours, holding his hand, promising over and over she would keep the dirt from burying his face again. In his nostrils was the liquorish odor of the fecund tropical earth that had buried him. It haunted him for years.

Military intelligence never did find any Chinese troops with superrifles.

Now as he sat in his airliner seat, smelling anew the humid earth of Vietnam, the claustrophobia slithered around just beyond his consciousness like guilt. For he had never in so many words thanked Parker for saving his life, never said how glad he was of his friendship, never had even indicated that he liked Parker. That was not the way Thomas was brought up.

He came from a Welsh family in New York City, descendants from immigrant miners. He was raised by his grandparents with a daily Bible session under the warning tick of an old wall clock. There was only one virtue: work. All work and no play makes dutiful, dour, humorless Welsh Christians, among whom no feelings were allowed to be shown. Emotionalism was a weakness. Stoicism was the protective leather cover that had been developed against the assaults of life and chance in the murderous mines of Wales.

Weeping was allowed, indeed it was irrepressible among the emotional Welsh, but they were locked-in people and weeping was done behind closed doors alone. In all his life, he'd never heard the words 'I love you' in his home.

And now it was too late to try to thank Parker. He had let his chance slip. Nor was it the first time. His inarticulateness had caused him unhappiness before – with a girl named Martha.

He and Parker had been young and green officers in Washington together when Thomas met her. She was from Connecticut starting a career as a government administrator. Thomas cared for her deeply. How much sleep he lost over her! He'd write lyrical letters and then, feeling absurd, throw them away. He loved to gaze at her beaming face, listened happily to her trilling laugh and yearned to take her to bed. But she was a quiet girl and he wasn't sure that she liked him.

So he worked at being charming, presented himself as the dashing young officer, told her amusing stories that made her laugh, and kept everything light. Humor was his long suit. He was a guaranteed good time on a date. But when he was alone with her, there always came a moment when he felt he should say something to her about his feelings. She would grow silent and watch him. He wanted to tell her how much he liked her amiableness, her sweet face, her merry laugh. He wanted to make passionate love to her and show her the volcano in his mute Welsh heart. Above all, he knew he should tell her he loved her. But he put it off. Instead, he arranged double dates with Parker and avoided the issue.

One night, they went dancing in a foursome, spent the evening tittering over Thomas's anecdotes. Then, on the dance floor, Martha told him she was marrying someone else.

His legs trembled and he danced close so she couldn't see his face.

'I hope you'll be happy,' he said at last.

'Oh, I'm sure I will,' she said. 'It's quite obvious to everyone he's crazy about me.'

Parker and Gorman treated it as a huge joke.

'Down in Texas,' Parker said, 'that's what they call courting too slow.'

'If you can't tell 'em you love 'em,' Gorman said, 'show 'em – in bed.'

In good Welsh style, Thomas hid his pain behind a series of quips that Parker and Gorman laughingly repeated all over Washington. One funny fellow, that Thomas. Shortly later, the dream team went off to Vietnam, where Thomas explored the consolations of the Saigon cribs. Prostitutes need no tender speeches. But humor was no longer Thomas's long suit; he had never gotten over her.

He glanced around the airplane at the passengers. In the darkness, many slept with their reading lights off, dark lumps in shadow; others were talking and drinking, one asleep on his wife's shoulder, a child under a blanket, one arm dangling, two men in shirt-sleeves mirthfully at cards, vacationers and travelers watching a movie. In the festive atmosphere, he felt like an intruder, a griever at a gala, sorrow in a party hat.

Doomsday Book. It wasn't a code term. What was a doomsday book? The Bible? An account of the end of life – all life? Or one life?

And who killed Bernie Parker?

In London, he was going to stop long enough to confer with his partner, Gorman, and to swap his tropical clothes for woollens and pick up two street men: Roland and Brewer. Then on to Germany.

The answer, Wynet had said, was in Cologne.

It was raining at Heathrow Airport when the courier stepped off the early-morning flight from Paris. His attaché case, as usual, was chained to a manacle on his wrist.

Inside the main building, the courier walked the long ramp to customs and passport control and then through the shuffling commuter crowds, past the shops and restaurants.

He followed the car-park signs, walking a path that he'd trod hundreds of times. With his free hand he buttoned his trench coat. In the parking lot he took out a slip of paper listing a license-plate number and a rank-and-file location, then hurried along in the rain, counting the rows of cars. Finding the license plate he wanted, he unlocked the door and got in. Rain rattled on the rooftop.

The courier started the engine and, with the attaché case still chained to his wrist, drove toward the M-4 motorway to make connection with the London Ring Road and the first of his early-morning deliveries.

In the attaché case was a number of envelopes containing bank drafts, bank transfer authorizations, stock certificates, bonds and other commercial papers and financial instruments of various types. Some of them were quite valuable to their owners but there were no negotiable securities, no cash.

As he crossed the A-3 Bath Road Bypass, a car fell in behind him.

The driver of the other car watched the courier curiously. 'He's almost sound asleep, Quist,' the driver said.

From the rear seat, Quist answered in a clear German accent, 'Good. Keep him that way.' He reached under the front seat and drew out a flat wooden case and opened it on his lap.

From its green satin nest he drew out a .38 Ballester Mollina revolver, milled and modified to receive a silencer – a long tubular affair that Quist screwed onto the end of the barrel.

'Too bleeding long,' said the driver. 'Everyone will see it.'

'Not the way I use it,' said Quist. He sat with the weapon in his lap and, looking past the beating windshield wipers, studied the back of the courier's head.

Any motion-picture casting director would have rejected Quist for the role instantly. He looked like a college student with fair hair and guileless blue eyes and a ready charming smile: the young man every woman wants her daughter to bring home from college.

The courier's car entered the M-4 motorway heading east and picked up speed.

'Perfect,' said Quist. 'Push him.'

The driver accelerated smoothly and drew up close behind the courier's car. The courier saw them and picked up his speed. The driver drew closer. The courier increased his speed.

'A little faster,' Quist said and waited as the speed increased.

'Faster,' Quist said again. Finally satisfied, he said to the driver, 'Take him.'

The driver pulled out and accelerated. He drew abreast of the courier car and cut him. When the courier swerved, Quist was ready by the open window. He fired once. The courier's tire burst, the right side of the car sagged and in an instant the vehicle slid on the rain-slick roadway, veered and tumbled. Trailing sparks, it rolled upright and crashed into a retaining wall.

Before his car had stopped, Quist was out and running back. Even from a distance, he could see that the courier's neck had been broken. The attaché case was on the floor, still chained to the dead man's hand.

Quist found the key ring in the courier's coat pocket, calmly selected the right one and opened the case. His nimble fingers searched the envelopes until he found the one he wanted. He slipped it into his coat pocket, locked the attaché case and returned the keys.

Several people came running now, and Quist straightened up. 'Dead,' he said. 'Poor chap.'

He glanced at their fear-filled faces, then walked back to his car and got in. He slipped the envelope out and looked at it again.

The printed legend on the envelope said: For Addressee's Eyes Only. Hand-Deliver. Obtain Receipt. No Reply Required.

It was addressed to Colin Thomas in Chelsea, London. The sender was Bernard Parker. No address.

Quist hastily took out a cigarette lighter and holding the envelope by the corner, watched the flames consume it. 'Drive on,' he said. Pieces of ash sailed through the open window, and at last he dropped the charred paper onto the wet roadway.

He glanced at his watch. Just enough time for breakfast before the return flight to Cologne.

2

When Thomas's flight landed at Heathrow, he shuffled through customs and wearily stooped into a cab. He was eager for sleep.

But the cab encountered a huge jam-up on the M-4 motorway to London and crawled a few feet at a time. All lanes were converging into one. There were a number of police cars parked on the motorway and a tow truck was hoisting a wrecked car. One side and the roof were crumpled and the windshield was crazed. On the door of the car was the legend, 'Pan Europe Bonded Messenger Service.'

'He didn't walk away from that one,' the cab driver said.

Thomas never noticed the soggy wad of paper ash that lay in a puddle on the motorway.

A few minutes later, the cab left the motorway and entered the streets of London. Thomas looked out at the endless sequence of rooming houses and small bed-and-breakfast hotels along Great Western Road to Kensington High Street. London in the rain: clusters of black umbrellas at the bus stops. Great red double-deckers crawling like circus elephants to such destinations as Hammersmith, Stoke Newington and Shepherd's Bush, Camden Town, Golders Green and Highgate. Home.

The London office of Excalibur Ltd never failed to impress Colin Thomas. It was a handsome brick town house of Regency design that stood in a quiet narrow street in Kensington, just off Notting Hill Gate.

When Colin Thomas and Frank Gorman had been in military intelligence, their collective net worth was less than five thousand dollars. Now they had come so far and so fast they owned this imposing building right in the heart of London, as well as two warehouses that sprawled across many acres north of London, crammed to the ceiling with every kind of small arms. It was one of the largest inventories of military equipment in Europe. Gorman boasted that overnight Excalibur could equip five divisions of modern infantry with everything including uniforms and helmets.

This time Thomas had little chance to take note of the building. He dashed from the cab with his head down, through the rain and up the steps and entered. Inside, smartly dressed London secretaries went to and fro amid eighteenth-century antiques and oriental rugs.

Frank Gorman was in his office, seated behind an authentic Hepplewhite desk. He was fashionably attired by the best London tailors, he spoke four languages, he belonged to the right London clubs, but still 'Yankee banker' was written all over him. He had a large dome of a forehead with thinning brown hair and a small purse of a mouth that bespoke several generations of New England banking forebears on both sides of his family.

Gossip in the arms world had summed up Excalibur in a single sentence: Thomas had made it work; Gorman had made it pay. And pay. And pay.

Gorman cried, 'Ah ha!' when he saw Thomas. 'The conquering hero.' He got up and thumped Thomas on the back. 'My God, Tommy, you really overdid it with the tan.

I got a great cable from our esteemed dictator. He states that you are an authentic military genius. And I think we scored some big points in Washington. Here. Sit sit sit.'

'You know about Parker?' Thomas asked.

Gorman nodded. 'We were trying to figure out how to tell you.'

'Wynet did. He yanked me off a plane in the middle of the night. He wants me to go to Cologne.'

'So I gather.' Gorman resisted the impulse to rub his hands together. He smelled a fat fee. 'How many men are you taking?'

'Roland and Brewer.'

'Charlie Brewer? Who do you want killed? Why not pick someone on our staff? There's—'

'Brewer's the man for this job, Frank.'

'Brewer's the man with the knife. I have a long memory.'

'That's why he's the man for the job.'

Gorman said, 'He lives here in London somewhere. Married a widow who owns a pub. He's retired for good, Tommy. You'll never get him to come.'

Thomas stood up. 'We'll see. By the way, here's the Galápagos letter of intent.'

Gorman scanned the list and inhaled softly. 'What a comfort in our old age, Tommy.' He reached into his drawer. 'And here's some light reading for your flight to Cologne. It's the most spectacular catalog we've ever done, don't you think? Four-color photography throughout with a heavy enamel chromecoat cover. From belt buckles to Armageddon.'

He stood up and came around to walk Thomas to the door. 'Doomsday Book. Isn't that a bit melodramatic, Tommy?' In his voice was still that severe, unforgiving tone whenever he spoke of Parker.

'You ever known Parker to exaggerate?' Thomas asked.

'You're right, I suppose.'

Gorman took a long searching look at his partner. His

eyes, shockingly pale now in his dark tan face, were as insolent as ever – pugnacious in fact. Men were often intimidated by Thomas's bold stare. It occurred to Gorman once again that he wouldn't want his partner as an adversary.

'By the way, Tommy, how much are we charging Wynet for saving the world from Doomsday?'

'You'll think of something appropriate, Frank.'

'No doubt,' Gorman said. As he watched Thomas's cab drive off in the rain, he already had a figure in mind. The price for Thomas's services would come high. It never occurred to him that Thomas might fail.

As he got into the cab, Thomas's thin blood and tropical tan shivered against the damp. Or was it anxiety?

Tired as he was, Thomas got a lift looking out at the streets of London. It was his favorite city as well as his home and he was glad to be back. He didn't want to go to Cologne, not for a while anyway; he knew he'd be haunted by memories of Parker there. Rather, he wanted to get off the merry-go-round, relax, go with friends to the theater and to dinner in the West End or talk whole evenings away in his favorite pub in Chelsea, the King's Head.

He had a thirst to prowl around London, go to a boxing match, see a soccer game, watch a horse race, go for walks through Mayfair to Piccadilly, stroll along Cheyne Walk by the Thames – far away from barracks and weapons and dead bodies. The smell of gun oil and sweat followed after him wherever he went.

This was a city he was always comfortable in – even when he was alone. Londoners with their well-bred reserve didn't swarm all over him as people did in America, where aloneness was equated with loneliness. He didn't have to apologize for sitting with a solitary drink in a pub. No Englishman would think of bothering him.

The cab drove down Park Lane, along the eastern edge of Hyde Park, stripped of foliage and sodden in the autumn rain, on to Knightsbridge and down Sloane Street. He watched the pedestrians hurry under their umbrellas and realized anew how cosmopolitan London had become over the years: olive-faced Arabs in flowing white robes, Sikhs in turbans, mahogany West Indians, Texans in ten-gallon hats and the London City man in his bowler and black umbrella.

Thomas's first residence in London was down that street he remembered, just off Sloane near Kings Road, a furnished bed-sitting room where that winter there had never been enough heat, and very little money because they were putting everything back into the business. Threadbare in London – but not for long, for it was in that city that the money had really started rolling in for him and Gorman.

He sensed once more his desperate need for a few hours' sleep as he flipped the pages of the new Excalibur annual catalog of new, used and recycled arms, starting with military uniforms, ceremonial swords and sabers. There were pages of sidearms, small arms, rifles and carbines including old Lee Enfields, Russian Kalashnikovs and US Armalite AR 18s, 5.56 caliber, plus models from Belgium, Japan and Italy. There were stylish four-color photographs of grenades and grenade launchers, radio-controlled anti-tank weapons, both missiles and rockets, and ammunition, also submachine guns, including the lethal-looking English Sterling L2A3 supplied complete with bayonet, bayonet scabbard, magazine and sling, and the US Ingram MAC 11, plus a broad line of machine guns both modern and old – even a World War II German Mauser MG 42.

The photography was stunning, done by one of London's top fashion photographers in dramatic low-key lighting. The models were London's best, lovely young women with golden falls of hair draped over khaki-green tunics. On one page a young tan weightlifter stood stripped to the waist and wearing crossed bandoliers and holding forth a Swiss SIG 530 rifle. Next to him stood a lovely black girl also stripped to the waist, wearing on a golden chain a hand

31

grenade that depended between her breasts. Her flashing eyes smiled at the reader.

Thomas's eyes skimmed past sniper's rifles and mortars, flamethrowers, mines (antipersonnel, antitank, trip wires and accessories), bayonets, knives, mine detectors, periscopes, range finders, passive night observation devices, flares, rockets and radar and finally a cross-reference index. The devil's toy box. Thomas cast it on the seat beside him and rubbed his eyes. How had he ever gotten in so deep?

Thomas had entered the arms trade almost without thinking. It had been obvious for some time that the three-man dream team was soon to break up: Parker was planning to leave the military to start his own arms trade newsletter, Thomas's insolence was getting him in trouble with the chickenshit ways of Washington, and the city reminded him too much of the long-married Martha anyway.

He wanted to get out of Washington, out of intelligence, out of his own skin if he could. Fifty years before, in the tradition of *Beau Geste*, he would have joined the French Foreign Legion and died wrapped in the tricolor in a desert.

Frank Gorman said, 'There's a lot of money in military surplus in Europe.' So seven years before, Thomas and Gorman and Gorman's wife, Emily, had started Excalibur Ltd with a second-hand microbus and practically no capital. They crisscrossed Europe, going from one arms auction to another, buying and selling and building an inventory, often cooking their meals on a camp stove and sleeping in the cheapest pensions. They quickly learned that Frank Gorman was right. There was money in it.

At first it was easy and harmless. They began by dealing in military uniforms to cater to the teen-age fad sweeping Europe's schools and campuses. That led to trading in helmets, mostly vintage, for dormitory decor, and that led to trading in antique small arms and collectors' items, which in turn led to trading in odd lots of rifles.

The trouble was they both were experts in modern ordnance, and they kept running into obvious bargains. So the odd lots of rifles became more dominant in their inventory, the customers changed from college-student outlets to international arms buyers, and their inventory gradually added military pistols, then ammunition, a few mortars, then some flamethrowers, antitank missiles, radar equipment, and at last they were inside the world of modern arms. Now they sold everything including tanks and jet fighters. Within seven years they had two well-stocked arms warehouses. Their four-color catalog was considered one of the best in the business.

Money rolled in, and with it came other things: corruption and violence. They learned to play the game one small step at a time, to make the standard fifteen percent kickback, the double invoice, the gifts and the numbered bank accounts in Switzerland and Liechtenstein, the smuggling on the moonless nights, the use of the influence peddler, finally clandestine business with Washington. And General Wynet. He considered his two boys a great success.

Thomas discovered a gift for military strategy and tactics. He began giving basic training to several small African nations beset by foreign guerrillas with communist backing. He had the satisfaction of helping them survive, and soon his services were in demand. He was now selling not arms but victory. And he never lost a battle – on three continents. He told himself that he was a freedom fighter or some such malarkey. But now there was this self-preening catalog that would sell anything to anybody. Excalibur's affairs included more and more body counts.

Gorman meantime had found his métier. He had a gift for business and he managed Excalibur in London from behind a museum-quality antique desk. He became the City man making his deals over cocktails in exclusive clubs. He learned financing, how to find credit for customers, and soon the business was roaring. He dressed the part, had his own London tailor and custom shoemaker, gave lavish parties with Emily in their London town house, bought an estate in Provence for long weekends with government leaders, power brokers, military figures, the whole roll call of people involved in the arms trade.

They were the perfect team, the tough street man and the elegant boardroom manipulator. But the body counts were increasing.

The cab drove down Sloane Street into Chelsea, where Thomas lived. He had discovered the district along the Thames during a summer vacation from college, and after an hour's stroll through its lanes and alleys, he had dreamed of owning a town house there.

The cab turned on to narrow Kings Road and drove in and out of traffic blocked by double-parked trucks and cars. Even in the rain, Chelsea was irrepressible. Three music students stood under a striped awning and played a stringed trio from Vivaldi to a crowd holding umbrellas. A man in a high black hat made of tin strolled benignly with a sandwich board that said 'Save Chelsea. Fight the Tower Block Builders.' Rain tinkled on his hat brim in syncopation.

Kings Road was filled with shoppers and tourists roaming in and out of boutiques, antique shops, hamburger joints and pubs. A salesman in a pinstripe suit stood under a large red-and-yellow umbrella and offered to sell a pale-blue, chrome-decked Rolls-Royce from a parked flatbed trailer to passersby. Men stared at it with evident love.

'Madame,' the salesman said to a woman in a flowered hat. 'You've earned this vehicle. All it needs is a chauffeur.'

The cab driver leaned out. 'I'll take the job,' he said.

A belly dancer with a bedraggled hair sat on a sopping camel led by a wet Bedouin with an incongruous red beard. The saddle blanket said: 'Tropical Holidays Ltd.'

Even in the rain Chelsea beat the stifling heat of Galápagos.

The cab turned toward the river and drove almost to Cheyne Walk. There at Battersea Bridge in Whistler's Reach, Thomas's eyes studied the colony of houseboats. A brightly painted Thames barge belonging to his friends, the Pennells, looked closed up and naked without its deckful of plants. The couple were probably still in the South of France.

As the cab pulled up in front of his home, Thomas realized anew how good the arms trade had been to him. In addition to the town house, he owned a secluded hillside villa overlooking the harbor of Portofino on the Italian Riviera, and he owned a forty-foot sailing sloop.

There had been long sailing vacations on that sloop with Bernie Parker, roving as far as the Greek islands. There had been many skiing weekends over the years, expensive hunting expeditions and fishing trips as well as a string of great European cities that they played in. All on the great profits of the arms trade. He had only a faint notion of his true income and Frank Gorman kept telling him that just ahead of them lay unbelievable wealth: there are no recessions in the arms trade.

As he paid the cab driver, he noted that Lucia had had the time-darkened front steps sandblasted; the marble looked new. The house was a good arrangement for both of them. Lucia got a free flat in her favorite neighborhood and he had a permanent babysitter for his house during the weeks and months he was away. Together they shared the same unconventional friends. And no strings attached.

He struggled out of the cab, feeling light-headed from the lack of sleep. After his bags had been put in the hallway, Thomas shut the door behind him. The building was quiet. He strolled along the hallway to the kitchen.

Lucia stood smiling at him. 'You're back,' she said happily. 'Yay team.'

'You like it? I bought it on Kings Road. I felt it brought out the real me.'

She turned slowly so he could take in all of the house gown. It was a royal blue and it clung to her full figure, cut very low across the bodice. 'And in case of fire,' she said, buttoning it at the neck. She approached him and kissed him gently. Then put her fingertips on his lips. 'How were the girls in Central America?'

'They send their regards.'

'I'll bet. I'm just brewing some tea.'

'No.'

'How about a back massage?' she asked. 'I'll be right up.'

He dogged his bags up to his living room and dropped them, then, stripping as he went, walked to his bedroom, opened the bed and fell face down. Jet lag: a three-hour nap was what he needed. He heard the rain tapping on the window: the wind had shifted and it was raining harder, a long wet autumn.

Sleep didn't come: Doomsday. Bernie Parker.

He heard her soft step upon the stair, and a moment later she was standing beside the bed, removing her gown. He felt her slip beside him, felt her warm breasts on his back, felt her lips kiss the nape of his neck.

Then she began to massage his back. 'Mmmmm. Tight,' she said. Her strong soft hands worked from the shoulder muscles down the long deep scar on his back. The muscles along the old wound pulled and fluttered as she worked.

'It was bad this time, I can tell,' she said.

He turned to her. 'What do you mean?'

She pushed him back onto his belly. 'You should wear sunglasses. Your eyes show too much. And when they don't, your back tells everything.' Skillful hands found all the tight muscles in his back. 'Stay awake for a few minutes. I want to welcome you home.'

'Bernie Parker's dead.'

He felt her kneading hands pause. 'Ohhh. Dear God. Poor Hilda.' Her eyes filled. 'Oh,' she said again softly. 'Oh.'

When he woke the rain was pelting the window by the bed and someone had spoken to him.

'It's one o'clock,' Lucia said again. 'Arthur Roland telephoned the address of a pub you wanted. It's up in Bloomsbury. He also says he has your airline ticket.' She walked out of the bedroom just barely in control of her tears.

Thomas got up and took a shower. The next step was to get Charlie Brewer. Frank Gorman was doubtful about hiring Brewer. Brewer wasn't cut to everyone's style. Gorman's boardroom manners and Brewer's street toughness didn't mix. They didn't like each other, and Brewer never bothered to hide his feelings. But personal feelings didn't matter, and Gorman knew it. Thomas needed Brewer. There was no one on the Excalibur staff with quite the same credentials.

Actually Charlie Brewer was still something of a mystery man to most people in the arms trade. He had appeared in Europe ten years before, speaking good German, passably good French and demotic Italian. He was working, he said, for Mann out of Zurich.

And that was interesting news, for that old Swiss troll was having problems. In his time, Mann had been one of the top European gun merchants. He'd gone everywhere, buying, selling, negotiating deals right at the client's desk, paying bribes in cash right out of his wallet, and shipping arms orders all over the world from his huge warehouse back in Zurich.

But Mann was getting old. Although he could still hit, he couldn't run anymore. Hypochondria had given him a list of illnesses. So he tried to do it all from Zurich by mail and phone. It didn't work: his competitors' street men who were on the scene beat him out consistently. It's hard to pass money under the table confidentially when you're on the long end of a telephone call that is usually monitored by your client's government.

So Mann became a grosser. He took to supplying the small-time gun hustlers who had no capital or backing of their own. It was a good idea. They're the gypsies of the trade, they go everywhere, they're chronically broke and

37

hungry, and they knock on a lot of doors, so when Mann turned to them he was quickly back in business, using their legs, his capital and his ideas. Soon the gypsies were wandering the world with Mann's catalog, stirring up profitable quarrels, dispensing fear, pushing arms, making the cash register ring.

But they're an improvident lot, and it's a big world with plenty of places to hide in, so without a thought for tomorrow, the gypsies began absconding with Mann's share of the money. If he couldn't make sales calls, he couldn't chase gypsies.

Enter Charlie Brewer: a quiet man, no talker, with an oblong face like a moose under a bald pate, jug ears and absolutely unblinking brown eyes. When he smiled he showed huge teeth like a Jack-o'-lantern. The gossips said he was a former US intelligence man, assigned for five years to the London office, but no two stories agreed on what branch. The CIA was most often mentioned, yet the CIA people in Europe denied him, and it was more likely that he'd been with the State Department, covert activities. All stories agreed he left the US Government under a very dark cloud. There was talk he had killed a man in a London pub with a knife.

No one knew what his specialty had been. They soon found out.

Brewer was seen everywhere – Hong Kong, Cape Town, Buenos Aires, San Francisco, New Delhi, a cat after the mice. As a result, some of the gypsies voluntarily quit the trade; others wouldn't talk but it was obvious that even the toughest of them were afraid – some were terrified – of Brewer. Some disappeared permanently. There seemed to be no hiding-place in the world that Brewer couldn't find. And soon Mann's money was flowing back to Zurich again. All of it.

Zurich was a good arrangement for Brewer until the old man died. And then Brewer retired to keep a public house in Bloomsbury up behind the university. The gossips said he really didn't need to work behind the bar, that his bounty-hunting fees had made him rich; and, of course, wasn't it strange that he, being an American, chose to settle in London? It suggested bad blood between him and his government. Exile may have been a penalty visited on him.

His wife was said to be built like a dumpling – a soft ample woman with good coloring and very shrewd dish-blue eyes and, behind the bar, a generous hand with the malt; a bed warmer, a helpmate and a one-man woman. But then Brewer would pick one like that. She could be as closemouthed as he.

Roland said that Brewer was retired and wasn't available, but Thomas frowned at that. He suspected he had a tough sale ahead of him, especially with a wife holding tight to the coattail. But when you're dealing with men who backshoot people like Parker on the steps of a Métro in broad daylight, you need a Brewer in your corner.

Thomas wondered if he was going to get him.

Charlie Brewer was working behind the bar himself. It was just after one in the afternoon and he looked around his pub to check the patrons' pints, then at the collection of dirty glasses by the sink. The little bastard hadn't come in yet.

He leaned over the end of the bar and looked down the rainy street to the green door by the grocery store. He straightened up. It was the same elderly crowd: the retired men of the neighborhood, slow beer drinkers the lot of them. When they talked they leaned close to each other and crooned stories of the old days into each other's closely held ears – the old days in the London neighborhood before Hitler's bombs blew it away.

At any minute, there would be the usual quarrel, a spilled pint, an upset chair, a slammed door: the tranquillity of old age.

He decided he'd best do some of the dirty glasses. He rolled up his sleeves and his two singularly hairy forearms reached into the tub of strong scalding disinfectant, screwing each glass up and down on the mounted brush.

Brewer looked at the burned-out old men and felt time closing in on him. He longed for another go while the legs and spirit were still prime. His stepson hurried through the rain, across the street and into the pub. Walking across the room to the basement door, he descended with barely a nod of greeting. Thirty-one days' truancy. After all the talk.

It was no use.

Words never moved anyone. Not in the history of the whole world. Adolescence was invincible. It was like a raging tropical fever, with no known cure, that had to burn itself out. The patient was either killed or cured by the terrible heat. Brewer felt in his impotent fury that if he didn't get away from the slack-mouthed, slobbering, heedless boy, he would soon kill him. In his guts stirred the longing for just one more adventure. One more go at the forces of darkness.

It wasn't far from the three-o'clock closing when a cab pulled up at the door. Brewer and his wife were working the bar together, with George earning his free grog by carrying the empty glasses from the tables to the dumb-waiter where they were lowered to the boy at the tubs in the basement.

The pub door opened. Brewer would have recognized the face anywhere. It stuck out like a lamp. Maybe it was the expression of confidence that set it off. Brewer watched him step up to the bar and put his arms on the mahogany. The same ready, quick hands. The smell of adventure rolled from him. Africa: two years ago.

Brewer smiled. His prayer had been answered. And he held forth his hand. 'Well, Thomas, ducks, you're a sight.'

Thomas smiled and shook his hand firmly. 'You look like you were born back there, Charlie.' He nodded affably to Mrs Brewer. 'Good evening.'

There was a glint of recognition in her eye. She nodded coldly to him.

'Well, we have some talking to do,' Brewer said. 'You still a bourbon man?'

'Fine.' Thomas watched Brewer's wife go upstairs.

'I lost track of you after Africa,' Brewer said.

Thomas nodded. 'I was in South America.'

Brewer studied him. Thomas was the born wanderer. Barracksroom bachelor. About thirty-four. Maybe thirty-six. Stayed in shape. He'd filled out. Looked bigger than a stevedore. Bulging shoulder muscles and heavy arms that filled the coat sleeves. The eyes were shrewder – tougher. But there was a flush in the cheek – an adolescent quality. Romanticism was it? And something else in the expression. Something Brewer didn't like. 'Looks like you do the drill every morning,' he said.

'How are you doing here, Charlie?'

Brewer glanced up the staircase behind the bar, then softly shut the door. 'What did you have in mind?'

'You look set up here. Pretty good.'

'Oh, it's grand. Practically runs itself. Something for my old age. What did you have in mind?'

'You ready for a little action?'

'Sure. Where?'

'How's your German?'

'I don't get boiled socks for an entrée if that's what you mean. This have anything to do with Parker?'

Thomas nodded. He wondered what all the gypsies in Cologne were going to do when Brewer walked in the door. Those cold hard points of light in Brewer's brown eyes hadn't mellowed one bit.

Brewer winced as a glass shattered in the cellar. 'Easy! Easy!' he called down the dumbwaiter shaft. Then he leaned back on the bar. 'When do we leave?'

'Tonight.' Thomas pushed an airline envelope across the bar at him. 'You still have friends on the Paris police?'

'Yes. You want to know about Parker?' Brewer looked at his ticket. Paris and Cologne. 'You were pretty sure of me, weren't you?'

Later, at closing time, Brewer's wife came back down. 'What did he want?' she asked.

'A chat.'

'He wanted more than a chat. I know a wild goose when I see one. He's a hard case, Brewer.'

'He's the very best at what he does.'

'And I know what that is. He has a haunted face. All your friends have the same look.' She watched him wipe the bar. 'When do you leave?'

Down in the basement, the boy shattered another glass.

Thomas had one more errand to do before he left for Cologne, one he was driven to by the pain in his back. Lying facedown on the examining table, he felt fatigue claiming him. If his back hadn't hurt so much, he could have slept. The doctor had cold, hard, almost flinty hands and when he placed the flat palms on Thomas's back, the chill made his muscles bunch.

'Relax.'

'I am.'

'That's not what I call it.' The doctor pulled the door open. 'Miss Guest.'

The nurse entered the examining room. 'See if you can loosen those muscles up so I can examine him.' He walked briskly out of the room.

Miss Guest, a hearty, flush-faced woman in a white nurse's uniform, approached the table and put her hands on his back. They were soft and warm and knowing. 'Lord love a duck. It's a bunch of sailor's knots for fair, isn't it? What have you been up to?'

'Living.'

'Well, love, turn the volume down. Otherwise, you'll ruin your back, won't you?'

She gripped him first by the two trapezius muscles that descended from the back of his neck across his shoulders. He felt the heels of her hands press and lighten then press again as she put her weight on her bent arms. 'My. Pure concrete.' Under her gentle firm hands his neck began to relax. The muscles relented.

Then her hands descended to the muscle on his right

42

side, down along the channel of the wound, pressing the scar tissue, forcing the muscle to stretch and relax.

'Marry me,' he murmured. 'I will give you all my wordly goods.'

'Will you now? No thank you, dearie. I just got rid of an idiot and I'm off men for a while. At least they're off me, I mean. I can really pick the losers, can't I?' She pressed harder. 'There it is.' He felt the muscle down along his side above the hip bone tremble and writhe. Then it knotted. Hard. Then harder. She got both hands on it and firmly, patiently, forced it to give, to stretch. 'Dear God,' she said. 'That's a British Navy knot and two half hitches.'

The muscle relented at last and stretched. His whole back relaxed, and he felt now the terrible fatigue that was in them.

'What was that?'

'It's called the gluteus medius,' the nurse said, 'and it's right at the end of your wound. You don't give it any sympathy at all, I mean, do you?' Her hands began to work back up to his neck again and he felt his eyelids getting heavy.

'I need you just to walk behind me and keep that up all day.'

'You're just going to tighten up again. You have to change whatever you're doing. You know you lost a lot of muscle tissue in the wound – mainly right here – feel it? Those are the rib muscles. That bomb just chewed up miles of it. Feel that? You were an eyelash away from a permanent basket. It's a miracle. Really. You know what you have to do?'

'What?' Thomas asked.

'Give your back a break.' She slapped a flat hand on his buttock. 'And do your exercises.' She walked out of the room.

He lay there watching the dabs of rain trickle down the pane and feeling the back muscles tingle and complain of fatigue. The doctor returned and put his cold, hard hands on the wound. Nimbly they worked downward. He took

43

Thomas's right arm and moved it up and down, probing the back muscle while he did so.

'Up,' he said. 'Over here.'

Thomas arose and went over to the freestanding chromium frame. 'Lift.' Thomas gripped the overhead bar and easily lifted his chin up level with his hands. The examination continued: he squeezed two handles on springs and watched the tension indicator record his hand strength. He lifted a weight on a pulley resting on his upper back. He made lateral pulls with his arms as the doctor made notes.

The doctor waited until he was dressed. 'Well. Physically your back's the same. Those exercises have put you in superb condition. Muscle strength and movement are excellent. You're as strong as a gorilla. The other back muscles have compensated very well. Your back should last you for the rest of your life – so long as you keep up the exercises. Now, I have a solemn warning for you. You can't endure that muscle stress much longer. Some of those muscles are in trouble right now. They're suffering from extreme fatigue. They're going to begin to give and fail, and the other muscles are going to pull your spine out of line and you can end up in a wheelchair or worse.'

'I've been doing the exercises regularly,' Thomas said.

'The problem's not in your back. It's in your head. There's a war going on inside there and your back can't take much more of it. Anyway, that's not my department. End the war or see a psychiatrist.'

Charlie Brewer eagerly left his pub that evening to catch the night flight to Paris but at Heathrow had a disconcerting experience: he saw a man who looked just like his father.

The man was struggling with a valise and stumbling toward the concourse to the Underground, drunk, staring popeyed at the ground and blowing breath through puffed cheeks. He even walked like his father in a large ruined body with bulking shoulders and thick neck. Seeing a

44

lookalike for his father was the black cat across the path for Brewer. He considered it the gravest bad luck.

Brewer boarded his plane reluctantly now, for the experience had aggravated his dread of flying. He ordered a stiff drink and tried to put it all out of his mind. But the resemblance had been too great – a twin in fact.

He sat back and thought about Paris. It would be good to be back in harness. The pub was safe, a snug harbor, he had some pennies put by and he should have been content. But he missed the trade and there was still a lot of go and shove in him yet.

He considered the assignment ahead of him. Thomas didn't have a hell of a lot to go on. But it was just the kind of job Brewer loved, what he'd been trained for in that secret camp in West Virginia. Cat after the mouse. Finding the lie-low sheepies. And he liked the time element. Right under the gun.

'How about if I freshen that up?' asked the steward, and he handed Brewer another small bottle of scotch and put another ice cube in his plastic glass. 'Water?'

'No. Just ice.'

Brewer relented and let himself remember. When he was fourteen, his mother had gotten him to make a birthday present for his father. It was a wooden stand to hold a shaving brush and he made it in the shop class in school. He made it reluctantly for he was afraid of his father, a large angry man, an inarticulate table pounder who became dangerous when he drank.

His father arrived home full of free birthday drinks and in an embarrassed rage smashed the brush holder with one blow. The present seemed to terrify him, and he went after Brewer with both hands, in the process battering his wife, who tried to protect the boy.

Brewer suffered a severely sprained left shoulder and a cracked wristbone. He waited on the stair landing outside the apartment door until he heard the long adenoidal snoring of drunkenness, the signal that it was safe to go to bed. His mother was having coffee with a neighbor: he could hear her weeping through the neighbor's apartment door. Mostly in later years he would remember his mother's tears – weeping as she tried to staunch the blood from her nose or weeping as she held an ice pack to a swollen bleeding eye and cheek. Love: she'd paid too high a price for it.

He didn't go to bed. Instead, concealing the terrible pain in his shoulder and wrist, he led his mother to a cousin's house two subway stops away and then returned to the apartment.

He found the metal trivet in the drawer by the sink, put it on the gas burner until it glowed red, and then with a pair of pliers carried it to his father's bed and placed it on the middle of his sleeping back. Holding his pain-filled arm, eagerly storing away in his memory the screams of agony and rage that reached his ears, he hurried down the stairs and through the dark streets.

Later he took a job that even the ghetto blacks wouldn't do: he swung a sledge for a cement company, breaking up old concrete with a five-pound hammer. One summer evening, he saw his father unconscious drunk in a bar. He went up to the table and lifted his father's head by the hair and looked at the besotted destroyed face, studied it like Hamlet holding Yorick's skull, then let it drop on to the powerful folded arms. One day, they'd meet.

In two years he grew four inches and put on thirty-five pounds. He worked off his fury with the hammer, still hating himself for opening up to his father like that. Other men avoided him. He grew calluses around his palms and his heart. He never quite trusted his emotions again. His one dream was revenge. One day, he learned that his father had taken the funds from his struggling construction business and absconded. Brewer was bitter: he felt cheated.

He found himself ever afterward watching the faces of men on the street. If he saw a man who resembled his father, he hurried to catch up. He never passed a saloon without looking in. When he went to intelligence school, he

46

gladly specialized in finding missing people, defectors, absconders, runaways. He'd learn how to find his father. As time passed, he wasn't sure why: to beat him or befriend him. That thought infuriated him, befriending the nightmare of his childhood.

It annoyed him now at forty-three that he was still looking at faces, even though his father had died in the emergency ward of the hospital in San Francisco years ago.

Brewer had no friends and liked it that way. It never occurred to him that he was lonely; he had little to say anyway and the long silences between drinks seemed to disturb his drinking companions. His first marriage was a disaster. Amalie was a different situation. One day behind the bar he slapped her rump. The impulse surprised him and it pleased her. He found her in his arms purring like a kitten. And that surprised him even more; behind her reserved, humorless demeanor she liked him and showed it for a moment although an hour later it was forgotten. He didn't know what to do about that. He liked her too but he was smart enough not to show it: love was a trap.

Brewer rarely had the experience of idle conversation on an airline flight. He just didn't look receptive to small talk. His heavy-limbed body looked too pugnacious: the bull neck, a result of his adolescent years with the sledge, too hostile. Thick black hair curled out from under his shirt-sleeve cuffs and stuck out in tufts from his collar. He was bald with a coal-black fringe and showed strong yellow teeth when he smiled, which he hardly ever did. He exuded an animal strength and vitality and looked at everyone with unblinking unsympathetic eyes.

His mind was never off duty. It had no reverie, no daydreams. It was constantly conscious and it saw everything. Relentlessly it read other people's hearts, searching out their secrets. And he had total recall. Brewer said he never dreamed, and it was probably true that his conscious mind never ventured into the dark places of his memory, not even in sleep.

47

An additional reason he had no small talk on this flight was his seat companion. He recognized the man instantly even after ten years and knew in turn he'd been recognized: one of Mann's gypsies that he'd chased to Jamaica. Dumb. Incompetent. Arrogant. Brewer remembered every single detail of the chase, what was said, what clothes the man wore. He was a small-potatoes gun trader always scratching for a score, an unimaginative thief, one of the many jackals that scrounged around the edges of the arms trade. All bound for Cologne. The man pretended to go to sleep.

Brewer sat patiently awake, waiting for the flight to end.

Osip Pavlovich Dudorov, the Soviet's KGB station chief in Amsterdam, got word of Parker's death from his intelligence counterpart, Guzenko, KGB station chief in Paris. The message came by teletype within an hour of the murder.

The moment he saw it, Dudorov summoned Gregov, then waited impatiently. Gregov had been irritating Dudorov for weeks. He was spending more time playing with that silly Russian travel agency they used as a front than he was on his intelligence assignments.

When Gregov arrived, Dudorov said, 'Get the bound file of Parker's newsletter and meet me in the computer room.'

Dudorov went down the old wooden stairs very slowly. He was feeling tired, weary to the bone. He admitted to himself he was getting old. The recent surgery had taken all the vinegar out of him. And he didn't think the doctors had told him everything. He suspected that he was dying. After forty-five years on duty. He had started during the terrible days of Beria in the old NKVD in 1939 and lived through the horrors of the German invasion, survived the repeated purges by Stalin, including the Jewish Doctors' Plot, and the de-Stalinification days under Khrushchev. He had survived everything but time. And the reason he was still alive and kicking: he had built his entire career on one thing: gathering more high-grade information than any other intelligence officer in the European sector. Even now, sick as he was, he ran a larger pack of illegals than any other KGB station on the continent – many of them buried so deeply inside European installations, including NATO, that no one would ever dig them out. And from those illegals, information flowed back to Russia in a torrent.

Dudorov knew he was vulnerable. After his surgery in Moscow he spent several weeks at the Lubyanka Center on Dzerzhinsky Street and realized that death, retirement, transfers, failure, disgrace and attrition had robbed him of all his good contacts. Worse, the new faces were almost beardless. Stalin and the old days were medieval history to these young middle-class brats. Everyone was dead and gone except his old adversary in German intelligence, Otto Dorten.

That was the only reason why Dudorov bothered about the Parker murder. Parker had been based in Cologne and that was Otto Dorten's territory. But even Dorten was sick now and out of the way. However, you never knew. When it came to Dorten, Dudorov always checked everything twice.

Gregov brought the binder of newsletters to the computer room. Beyond the painted window, he could hear the soft purr of an Amsterdam tourist boat cruising along the canal, hermetically sealed under an all-weather glass dome, and knew the guide was saying to the staring faces: 'And that building houses the Russian agency responsible for all European travel tours to the Soviet Union.' Gregov smiled to himself. The travel business to Russia was very slow.

He watched old Dudorov punch his coded call letters on the computer keyboard to authorize transmission. It had taken Gregov nearly a year of close observation to finally figure out Dudorov's computer code number. And someday, well, one never knew.

The two men watched as the computer screen displayed

the summary of Parker's biography. First came the file numbers, then the related file numbers, the computer access code and then data itself on Parker:

Parker, Bernard D.: US citizen, age 34, born in Springtime, Missouri. Six feet, four inches, 232 pounds. Mole on left side of neck, star-shaped scar left wrist. Education: University of Virginia, George Mason Campus, BA degree in political science and philosophy.

BG: Four years United States Army intelligence, Washington DC, Paris, France, Brussels, Vietnam. Seven years: Founder and Publisher, Parker's Arms World Newsletter, Cologne. Federal Republic of Germany. Subject: World Arms Trade. Parker believed to be still closely connected with USAI. Complete set of fingerprints and ID photo on file. Detailed biography available. Signal for transmission. Cross reference (see alpha numerical file directory for designated file numbers): Thomas, Colin; Gorman, Frank; Excalibur Ltd, London, England; Wynet, Claude, General USIA. Also refer: KGB and GRU USAI EOM Reports Washington DC for years 1971-74. See also media data file, ref., European Publications, Political and Economic, for circulation and editorial summary of Parker's Arms World Newsletter.

Dudorov turned off the display screen. 'Just a hunch,' he said to Gregov. 'I always watch for connections with Otto Dorten. Listen, ask Paris for more details on Parker's death. See if they've found out who killed him and why.' He looked up at Gregov thoughtfully. 'Soon enough, you'll be back home in Russia. Away from your cranky old Bolshevik boss.' He walked off with the bound file of Parker's newsletter under his arm.

Back home in Russia: Gregov suppressed a shudder. What was taking Gorman so long? Days counted now. If Washington didn't move fast, his chance would pass. He returned to his desk filled with dread.

3

Thomas woke late the next morning and lay with bright sunlight falling across his bed as he struggled to remember where he was.

It was Sunday; he was in the Hotel Central in Cologne, and as if in confirmation, he heard the snort of a barge horn on the Rhine. Then the sadness returned when he recalled Bernie Parker's death.

Thomas looked from his hotel window out over the Cologne skyline dominated by the largest Gothic cathedral in northern Europe with twin spires well over five hundred feet high. Below, his eye picked out the two main shopping and business streets – Hohe Strasse and Schildegasse – lined with shops and crowded with banking and insurance offices. He'd walked many times with Parker down there.

Parker had settled in Cologne with his newsletter because, for one thing, he felt it was the geographic center of Europe. Berlin was only 295 air miles away; Paris 250 air miles, Brussels 150 miles, London 325, Rome, 750. Bonn, the West German capital, was only 21 miles upriver. It was also a short flight to his favorite Alps ski resort.

And Cologne was a crossroads city, a major north – south and east – west rail junction and the major terminus on the Rhine for traffic coming upriver from Rotterdam and the North Sea.

Moreover, Cologne was Parker's kind of city. It was centuries old and yet brand-new, much of it having been rebuilt after the 250 Allied air raids of 1944, a combination of new wide streets and old twisting cobbled lanes. Everything Parker wanted was packed into the city's old section between the sweeping bend of the Rhine and the

Ring Road that followed the course that once the old Roman wall had made. Excellent German restaurants were there, and a number of first-rate hotels. Down the street was the new opera house, where he went often, and his favorite cafés where he would sit with Hilda and his friends and drink chilled Riesling wine and eat black bread with butter.

The river had its lure. He was a river man himself, from Springtime, Missouri, on the banks of the Mississippi, and he often dragged Thomas to the spacious promenades of the city to look out on the river traffic. From dawn to dusk, the river was never empty. 'Busier than the Mississippi,' Parker said. And he would stand fascinated as he watched the low-slung freighters, the towed barges and riverboats by the dozen. With his love of cataloging, he would call off the products carried on the Rhine. 'Grain and coal and ore and wine, porcelain, drugs, leather, dyes, chocolate, Eau de Cologne, steel, chemicals, electric generators, automobiles, railroad cars, machinery – and hordes of tourists.'

But Parker had selected Cologne to live and work in for a far more important reason. Cologne was one of the principal espionage centers of the Continent, a never-ending source of information on arms and munitions – abundant newsletter material.

Thoughtfully Thomas gazed at the streets. Everywhere he went down there, he would encounter memories of Parker.

Awake now, Thomas remembered: he knew where to find the Doomsday Book. All he needed was a rented car to go and get it.

Eight years before, Parker had begun collecting news on the arms trade. Soon he was subscribing to over forty publications – business and financial and also trade magazines, in four languages. His apartment began to overflow with cartons of manila files, and he couldn't manage all the information that was pouring through his mailbox. Obsessed, he rented a cheap office up near the

Sacré-Coeur and hired a librarian-researcher to help him.

Parker found collusion, corruption, bribery, sellouts, national betrayals everywhere; his first success was the documenting of a conspiracy to sell an unwitting African nation arms it didn't need for money that it should have spent on food and social services. After the sale, the country had its first famine.

Soon Parker began to receive phone calls from other intelligence men, other intelligence services. Mounting pressure for more information led him to issue a monthly summary of arms auctions, large munitions sales, illegal arms movements, undercover intercorporate deals and events like the African famine.

The demand for his report was almost overwhelming. Since his costs were taking a large bite out of his personal income he now charged a subscription fee. The money came in, the demand for more information rose and almost by popular demand Parker was out of military intelligence and into newsletter editing.

Four months before, when Thomas had last visited Parker's offices, the flow of information had grown to such a point that Bernie Parker had three full-time researchers processing it. And file space had become so tight he had two full-time photographers putting everything on microfilm. The newsletter was now the scourge of the arms field.

Parker had dossiers on everyone, on all the executives in all the munitions firms, on all the ex-military men who had gone to work for those companies, on the major figures in the defense departments of most arms-buying countries, on the smugglers and the influence peddlers and their contacts.

Lastly, Parker had created a network of informers. Many were prime contacts in high places, friends and former colleagues. Many others were information sellers who charged fees for what they picked up in their travels. Parker was constantly meeting people in hotel rooms, in back bar rooms, in cars in parking lots, in men's rooms in train stations and airports. He had become a one-man free-lance intelligence system, the first person to report to the world regularly on the awful events occurring in the arms race.

He now charged $100 a year for a subscription, and he had many thousand subscribers. Each year his files grew fatter; each year his income grew higher; each year his list of enemies grew greater. Thomas wondered who would be insane enough to want to succeed Parker in that lucrative, short-term career. For Parker had led a dangerous life. He'd dissected the most dangerous and secretive trade in the world.

Arms traders hate publicity and so do their customers: nations secretly arming against their neighbors; officials paying and taking bribes; bagmen making standard 15 percent kickbacks under the table; dealers smuggling weapons over sealed borders; government ministers tucking packages of money into Liechtenstein bank accounts – the whole business was a sewer rats' paradise where light was anathema. And Parker had brought light.

As he got out of his rented car and stood before the building that housed the newsletter, Thomas was aware that he was the only intelligence man around who knew how Parker's filing system worked. More important, he was the only one who knew how Parker's mind worked: he had understood instantly that Parker's dying words referred to a folder in his file.

Thomas glanced up at Parker's office windows that reflected the afternoon sunlight. Up there in the files, there would be a folder waiting for him titled Doomsday Book. In a few minutes he would have the answer to the riddle.

As he expected, one of the keys on Parker's ring fit the office door. But when Thomas pushed the door, it opened only a few inches. Something was pressing against it. Thomas pushed a little harder and the door grudgingly opened a few more inches. But the resistance increased.

Somewhat blinded by the brilliant sunlight, his eyes at first were bewildered by the sight: the entire office floor was covered with paper confetti at least a foot deep. He stared at length at it, wondering who would have carried such a quantity of confetti up the stairs to dump all over the floor. It could hardly have been a practical joke.

Then he saw the paper shredder and understood. It was an electrically operated contraption standing on the secretary's desk, common enough in every government office where confidential papers were processed. Everything thrown into the wastebasket had to pass first through the shredder. He stooped down and seized a handful of confetti, bits of every kind of paper, bits of cardboard, and bits of cellophane, dark like negative film. The confetti was shocking, out of place, giving the office an ominously festive appearance.

Thomas stepped up on a desk and jumped down into a doorway leading to the file room. This room was also a foot deep in confetti and on a researcher's desk there was another paper shredder. On the walls, left and right, were banks of file cabinets. By the windows were several desktop microfilm projectors.

All the file drawers were standing open. On the top of them the narrow drawers of the smaller microfilm cases were also standing open. Every piece of paper in the files, every memo, every magazine clipping, every newspaper clipping – everything, including the manila file folders themselves, had been shredded. And along with them, every last inch of microfilm, too, had been shredded. It must have taken several days of steady work by both machines to do it. But they'd done their work: Parker's gold mine – seven years of grinding labor – was irretrievably destroyed. The furtive tracks of the arms trade had been covered over once more.

It took Thomas a few moments of standing in the midst of the vandalism to recover. What he was looking at wasn't an act of rage, a deliberate smashing of things. It was a calm hours-long labor to destroy information. He had been right: in those millions and millions of bits of paper and film was the information that Parker wanted him to have, the explanation of the Doomsday Book. Parker's files had been as deliberately erased as his life had been, and Thomas suspected that without those files, his quest was hopeless.

While he stood there ankle-deep in confetti, a man with binoculars and an instant camera with a telephoto lens watched him from a darkened office across the street. And when Thomas left, the man drank some cold coffee from a cardboard container while studying the pictures of Thomas he had taken. A few moments later he, too, appeared down in the street where he got into his car and drove off.

The photographer's route took him southeast of Cologne, along the Rhine River on the A-7 motorway past Bonn and into the rolling wine country of the Moselle region. He reluctantly reduced his speed after he entered a long twisting country road; then as he approached his destination, he slowed even more.

Cars were parked on both sides of the narrow road and he searched among them for a place to leave his car. At last, patience spent, he drove up under some trees, parked and set off on foot, still hurrying. The photographer walked nearly a mile before he turned off on to a rutted lane. Cars here were parked everywhere, anyhow, all over the perimeter of a small airfield.

He was in the midst of a Sunday air show. Many private planes had been flown in and were stowed around an old hangar as close as fighters on a carrier deck. Every available square foot of space was occupied. Down along the flight line, a dozen air force jet trainers, flown in for the arms auction, were being inspected by a crowd of arms dealers. They all carried thick copies of the auction prospectus as they talked with the pilots and climbed up to peer into the cockpits. The next morning a number of them would submit a sealed bid to the office of the Ministry of Defense.

The photographer paused, doubtfully staring about him. Throngs stood on the grandstand or strolled about, looking at the private planes, at the jet trainers and at the vintage aircraft that were participating in the air show. By far the largest crowd surrounded the World War II Messerschmitt 109. Another mass of people milled in awed silence around a World War I Fokker DR I, a three-winged craft in violent red, identical to the Fokker flown by the legendary von Richthofen – the Red Baron.

Officials in distinctive red caps, holding up blackboards with block-lettered legends, followed a strict timetable as loudspeakers called off the events. The air was filled with the sounds of aircraft engines warming up. The weather was ideal: the wind socks barely stirred in a faint southeast ground breeze and the sky was cloudless.

Gustav Behring, chairman of the board, Fund Exchange Bank of Germany, stood apart from the crowd on the grandstand. A stout, affable man, he looked benignly at the crowd with shrewd blue eyes and a pink political smile. But when he looked at Manfred Fritzsche standing before a group of stunt pilots, he felt little like smiling. In fact, he told himself anew that he would have to kill Manfred Fritzsche.

There was a solemn irony in this. Gustav Behring, aside from being a very influential banker, was believed by many to have one of the canniest political minds in Germany – Mr Playmaker himself, Mr Behind-the-Scenes, the Great Compromiser who could bring God and the devil to harmonious agreement. Murder was, therefore, a form of failure to him and this murder in particular would be doubly ironic, for Fritzsche was one of Behring's two best friends: forty years of the closest possible contact with never a serious quarrel.

For the moment, Behring tried to avoid the pain of thinking about Fritzsche. But his mind could find no rest anywhere. Even thinking about his son brought no relief.

After the air show he was planning to drive out in the fine autumn weather to visit him at his private boarding school. The boy had just made the school soccer team and deserved congratulations with dinner at a good restaurant. But thoughts of the son, his firstborn and the apple of his eye, brought thoughts of his wife, who was away to the south

57

of Italy for a holiday. She was his second wife and many years younger. He saw her clearly in the Sicilian night, saw her bare writhing thighs and eager thrusting pelvis, holding one young Italian lover in her arms while her eyes were casting about for the next. She had a preference for waiters.

Be discreet, Sophia, he begged and sought to turn his mind to some happy corner away from all the pain. He ached for a drink and wished he dared take a nip from his pocket flask.

Then his heart chilled. The photographer was stepping through the crowd toward him. Someone had entered Parker's office. He suppressed an impulse to back away as though to escape the leper's touch. The man could not be bearing good news. What a catastrophe Fritzsche had caused. Behring glanced over at him and felt anew the anger that had coursed through the veins like bile the last two days.

There was no avoiding it. The photographer mounted the grandstand, came right up to him and nodded a silent greeting.

'What is it?' Behring asked.

The photographer reached into a coat pocket and brought out an envelope. Behring's hands were shaking. He opened the envelope as though it contained the jury's verdict. There were five or six photographs and he looked fearfully at the topmost one.

'Oh dear God,' he said with a profound sigh. It couldn't have been worse. He was looking at the face of Colin Thomas. Even in the graininess of the photo, there was no mistaking the facial scar and the stubborn set of the lips. He nodded at the photographer and the man left.

Behring never felt more alone in his entire life. If Otto Dorten hadn't been flat on his back with a heart attack, he would have handled this – as he had handled everything else since the first day the three of them had hatched their conspiracy. Indeed, Fritzsche's baboon wouldn't have killed Parker at all if Dorten had been well.

58

Behring looked yet again at Fritzsche. He had pictured himself over and over during the past two days shooting that ungovernable fool right through the head. Executing him. And the image caused agony in his gut. He was not sure he could bring himself to do it. He had to, of course. Otherwise Fritzsche was going to ruin everything, expose Behring and many dozens of others and probably bring on a final confrontation with the Soviet Union. Well, he had to break the news to him.

Fritzsche was telling a parting anecdote to the young stunt pilots. When he finished, they laughed and straggled down the steps of the grandstand. The loudspeaker system was calling them to their positions.

Fritzsche was a vigorous, straight-backed man in his sixties. An important industrialist and celebrated war hero who had fought with a tank unit at the Russian front, he was a somewhat forbidding figure standing there in his blue marshal's sash with the gold lettering. He had small dark-brown eyes, humorless and judging, that were set in a triangular cat's face. When he smiled, rarely, his eyes acquired only a faint hue of warmth before the smile fell like a dropped curtain.

Behring handed the packet of photographs to him. Fritzsche had enjoyed the attention he'd gotten from the young pilots and he was in high spirits. He took the packet almost with a smile.

'What's this, Gustav?' He took out the photos and studied them. 'So?'

'That's Parker's office. Do you know who that man is?'

'No. Should I?' Fritzsche asked.

'It's Thomas.'

'Hmmmm.' Fritzsche looked at the photos again. 'So that's the creature of your nightmare. I see no horns or scaly tail.'

'Don't make light of it, Manfred.'

'I don't make light of it. He must be dealt with. Immediately.'

'Manfred,' Behring said, 'there can be no more killing.'

'Do we have a choice?' Fritzsche replied. 'As you feared, he's here. He's very, very dangerous, you say–'

Behring looked at those small brown eyes and shook his head. 'That's how we got into this mess, Manfred. Taking care of Parker. You've stirred up a beehive.' He looked again unhappily at the photos of Colin Thomas. 'And this man is the last one I wanted to see here. They've sent in their heavyweight.'

'Don't look so unhappy, Gustav. He's just a gun seller.'

There was bitter anger in Behring's eyes. 'You read that report on him. He's not just a gun seller. For us, he's the most dangerous man in Europe. He certainly slows things down.'

'Slows things down!' Fritzsche protested. 'That's absurd. We cannot waste another moment.'

'No,' Behring said. 'We'll have to wait a few days until the auction is over – until he leaves.'

'Don't talk nonsense!' Fritzsche said. 'We cannot wait one more minute. The Book is ready. Everything is ready. Nearly forty years' work. Kill him, I say. Now.' A purple flush of anger crossed his cat's face.

Fritzsche's words were like a pronouncement of doom to Behring. This heedless bullheaded man could ruin decades of infinite labor and destroy the lives of so many important men. And Russia.

Behring looked eastward. There was no natural defense for Germany against Russia: it was one vast meadowland all the way to Moscow. He took back the photos and put them in his pocket. Then he went down behind the grandstands and took a long, gratifying pull on his pocket flask. He drained nearly half of it. He had to think.

There was only one hope: Otto Dorten. He was the only man who could restrain the Great Tank Commander of the Eastern Front. If Otto was well enough to see the two of them, he would talk sense into Fritzsche. Half dead, he was smarter than Fritzsche and Fritzsche knew it. And, half dead, he could still rise up and kill Fritzsche. And Fritzsche knew that, too. Otto Dorten was the ring through the bull's nose.

Behring studied the pilots standing down on the field talking to the red-capped managers and referees and easily found her: Dorten's daughter, Kaethe, standing next to her uncle. She wore riding pants, jodhpur boots and a white silk blouse and held her helmet and goggles in her hand.

Quickly, Behring went down to her and led her aside. 'Kaethe, you know I wouldn't disturb your father without the profoundest cause. I have an urgent need to speak to him. Do you think that today–'

She shook her head. 'He's very sick.'

'For a few moments.'

She reflected. 'Well, I'm going to see him after the air show. You can come to the house and wait in your car. Maybe – well, we'll see.'

Behring pushed an anxious hand through his hair and nodded. 'After the air show.'

He went back up on the grandstand. 'Manfred, there's a chance we can see Otto today – after the air show. I think we ought to have him straighten this out.'

Fritzsche's small brown eyes studied Behring's face. He nodded once. 'For whatever good it will do.'

Whatever good it will do: it might save your life, you pigheaded old man. Behring stepped away.

His mind could find no place of peace to hide in today.

The first plane to take off was the red Fokker DR-I triplane. The crowd shouted and waved at it as the familiar black Maltese Cross on its white field flashed by. The pilot, his white scarf trailing behind, waved back.

Many observers had the prescribed sequence of aerial maneuvers drawn on graph paper with arrows and dotted lines. Lying on the ground, they held the paper up and compared the Fokker's flight pattern with the graph. Others held up a piece of clear plastic with circles and other flight patterns etched on its surface. They watched the flight through the plastic.

'Perfect!' many people shouted when the Fokker had finished.

More planes took off to fly their patterns. Then a trio of biplanes with thick smoke trails – the Blue Devils – performed one intricate pattern after another, finishing with a spectacular bomb-burst maneuver. The crowd shouted its approval.

Experimental planes performed; homemade, skeletal one-seaters with small gasoline engines, improbable as dragonflies, skimmed by. Then vintage aircraft of all types. The afternoon wore on as one exciting event followed another, all rigidly controlled by the officials.

Kaethe Dorten appeared on the flight line. As she approached the Messerschmitt a number of older men, some wearing in their lapels Luftwaffe insignias from World War II, applauded her and called encouragement. 'Get him, Kaethe.' With noisy good nature, they booed her uncle, the pilot of the English Spitfire who walked with her.

'Karl,' one man called, 'you'd better lose or there will be no wienerschnitzel for you tonight.' That led to another round of shouts and applause.

One man touched the German insignia of the Messerschmitt with tears in his eyes.

An official appeared before the two planes, waving his blackboard with instructions. When another official made a spinning motion with his finger, the two planes started their engines and slowly rolled in ungainly fashion along the uneven turf toward the flight line.

The level of crowd noise rose perceptibly. Kaethe Dorten was clearly very popular with the German crowd, and many called her name as the Messerschmitt rolled onto the airstrip, picked up ground speed and lifted off. Right behind it, eagerly, the Spitfire followed. They flew south toward the Hunsrueck mountains, becoming specks as they climbed higher and higher.

A few minutes later, the loudspeaker announced the approach of the two aircraft, and the crowd settled down to watch, sitting or lying on the ground all around the airstrip, many on cars and vans, binoculars upraised.

The Messerschmitt had given the Spitfire the advantage, flying ahead of it and a hundred feet lower. With an eager pounce the Spitfire peeled off and made a power dive. The Messerschmitt did a wing-over and dove and the dogfight was on, directly above the airfield.

Kaethe Dorten revealed her personality in every move of her Messerschmitt. She was utterly reckless, flying with a wild abandon that threatened to tear the wings off the plane, yet every move was premeditated. Like a skilled chess player she had thought ahead three or four maneuvers. Most of all, her flying exhibited an almost demonic will to win.

Her uncle, in the Spitfire, matched her action move for move. The simulated dogfight lasted no more than twelve minutes, but it left the crowd shouting with excitement. The Luftwaffe pilots gave Kaethe the edge. Much to the joy of the German crowd, the judges deemed that the Messerschmitt had won.

Kaethe Dorten drove fast in the waning daylight along a network of back roads to get to her parents' home before Fritzsche's limousine did. On the final stretch, the road crested and began a long curving descent toward the river that lay shimmering red in the late-afternoon sunlight. At the end of the road she could see the house on the near bank of the river. The whole valley was given over to earth colors, duns and umbers and beiges, and the fields had a raked and trimmed look, ready for winter. Shadows filled the low spots and an evening chill was spreading. For her this was once the road home.

As the car descended, she could see the details of the ancient farmhouse and the disused brick barn beyond it under some old trees. Drawing still closer, she could see her father in the meadow reclining on a chaise. He was lying under a blanket, a lone figure in the middle of the meadow behind the house, gazing into the distance as though trying to see the future before anyone else did. A pair of binoculars lay on the ground beside him.

She parked near the old paddock and walked by the empty stables along the brick path to the back. From under a copse of young birches behind him, the wind carried a sudden dervish of brown leaves and sent them scurrying like field mice. The weather was going to change soon. She kissed him quickly on the forehead. 'How are you?'

'I am well.'

She studied his face, gazed at his eyes and the circles under them.

'I am perfectly well,' he insisted.

His face was thinner. Even his hair seemed thinner, combed straight across the skull, the remnant of an army lined up for the last battle. But the eyes flashed, two furies trapped in a dying body.

'Fritzsche's coming with Behring,' she said. 'Are you up to that? I can send them away.'

He smiled. 'Send away the German banker's banker and the single most powerful industrialist in the country? Yes, you would.' He shook his head at her. 'Boldness. You would have made a great career for yourself in intelligence.'

Intelligence. She smiled at him. He'd told her that before. It's what he had done. By the time he was twenty-three, in the Abwehr in Berlin he had already had a brilliant name – for intuition, clairvoyance in fact, most notably when he warned Hitler weeks in advance that Siberian troops would be moved to defend Moscow against the blitzkreig. And after the war, when Germany was torn in two, during the years of the Berlin airlift and the Berlin Wall, and the near-collapse of the British intelligence system, he had received the ultimate compliment from the Russians: they attempted to assassinate him.

'They'll be here in a minute,' she said.

'How did the flying go?' He'd changed the subject.

'I won.'

'Karl let you.'

'He never had a chance.'

'I tried to watch with the binoculars but you were too far away – beyond the horizon.'

'It would have made you nervous.'

She went off to greet her mother. Through the window he watched her two hands flying, banking, diving, hot pursuit, the Spitfire tighter in the turns, the Messerschmitt faster in the climbs.

'How is he?' Kaethe asked her mother.

'Mending. But his career is over. His heart will never stand it again.'

Kaethe looked through the window at her father. He should have died; she dared to think it. When his career ended, he should have ended. He was going to make an impossible invalid. One day, like a man pulling the pin on a hand grenade, he would simply explode inside, willing his own death.

He was born to walk the tightrope over the abyss, content only when he was daring death. She discovered that in him only after she'd discovered it in herself – when she was fifteen, the day her uncle Karl had begun her training as a pilot. She discovered in the cockpit her almost fatal love of recklessness. It was a narcotic to her as it was to him, the thrill of being millimeters away from death and getting away with it, the suicide betting on being rescued. Her mother warned her that she had a death wish.

In her adolescence she considered flying her career. By eighteen she was barnstorming across Europe at air shows with her uncle and a team of stunt pilots. But it was too intoxicating; twice she nearly crashed. The plane, unable to do the wild gyrations she asked of it, had gotten away from her, and she saved herself only with her considerable flying skill a scant few feet above the ground. But the second time, she nearly killed one of the other pilots as well and she voluntarily grounded herself for months.

She turned to racing cars, and the drivers quickly dubbed her Mad Kaethe Dorten. For even at top speed on wild hairpin turns, the thought of dying didn't frighten her enough to restrain her, and she knew she would eventually kill herself. She felt inside that she was going mad.

She met a young actor whose audacity on the stage fascinated her. Each night in front of an audience, he would play the same part by building an entirely new character for it in the air, improvising as he went, a man on a tightrope, then when the whole creation seemed ready to collapse, he'd bring it off, inches from disaster. She'd found a kindred spirit but the theater wasn't for her.

She'd always thought she'd gotten her fascination with danger from Karl, her mother's brother, until in her adolescence she discovered her father at his games. There was an expression that appeared on her face whenever she pulled off something exceedingly dangerous, a flash of victory, a feeling of invincibility. And one day she saw it on her father's face. She knew then that he was a fellow addict. And she began to pay close attention to him. She watched him: at the dinner table with guests, alone by a window seat conferring with a famous politician, receiving a report in his study from an agent late at night. In the world of postwar politics, in a wrecked Germany, trusted neither by the West nor by the East, with an intelligence system that was nearly nonexistent, her father had to play a solitary and dangerous game, gathering the information West Germany needed to form its policies. For thirty years he occupied that gray zone between politics and intelligence, 'living in the cracks,' he called it.

All through her childhood, there was a parade of people in her home – in the country house and in the town house in Bonn – people from all over the world, the famous and the infamous. At the dinner table, the politics were still over her head but she understood by reading faces and heeding voice intonations who was in power, who was slipping, who was trying to package a deal, and she watched her father listening for the verbal slip, the unconvincing lie, the planted fact.

Then he would be gone for weeks at a time, the man of mystery even in his own home. When he returned he would often have that exhilarated expression on his face, and she knew he had narrowly beaten the odds again somewhere.

All his activities seemed to center around Russia.

Kaethe intruded into his life as far as he would permit, even visited his office frequently. For a time he thought she would be drawn to intelligence with her two brothers and he began to teach her. He told her things he'd never told another, tales mainly from his career, and at nineteen she had enough of his experience stored in her head to have become a successful politician or spy.

One day he watched her fly. 'Recklessness,' he said. 'Don't drink too deeply from that bowl. You know what kills reckless people? Boredom.'

Boredom: she drifted away from school and went looking for a vocation that wouldn't be boring – something like her father's secret game that would be her own.

She met a friend in Cologne one day, near the Dom. Just back from the Riviera, the girl was becoming a beautiful butterfly, spending her days shopping, her evenings pursuing an eligible young man of wealth and grooming herself for a comfortable life as a matron in Cologne society.

Kaethe, for no reason, said she was looking for a job. 'Something exciting.' Her friend's brother worked for a successful public-relations firm in Cologne. It sounded as though it had all the elements of a circus, and Kaethe went for an interview. Within the first hour of the first day on the job, she knew she'd found the game she wanted to play. She had laid her hand on power and knew exactly how to manipulate it.

The public-relations business is composed of people with ideas. The inventory, it is said, goes down the elevator shaft at five every night and returns at nine the next morning. How to promote a new product; how to put over a new style; how to put a corporation in a good light. With an increasingly sophisticated German population, the old and coarse methods of molding public opinion no longer worked. Subtler methods were needed. Kaethe soon revealed a gift for taking abstract ideas and packaging them inside engaging people. She got corporation presidents to take lessons in speaking and gesturing, learning to purvey charm and wit as effectively as politicians.

And she revealed an uncanny sense of market control. A new feminine spray was failing. The agency recommended that the price be cut and a more discreet package be designed. The client was unhappy with the idea. Shrewdly he took Kaethe to dinner and asked for her suggestions.

'Raise the price,' she said. 'Double it. And make the package bluntly sexual.'

He did, and from near-collapse the sales rose steeply, the client had a hot new product and suddenly Kaethe owned her own public-relations agency with one account. She was twenty-four. A small cosmetics account is very challenging, but it's regarded as a bit frivolous by the major industrial firms. She turned down three other cosmetics accounts that would have made her a large sum of money but would also have type-cast her agency. She was after bigger fish. And she found it in Fritzsche Aircraft. Fritzsche was involved in a sharp contest to sell a specially designed coast guard plane to Holland. The English were squeezing them out. Kaethe found that the Germans were talking to the wrong people. From her tutelage under her father, she knew that power did not always reside with the title. Often it was behind the scenes.

'Find the one man who can say yes,' he said; 'that's the first step in control. Get past the men who can say no but cannot say yes.'

She found him – hidden away on the corporate board with no title – the man who could say yes. Then she turned her attention to the Fritzsche sales presentation. It was the traditional kind – an easel with a pointer and hand-drawn charts. It was dull, unconvincing, not a sales talk but a stern Teutonic lecture. She threw it away.

She introduced American sales methods, stored the easel and the lectern, adopted a tone of informality, used slides and film clips and humor and showed the salesmen how to highlight their facts, then with glossy cinematic footage made the German plane seem like the guardian angel of all the Netherlands.

Fritzsche made the sale, and Kaethe Dorten had her first big industrial account. She'd gotten inside the charmed circle. Soon she picked up one major account after another. She'd reached the stage where she could literally invent a new product, plan a marketing strategy, design the packing, develop the sales program and present it all neatly gift-wrapped to her client. The lines between industry and politics blurred. She made a special study of British and American political campaign methods, learned how to use television and how to package a politician and soon scored a series of notable upsets at the German polls. She had become as skillful at politics as she was at marketing and publicity. Her fees became astronomical but so did the number of clamoring new clients. At thirty she was one of the most successful women in Germany.

Unexpectedly at the peak of her fame, the old malaise seized her. Boredom. At those moments, she'd recall that flush on her father's face and wish she was part of it – whatever it was that was going on secretly among the three of them – her father and Fritzsche and Behring.

Inside his limousine, Manfred Fritzsche glanced at Behring. The aging affable German banker was separated by many years from his fiery youth when he was a feared Luftwaffe pilot.

'Gustav.'

'Yes.'

'I think you've lost your nerve.'

Behring shook his head and smiled. 'No. I've merely changed my tactics.'

'It's the same thing.' Fritzsche looked contemptuously at the passing fields.

'Are we going to bicker again, Manfred? Let's see what Otto has to say.'

'What can he say? What can he do? He lies there in his

old farm with a ruptured heart. Helpless. He'll never be back. Never.'

Behring studied Fritzsche's face with a severe expression. 'He'd better be back. We simply cannot make it without him.'

Fritzsche nodded almost perfunctorily as he glanced out at the winter-ready landscape. The sun would set in a short time.

'Gustav. You remember when the three of us stood in Berlin and watched the Russian troops on parade?'

Behring nodded. They'd stood by the bomb-battered Brandenberg Gate near the freshly patched broad boulevard of Unter den Linden. Berlin was flat. Flat flat. The buildings all around the gate were down. Gone. Rubble. They had stood watching the victorious Russians, three defeated young men from a defeated army in a defeated city in a nation halved, occupied by four conquerors, its industrial capacity crippled by bombs, its economy wrecked, the finest army ever assembled buried rank on rank in foreign graves, each fiendish sin of the Nazis exhumed, unwrapped and held up in daylight in Nuremberg to a soul-sick world, while Russian tanks rumbled by, shaking the earth in Berlin like vengeance.

Fritzsche put his hand on Behring's sleeve. 'Don't forget that day, Gustav.'

Fritzsche's limousine drove up the long graveled drive between Swedish pines and stopped by the old brick barn.

'Well?' Fritzsche said.

'Wait.' Behring said. 'Here.' They sat in silence behind the chauffeur and Behring could hear the faint ticking of the dashboard clock. He exhorted the perverse powers that govern the affairs of men to help him. If Dorten turned them away now, he would have to sit down this evening and plan how to execute the man sitting next to him.

Ever since Dorten's heart attack, Fritzsche had been on a rampage. A lot of the bluster was fear. The thought of going on without Dorten was as frightening to Fritzsche as it was to Behring. But he was also exhilarated. He was eager to take charge; after all the years of deferring to Dorten and his brilliant mind, Fritzsche hungered to assert himself and prove himself in the eyes of the group. He wanted Dorten to live; he wanted Dorten to die.

And he had forced himself to cross his Rubicon by having Parker killed. Fritzsche trying to become Dorten; the mace trying to become the épée.

Behring watched the front door of the old farmhouse, his hands clenched desperately in his coat pockets. Fritzsche shifted impatiently.

Unexpectedly, Kaethe Dorten came around the barn. She was bringing the verdict. Yes. No. More and more, people were approaching him these days with verdicts. He had to school himself to wait with patience.

Her face leaned down to the open window. 'He can see you for just a few minutes.'

Her face never looked lovelier to him. Oh, to have such a wife.

The chauffeur opened the door of the limousine, and Fritzsche and Behring stepped out to walk around the stables to the back, Fritzsche with his imperious straight back and barely concealed military strut and Behring with his outgoing politician's stride. Dorten lay on his chaise, immobile, staring off, and Fritzsche wondered if the heart attack had dampened his fires, made him cautious and fearful. Another timid soul like Behring could ruin everything.

When they reached the recumbent figure on the chaise, Fritzsche was relieved to see that the fierce glint in Dorten's eye was undiminished. His craggy face and thin hair gave him an indomitable, weathered look. Still defiant, the one man who shared Fritzsche's obsession.

'Otto,' Fritzsche said, doffing his hat. 'Kaethe tells us you are stronger today.'

Dorten nodded them toward the several empty chairs. 'What is the problem?'

As he sat, Fritzsche was struck how much Dorten had aged. He was only – what? – sixty-two.

Dorten said, 'I see by your expression that my face looks as bad to you as it does to me.'

'You look more unconquerable than ever, Otto.'

'I am more aware of time than ever. There's not much left. For any of us.' He looked from one face to the other. 'I can guess what the problem is. Who walked into Parker's office?'

Behring reached into his pocket and laid the half dozen photographs on the blanket on Dorten's lap. Dorten fanned them like a poker hand. 'Thomas.'

'Our worst fears,' said Behring.

Fritzsche gave a frustrated little sigh. 'The politicians are having qualms.'

'Not qualms,' said Behring. 'Caution.'

'Caution. That's what Hitler felt that August when we were driving into Russia. A whole month of caution. Waiting! Cost us the war and brought about our defeat. Caution is a sickness.'

Dorten gazed at the photos. 'It had to be Thomas. Wynet is getting predictable.'

Fritzsche found Behring's solemn gaze on his face. 'What would you have had me do!' he exploded. 'Parker had our secret and was running like hell for Washington. Otto's in his sickbed and you're at a NATO meeting in the Netherlands. I had to do something and I did. I shut his mouth and destroyed the document.'

'Tank Commander Fritzsche to the rescue,' murmured Behring. 'The man's executed in public, a hue and cry is raised, even the Russians are bound to come and take a look and we know nothing. Nothing! How much did Parker know? We don't know. Who was he working with? We don't know. How much did he tell others? We don't know. How much does this Thomas know? Ah – Manfred, you burned his letter to Thomas. The one thing that would have told us where the leak was. Without reading it. Your man burned it without reading it.'

'Did he have any choice? He had to destroy it before the British police got him. There was no time to read it!'

Behring shook his head. 'Everything for you is aim the cannon and blast away.'

Dorten cast aside the blanket and stood up.

'Take it easy, Otto,' Fritzsche said and hastened to put his arm around Dorten's shoulder. 'I don't want to lose you now.'

'You won't be rid of me that easily.' Dorten casually brushed Fritzsche's arm aside and led the way into his study. 'Come.' He was chilled to the bone.

There was a fire going and the last rays of sunset were shining vertically through the window, casting golden squares on the paneled walls. Fritzsche gazed fondly around the room. It had been born here, the plot against the communists. It had been just the three of them then and a large sand table in the center showing the terrain of Poland and western Russia. In this room, they'd taught themselves how to destroy Russia.

Dorten stood with his back to the fire and addressed himself to Behring. 'You want to delay?'

Behring nodded. 'Wait until Thomas leaves.'

'Thomas,' Fritzsche interrupted angrily. 'He's just a gun shill.'

'He's far more than that,' Behring said. 'And he's here looking for us.'

'The Book is ready for presentation to the Chinese,' Fritzsche exclaimed. 'I must see Fox immediately. Minutes count.' Fox was the code name for a Mr Wang. Even Chinese surnames were avoided in their plans.

Behring made a skeptical face.

'Minutes!' Fritzsche insisted. 'Look.' He pointed a finger through the window eastward toward the encroaching darkness. 'You could roll a bowling ball that way and it wouldn't stop until it rolled into the doors of the Kremlin. We have no natural barriers against the Russians and they are overly armed, beyond all reason. They could overrun us in a few days. We are in danger every moment.'

'We've been over this so many times.' Behring sighed and slumped in a chair.

'How long can we keep all this a secret?' demanded Fritzsche. 'Far too many people know now. And Parker knew. Secrets don't keep!'

'If we're not careful,' Behring murmured, 'we could cause the destruction of the whole world.'

'I don't care a fig about the rest of the world!' Fritzsche exclaimed. 'Does the world care about the reunification of Germany? No. Only we Germans do.'

'And the Russians.'

'Oh, of course, the Russians,' Fritzsche replied. 'They will keep us cut in two forever. And everyone else has gone off about his business, with our reunification completely forgotten. Listen. We have sworn to reunify this country – even if we have to risk another world war. We will not let the rest of the world have another moment's peace until we become a whole nation once more. We reunite or the whole world pays.'

'Or dies.'

'So be it!' Fritzsche pounded the chair arm.

'Oh come, Manfred. A short delay—'

'We delayed with Russia in 1941,' Fritzsche shouted, 'and Russia won half of Europe for a prize. Delay now and she'll take the other half.'

Behring said, 'I say we should wait a day or two. If Thomas should discover what we are up to, everything could be ruined.'

'Then kill him,' Fritzsche cried. 'He should have already been killed the moment he stepped foot in Parker's office.'

'Piano,' said Dorten in a low voice.

'Pardon?'

'Piano. The soft game. Deftly. Deftly.' Dorten stroked the air. 'We mustn't use force on Thomas. Since you bring up Russia, Manfred, remember how they broke our game.

They danced away from our pincers. They retreated too fast for us. We couldn't catch them. That's what we need to do with Thomas. Stay out of reach. Let his nets come up empty. And he'll leave. Meantime Manfred is right, Gustav. We must not delay another moment. The Book is ready. We must pursue our plan with the utmost speed. It must be accomplished before Russia realizes it. No delay.'

'But what about Thomas?' Behring demanded. 'Who will handle him?'

'I have just the person,' said Dorten.

'Who?' Fritzsche asked.

'Kaethe!' Behring exclaimed.

'She can handle Thomas,' Dorten said.

'It's too delicate, Otto!' Behring insisted. 'Dozens and dozens of people – some of the most important people in the country – the whole thing in the hands of an inexperienced girl.'

'Trust me, Gustav. I will run things. Kaethe will be my legs.'

'I don't care how you handle it,' Fritzsche said. 'Play pattycake with him or kill him. If he gets any closer, I will kill him without hesitation.'

'No you won't,' Dorten said.

Fritzsche's cat's face flushed in sudden anger. He glared. Dorten was the only man who could take such a tone with him.

Dorten raised a finger. 'It's your impetuousness that's caused this problem, Manfred. Now you damned well better keep your hands out of it or we'll all be ruined.'

Fritzsche slammed a hand on his thigh and stood. 'I don't care what you do. I'm not delaying another five minutes.' He could read Dorten's thoughts. 'I won't fail.'

Dorten watched him leave, followed by the unhappy Behring. It was growing colder outside. As he poked the fire, the sun was almost gone and the darkness in the east had spread as black and impenetrable as the future. The future: where the bad news came from.

Otto Dorten walked down the corridor to the kitchen to find Kaethe. It was done. They were all riding the tiger now.

In his gruff way, he tried to make her comfortable. Dorten put Kaethe in the chair by the fire, the chair where he'd sat and read all the books that lined the shelves that rose to the ceiling on three walls. All the books shared one subject: Russia.

He got out a bottle of brandy, forbidden to him, and he poured two glasses.

He saluted her. 'To your health.'

Then he commenced speaking to her in his terse telegram-style German, often without adverbs or adjectives.

'I'm dying,' he said. 'A good sneeze will do it.'

She sat up to protest.

'Enough. That's not what I want to talk to you about.' He drank off the rest of his brandy. 'There's a war coming.'

'War!'

'For the reunification of Germany.'

The idea was so preposterous, her mouth fell open.

'It will mean the destruction of Russia,' he continued. 'I helped engineer it. But I won't live to see it.'

'See what, Father?'

'The war against Russia.'

She was sure he was mad. The heart attack had probably involved a stroke, brain damage. The hallucinations of the senile, seeing conspiracies everywhere.

'After all these years, we are ready to crush Russia.'

She shook her head. 'Father. Germany is only half a country, less than twenty million people. You have no army. And there are two hundred and fifty million Russians. Germany couldn't crush Liechtenstein. How could you possibly crush Russia?'

'How? I will tell you, Kaethe. I discovered how forty years ago. And we've been working on it ever since.'

Kaethe squirmed in her chair. He was far sicker than

76

she'd thought. Her mother hadn't given her any inkling of it. She felt a profound sadness for his fine mind baffled by brain damage.

He tapped her knee with his forefinger. 'Listen. In late nineteen forty-five, Fritzsche and Behring and I were in Berlin, home from the wars. Things were in a great mess. There we were, two young officers and an ex-intelligence agent specializing in Russia. Three young men out of service with no civilian trades, in our twenties, defeated and confronted with a partitioned Germany, half of it being stripped of every factory and tool Russia could lay its hands on, with four foreign armies in occupation. No jobs. No future. Many of our families and comrades dead. We cursed ourselves for taking on the whole world in war. It was a time of despair for us.

'And Berlin wasn't the place to be. All that rubble. More than four hundred Allied bombings destroyed it. And uncounted thousands of Russian shells. Then street-to-street fighting finished it off. There didn't seem to be much left. You know what we were doing? We were watching the Russians parade through Brandenberg Gate. Gustav Behring was weeping with anger. Boom boom boom went the goddamned Russian drums. There were hardly any Germans watching. The crowd was all Russian soldiers, all cheering.'

Dorten poured himself another brandy, then filled her glass.

'So I stood there and I looked at all those Russian soldiers. And I thought about what a ragtag army it was, a piece of this, a dash of that. There were Ukrainians and Estonians and Latvians and Russians and Belorussians and Karelians and Georgians and Kazakhs, Armenians and Azerbaidjanis, Bashkirs, Mordvinians, Tartars, Irkutsks, Uzbeks, Mongols, and Cossacks and lots of others. They didn't have the same uniforms, they wore all kinds of different hats, different pants, all sweat-stained and filthy. They rode on ponies and horse-drawn carts and bicycles and motorcycles. They spoke different languages and couldn't understand each other. They didn't know what plumbing was or toilets and the streets stank with their urine and shit. There were more than a hundred and fifty completely different tribes and clans and nations. As I watched them I knew for a certainty that Russia would never again let Germany reunite. Partition was permanent.

'Then the words just tumbled out of my mouth. As the Russian band went boom boom boom, I said to Fritzsche and Behring, "I know how to put Germany back together." And just like that Gus Behring put his hand over my mouth and they led me away from there.

'Behring's grandmother's house was still standing and it was in the American sector. We got a bottle and we went there to his bedroom.

'Then Fritzsche said to me, "All right. Now, how do you put Germany back together?"

'"Very simple," I said. "Pull Russia apart."'

Otto Dorten looked at his daughter with very lucid eyes. 'And that's what the three of us have been doing for forty years, preparing to pull Russia apart.'

Slowly, as he talked, Kaethe realized he was rational and absolutely serious.

That afternoon, in Behring's bedroom in his grandmother's house, using an old prewar map of Russia, Dorten had explained what he had learned about the Russians during his wartime intelligence work. He explained the diversity of customs and religions, he dwelt on their traditional internecine animosities and recalled the tens of thousands of them that greeted the German soldiers as liberators during the invasion of Russia – until Nazi mistreatment turned them against the Germans.

What Dorten was suggesting was a plan to create such internal strife inside Russia that it would collapse into 150 small countries.

Two things were clear to the three that day in Berlin: Dorten's plan could work, and it would take an enormous amount of planning and labor. And suddenly the despair of the Brandenberg Gate was gone. They had a mission. It seemed an impossible one but the more he talked about it, the more convinced they became. They weren't aware that it would take forty years.

By darkness, the three men had formulated a plan. Behring was to enter politics. Fritzsche would enter industry. And Dorten would rejoin German intelligence and help rebuild it so that he could have secret windows into every corner of Russia, to become an expert on those 150 diverse fragments inside Russia.

They had started, before Kaethe was born, with an ordinary sand table right in the study where he was now talking to his daughter. First on the sand table they re-created the terrain of Poland and western Russia and reenacted the German war in Russia 1942–45, studied every move of every military unit, German and Russian, learned every mistake by heart, learned every lesson. When they felt they had discovered as much as they could about the habits of the Russian mind, they turned to the next subject: the art of supplying and operating terrorists and guerrillas inside Russia, the art of taking apart a patchwork quilt.

Meantime their careers developed. Dorten was instrumental in building an intelligence system that helped the new West German government formulate postwar policies toward Russia. Fritzsche struggled for years, without complaint and without flagging, to build an industrial base. And Behring discovered a real aptitude for manipulating politics behind the scenes and rose rapidly. And his career in banking thrived. The two worked in tandem. As he grew more powerful in banking he grew more powerful in politics that would help him continue his governmental climb. He was now head of a major German bank and a power behind the throne.

But after years of study and preparation, they began having trouble with their Russian conspiracy. They met two or three nights a week whenever possible in Dorten's study and pored over the volumes of material that Dorten's

Russian intelligence staff was gathering. Somehow the internal dissension they projected inside Russia wasn't strong enough. There was some element missing.

They needed more help. One night they agreed to bring in another man, a close friend of Dorten's who was a key figure in the new West German Army. Dorten didn't give Kaethe his name.

'We had him work a few theoretical military questions with us on the sand table; a guerrilla force fighting a conventional army was still a new concept then. He was a very shrewd man and a brilliant military strategist and he soon got the drift of our activities. He was eager to join us. In fact, he belonged to a clique of officers who dreamed of a reborn Germany. They took our military questions and formed their own study group to solve them.'

In a few weeks, the officer was back. The problem was twofold, he told them: First logistics. They had to design and develop new kinds of weapons and supplies – radios and explosives – and technical information for guerrillas and terrorists, and they had to develop techniques for smuggling supplies and information across Russian borders to the dissidents. Second, if the dissidents succeeded in pulling down the Russian empire, chaos would follow, civil wars, famines. Other powers would be drawn in like a newly independent Poland, and Hungary seeking revenge, and East Germany, and a major war would break out. At a key moment a disciplined outside army was needed to enter and take control in order to carefully dismember the empire and turn it into a balkanized collection of small and harmless nations.

Where could they get an outside army? The West German Army couldn't do it, it would have to travel too far across East Germany and Poland to get at Russia. And Poland would never permit that, not with the memories of World War II ever green.

The military study group examined various alternatives, through Sweden and Finland. Impossible. Up through

Iran or Turkey or Pakistan and Afghanistan. Unthinkable.

After years of enormous effort and planning and preparation, they were stopped. The military study group slammed door after door. The project would have to be abandoned.

Dorten was the believer, the man of faith who kept the spirits of the others up. And he had clung to a belief, like an article of faith pinned to the underside of a lapel, that when a new problem occurred, a new solution would appear with it. Now, for the first time, even Dorten's faith faltered. They could scotch the snake but not kill it.

To help solve the problem, they inducted the famous geopolitician Dr Hesse. His studies probed the same paths into Russia – through Poland, Finland, Czechoslovakia, Turkey and middle Asia – and he, too, shook his head.

Then one morning while shaving, Dorten, who always drew heavily on hunch and intuition, thought of a solution to their problem. His beard stood up through the lather so thickly that it stopped the razor. Half shaved, with the lather drying on his face, Dorten hurried down to his telephone and called Dr Hesse. He whispered one word to him and went back to his shaving.

Several weeks went by. At 3 a.m. one cool autumn night he was lying in his bed awake next to his sleeping wife, brooding endlessly on that Russian bear, the obsession of his life for nearly, then, thirty-five years.

He heard a car racing up the long tree-lined drive to the old farm, scattering gravel and raising autumn dust in the moonlight. The headlights flooded his bedroom windows, then turned away as the car entered the turnaround in front of the building. A moment later, he heard the heavy brass knocker banging. It pounded again. And again, urgently. A few moments later, his manservant knuckled his bedroom door and murmured apologies. 'Most urgent, sir.'

He rose, barely heeding his wife's whispered questions, put on his robe and descended. A very heavy man in a wrinkled business suit was standing in the entryway in great agitation. Dr Hesse. He held two fat fists trembling before him. 'We have it! You were right!'

And eagerly he guided Dorten out of the house and walked him up and down the long drive, babbling his information. 'It was so obvious. The rest of us were still blinded by doctrinaire similarities.'

Before anyone else in the West had grasped it, Dorten had recognized as fundamental and final the break between China and Russia. Dorten had found the road to Moscow – and a ready-made army to boot. China.

Dr Hesse walked Dorten up and down until dawn, described the geopolitical studies they had conducted, the diplomatic and economic questions, the magnitude of the rift between Russia and its eastern neighbor. 'It is the most significant political event of the twentieth century.' There had also been preliminary and tentative military studies that were all positive. China was an ideal ally of Germany. A match made in heaven. Dr Hesse talked volubly, overly excited, a thin blithe spirit trying to cavort and soar in a too-heavy, clumsy body, waving thick short hands, swaying, rumpled, intoxicated with glee in the moonlight, believing they were about to alter history.

Dr Hesse suffered from total recall, and he had to tell every detail. He was clearly overwhelmed by the significance of it all. Half of what he was saying Dorten didn't hear, the primitive road system, the backwardness of the Chinese soldier, the terrible winter weather, the mountains and impassable terrains. The doctor's babbling gave Dorten time to think, to grasp the enormous implications.

At that moment Russia's ancient nightmare – two armed fronts, east and west, combined with internal separatist movements – the nightmare stood up, a huge and bulky shadow of terror, and began to shamble toward the gates of Moscow. With the incredible swiftness of history, the tide had turned. At last, they had the wherewithal to destroy their enemy.

Thoroughgoing China studies began in earnest. The military group set up several huge sand tables containing a model of the Asian land mass. At night when the rest of Germany was sleeping, they went seeking the readiest route through Russia to Moscow. They studied the Chinese army and determined what equipment it would need. The political study group assembled composites of the Chinese leadership, did psychographs on their attitudes and computerized their previous decisions and reactions.

The picture was clear-cut. The Chinese leadership thirsted to attack Russia.

The next step was obvious: a massive proposal to be secretly made to China, complete with maps and war plans and economic studies. West Germany would provide the infrastructure of terrorists and guerrillas, would arm and train them to paralyze Russia from within, would raise similar groups to take over in Poland and Hungary and Romania and Czechoslovakia and elsewhere, would provide technical advice and assistance to the Chinese and, most of all, secretly arm the Chinese with a modern army, including radar and aircraft and telemetry, and rockets and even cruise missiles that would carry Chinese nuclear warheads.

Meantime, West Germany would also, as a member of NATO, sound the alarm to ready a European army to pressure Russia from the west. The huge beast would be beset from every quarter, wolves from the outside, debilitating worms within.

Dr Hesse essayed a waltz. 'Think, Dorten, of the homecoming! A reunited Germany. Herrenvolk in East Prussia, East Germany, Austria, Czechoslovakia, France, Holland, everywhere one huge nation to dominate Europe right to the Chinese border!'

His thick feet scuffed dust up from the gravel and he dabbed his handkerchief on his fat throat. The full German moonlight seemed to work on him like catnip.

There was only one question that raised doubts. Would China be willing to pay for the purchase of a modern army?

A special group of economists, geologists and industrialists examined this. They found ample mineral deposits, even abundant oil and industrial diamonds, a whole spectrum of raw materials that Germany's industrial plant could use in return for military equipment.

Other questions seemed insignificant – how could Germany manufacture such a magnitude of military supplies for China right under the very nose of Russia and then secretly ship them half way around the world?

They had to be most convincing with the Chinese. If the Chinese felt the cost was too high, if they refused – but it was too dismaying to think about that. Yet privately each of them walked the floor at night worrying about a Chinese refusal. To have gotten this close and then miscarriage. Men tore their hair in darkness.

The cabal of conspirators grew, for questions elicited answers that only spawned more questions. They had to anticipate every Chinese question, blunt every possible Chinese negative. Like tentacles the cabal now reached into every department of government and science and industry and even medicine for experts who could help.

The Chinese would ask searching questions about the internal terrorist groups. To answer them, the cabal needed more and more accurate information about the internal working of Russia. More and more trips for Dorten.

'I have been in Russia many times,' Dorten told his daughter, 'under a number of different names.'

Recognition lit her face: now she knew why he had worn that expression of triumph so frequently when she was growing up: each time he'd beaten the odds, each time he'd emerged from Russia with essential information and his life.

He found everywhere in Russia enormous discontent and discord. Not enough houses, too little food. Too much national treasure spent on superabundant arms – treasure that should have been spent on homes, better diets, farming equipment, new factories. Communism didn't work. Protesters were exiled, or jailed or shot in their cells. Tens of thousands languished in prisons. Massive resentment was barely concealed. Defectors climbed walls all along the border. East German Volpos, Russian scientists, ballet dancers, doctors, poets and farmers – all were clamoring to get out. Poland was smoldering, East Germany was ready to defect en masse. Czechoslovakia was held down by a large Russian army of occupation. The list was long.

Dorten played his mad, reckless game, seeking out dissidents everywhere inside the Iron Curtain and getting them in readiness, anyone who would agree to feed his staff information and also help form nucleus groups of five or ten.

'Every night in Russia when the sun goes down – now, tonight, when it gets dark outside,' he said to her, pointing at the window, 'these groups gather in kitchens or cellars and they study methods of sabotaging telemetry systems, memorize the construction of missile silos, rehearse techniques of attack on armories to secure arms and equipment, learn how to plant explosives and disrupt lines of communication, operate underground newspapers. Thousands of them. I did that – almost singlehanded. And one of these nights, the final campaign will begin when the very doors of the Kremlin are blown off their hinges and the air is filled with the sound of sharpening knives.'

After years of secret labor, it was ready: the proposal to the Chinese to make common war on Russia. Everything was in it, the answers to all their questions including a design of a modified jet fighter for the superlong ranges of the Chinese-Russian border.

'It's that thick.' He held his hands about four inches apart. 'Fritzsche calls it the Doomsday Book.'

This, he said, was the critical moment. Fritzsche had to meet in the utmost secrecy with the Chinese. No one on earth must know of it.

'The Chinese may turn us down. We can't succeed without them. Everything hinges on it. A lifetime of work collapses and a whole vast network inside Russia withers and dies, or maybe the Russians will penetrate it and destroy everyone. Three or four generations would pass by before such an opportunity would present itself again. Meantime Germany would disappear.'

Dorten poured another forbidden brandy for himself. And one for her. 'So here we are.' And he told her about Parker and Thomas. 'It's a hell of a mess Fritzsche made. It's going to take the greatest skill to cover it all up and prevent Thomas from finding anything. Worse, if we don't get it all smoothed over again, the Russians will certainly come sniffing. They must have taken note of Parker's death. That Dudorov in Amsterdam – like a buzzard he'll be here.'

He touched her arm. 'It requires the deftest touch. Thomas must not know he's being manipulated, or watched or decoyed. He must be lured into following a red herring right off the continent. Let him find nothing. Let him pounce on air. I will give you four of my best people. They will come to your apartment.' He studied her doubtful expression.

'Do not be afraid, Kaethe. I'll be right here and my people will know exactly what to do.'

'Then why do you need me?'

He frowned at her. 'There's a leak in our communication lines. Parker found it. We have to find it and plug it up before Thomas finds it. Be my eyes, ears and legs – before he ruins everything.'

She studied his face for a trace of mirth. There was none and she frowned in perplexity. 'Are you serious?'

'All these years I've kept a ring through Fritzsche's nose. Now that I'm flat on my back, he's pulled loose and he's out of control. Behring can't handle him. And your brother – well, his way of handling Fritzsche would be something violent. I've reviewed all the others, all the people involved in this plan. But I need someone nearby – close, that I can trust implicitly, that will be my surrogate in Fritzsche's eyes. Just don't let him think you are afraid of him.'

She refused more brandy. 'What do you want me to do?'

'First, put a ring through Fritzsche's nose and hold him back. Second, you have a hell of a mess to clean up that Fritzsche made. Third, find the leak before Thomas does. You have to meet this Thomas. Stalk him. Discover how much of our Russian plot his people know about. And decoy him. Lead him away from Fritzsche and the meeting with the Chinese. In the next day or two, Fritzsche will call a meeting with you and Behring to discuss security during the night he meets the Chinese. If Thomas uncovers that meeting, it would be an incredible disaster. He mustn't even guess that the people we're meeting with are Chinese.'

Dorten felt desperately tired. He knew he should be in bed but there was so much still to tell her. 'All of these years, I dreamed of dying in my father's house in Berlin – that's how much I believed in our Plan. A Communist lives in it now – a factory head, a Pole. When I'm in Berlin, I can stand near the wall and with binoculars can see the old house. They painted the shutters green. Imagine. Green. Ironic, isn't it? I'm free but my house is in jail.'

When she left, he saw that she was stunned. Her lips were almost white. Under normal circumstances, he would never have dropped the whole burden on her like that. But she was the only one in all of Germany he could turn to.

But so little time – and so much for her to learn. He feared that even she couldn't imagine it. Now she was another one riding the tiger with them – and the tiger was running in full flight. The pains in his chest were back. He felt too weak to find his way to bed.

He looked eastward through his window at the darkness toward Moscow. 'I will get you. I will get you even from the grave.'

He poured himself another brandy. Recklessly.

When Kaethe left her father, she was in shock. Awed.

There was no mistaking her father's message: she was to take up his part in the effort. As she drove back to Cologne, she sensed that all about her in Germany were hundreds of important people who were secretly part of this desperate cabal. And inside the Russian world were thousands more getting ready. The next few days were critical.

She felt exactly as though she'd been led into the Berlin Philharmonic Hall before a full house and handed the baton to conduct the symphonic orchestra. She couldn't read a note of music.

She stopped her car and got out. Eastward toward Russia she looked as though she expected to see a line of Cossacks come riding over the horizon directly for her, swinging their cavalry sabers: Ivan, the raping Russian soldier – the loose and baggy monster of her childhood. She thought of her father prudently watching the Russians over the years, counting their growing hoard of Red tanks, noting their increasing numbers of Red jet fighters and bombers, fingering the lengthening lists of Red Army divisions, names, type, number of troops, and knowing, sooner or later – more likely sooner – that that marauding mob would sweep across Germany.

She'd been to Berlin a number of times, and each time she saw what her life would be like under the smothering, ruthless hand of communism. In East Germany, every child from the fifth grade on studied Russian by law. She looked eastward once more and knew she would help the cabal with all her heart.

'We have no choice,' she said aloud.

Fritzsche was alarmed. As he rode through the darkness in his limousine, he was worried by Dorten's condition. You didn't have to be a doctor to know that Otto was desperately sick. The whole plan was in jeopardy. The one thing in their conspiracy that they'd never factored in: personal mortality. And of all people – Dorten.

Fritzsche recalled the many nights at the sand table going over the campaigns of the German Army Group Vistula – at Moscow and Stalingrad and Leningrad – moving the little flags of the German and Russian armies. In the early years their progress had been painfully slow and the bleak winter nights made their hopes flag. The snow-filled wind that thrashed at the February windows of Dorten's study, raising memories of the frozen Russian front, scorned their petty efforts. Russia was growing stronger those years and developed atomic warheads and rocketry and missiles and put men into space. It was as though they were running on foot after a racing locomotive. On those bitter nights it was Dorten, always Dorten, who got them up, got the blood pumping, renewed their fanatical resolve, then led them back to the sand table to dream and plan.

Time and time again over the years, it was Dorten who kept things glued together, found the way around impossible obstacles, kept them moving ever closer to their goal.

With him gone, who would take his place?

At an intersection in Cologne, the limousine stopped and a muscular figure stepped from a doorway. He leaned his head close to the window.

'Get in,' Fritzsche said. And Quist got in and pulled the door shut behind him. The chauffeur drove on.

Fritzsche pulled from his pocket a photograph. 'Here. His name is Dancer. He's a gun runner and a drinking pal of Parker's and he knows too much. You'll find him in the main cargo hangar of the customs compound in Heathrow Airport in London.'

Quist's youthful blue eyes studied the photo while Fritzsche wrinkled his nose: Quist wore too much after-shave.

Quist said nothing. He simply nodded and put the photo in his inner pocket.

'Do it tonight,' Fritzsche said.

Quist nodded again.

The chauffeur let him out at the corner. When the limousine drove on, Fritzsche opened the window to change the air. The aftershave was cloying.

Fritzsche's chauffeur drove toward her apartment even without consulting his employer. And Fritzsche impatiently watched the streets pass by, eager as an addict. He couldn't get enough of her. How would he ever let her go? Each day as the terrible pressure mounted from the China plan, he fled at dusk to her arms and innocence.

He had taken his first mistress when he was forty-five and it was done from pure lust. Even a few years before, he would never have permitted himself an adulterous liaison. It was immoral. But at forty-five, having weathered the trying years of building his enormous empire with iron discipline and total dedication, he wanted a reward. Something undisciplined, self-preening, forbidden, something beyond money and power. He yearned for affection and admiration. He had earned it.

Progressively, as the years went by, the mistresses got younger. And now, at age sixty-one, he had a mistress of sixteen. And with her, he had made the tragic blunder of the aging. He literally worshipped her. Only with the sternest discipline was he able to stay away from her and tend to his business.

Each evening when he wasn't traveling, he would hurry to her side, touch her hair and throat and listen to her prattle about her day. She lived a quiet life since he was jealous of the world's attention, and when he arrived she was eager to talk.

She was exquisite. Her small full figure and beautiful limbs were guided by an instinctive grace of movement that he could picture just by shutting his eyes. She was a passionate creature and her passion renewed his. He was, in fact, insatiable, hungry for more sex than he was capable of.

She also fulfilled his need for rambling unguarded talk. He knew she heard with only half an ear what he was saying but she made the appropriate noises and nods while she played with the latest bauble he'd brought her. He had showered so many presents on her that her apartment was bulging. He'd made her rich in every way except cash. His secret dread was that if she had enough money, she would leave him.

And in his lucid moments, he knew she would – that she should. Even though she went to art school every day she was growing up alone, away from young people her own age, and when he took her out he noted the sidelong glances she cast in every direction.

'Next week,' he told himself, 'I will talk to her about her freedom.' But the thought of it caused panic in his heart and he thought next week would never come. He refused to ask himself what he would do when age bent his back, when he would become stooped and slow and smell of liniment and talk of his doctor and grandchildren and love his bed.

As he got out of the limousine and looked up at her lighted window, he admonished himself again not to let his silly babbling reveal anything about the China plan. That could produce a catastrophe. Not one word to her. He promised himself he wouldn't. And he hurried up the stairs to her child's arms.

Fritzsche entered the apartment with his own key and discovered Tatzie sitting in his favorite chair, thumbing a fashion magazine. She was wearing the boudoir gown he'd purchased for her in Paris and strode with a delicious rustle across the room to him and kissed him with the ingenuous joy of youth. She began talking at once. There was a long article on the latest dress collection of a young German in Paris. An important new designer they were calling him.

Eagerly Tatzie flipped the pages, to find his picture. 'He was one of the first graduates from our design school. Aren't his gowns and frocks beautiful?'

He looked with relief at the face in the photographs – homosexual – then dangled before her eyes an extremely thin and delicate gold chain holding a small ruby in a filigreed gold claw.

'Oh, it's beautiful!' Quickly she turned her back and pulled the gown away from her shoulders almost to her waist. He put the chain around her neck and clasped it at the base of her neck. It hung below her throat just above the cleavage of her swelling young breasts. Her flawless skin was like a painting by Renoir.

'What did you do today?' he asked her softly as he watched her examine the new ruby in the mirror.

'Oh, I went out with the girl down the hall.'

'Oh, who's she?'

'She's a secretary and she's married and she took the day off – sick leave, you know.' They'd gone shopping together and then to a film. The secretary's husband was building his own business and was frequently away. The woman was lonely. 'We went to a restaurant. And two men tried to pick us up.' She laughed. 'Very clumsy. We laughed at them.'

Then she reported that they had a new janitor. Fritzsche had taken one look at the previous one, a young man with bulging muscles and a jaunty air, and had gone immediately to the rental agent with a small gift – an envelope with money – and the young janitor disappeared. 'This one is bald with a paunch and smells of beer and sausage,' she said. 'He has bad teeth.'

'What became of your school friend – what's her name – Mitzi?' he asked. The homely girl with an incipient mustache.

'Oh, tomorrow, after design class, she and I are going to see an exhibit of new fabrics. We have a new instructor in fabric design and he's arranged it.'

A new young man. The words filled Fritzsche with dread. Always the first reaction is dread: is this the first mention of the youth who finally will carry her off? He shifted in his seat to ease the pressure of his stiffening back. Life was closing in like nighttime, shrinking his horizons, his fierce hawk's spirit being caged inside his own calcifying skeleton.

He listened to her prattle in her child's voice – she sounded around ten years old at times – going on about designs and instructors and the French influence this year. His eyes studied her face, feature by feature, the unbelievable perfection of her ears and throat and the rising young breasts. He touched the fine bone in her shoulder.

'Pardon?' he said, rousing himself.

'I said, what was your day like?' She was removing his tie. Her nimble fingers opened his shirt. She put her two hands on his chest, stroking, watching the thick gray hair curl up between her fingers. He felt her soft lips on his neck, felt the first stirring of lust.

'Ah, Tatzie, the world's a bad place. You must learn to read the secret hearts of people. You have to learn to see the hidden evil or they will destroy you. Today I planned with some of my friends to help make Germany stronger for the future – for you, for young people, for the coming generations, for your children even.' The thought of seeing her pregnant with his child filled him with love – the new Germany. Alas, he was too old for that.

She nuzzled his throat again and stroked his chest. He relaxed. He felt a suffusion of comfort and safety in her arms and he talked about the new, reunited Germany. 'I am going to leave you that, Tatzie. It is the dream that keeps me awake nights. My generation caused the sundering of Germany. We should put it back together before we leave. Ah, we have such a marvelous plan afoot to unite Germany. It is more than a dream. You will tell your grandchildren about it.'

But now she had his trousers open, and passion silenced him. He was grateful: he'd almost said too much. He followed her, hobbling with his half-fallen trousers to the bedroom, eager to see the ruby on her reclining nude figure. The renewed youthful vigor of his erection astonished him.

4

After finding the shredded confetti in Parker's offices, Colin Thomas spent several hours in his hotel calling Parker's apartment. He was hoping that Hilda was there. There was no answer. Then he became apprehensive and he set out in his car, afraid of what he might find there.

Parker had been a big man who took gargantuan bites from life and his ideal girl was big too, a 'double handful' with a sunny disposition and placid aspect who would be unperturbed by his highly irregular habits. Hilda was all that and more. She had a rich and deep, sensuous giggle, a quick sense of humor, enormous patience and the gusto to carouse with him all night, then jump into a car and drive to a distant city where Parker could buttonhole a man for a piece of information on the arms trade. She could just as easily pack and be ready in minutes for a weekend in Paris or a prolonged stay in Africa. Like Parker, she treated life as a banquet. Hilda was the only woman Bernie had ever proposed to.

They lived in a fairly new apartment complex, low blocks two stories high surrounded by herringbone patterns of parked cars. Thomas drove by their apartment and saw that the windows were dark. He circled around several times as though seeking a parking space while his eyes checked each parked car for shadowy figures on watch. Several lots away from the apartment he parked and walked warily from one streetlamp to another.

It was a fine autumn evening in the Rhine Valley, the moon was approaching full and under a cloudless sky the stars crowded together like spectators. In practically every street-level apartment, he saw the flickering colors of a television set. All of Germany seemed to be watching. The American disease.

It had been only a few months since his last visit, just before he'd gone to Galápagos, in fact, and he and Parker had come as close as they ever had to an angry quarrel. Parker called the Galápagos regime a pack of Al Capones – hoods, mobsters, racketeers, 'milking, bleeding that country into unbelievable poverty! Monsters!'

Thomas had argued that the middle class was just large enough to qualify Galápagos as a civilized country. They were the only future that the country had. 'If those Castro Reds get in, there'll be a mountain of middle-class bodies and economic stagnation. The dead hand of communism.'

'We're getting married,' Hilda put that flowery wreath on the table between them like a peace offering.

Thomas was delighted and he kissed her. 'You've got real guts, lady.'

Hilda watched Parker as he spun his wineglass, then slouched angrily. 'He wants you to be best man,' she said, 'if he can stop talking guns long enough to ask you.'

'I accept.'

'Goddamned gunrunner.' Parker accepted his handshake with a sour grin.

Thomas asked about the honeymoon and saw them exchange glances and read the signals. 'Take the *Sea Breeze*,' he offered. It was his sailboat, a forty-foot sloop, moored in Portofino. Hilda clasped her hands ecstatically.

'Why the hell didn't you just ask for it?' Thomas asked. 'You know I'd give you two anything I have.'

'Just don't get blown away in Galápagos,' Parker said. 'Those brownshirt thugs aren't worth one of your fingernails.' And they were off again. Parker was completely humorless about the arms trade. 'All this arming can have only one outcome. Mindless heedless bastards. Never learn.'

It was the same old argument between them. Thomas

defended the West: after 1945, the whole world was spent, and the Russians were on the move, snapping up any unguarded real estate everywhere. What stopped the Reds was the free arms program of the United States. 'Guns and lots of them stopped the Reds. Even Greece would be a communist country today if it weren't for the United States. Part of the Dismal Empire. If we can contain it long enough, it'll collapse from stagnation and boredom.'

'Bullshit. You talk like Dulles.'

One of Parker's bêtes noires was McNamara, Kennedy's Defense Secretary, who had changed the arms giveaway program to an arms-sales program in 1961 and thereupon created an aggressive sales organization inside the Pentagon to knock down doors, selling arms as McNamara had learned to sell cars, Detroit style.

The age of the American Gun Huckster had arrived. Guns were no longer a bulwark of democracy. They became a major item in the United States' trade balance. They could just as easily have been anvils or slippers. The sale of the Starfighter jet to Germany was one of Parker's favorite cases in point. The monumental Lockheed scandals were another.

Thomas never yielded to Parker. 'The world has armed because of Moscow. They're the cause of the arms race. In fact the West's problem is it's underarmed to fight a conventional war.'

'Bullshit.'

'I think I'll have a baby,' Hilda said, pointedly taking the bottle of wine from the table. Parker was turning his glass intently. She put her arms around Thomas's neck and kissed his cheek. 'Would you like to be the father of my first child? We could all go on the honeymoon together.'

Silenced, Parker shook his head, still full of things to say. Thomas decided not to tell him that he had become a public scold, a monomaniac on the subject of arms.

'There's a terrible war coming if we don't stop,' Parker said as a coda.

Before he left, Thomas touched upon another point of

dispute. 'Hire a bodyguard,' he told Parker. 'Christ knows you're making enough money. You could hire a private army.' He pointed a finger at Parker's stubborn face. 'You've made a lot of enemies. Someone is going to put a contract out on you.'

And someone had.

As he approached the Parker's apartment he saw a shadow of a head bob down in the midst of a row of cars. Was it inside one of the cars or beside it? Thomas walked slowly past, looking through the windows. But there wasn't enough light and he didn't want to announce his awareness. He passed on: it could have been a tree shadow.

The Parkers' windows were still dark. No one answered the doorbell. After the shock of Parker's office, Thomas felt a tingling of apprehension as he unlocked the outer door and mounted the stairs.

He tapped with a knuckle several times on the inner door, then put his ear to it. At last he opened it and looked inside: there was no sound, no movement. The apartment was totally dark.

All of Excalibur's salesmen were housed in the Hotel Central near the Cologne cathedral, and when Brewer arrived from Paris late Sunday afternoon he went directly there by cab. The arms auction had drawn a crowd. Restaurants were overbooked; hotels were filled; stores and shops sold their stock at a brisk pace.

A long line of cabs kept arriving at the Hotel Central from the airport, dropping their fares and picking up new ones, assisted by two doormen. The crowds strolled in, weaving through the crowds that strolled out. The lobby was packed, and there were lines waiting to get into the three restaurants. The arms trade was there in force, and everyone carried a half-inch-thick, white-bound list of the matériel to be auctioned by sealed bids.

Brewer knew what was on that list – page after page of bayonet scabbards, military shoes, pup tents, mess kits, parachutes, spare parts for trucks. But the magic listing, the items that attracted the arms dealers, was the weaponry, and there would be every kind, pages of it, titles that read like a malediction against mankind – rifles, hand grenades, jet trainers, bombs, dynamite, mass destruction. The German military was having a garage sale.

The area around the several banks of elevators teemed with arms people. At the registration desk, the bells kept ringing, and the service staff was deliberately calm, obviously hard pressed. People stood over their bags or sat on them waiting – waiting for registration, waiting for a porter, waiting for a cancellation, waiting for the airport limousine or a rental car.

By the front window, Brewer saw a familiar figure. Georges. A French-Syrian, a fat self-announcement of availability like a three-dimensional sign over a shop. He was ready to smuggle anything across any border. Satisfaction guaranteed. From behind a newspaper his eyes never missed a single face that passed. They noted Brewer's presence and moved on.

Brewer got the key to his room and the minute he opened the door, he remembered anew why he'd married and left the arms trade.

The room was almost a carbon copy of the room in Paris he'd slept in the previous night. The bucolic painting over the bed was unforgettable: he'd spent six days in San Diego once, staring at it.

The depressingly cheerful orange coffee table, the by-the-mile carpeting, the factory-formula furniture, the drapes, the television set, even the television shows were he to turn on the set – all were identical to thousands upon thousands of other hotel rooms around the earth. It gave him a depressing feeling of being alone and forgotten. In these rooms, it was always a solitary Christmas day in a strange city. He had a terror that he might die alone some night in a room like this. Brewer almost wished for his home over the pub in Bloomsbury until he thought of the boy; then he recovered again the feeling of holiday, of escape and freedom. He looked out on the city, at the Dom, Cologne's

98

celebrated twin-spired cathedral, at the bridge and at the sun-bright Rhine River. The circular road, where once the Roman wall stood, was crowded with Sunday traffic.

Brewer left the room and went in search of Thomas.

Using a flashlight, Thomas entered Parker's apartment. He checked the living room and kitchen, then walked over to the bedroom. The bed was made; Parker's clothing hung in one closet, Hilda's in another. Their suitcases still lay on the closet shelves. Underclothes and shirts still filled the bureau drawers. He went back to the kitchen. There were a few soiled dishes on the counter, a cold half pot of coffee on the stove and a cup of cold coffee on the kitchen table with a newspaper and some mail. The whole apartment gave the impression that Hilda had abruptly gotten up from her cup of coffee and stepped out of the apartment. Fled? Or captured?

He shone the flashlight on the desk. Parker's personal checkbook was there with some unpaid bills tucked under the flap. There was an envelope with about fifty dollars in currency in it, a small jar of coins and some stamps. The three drawers on either side of the kneehole were partially open and empty. Someone had taken all the papers from the drawers and carried them off. Along with Hilda?

In the darkness the walls now seemed to be pressing inward and a vague sense of his old claustrophobia stirred just over the borders of his consciousness. Like a distant cloud, the claustrophobia was never really near but never really gone, something menacing that waited for a chance to attack.

Then the phone rang. In the dark, it was like a scream. It rang eight times, as unnerving as a burglar alarm; then it stopped. He knew he ought to leave. He had no weapon and the people who had cleaned out Parker's desk drawers would surely come back to complete the search of his apartment.

Thomas let his eyes rove and tried to think where Bernie would hide things. Apartments were too easy to search, and

Parker probably used other places, but if pressed, Parker usually went for things tubular.

So Thomas went over to the two living-room windows and looked speculatively at the shades. He pulled one down full length until the wooden shaft was exposed. Then he rolled it up again. He stepped to the other shade and pulled. Like bats, small squares of paper fluttered around his head. He stooped down and shone his flashlight on them. Money: there was about two thousand dollars in German currency. That had to be Hilda's doing.

He went next to the bathroom to check the cardboard core of the toilet paper. It was there, as he stood in the darkness probing a finger into the core, that he heard a scraping at the door lock. He'd stayed too long. He was trapped. Quickly he stepped over to the window drapes and drew them, shutting out even the faint street light. Then he hurried to the door and stood beside it flat against the wall.

The lock turned with slow care. The door softly opened. Two voices whispered. A pencil type flashlight lit the rug. Two figures entered, still whispering. They stood beside him flashing the light over the furnishings. Then they moved by him and went into the bedroom. A moment later he heard drawers sliding open and a bumping. More whispering. The bedroom was faintly lit by the streetlamp and he could make out the two figures. He pushed the wall switch and the overhead bedroom light went on.

Two women gasped at him. They were bent over the bed, putting things into a suitcase, clothing mainly and cosmetics.

'Tommy!' Hilda gasped. She put her hands to her mouth in joy and dismay.

'The light,' said Hilda's sister, pointing. 'Put out the light. Quickly.'

In the darkness he felt Hilda's hands around his neck, her face weeping at his throat. He had never known her to cry before and he put his arms around her.

'Oh God,' she said. 'I can't get a hold of myself. He would have been so angry.'

They refused to put on any lights. Hilda made coffee by flashlight and, still sobbing, her hands washed the soiled dishes as if disconnected from the face that wept. 'I had to come back here,' she said, 'for clothes. I have to fly to America for the funeral. I hope the plane crashes in the sea.'

Thomas got her to talk about the night Parker ran to Paris. 'He ordered a present for you as best man,' she said. 'It was a ship's chronometer for your sailboat. And he was supposed to pick it up that day in Cologne. There's a shop by the cathedral and it was that night – the day before yesterday, was it? – when he didn't come back. It got later and later. I wasn't worried. He often stayed out to two or three in the morning. Then he called me. Out of the blue it was, there was nothing wrong before that. And he said over the telephone, "Hilda, get the hell out of there. Go stay with your sister until I call you. They're chasing me." "Who's chasing you?" I said. And he said, "It's World War Three, Hilda." And he hung up the phone. And that was the last I heard from him.' She sobbed again and the hands began furiously to wash the same dishes over again in the darkness, lit only by the pocket flashlight as the coffeepot gurgled mournfully.

And that was it. She knew nothing else. Parker never talked about the newsletter, never told her any of the gossip and information he picked up. He received phone calls at all hours. He often went out to meet people late at night in bars or restaurants or even at a phone booth at some remote place. He never mentioned World War III to her before. She'd never heard of the Doomsday Book.

Thomas let her talk while her sister morosely drank coffee. She was preoccupied – worried, was it?

'I haven't told you the best part, Tommy,' Hilda said. 'When we decided to get married, I celebrated by getting pregnant. You should have heard Bernie laugh.'

The three of them sat in the dark in the kitchen, solemn

101

as though at a wake, portions of their faces lit by the inadequate flashlight, a grieving cheek and ear from Hilda's averted face, the bowed sullen brow of her sister, the merry twinkle of Hilda's diamond engagement ring, Thomas's dull coffee spoon.

'It's not safe here,' Thomas murmured at last. 'They're still searching for something and they're bound to come back.'

'I'll just do up these cups.' Hilda sat up, then paused. 'Is it safe on the streets of America? In Cincinnati? Is his mother – will I like–' She stroked a flat palm on her kitchen table slowly as though to soothe it.

'You're worrying about the wrong things,' her sister said. 'In five months you will have a baby to take care of.'

'Shhhhhh.' Thomas put a silencing hand on her arm. 'Listen.'

It was a faint sound, furtive in the darkness. Thomas recognized it: a lock pick deftly inserted in the door lock. He put out the flashlight and moved to the wall by the door and flattened himself there. The lock clicked.

The door moved barely an inch, admitting pale light from the hall. It opened a foot and the light lay across the entryway rug. Then it swung fully open. A thick powerful figure in silhouette filled the doorway and the man regarded the two immobile staring women at the table.

'It's okay, Charlie,' Thomas said.

'Found you,' Brewer replied.

Kaethe Dorten dressed for the evening while her mind dwelt on her father. All those years while she was growing up, doing her homework, reading children's books, playing children's games in her bedroom, a few feet away in the study, her father and Manfred Fritzsche and Gustav Behring were planning, night after night, the complete destruction of one of the most powerful nations in history. Their audacity awed her. And her father's plan astonished her. It was either mad or brilliant.

Her quick mind was racing, as it kept discovering more

and more implications. Finally she had to try to block it out of her thoughts. 'Later,' she told herself. 'I'll think about it.' She needed to turn her attention to Thomas.

She bathed and tried on four different evening gowns before she selected one. And that was the most daring of the lot – white silk that showed off the smooth skin of her fine arms and back. Studying herself in a mirror, she thanked her mother and grandmother for her figure.

Again, the thrill in her throat occurred when she thought of Thomas, only now it extended down to her belly. It was a form of stage fright and that amused her. 'I feel,' she told herself, 'as though I'm hunting my first tiger.'

She got out the dossier on Thomas her father had given her. It was a masterpiece of vagueness, written in the sterile, factless language of the hardened bureaucrat; she found some interesting parallels between them. Like her, Thomas had built his own business with his own hard labor. Like her, he had a reputation for innovation and unconventional methods.

Thomas had entered military intelligence after attending Dartmouth College, where he majored in economics and banking. Six months in the Federal Reserve System in Boston made him restless. He took a commission in military intelligence after meeting General Claude Wynet at a Washington cocktail party.

In the military he served with both Frank Gorman, his future business partner, and Bernard Parker. Thomas was wounded in Vietnam ('severely'), evidently in the back (the source of the scar on his face probably). The three men left the service about the same time with distinguished records (no details).

The dossier noted that when Thomas had entered the arms business, the principal sales techniques were fear and bribery. By introducing modern methods, including economic-impact studies, objective military estimates, financial and credit recommendations and military training programs, Thomas and his partner, Gorman, rather than selling whatever noisy and shiny hardware could be pressed on the client, sold a complete military package based on client needs. Their competitors paid them the highest compliment, they all copied Excalibur's methods – with little success.

Meantime, Excalibur Ltd had grown so large and powerful it now sold directly in world markets against such giants as the United States Government. In its warehouses, Excalibur was reported to have enough inventory to outfit infantry divisions. Principal credit for the company's success went to Thomas's business methods (sharp, aggressive, resourceful).

The dossier summed up Thomas's personality profile with such words (selected from a suggested word list) as dedication, intelligence (exceptional), resourcefulness (singular) and courage. But it didn't supply any instances from Thomas's career to document these words. There was no anecdotal material, particularly no hard facts beyond dates and place names. Under 'Remarks, Psychological,' again without elaboration, it noted: incipient claustrophobia. The character profile concluded with one word: formidable.

The writing was more like an alarmed warning than an objective report. It seemed to have been written by a hysteric. She could picture her father ordering that the report be couched in the strongest terms as a stern admonition to her. When he had handed the dossier to her, he'd said: 'Be careful. He's an exceedingly dangerous man.' But nothing in the report documented it.

She sat on her couch looking over the night lights of Cologne and their reflections on the Rhine and composed her thoughts. Fritzsche had really botched things with his Panzer tactics. He had killed Parker in a public execution, without finding out how much Parker knew, what his sources were and who he had been working with. He had burned Parker's letter to Thomas unread. He had shredded Parker's records, which made the murder a silencing rather than an act of revenge and so narrowed Thomas's investigation extremely; he had drawn into Germany one of the United States' smartest agents. And she suspected that Fritzsche had also done some other things he hadn't yet mentioned.

So her assignment was threefold. As much as possible cover up what Fritzsche had done. Find out how much Parker knew and discover his sources. And prevent Thomas from learning anything.

Kaethe's doorbell rang shortly after eight. Three men and a woman entered her apartment with terse nods. Her father had said they were the four best street people in Germany. One of the men looked like a banker. The second was as pale as a pallbearer. And the third looked like a thief: his shifty eyes never met hers. The woman looked like a housewife come to dicker about her water bill.

They were unlike any intelligence people she'd ever met. There was something between the banker and the housewife: he avoided looking at her and she watched him with angry eyes – or were they hungry eyes? The pallbearer seemed somnolent – probably on drugs. And the thief's eyes never stopped taking inventory of her apartment. They didn't give their names. They sat stiffly on their chairs and waited for her to speak.

'My father regrets that he cannot meet with you,' she told them. 'He is relying on me to be his messenger until he's on his feet again. Now – an American agent arrived in Cologne yesterday. His name is Thomas.'

'Colin Thomas?' asked the banker.

'Yes. You know him?'

They all nodded. 'Oh yes, he is well known.'

Carefully Kaethe told them of Bernie Parker's murder and concluded by saying, 'His death was a terrible blunder and we have to cover over his trail. Colin Thomas must not be allowed to find anything.'

'He's notoriously relentless,' the banker said. 'Thomas never gives up. Have you considered assassination?'

'No! Parker's death has already caused a sensation. Thomas's murder would be a catastrophe. Just be sure we

105

have covered Parker's trail thoroughly. Now, how about Parker's office staff?'

The banker looked at his watch. 'They left by jet for Greece two hours ago, just as your father ordered. Four ladies. Three weeks in the Greek islands, all expenses paid. Their tour guide is one of our people. He will make sure that no one questions them in Greece about Parker. Their neighbors have all been told that the ladies won a sweepstakes trip to Spain. Thomas will learn nothing from them.'

'How about the man who was with Parker that night?' Kaethe asked.

'Dancer,' the banker said. 'He's a small-time gun smuggler and an information peddler.'

'Where is he?' Kaethe asked.

'We're seeking him,' the banker said. 'He seems to have gone into hiding.'

'That's ominous. Why would he hide? We have to find him. Put more people on it – as many as you need. Just find him.' She gazed at their intelligent, capable faces. Their calm professionalism was reassuring to her. 'Now, we have to learn what Thomas knows. He has two men with him – Brewer and Roland. Know them?'

They all nodded.

'Roland,' the banker said, 'is a first-class agent. Very smart and resourceful. Brewer is dangerous – smart and completely ruthless. He's a killer.'

'I want their rooms searched – Thomas's and Roland's and Brewer's. We have to do a thorough job and that means getting them out of their rooms and keeping them out. Every inch of their rooms must be searched. I want photographs taken of all their papers, no matter how insignificant, including their passports. Who's the photographer?'

The woman nodded her head.

'Good,' Kaethe said. 'How will you get into the rooms?'

The woman looked at the pallbearer. 'Him,' she said.

'He will also be my hallway sentry. He will warn me if anyone comes.'

Kaethe Dorten looked at the banker and the thief. 'Can you two handle Brewer and Roland – make sure they stay away from their rooms?'

The banker nodded. 'Yes,' he said tersely.

'Use physical force only under extreme stress.'

'Pardon,' the banker asked, 'but who will keep Thomas away from his room? He is the most dangerous of the three.'

'I will,' Kaethe said and watched them exchange doubtful glances.

Roland arrived on the evening flight from London, and after checking into his room, he and Brewer went to Thomas's suite for a meeting.

Roland brought a half bottle of whiskey and some plastic glasses with him. He sat back on a sofa, put his feet up and spilled some whiskey into a glass, then held the bottle up, offering it to Thomas and Brewer. They shook their heads and Roland put the bottle between his thighs.

Thomas started by pointing at Brewer. 'You pick up anything in Paris, Charlie?'

Brewer nodded. 'Sure.' He told his story quickly. He had friends in the Paris police administration. They let him see the car. They let him see Parker's corpse. They let him see the bullet hole in Parker's back. The vehicle had been abandoned in the Eighteenth Arrondissement up behind Gare du Nord. Mud coated much of the body, turf had been forced up into the chassis, and the wheel wells were clotted with dirt and twigs, indicating that it had been driven hard over back roads and open fields. It had one flat tire when the police found it abandoned in an alley.

'The car was a rental,' Brewer added. 'From the Bonn Airport. I think he was going to take a flight out, maybe on his way to Washington. But they were watching for him at all the airline gates. So he rented a car and they saw him and followed him.'

'All the way to Paris? That's four hundred miles,' Roland was skeptical.

'And chased all the way, Roland,' Brewer answered.

'I did a little checking this evening,' Thomas said. 'It seemed to me that there would be one man at this auction without fail.'

'Dancer,' Brewer said.

'Right,' Thomas replied. 'Dancer. He should have been here scabbing up some gunrunning jobs and freeloading drinks from Parker. So I sniffed around and found out that he was here but he checked out almost at the same time that Parker was being killed in Paris. See if you can find him, Charlie.'

Brewer nodded.

'It won't be easy. I think he's scared and on the run.' Thomas looked at Roland. 'How about Parker's office staff? It's Sunday night. They're probably all home, Arthur. Go pump them. Find out what Parker was working on. If you learn anything I'll be right here in the hotel mixing it up with the traders. I want to see if I can find anyone in the trade who saw Parker that night. Okay? Go.'

Thomas went down to the exhibition hall of the Hotel Central. It was packed. Ordinary-looking men with bald spots and slight paunches and women in rumpled travel clothes shopped the new lines of weapons and military equipment as benignly as toy buyers. Some couples strolled through with their children.

It might have been a harmless yacht show. At each booth eager to demonstrate their product lines were salesmen wearing each on his lapel a card in plastic, 'Hello there, my name is—.'

They were aided by continuous-reel, full-color movie projectors that threw on the screens footage of war matériel in action, bombing, blasting, whizzing through air, riddling targets, dealing out mayhem and slaughter, conquering everything. There were eyestopping posters and four-color brochures and catalogs and scale models and automatic slides with sound tracks.

At many booths, pretty girls from the local modeling agencies greeted everyone and gave away lapel buttons with company slogans.

'I've seen the new Clauseon Sky Raider Rocket' was the most numerous on the lapels of the shuffling crowd. People had a choice of French, German or English.

Thomas saw a complete cast of characters from the arms business: the military attachés from the Bonn embassies, salesmen from the big munitions-manufacturing firms, military officers drawn from countries as far as Africa and South America and independent arms dealers come to buy for inventory, all squeezed in with the fringe characters of the business – the gunrunners and the smugglers, the fee men and the bird dogs, the boosters and the tipsters, the professional patriots and the desperate exiles, the camp followers and the mercenaries looking for a war.

Thomas talked to many of them. Then he went up to the ballroom.

The beat of the music dominated everything. Excalibur was having its disco in the main ballroom of the hotel, and it seemed everyone in the arms trade was planning to attend. The ballroom was filling rapidly. There were four bars, one at each corner; the disco equipment was on an island in the center. Overhead, strings of light flashed with the beat.

Travers, Excalibur's German representative, was in charge of the disco, and he moved among the crowds like an impresario. 'I decided on a dance rather than a cocktail party because it loosens them up faster,' he told Thomas.

Thomas frowned slightly when he saw Travers signal the disco operator to make the music louder. It was already deafening. Then he saw Kaethe Dorten enter.

She created an immediate flurry: everyone seemed to know her and greet her; the crowd became brighter and more enthusiastic. Completely poised, she had the politician's gift for making each person she greeted seem like a personal friend. People pressed around her, most to salute her, all to stare at her figure in the fitted evening gown. By the time she'd reached the disco island, she had converted the party to her own.

'Who is she?' Thomas asked Travers.

'I don't know.'

'You seem to be the only one who doesn't.'

Travers shrugged. 'The man she's with is a midlevel administrator with the German Defense Department. Name's Kosney.' Kosney was about thirty, well over six feet tall, thin and darkly good-looking in an evening jacket. But he had the ungainly walk of a marionette: Thomas doubted that he'd come to dance.

Kosney approached and introduced Kaethe Dorten to Travers. Travers introduced Thomas. Kaethe shook his hand with a surprisingly strong grip.

'Are you with Excalibur, too, Mr Thomas?' she asked, raising her voice above the din.

'Yes. I am.'

'Your party seems a huge success.'

'Yes, well, it's to introduce our new line.'

'What new line?'

'Hearing aids.'

She laughed and said, 'I'll take two.'

He looked at her thoughtfully. 'Dorten,' he said. 'That's a familiar name. What does your father do?'

It was the one question she dreaded. Had he guessed her identity that quickly? 'My father's retired. Dorten's a common name. I doubt if you know him.'

'Retired from what?'

'From a busy life, Mr Thomas. You may be interested to learn that you and I are competitors.'

'Is that so? In hearing aids?'

'No. Arms.' She laughed again and he listened with pleasure. Her laughter reminded him of Martha. 'My firm is doing the sales presentation for the Essen Arms Company.'

'Oh, the Spanish contract?' he asked.

'Yes,' she said.

'Do you expect to get it?'

'Of course. Do you?'

He smiled. 'I had some hopes in that direction. What do you do? Writing? Sales?'

'I own the company, Mr Thomas.'

He was clearly surprised. He grunted. 'And you expect to get that contract?'

'Yes. Of course. It's a foregone conclusion.' Her smile broadened and she raised her chin to challenge him.

He shook his head. 'I'm sorry, but that's very doubtful.'

'Are you a betting man?'

'Oh, I would hate to take your money.'

'I won't hate taking yours, Mr Thomas. Is it a bet?'

'You're going to lose your money.'

No, she wasn't going to be like the mild-mannered sweet Martha. He sensed she was more like the girls they used to call tomboys.

'Would you like to bet a bottle of champagne on it, Mr Thomas?'

They shook hands, then stood smiling at each other. She'd skillfully steered the conversation away from her father.

Kosney touched her shoulder. 'Dance?' he asked her.

Kosney was an ungainly if enthusiastic dancer and to the beat of the disco he wiggled like a whip. To keep from laughing, Kaethe looked away from him. She found Thomas's eyes on her.

Those pale eyes, she decided, made his face charming, especially when he smiled; and his thick curly brown hair was the kind that many women would have given a ransom to get. His pronounced jawline suggested pigheadedness, but the nose was well shaped and masculine. The scar on his neck and cheek should have conveyed an air of romance;

instead it seemed more like a warning. She remembered the word in his dossier: formidable.

She tried to sort out her various reactions to him. During their conversation, she had peeled layers of impressions like an onion. First, he struck her as friendly and warm with those dancing pale eyes as he joked about the hearing aids. Then came blunt suspicion when he'd asked about her last name. She next recognized his highly competitive nature when she challenged him to a bet. And when they shook hands to seal the wager, she felt a tingle of fear along her back: he was going to be a formidable adversary. Inside him there was a deep core of ruthlessness. But then as she turned away to dance with Kosney, she saw, almost at the corner of Thomas's eye, a fleeting expression. If it wasn't loneliness, it was certainly aloofness. It was clear to her that few people ever got to know the man inside Colin Thomas. She suspected there was carefully bricked-up vulnerability in there.

But beyond all that was another attribute she wasn't able to identify. Was it cruelty? No. Something else. And that unknown attribute was the one that intimidated her most.

Kosney was enjoying himself hugely. He held his hands up and his body whipped back and forth even more. He looked just like a crane taking flight. She turned away chuckling, then cast her eyes about for her people. She saw the banker by the main entrance. He wore a lapel button that said, 'I've seen the new Clausen Sky Raider Rocket.' He was standing near Charlie Brewer and his banker's face was completely impassive. She knew he was listening to every word that Brewer said to people.

The thief was in the hotel bar observing Roland and maybe picking a pocket or two.

Up on Thomas's floor, the woman carried her paper shopping bag by the twine handles down the hall accompanied by the lean and anxious undertaker. He unlocked the door to Thomas's room for her, let her in and pulled the door shut to stand and wait like a mourner at a graveside. The woman set her bag down and gazed about Thomas's room. She decided to start by stripping the bed.

Kosney led Kaethe off the dance floor at last and she noted that Thomas had taken the bait. He strolled toward her.

'Would you care to dance, Miss Dorten?'

'Yes. But I'd rather hear how you plan to take the Spanish contract.'

'You can't hear anything here.'

'Then I'll listen in the bar.' She patted Kosney's arm. 'I'll be back. Business first.'

She noticed her thief seated at the bar near the booth where Roland was sitting with three other men. It was obvious Roland had been drinking heavily.

'How do you plan to win your bottle of champagne, Mr Thomas?' she asked when they were seated.

'Wouldn't you rather be surprised?'

She shook her head. 'I hate surprises.'

'And I hate to disappoint you, but I think you're in for one anyway.'

'I see. Isn't there an American expression, talk is cheap?'

'There's a quotation I like better. There's no substitute for victory. Courtesy of Douglas MacArthur.'

She smiled again graciously. He wasn't going to tell her anything about his strategy. She wondered how they were coming along upstairs in Thomas's room. Maybe she could lead Thomas away from the hotel. Now that she'd met him she realized he would not be easy to dissuade if he decided to go to his room for some reason.

'Would you like to go to a party, Mr Thomas? I would like to show you how I'm going to get that Spanish contract.'

'Really?' He smiled at her as though he were going to say no.

The woman found a large brown envelope under Thomas's mattress. Inside were a half dozen typewritten pages. No salutation on them, no identifying letterhead. Just plain white sheets covered with typing. At the head of the first page was an underscored line: 'Bernard Parker: Comments Taken from Various Official Reports During the Recent Year.'

The six sheets appeared to contain extracts of reports filed by a number of different agencies in Washington, all concerning Bernard Parker. On the last sheet in pen was written: 'Thomas. Best I could do. Wynet.'

The woman took out of the shopping bag a tripod and a camera with a close-up lens and flash. Then she paused and opened the door.

'How's everything?'

'Hurry up,' the pallbearer said.

Thomas followed Kaethe Dorten to her car. She drove fast with complete assurance, across Cologne to another hotel, then led him inside to a formal cocktail party. A quartet was playing Viennese waltzes, and waiters were passing among the guests with trays of hors d'oeuvre. She led him up to a round-faced man with a sharp bill of a nose and thin black hair. The man happily placed a courtly kiss on her cheek.

'Mr Thomas,' she said. 'I should like you to meet the Spanish Ambassador to Germany.'

The ambassador shook Thomas's hand. 'Welcome to my little soiree, Mr Thomas.'

Thomas nodded and smiled at Kaethe Dorten, for he saw around him a number of ranking members of the German Government.

'May I get you a drink?' she asked.

When she returned, she found Thomas talking to a group of German government officials. The Spanish ambassador was introducing him to several others. They all politely exclaimed at his excellent German accent.

'Uncanny,' one said. 'I can shut my eyes and swear I was hearing my old professor of geopolitics.'

'Mr Thomas tells me he expects to receive the Spanish arms contract,' Kaethe Dorten said.

The ambassador smiled. 'Then here's to you, Mr Thomas. One never knows about these things until all the bids are opened.' As he drank, his eyes looked above the glass rim at Kaethe Dorten.

'Would you care to dance, Mr Thomas?' Kaethe asked.

It was a waltz and she held him in her arms and sensed his great physical strength. Yet he was very light on his feet, an excellent partner, completely relaxed. She wondered if she was going to get silly about this man. All her alarm systems were warning her but that just stimulated her recklessness.

When they came out of the hotel, it was pouring rain and her car was parked a block away on a side street. She frowned at it thoughtfully; she wanted to get him somewhere where she could try to pump him.

Thomas said, 'Suppose you let me get the car while you wait here.'

'Nonsense. We can run. A little rain will never hurt.' So they ran, or at least she attempted to, carrying her evening slippers in one hand and holding her skirts above the puddles with the other. By the time they'd reached her car, she had contrived to get them wet through.

She laughed at him. 'I'm sorry I got you soaked. But I know a nice place where we can get a brandy and dry off.' She seemed to have completely forgotten about her escort, Kosney.

The nice place was her apartment, a large suite on the top floor of a high-rise building. There were few interior walls. A number of clear-glass panels served as area separators and gave the suite a sense of great spaciousness. The furnishings were all contemporary and looked like something from an architect's magazine.

She got Thomas's jacket off and handed it over to her housekeeper to drape over a chair by the kitchen oven.

'Here's to business,' she said, toasting him with her brandy. 'I love it. And I love winning.'

He grinned at her and at her damp hair. 'I know that feeling well.'

'How did you get into the arms business?' she asked.

He hesitated and that surprised her. 'I just tripped and stumbled into it. I was trying to get away from something else.'

Her intuition told her that the 'something else' was a woman. 'I see,' she said. 'What do you do? I mean how does the arms business work?'

'Very badly.' Again he'd grown evasive. So she switched tactics and talked about her business – of clients and publicity. He listened attentively, laughed at her anecdotes and made several incisive observations. Then she tried to switch him back to his field. But he ducked again.

Instead he asked her about Cologne. She walked over to the huge glass windows. 'Oh, I love Cologne. The city and I grew up together. All through my childhood Cologne was being rebuilt from the war. It seemed every week they had another ribbon-cutting ceremony.'

The sky was dark and turbulent with clouds, and the showers were not through yet, but the moon, three quarters full, broke through at times and silhouetted the cathedral and made the Rhine River glitter. 'It was a miracle the cathedral survived,' she said. 'The Allied bombers tried not to hit it. But the original bridge behind it went down. See the four bridges? All of them were built since the war. And over there see the new Opera House? It's one of the finest in Europe. And Hohe Strasse–' She pointed down to the blaze of neon lights that lay in the old city off the cathedral close. Even at this late hour it was packed with people. 'I love Hohe Strasse. I always have a feeling of excitement when I walk through the throngs there. In fact, my office overlooks it.'

She watched his eyes look over her city. She'd never met anyone quite like him before. She knew stunt pilots and daring racing car drivers and businessmen of all types who

116

took great risks with gusto. But she couldn't picture him doing any of those things. He would never be content to be confined to an office, never happy as the head of a large corporation, or a bank, never would stay put as a package designer or as a boardroom salesman in a pinstripe suit discussing columns of sales figures on a chart.

In fact when she tried to picture him in action, it was in some exotic country with camels or rickshaws in the midst of men and sweat and machine oil and guns. She realized she was picturing him as a mercenary soldier. And that's what he was. A gun for hire. But inside him there was something that was unhappy with that role. She sensed it.

She gave one last try. 'Did you know that Cologne man who was killed in Paris? He wrote a newsletter on the arms business.'

'Parker? Yes.' He turned away from the window and looked attentively at her.

'I subscribe to his newsletter,' she said. 'He seemed genuinely concerned about the amount of arms in the world.'

'Yes,' Thomas said. 'He was.' And that was the end of that conversation.

He was a very tough man to win a bottle of champagne from.

Thomas couldn't sleep. He lay in the dark thinking about Kaethe Dorten. Strange, her laugh reminded him of Martha's, although they were totally different in all other respects.

He could easily picture Kaethe Dorten's face. Under silky light brown hair, it was marvelously alive and constantly moving. Of course, the dark brown eyes were a key reason for the vitality; they were vivid and full of hell. And the mouth had a complete repertory of emotions. He'd seen it register skepticism, competitiveness and mirth. He wondered what anger looked like; and passion – he tried to picture that. It was a sensual mouth, he decided, delicious

117

looking. Enticing ... if you could get her to lay aside that feisty-terrier streak long enough to kiss her. That was the one drawback: the competitiveness. How could you make love to a woman who was trying to beat your brains out in a business deal? He hadn't forgotten about the Spanish contract.

Sleep wouldn't come. It was the claustrophobia he knew. He lay in the dark watching the strip of light under the hallway door. As long as there was a spot of light, the black walls couldn't close in on him; the damp earth of Vietnam couldn't suffocate him. But this time the spot of light wasn't enough. Sleep evaded him.

He knew what to do. He dressed and went down to the bar. The place was still packed with arms people, and his eyes searched the faces in the crowd. With one glance at the expression on her face, he made contact: she smiled at him. Young and superficially pretty, she wore her price in her eyes.

'Welcome to Cologne,' she said. 'Are you staying in the hotel?'

'Yes. I'm here on business.'

'Here's to business success.' She clinked her glass against his. 'Is this your first trip to Cologne?'

'No. But I have a lot to do in the morning and I have insomnia.'

'Oh, poor Fritz. Maybe you don't like being alone.'

'That's right. I have a bottle in my room. Would you like to come up for a drink?'

She leaned her lips close to him and whispered the price that he'd read in her eyes. He nodded and they left the bar.

On the elevator she asked him, 'Are you from Prague?'

'No. I'm American.'

'Oh? You speak German with a Prague accent. Very nice.' She held out her hand as he counted out the money.

He slept in her arms. His head was against her breasts, hearing faintly the beat of her heart, and he dreamed all

118

night about Bernie Parker while her hand held his as the nurse's had done in Vietnam to save him from suffocation.

When Charlie Brewer left Thomas's hotel suite that evening, he went in search of Dancer, the gunrunner. Typically Dancer would follow the same pattern that all the gypsies had when they were absconding with the old Swiss troll's money.

No matter how carefully they hid themselves, in Hong Kong or Chicago or Tahiti, they all made the same simple mistake: they told someone where they were. It was a mother, a brother, an insurance company in Connecticut, a stockbroker, a Swiss bank, a mail-order house, a woman, a friend, an offspring. That thread, that single contact, was all Brewer needed. He had never once failed to find his quarry.

There was one sure way to find Dancer quickly, and Brewer went looking for Folger. Cologne was similar to every other convention city. There were many places to go in the night. There were the big commercial places, the expensive restaurants, the intimate gourmet restaurants, the night spots, the illegal gaming places, the call houses, the cafés and the low saloons. The men who attended conventions quickly sorted themselves out by social standing, income and breeding. Folger had very low standards.

In fact he was an easy target. He was an ignorant man from rural West Texas with no education and a fund of improbable stories about his days as a cowboy. Most of his stories were taken from Western novels and centered on cattle customs that had perished long before Folger was born. He talked for example of long cattle drives across the great plains to Chicago, a practice the railroads and refrigeration had ended decades ago. Folger had a big mouth, and he drank too much. But he was strong and tough, he was mean when he drank, and he was completely loyal to Dancer, his partner. But right now he was somewhere in Cologne, and Brewer made the rounds sniffing after him.

Everywhere Brewer went, he found members of the trade, drinking and talking or sleeping in a chair or pawing an obliging hooker. Brewer's questions led him from dive to dive, for Folger was an itinerant sponge who left a noisy wet trail behind him.

He found Folger, at length, in a café by the river across from Cologne, in his soiled white cowboy hat. His face had the familiar flush, his breathing was shallow and his eyes were glazed. As expected, he was talking. He sat in a booth against a wall and a middle-aged woman had fallen asleep against him while he talked to a German workingman who spoke some English. Folger was telling a plot from several novels about himself and the German was translating it to other workingmen who stood, listening with awe. Folger was being chased in a thunderstorm across the prairie with a stampeding herd of cattle and a pursuing band of murderous Apaches.

Brewer poked him with a finger. 'Folger. I need to see you for a moment. Outside.'

'Go fuck yourself, Brewer. Can't you see I'm talking?'

'It's important, Folger, and it will only take a minute.'

'Turn blue.'

Brewer looked at the workingmen. 'Did he get to the part where they stick a tomahawk up his ass?' he asked in German. The men were shocked, then understood and laughed uproariously.

'Brewer, goddammit, what did you tell them?'

'Learn German, Folger.'

Brewer went outside and waited. He'd given Folger a chance to do it the easy way.

After a few minutes, Folger came out amid a background of laughter. He'd lost another audience and he stood indecisively with balled fists at his side.

Brewer went up to him. 'Folger. I'm going to ask you once. Where's Dancer?'

Brewer was exactly what Folger wanted. He threw a

punch. It was quick and unexpected and it caught Brewer on the side of the head. Brewer recovered his balance and ducked under the next punch and tumbled Folger down the old stone steps to a boat landing. When he got down to the bottom, Folger rolled, jumped up and threw an overarm punch that landed in the middle of Brewer's back, and almost drove him to his knees.

Brewer's powerful arms seized Folger around the legs and spilled his head and shoulders into the river. He quickly pushed Folger's head under. He counted slowly while Folger struggled. Up at the top of the stone steps, four Germans stood and stared in wonder and exchanged questions.

Brewer pulled Folger's head up from the water. 'Where is he, Folger?' He let the man suck in a lungful of air and waited a moment longer. Then he plunged the cowboy's head into the water again. One of the Germans took several steps down but was called back by the others.

Brewer pulled Folger's head up. 'This is last call, Folger. Tell me or drown. When I count three. One. Two.'

'Heathrow. Heathrow, goddamn it. He's flying cargo to Shannon.'

'You wouldn't be dumb enough to lie to me, Folger, would you?'

'Heathrow, I said.'

Brewer pushed Folger's face into the water with his foot and mounted the steps, shouldering his way through the four men. Behind him, Folger shouted vows of revenge.

'I'll get you, Brewer. So help me God, I'll get you!'

Shortly after nine that evening, Quist got out of a car at the Cologne/Bonn air terminal and waved the driver off. He had no baggage, not even an attaché case. On his head raffishly cocked to the right rested a peaked tweed cap. He wore a travel-seasoned trench coat, the belt casually knotted at the waist. From the youthful face, his mirthful blue eyes glanced at all the girls. He might have been a college student, star of the varsity soccer team. In his pocket was a counterfeit passport.

The job was a piece of cake. He reviewed it once more in his mind. Landing at Heathrow, London, he was to go to the entrance of the causeway to the London Underground. There he would meet a messenger in a chauffeur's livery. In a beribboned florist's box, he would receive a .38-caliber assassin's pistol with a silencer. He was to proceed to the air freight terminal, where he would locate a man loading an antique DC-3. At the propitious moment, he was to waste the man. Then he would return to the terminal, hand back the pistol to the messenger from London and board the return flight to Cologne. He had an hour and twenty minutes between flights to get the job done.

In his trench coat pocket was a clear photograph of the man. Immediately after making positive identification, he was to burn the photograph, and, on his return to Cologne, once through customs, he was to destroy the counterfeit passport.

Quist walked into the terminal in his loose, athletic gait. He sensed that people were looking at him, the hero in an espionage film on a secret mission. He looked at them all with insolence. He pushed his passport across the counter to the desk clerk who confirmed on a computer display screen that Quist, L. P., had reserved a seat on the evening flight to London. There was the usual rigmarole of papers to fill out and the fuss over cash.

The clerk was distressed. 'No credit cards, sir?'

'No. All I have is cash.'

The clerk examined the passport, comparing face with photo, then returned it along with the round-trip ticket and boarding pass. As he turned away from the counter Quist brushed past Charlie Brewer, who was booked on the same flight. Brewer picked up his ticket, then walked along the concourse behind Quist, watching his swaggering gait. There was a touch too much of the professional about him that didn't go with the boyish face.

They passed through the weapon-detecting station and through the doorway to the ramp. Quist selected a window seat near the left wing. Before sitting, he balled his trench coat and pushed it into the overhead baggage compartment, then shut the door. When the plane was airborne, he slumped in his seat and slept. Brewer sat on the aisle seat in the same row as Quist.

Twenty minutes after they took off Brewer stood up and went to the lavatory. On his return he opened the compartment door and drew out Quist's trench coat. Casually, as he watched Quist's sleeping face, he went through the pockets. He drew out a book of matches, the flight ticket, the passport and a photograph. Brewer took a long look at the face in the photograph.

He returned the material to its pocket and put the coat back in the compartment over his head then sat again in his aisle seat. Counterfeit people had the same false ring as counterfeit coin. The pink-cheeked college boy was somebody's executioner. And his target was Dancer.

It had been a long day for Brewer and it looked like it was going to be a busy night – a real footrace. He glanced at the sleeping man-child next to him: amateur night at the shooting gallery.

When the plane landed at Heathrow, Brewer stayed right behind Quist as they stepped along the aisle and down the boarding stairs. He followed him through several concourses past the baggage-claim area then queued behind him through the passport control station.

Quist turned and commenced following the signs with the barred red circle for the London Underground. Ahead about sixty feet, Brewer found his opportunity. A terminal porter entered a swinging door. A moment later, another emerged. Adjusting his stride to Quist's, Brewer drew closer, grabbed Quist's elbow and turned him to the doorway and rushed him through. Before Quist could turn, Brewer struck him at the base of his neck and sent him sliding on his knees. Brewer pulled him to his feet and swung his fist into Quist's solar plexus. Quist went down doubled over. Before the startled porters could make a move, Brewer was back through the doorway and hurrying away. He got a cab at the cab stand and headed for the air freight terminal.

After a few minutes, Quist's head began to clear and two porters helped him to his feet. The wind had been punched out of him, his gut hurt and his neck throbbed with sharp pain. He sat down, rubbing his neck and fighting nausea.

'What did he look like?' he demanded.

'Why. Bulky, I suppose, sir. In a raincoat and a hat. Dark complexion, I would say, wouldn't you?'

The other porter nodded. 'Middling dark. Black brows.' He held Quist's peaked tweed cap.

Quist shrugged away from his helpers and strode furiously through the door and hurried along the concourse to the Underground entrance. There stood the liveried chauffeur with the beribboned box of flowers.

'I'll take it,' Quist said.

'Pardon.'

'Lohengrin, God damn it.'

'A dozen roses, sir.'

'And'–Quist snapped, his fingers groping – 'a bouquet of lady's-slippers.'

The chauffeur handed over the box. 'I'll wait right here sir.'

Quist pulled the broad blue ribbon from the box and flung it in a ball on the ground. He stepped into a cab.

'Air freight terminal.' He opened the box. The .38 pistol and the silencer were in a specially made leather holster on a neck belt. Quist opened his trench coat and suit jacket, then bobbed his head down and slipped the holster strap over his head. His neck radiated shooting pains and he felt his fury increase. Quickly he rebuttoned his jacket and coat over the dangling weapon and sat back.

He took a deep breath and let his careful field training reassert itself. All anger and passion were to be subdued; clear deliberate thinking and uncluttered awareness were paramount. He felt his rage gradually subside. He had to

124

evaluate the significance of the attack on him and discover its connection with the job ahead of him.

Cargo planes from all over the world were busy loading and unloading under banks of night lights. Inside the receiving buildings, forklift trucks were transporting cargo on palettes and containerized shipping units to storage facilities. It seemed like chaos to the outsider, but every item was under the surveillance of British Customs.

At the end of a long building, Brewer found Dancer's old DC-3. It was such an antique that pilots and crewmen strolled down to look it over. Dancer was nowhere in sight. Brewer jumped up on a loading platform and ran inside where a group of cargo handlers were having tea.

'I'm looking for Dancer,' he said. 'The DC-3.'

'Right up them stairs, mate, just past the loo. You'll find a room with some beds in it. He'll be in one of them.'

Dancer was wearing a pair of white overalls and slumbered deeply, half wrapped in an old British Navy wool blanket. Brewer sat on the bed next to him and pushed his shoulder. 'Dancer.' He pushed again. 'Hey. Dancer.'

Dancer opened his eyes, momentarily disoriented, and stared with disbelief at Brewer. He worked his mouth several times. 'Well, I know I haven't died and gone to heaven. That's clear.' He rubbed his eyes. 'What time is it?' He pulled the blanket back and sat up. 'It is you. After all this time. Tell me, Brewer, you didn't come looking for that fiver I owe you?'

'Why didn't I?'

'Because I don't owe you a fiver, Brewer, that's bleeding why.' Dancer sat up. 'I've been living in that lumping old bird for days. I can't remember when I slept last, washed last, ate last.' Decades away from Belfast, the North Ireland accent was still unmistakable. Dancer was a thin, sharp-faced man with thin pale hair and a habitual sour leer on his face. He groped in a breast pocket for a package of cigarettes and lit one. 'Now I'm ready for the bad news.'

'What bad news?'

Dancer snorted cynically at him. 'People never come looking for you in the middle of the night with good news. Let me have it all in one go.'

'You're full of shit, Dancer. I came around to inquire about your health and well-being.'

Dancer rubbed his face in his hands. 'Sure, sure. Tell me, does this have something to do with Parker?'

'It may. What are you up to here? What are you doing?'

'Air cargo. And all legitimate. I'm hauling all kinds of goodies from here to Shannon for the duty free shops. Two wonderful weeks' work. I've flown back and forth so much the bird knows the way without me.'

'Grand,' Brewer said. 'Where'd you pick up that job?'

'Tell me why you're asking.'

'Nothing important, Dancer.'

'Bullshit yourself. You come here in the middle of the bloody night from God knows how far and ask me about what I'm doing and it's nothing important? You haven't changed a bleeding bit, mate.'

'You were one of the last people to see Parker alive.'

'There! Didn't I tell you?' Dancer stood up. 'If I have to sing that song, then I'm going to have to have some tea to wet my pipes.' He pushed his feet into a pair of paint-stained slip-on shoes and shuffled away with Brewer following.

The cargo handlers were still drinking tea and chuckling when Dancer arrived. Sleepily, he poured some warm tea into a cup and stuck his lips into it. 'Bah,' he said.

'Dancer, you want me to wind up the rubber bands on your bird?'

'She works just as well on fart power, chum. Fill her up.'

The group arose chuckling and dispersed. Dancer proffered an empty cup to Brewer.

'No thanks,' Brewer said. 'You were saying–'

Dancer found another cigarette. 'It's quickly told and

126

not much help. I flew into Bonn that morning and I don't mind telling you I didn't have the price of enough fuel to fly back out again. I hunted old Parker up around four or five – I disremember. In time for a stein or two anyway. He said he was killing time so we drank some more and we had somewhat to eat.'

'Where?'

'Where? Let me see. In Cologne. A snug – when you come out of the cathedral you go left for two blocks and turn left again and there it is with a stained-glass window with a stained-glass pig in the middle.'

Brewer nodded. 'And–?'

'And that's about it. We talked about this and that. I got him laughing pretty good–'

'He was in a good mood?'

'He was as relaxed as a dirty sock,' Dancer said. 'He told me he was taking Hilda skiing some bleeding where in Switzerland. For the weekend, you know.' Dancer sat back on a bench and rested his back on a wall to look at his cup. 'I wonder if this is warm gasoline.'

'What time did you break up?'

'Around eight. He had to go. He said he had to meet someone in a club.'

'Did he say what club?'

'As a matter of fact, he did, Brewer. And isn't it a miracle I remember the name of it? The Bismarck Club.'

'Bismarck? Where's that?'

'I'll never tell you. Probably not far from where we were drinking.'

'Was he sober?'

'I've never seen the man drunk. I've seen him wreck bars and tear down buildings and throw people at the moon, but I have never seen him drunk.'

'Was he driving his car?' Brewer asked.

'I'll never tell you,' Dancer said. 'He walked out, turned left and that was that.'

'Did you get your fuel money?'

'Some. Parker will never leave a pal in a lurch.'

'When did you leave Germany?'

'The next afternoon,' Dancer replied. 'I was over in the hotel – the new one.'

'The Central.'

'That's it. I was scraping around looking for some action and I got it.'

'Got what, Dancer?'

'This job.'

'Interesting. Who gave it to you?'

'Fritzsche Air Cargo.'

'In Bonn?'

'Yes.'

'An air cargo carrier gave you a job carrying air cargo. Why didn't they handle it themselves?'

'Scheduling problems, mate. Happens all the time. They take the work, then subcontract it out.'

'You got the job in the hotel?'

'No, no, Brewer. The downtown air freight offices of Fritzsche, they called me on the phone. I went nipping around and signed the papers right there. It was hot.'

'How much longer are you going to be?'

'Another week. Ten days maybe. It'll pay for a complete two-hundred-and-forty-hour check on both engines and an overhaul.'

'New rubber bands.'

'Yeah. New rubber bands.'

Brewer paced up and down a few times, looking out expectantly on the loading platform.

Under the light, Dancer watched him. 'Who you working with, Brewer?'

'Thomas.'

'Excalibur? I've been waiting to hear from them. You tell him I'm waiting.'

'He knows, Dancer. He knows. Tell me. Did Parker mention anything about a Doomsday?'

'You kidding?'

'I never kid about Doomsday, Dancer.'

Dancer shook his head. 'I left him laughing, Brewer.'

'That's what I'm going to do for you, Dancer. Leave you laughing and alive.'

'Alive?'

'Is your bird ready to go?'

'Yep.'

'Then go. Don't even stop to pick up your dunnage. Just get up and go.'

Dancer put the mug down and stood – the survivor ready for flight. 'What's up, mate?'

'They sent someone after you, Dancer. I slowed him down but he's not far behind. File a flight plan to de Gaulle. After you're airborne, change it to Amsterdam. You'll pick up a load from Excalibur – for Spain. Lie low until you hear from Thomas.'

Dancer took two steps, jumped off the platform and ran toward his DC-3.

Quist ran along the loading platforms, dodging in and out of trucks, forklifts and airport vehicles, holding the florist's box like a football. A rose fell out as he ran, then another.

He jumped up on the loading platform and inside saw a man pouring a cup of tea.

'Dancer! Have you seen Dancer!'

The man pointed out on the line. Quist turned and saw the old DC-3 engines warming up. He could see Dancer staring at him and the old plane began to roll down the taxi ramp. Quist jumped off the platform and ran at the DC-3. Approaching, he pulled the revolver out of its long leather holster and raised it to fire.

A forklift truck turned a corner and rushed toward him at top speed, its horn hooting. Quist dodged clear of it and heard the driver shouting. When it passed him, the plane had gotten out of range. Its running lights went off into the darkness and Quist stood on the runway, staring after it, panting, the gun hanging at his side. Behind him Charlie Brewer parked the forklift. The last roses spilled from Quist's florist's box and fell at his feet.

Quist wasn't hard to follow. Brewer observed him give the florist's box to the liveried chauffeur, then strolled behind him to the check-in line for the flight back to Cologne. If Brewer had had time to get a backup man, the chauffeur could have been followed.

In the passengers' lounge, which was being cleaned by a housekeeping crew, Quist walked up and down. Then he got an airline schedule from an information desk and fell to studying it. Brewer could easily see the title on the cover. London/Madrid. Quist looked at his watch, took out his wallet and checked the contents, then thoughtfully paced again.

The Cologne flight was called on the public address system, and the sleepy passengers moved in a ragged string toward the boarding gate. Brewer remained seated, waiting for Quist to make his move. Quist was agonizing. He crossed and recrossed his legs, drew a hand across his mouth, stood up, sat down, then looked longingly after the other passengers.

Abruptly he stood and walked quickly to the boarding gate to Cologne. Brewer was right behind him.

He sat two aisles behind Quist and kept him under surveillance all through the return flight. Quist was in trouble. He had failed. By the way he had strutted through the Cologne airport on his way to England, he obviously had felt he had a pushover assignment. Cocky. Inattentive. He'd let his mark get away, a mark with dangerous information. He faced a rough time back in Cologne or he wouldn't have so carefully considered fleeing to Madrid.

Quist began to fidget about fifteen minutes before touchdown. He was clearly rehearsing a speech, shifting in his seat, crossing and recrossing his legs and brushing his fair hair endlessly with both hands.

Brewer followed him through the terminal, a man reluctantly going to his fate, heavy-footed, in a disconsolate slow stroll.

He stopped and made a phone call. He shook his head

as he talked, then held out a pleading palm, grew red-faced, raised his voice and furiously hung up the telephone.

Brewer stayed right with him, aware that this might be the break he was waiting for. If he was very careful, very professional, he would be able to follow the distracted Quist to his destination.

Quist waited by the main passenger entrance near the cab stand. He must have been expecting to be picked up. And Brewer had his choice of available cabs for following Quist.

Quist paced in agony for nearly twenty minutes. Then two cars rushed up to the entrance and stopped. Quist went through the doorway toward them as the doors opened and five or six men stepped out. Brewer was tagged.

The men scattered toward various exits. Three hastened purposefully past Quist and through the main entrance. Brewer ran. He moved through the passenger lounge, past sleeping figures and around the cleaning crews, to the exit. He got to it as one of the men came through it after him.

The man wasn't much. Out of shape and not young, but he was heavy with strong arms and he managed to slow Brewer down. Brewer got him with a kick in the kneecap but by then another man had come up and propelled Brewer through the doorway and out on the sidewalk. Two more were coming up fast. Brewer made himself pause until he took measure of his assailant. He was younger, stronger than the other, in good shape and he knew what to do with his hands. Twice he narrowly missed driving his beefy elbow into Brewer's gut. Now another man had arrived and he was full of business, a knife in his hand.

'Hold him! Hold him!' he called urgently, eager to thrust the blade.

Brewer turned his man with a violent swing, then shoved him at the knife wielder. It didn't completely work but it gave Brewer a three-step head start and he turned and ran. This was one he owed Quist. He was surprised at how slow they were. Instead of chasing him, they were waving for the two cars to come up. Brewer settled down to an easy trot,

131

moving toward the huge parking lot, through the gate and amid the many parked cars.

A few moments later, the two pursuing cars raced through the gate and went in two directions, searching for him. Brewer kept low, running between cars with his head down. He kept trying door handles.

They were pros. They got out of their cars and crouched and lay down scanning the ground for moving legs between the cars. They spread out and moved methodically through the cars like an infantry unit on a sweep. Now they walked with handguns held at their sides.

Brewer promised himself that if he got out of this one, he would return immediately to his snug little pub in Bloomsbury and never stray again.

It was a mistake to have entered the car park. The entire area was encompassed by a cyclone fence. A climber would have made an ideal target. He was trapped. The only way out was the way he had come in. He tried a few more car doors, then he turned to face his pursuers.

He would concentrate on just one of them: the one with the knife. The man was big and he hurried on the balls of his feet in short mincing steps, peering like a hunting dog in car windows and squinting under chassis. In shadow, Brewer stepped across several rows of cars to intercept him. He paused by a small stake truck with a tarpaulin over it. It was an obvious place to hide in, an easy place to search.

Brewer waited behind a microbus, listening for those quick light steps. And softly they came. They paused. The man lifted the tarpaulin and peered inside, then probed with the knife blade. He put his head in.

Brewer moved. He stepped up behind the man and pressed him against the tailgate, pinning the hand that held the knife. Brewer put his forearm around the man's windpipe. The man tried to turn, tried to get away from the tailgate to free his arm and knife. Brewer slowly began to strangle him standing up.

The man was powerful with a great chest and thick

132

muscular arms and he fought violently. He tried several times to cry out but Brewer's forearm had shut his windpipe completely.

Something sharp touched Brewer's ribs. The man was probing desperately with his knife from under his own armpit. Brewer was able to shift his body only a scant inch but the knife blade found him. It sliced along his rib, probing for the space between, trying to push the long blade through the ribs and into his heart.

The searching blade sliced again, cutting the flesh. Brewer pressed the man harder against the tailgate, trying to prevent his wrist with the knife from rotating. The man struggled to keep it free. Brewer brought his head back and banged it against the man's skull, trying to shift his weight away from the seeking knife tip. Another sharp thrust and the knife skated along another rib bone. A micromillimeter lower and it would slip through. Brewer banged his head against the other's again.

The man gathered all his strength and tried to back away from the tailgate. He almost lifted Brewer off his feet and Brewer gripped the edge of the tailgate with his other hand and held firmly.

The two of them trembled with exertion in the dark, in the absolute silence, each pitting every bit of strength against the other. The knife blade came around again and sliced through his raincoat and jacket and shirt and found the space between two ribs. Brewer twisted and moved but the blade held its place. A quick thrust was all that was needed.

But it never came. The man slumped in Brewer's arms. When he was lowered to the ground he was dead. Brewer hurried up the aisle toward the exit gate.

Moments later, he heard an outcry. The body had been discovered. All the searchers converged there on the run and Brewer sprinted toward the exit gate. He passed the two pursuit cars, abandoned by the gate, their doors all standing open, and hurried back toward the cab stand.

He ducked into a cab. 'Take me to a doctor,' he said. He

133

pushed his hand under his shirt and felt it covered with warm blood. The several wounds were bleeding freely. Brewer had completely forgotten his vow to return to his pub.

Brewer went directly to Thomas's hotel room and knocked. It was 4 a.m. To his surprise, Thomas was up, seated beside a room service tray with a pot of coffee, reading Bernie Parker's telephone bill.

Brewer sat down and poured himself some of Thomas's coffee. 'I found him. In Heathrow. Flying air cargo just as Folger said. And I was just six steps ahead of a grunt named Quist.'

Thomas listened to Brewer's report, frowning skeptically throughout. 'That sounds fishy as hell,' Thomas said. 'A big air freight operator hires a known gun smuggler with a doddering old DC-3 to carry valuable cargo? Come on. That was a setup to get Dancer out of town.'

'Then,' Brewer said, 'who sent Quist after him?'

Thomas shrugged.

'How did Roland make out?' Brewer asked.

'Somebody hustled Bernie Parker's office staff out of the country. But Roland came up with a real winner anyway. This is Parker's office phone bill – it's a gold mine. You know Anton Boxx?'

'Boxx?'

'I went to school with him. He's with a big bank in Paris.' Thomas pushed the bill across the coffee table to Brewer. 'Parker made a lot of phone calls to Boxx in the last month. More than twenty.' He looked at his bedside clock. 'I wonder what time Boxx gets up.'

Brewer felt the fatigue deep in his shoulder muscles. 'I'll see you in a couple of hours.'

Fritzsche's man awakened him at four-thirty in the morning. Quist was waiting in the hallway downstairs. Fritzsche had a premonition of bad news when he put on his robe and slippers.

'Well,' he said in his loud voice halfway down the stairs. 'What happened?'

'You didn't hide Dancer well enough,' Quist answered.

'What does that mean?'

'Thomas's man got there first. Brewer. And warned Dancer off.'

'He escaped?' Fritzsche felt the blood of rage throbbing in his face.

'That's exactly what I'm telling you. Thomas has him now.'

'Find him!' Fritzsche shouted.

Quist started to leave, then paused. 'Oh. Brewer also killed one of the security staff from the club.'

'How?'

'Strangled him. In the airport.'

Fritzsche sat down in a chair by the railing. 'Wait.' Quist waited and Fritzsche sat and thought. Dancer had escaped. Dorten would hear about this. And he would realize what a blunder Fritzsche had made. And he would have Fritzsche's head on a tray. Dorten was the one man that Fritzsche feared. Dorten would not hesitate to order his execution. And Dorten would be even wilder if he discovered that Thomas had gotten a lead from Dancer into the Bismarck Club. Fritzsche had to move – and fast.

'So,' he said to Quist, 'Brewer was too much for you.'

'No.'

'Yes. He settled your hash in London and you turned out the security force to get him and he fixed them too. Don't lie, Quist. I'll get the whole story when I go to the club.'

Quist clasped his hands in anger. 'That's not the way I read it. You didn't tell me that Brewer was on Dancer's trail. He took me from behind right in Heathrow.'

'And how did he get the security man? Tell me it was luck. Those security men are all handpicked. You don't get lucky around men like that. Maybe I should fire you and the security staff and hire Brewer. He seems to be better than the lot of you.'

Quist's face flushed red and he rocked on his feet.

'Tell you what, Quist. We can't play patty-cake any-more. You get as many security people as you need and you get Thomas. I want him for lunch – dead. Don't tell me how. Just do it. And don't miss.'

Quist turned and stalked out. He slammed the door so loudly he awakened all the servants on the third floor.

5

The first thing Fritzsche thought about when he woke up that morning was his appointment with the Chinese contact to set up the secret meeting.

But first was his regular morning ceremony. Every morning upon arising, Manfred Fritzsche recited to himself without fail the five fatal errors of Operation Barbarossa, the drive of the German Group Vistula to conquer Russia in the summer and autumn of 1941. Like a rosary, at each stage of his morning toilet he would focus his mind on one of these major mistakes.

Upon awakening, Fritzsche would gaze at the ceiling and tell himself, 'Hitler started too late – June twenty-second.' And Hitler had the benefit of Napoleon's example – who started too late on June 23. Of course there were mitigating circumstances. Stalin had grabbed Romania and Hitler was worried about his oil supplies so he spent five precious weeks on a brilliant drive into Greece. And of course the thaw in Russia was late and Hitler could hardly have started much before June 22 any way. Still, it was a major blunder.

When he brushed his teeth, Fritzsche considered Hitler's second grave error. With three armies driving into Russia, the right flank aimed at Leningrad, the center aimed at Moscow and the left flank aimed at Kiev, Hitler hesitated.

136

Each target was enticing; but he couldn't take all three simultaneously. Which one to concentrate on? Hitler and his generals spent a month during July and August bickering. The decision should have been made before the war was launched. The decision – to take Moscow – was too late. Winter arrived in Moscow before they did. The month's bickering cost Germany the war, not just Moscow.

After his manservant had drawn his bath, Fritzsche sat in the warmth of the tub and thought about how totally unprepared Hitler was for the terrible Russian winter. The troops had no winter uniforms; there was no antifreeze for their vehicles; no shelter for the men. The German troops froze in the open fields of Russia while Siberian winds cut them to ribbons and their mechanized mobility was buried in the deep snow. Many of the troops had only the garments they took from Russian corpses, and the tanks and trucks froze solid and wouldn't start.

As he shaved, Fritzsche looked himself in the eye and remembered the fourth fatal error. The brutal behavior of the German soldiers disaffected hundreds of thousands of ethnics who would have fought gladly alongside the German troops against their Russian exploiters. German brutality hammered and annealed the friendly ethnics into a wild army intoxicated with hatred for Germany.

And he finished his morning litany like a secular devotee making the stations in a church while tying his tie. 'Hitler had inadequate intelligence and he didn't believe what little he did have.' Hitler launched 100 German divisions against a supposed strength of 200 Russian divisions. Then he discovered there were 360. If he had listened to his intelligence men he would have realized that it was impossible for him to beat Russia with the equipment and troops on hand.

Before he left his bedroom, Fritzsche recited several times over like a chorus, 'Russia can be defeated.'

This morning, after his recitation he hastily consumed his roll and butter, drank his single cup of black coffee and left home somewhat earlier than usual. He had his chauffeur drive him to a remote, parklike area on the Rhine River a few miles above Bonn.

And there he took a short stroll through a little wood to a narrow lane where he found a car parked. He stood by the window, seeing his breath in the chilly air, and spoke through the open window to the driver. 'There must be no telephone conversations,' he said. 'And the meeting place must be absolutely secure from eavesdropping.'

The driver of the car said, 'Mr Fox has arranged everything. The meeting is tomorrow night.' He extended a slip of paper. 'This is a map of the meeting place. Do you know it?'

Fritzsche studied it. 'I'll find it.'

'Be sure the map is completely understandable.'

'It is.'

'If for any reason Mr Fox needs to cancel the meeting, I will send you a message saying that the air freight meeting in Paris is canceled. If you need to cancel the meeting, send me a message that says you cannot attend the air freight meeting in Paris.'

With that, the car drove off. Fritzsche strolled back to his limousine, memorizing the map and praying for resolve and courage. He was nearing the point of no return.

Thomas waited until ten and called Anton Boxx's office in Paris. The secretary told him that Boxx was in Bogotá and would be back in two days.

Thomas switched his thoughts to Manfred Fritzsche. Why had he hired Dancer to go to London? Thomas was getting ready to go to the library to research Fritzsche's background and business connections when his phone rang.

'Mr Thomas?' a woman's voice asked.

'Yes.'

'Mr Colin Thomas?'

'Yes.'

'I have some information for you and I have something to give you.'

'What is it?'

'I have Bernie Parker's appointment book. Would you like to see it?'

'Who is this?'

'He didn't bring his appointment book with him to Paris, Mr Thomas. He left it in my apartment.'

'Who is this?'

'I was a friend of Bernie's. A good friend. And I want to help you catch the men who did it.'

'Go on.'

'Meet me somewhere safe. Somewhere public. And you must promise me you won't follow me after we meet.'

'How tall are you?'

There was a pause. 'What – why do you want to know that?'

'How will I identify you?'

'Don't you think we ought to pick a place first?'

'You've already done that and I'm guessing it's the cathedral.'

'That's as good a place as any, wouldn't you say?'

'How tall are you. What do you look like?'

'I am five feet two and I weigh one hundred ten pounds and I have short brown hair and brown eyes and I'll be holding a newspaper in a roll under my left arm. You carry a rolled newspaper too. Meet me at the center door of the cathedral, in, say, half an hour?'

'Yes.'

Thomas went up and roused Brewer. 'It's a setup,' he told Brewer. 'Parker never in his life had a girl friend that small. But right now, it's the best lead we've got.'

Brewer was kicking on his pants. 'If it's that Quist again, I can spot him a mile off.' He paused and considered Thomas. 'Maybe we shouldn't show up. This makes it too easy for them. You stand on the steps of that cathedral and you might as well help them aim the gun at your head.'

'I'll be very careful.'

Brewer snorted at him. He quickly finished dressing.

'Roland will meet us in the lobby,' Thomas said.

Quist walked purposefully toward the cathedral. But he was early and he paused at a shoe store. He liked the smell of leather; it reminded him of his childhood and happier days. When he raised his eyes from the window display, he found a woman staring frankly at him. A large Viking type she was, statuesque, heavy-breasted and very well dressed in a light wool afternoon frock – rather pretty, about thirty-five or forty.

Women were easy for Quist. It usually took only a look. When he wanted one, he simply walked along of an evening until he made contact. There was no selling, no maneuvering, no false protestation, just an open encounter. As a rule it all was sealed with a good hard smack on the rump; then she would follow him to the hotel.

Once he'd met a woman on the street, strolled with her along the Rhine River for a short while, escorted her to a hotel and gotten his back raked open by her fingernails during abandoned copulation, then parted with her again on the street, all without one word passing between them.

He glanced again at the Viking woman. This one would be very physical. Alas, duty called. He had a rendezvous at the cathedral. As he walked past her, he drew his finger across her back.

Ahead, the first cathedral tour buses were unloading. A florist was pouring water on bunches of cut flowers outside his shop window. Quist glanced back and commenced smiling broadly. The woman had followed him. Her sidelong glance met his. And when she stepped past him, he felt her finger drawn across his back.

Quist abruptly crossed the street, his eyes searching the cathedral steps.

Roland balked at the whole situation. He stood in the lobby

140

and argued with both Thomas and Brewer, and was clearly afraid.

'It's a setup,' he insisted. 'We opened too many closets yesterday and someone wants us out of the way.'

'It's a lead,' Brewer said.

'A lead? It's an execution. Who's the target? Thomas? You? Me? All of us? Oh, come on.'

'Do you have a better suggestion?' Thomas asked.

'Survive!' Roland replied. 'Skip the whole thing.'

'If I were going to ace someone,' Thomas said, 'I wouldn't choose the steps of that cathedral. Have you ever seen the crowds of tourists that pack in there?'

'You two have more courage than brains,' Roland said. 'Each one of you is crazier than the other.'

'Maybe you're right, Roland,' Brewer said. 'This job really needs only two of us.'

'If you go, I go,' Roland replied. 'But if someone gets killed, remember what I told you.'

He said no more but he wore a mournful expression on his face like a condemned man as the three of them walked up the always crowded Hohe Strasse toward the cathedral.

They waited nearly an hour and Thomas had a growing sense of vulnerability. Maybe Roland was right. Anyone could walk up to his target, kill him and escape on foot through the crowds.

The cathedral in Cologne – the Dom – is one of the most celebrated in Europe, an example of pure German Gothic style. It is enormous, with two spires over five hundred feet high, that can be seen for great distances over the German countryside, a somewhat battered survivor of World War II.

The cathedral stood with its back to the Cathedral Bridge over the Rhine. It was a major tourist stop and when Thomas and Brewer and Roland approached it, the day's visits were in full swing. Groups on tours were herded by tour guides waving furled umbrellas. They paused everywhere, at the foot of the steps, by the three front entrances and at the many points of interest inside.

Thomas and Brewer and Roland strolled by the front of the enormous structure. But they didn't see a woman standing with a rolled-up newspaper at the middle entrance. On foot they reconnoitered the area. Assassination would be easy. When they turned and came back, they saw a woman in the midst of the shuffling crowds stand with a rolled-up newspaper under her left arm. She was slight with brown hair. Patiently, she studied the faces in the crowd. Not Parker's type at all.

While Thomas and Roland waited, Brewer went up the steps into the cathedral foyer by the left-hand door and emerged moments later by the far right door. He shook his head at Thomas. No Quist. Thomas took a last look around and mounted the steps to the woman.

He got the barest glimpse of Quist, who leaned out from the left doorway. The man stepped clear and brought up a handgun. Holding it with both hands, he drew a perfect bead on Thomas's head and fired. Roland shouted and pushed Thomas down, then fell on top of him. A great outcry panicked the crowd. Thomas sat up with Roland lying across his lap. Roland never knew what hit his temple. The shot killed him instantly.

Brewer darted past the fallen Roland and after the gunman. Thomas was right behind him. At the corner of the building they saw Quist riding on the back of a motorcycle, hugging the driver. It roared down the street. The only thing that could pursue it through the crowded streets was another motorcycle.

Thomas and Brewer turned and watched the crowd cluster around Roland. The woman with the newspaper was gone.

Brewer walked Thomas around Cologne for nearly two hours. In the beaming sunlight, they paced the broad promenade along the Rhine River, past the carefully preserved rows of historic buildings that had somehow survived the bombing. Thomas's eyes looked at the heavy boat traffic on the river without really seeing it. Even the imposing steel work of the Cathedral Bridge failed to intrude on his thoughts.

'There was a strain between us,' he said to Brewer at last. 'I was meaning to talk to Roland. I wanted to tell him I didn't dislike him. I wanted to say actually that I liked him well enough. He was a pro.'

'Why didn't you?' Brewer asked.

Later Brewer went off to the library and searched for the biography of Manfred Fritzsche. He returned at early evening. Thomas had been making phone calls to London and Washington.

'There's lots of material available on Fritzsche,' Brewer said. 'He's a public figure. They write magazine articles about him all the time. Okay? Very big industrialist. He was in the German Army in World War Two, in a Panzer group under Guderian, first in France and then later in Russia. All kinds of decorations. He's a big war hero, lots of stories around about his daring deeds. Okay? Comes from an old Prussian family. Very military. But after the war, he went into business and he built three big companies and who knows how many others, counting all the corporate divisions.'

'What three companies?'

'First, an air freight business. Called Fritzsche Air Freight. It has a subsidiary that makes specialized military aircraft like coast guard planes. Okay? Then an electrical harness company – makes wiring harnesses for jet fighters. And now, microminiature components for military hardware. Very profitable. And that's it.'

'Where are his headquarters?'

Brewer turned and pointed out of the window past the twin cathedral spires. 'Right there. It's called – are you ready? The Fritzsche Building. Here's the address.'

'Where does he live?' Thomas asked.

'That I couldn't get. One thing. He's famous for his

143

Mercedes. Custom made. Big as a yacht and everyone in Germany knows it.'

'How about the Bismarck Club?'

'Any tourist guide can help you with that one.' Brewer took out a colorful brochure. 'The Bismarck Club is in a famous old manor house. You can tour the outside of the buildings and the grounds but you're not allowed inside. It's a private club. Founder? Guess who. Manfred Fritzsche.'

Kaethe Dorten had a dinner appointment and she arrived back in Cologne from a client meeting in Hamburg with just enough time to make it.

She found the woman there with her familiar paper shopping bag. Kaethe quickly shut her office door. 'What is it? What happened?'

'Arthur Roland has been killed. Quist shot him on the steps of the cathedral.'

Kaethe sat down and stared openmouthed at the woman. 'He's insane. Fritzsche is suffering from senile madness.'

'He's trying to cover up a mess he made,' the woman said. 'But he's just making things worse. Roland was a very good agent.' The woman hesitated then said: 'Quist was aiming at Thomas.'

'Thomas?' The woman knew. She saw Kaethe's feelings flood her face like a blush.

'And that would have been a real shame,' the woman said. 'These Americans are not our enemies. Fritzsche has distracted everyone from our assignment against Russia.'

Kaethe read something in the woman's manner. 'There's more, isn't there?'

'Yes. Brewer found Dancer in London. And now they've put him in hiding.'

'Oh, can there be any worse news?'

The woman said, 'We located Dancer's DC-3 last night. But Brewer got to Dancer ahead of us. It's just as well. Fritzsche had sent Quist to kill Dancer.'

Kaethe almost laughed. It reminded her of a
bad German joke about a string of calamities on a

'Thomas is too clever for Fritzsche,' the woman
tinued.

Kaethe Dorten knew that she'd better see her father.
This was much too much for her to handle. But first, she
decided, she'd better confront Fritzsche. If her father had
to take charge again, it might kill him.

'I'll take care of it,' she told the woman.

The woman nodded, stood and silently departed.

Kaethe put her hands to her mouth as an idea took form
in her mind. Gustav Behring had made a prophecy. He said
someone would have to kill Manfred Fritzsche. That senile
old man and his boy killer. What a devastating team. But
not her – she couldn't kill. Could she?

Roland's death rousted Dudorov, the KGB station chief in
Amsterdam. Following so closely upon Parker's murder, it
set all the alarm bells ringing in Dudorov's head. He read
and reread the teletype message from the KGB station chief
in Bonn. After he'd seen the computer summary on Roland,
he was even more alert. The two deaths were connected
with Excalibur Ltd of London and who knew what else?
Was Dorten, sick as he was, up to something?

Dudorov knew he would have to shake off his weariness
and go to Cologne. Nothing less than a clandestine
face-to-face report with his illegals there would do. He
asked the computer for the most recent reports on Dorten
and also on the Bismarck Club. Then he called Gregov.
'We're going to Cologne,' he said.

Colin Thomas had one name – Fritzsche, who owned some
factories – and one address – the Bismarck Club, a private
organization that Fritzsche had founded. The only connection that had with Parker's death was Dancer's word that
Parker was on his way to the club when last seen.

The next logical step was to put a tap on this Manfred
Fritzsche's telephone – his home telephone. And since they

had no home address for him, the logical way to reach it was to let him lead them there.

Thomas and Brewer arrived at the Fritzsche office building before five with a trunkful of used telephone tap equipment and tools that Thomas had gotten through the assistance of Excalibur's German representative, Travers. Then they waited as they had done so many times in their careers. They were parked a half block behind Fritzsche's Mercedes. Nearby, in full view, Fritzsche's chauffeur stood talking to another chauffeur. Fritzsche emerged around six.

Following the limousine was easy. The chauffeur drove in a proper four-square style at moderate speed south along the Cologne-Bonn motorway for a few miles then turned off into an area of high-rise apartments. It was not a neighborhood where a wealthy man like Fritzsche would live. Brewer's cynical mind identified the destination of the limousine immediately.

'A love nest,' he said to Thomas.

When the limousine stopped and parked at the curb of one of the apartments, Thomas got out and hastened to the entrance. He walked in right behind Fritzsche, who had unlocked the front door. They entered the elevator together. Fritzsche pushed the fifth-floor button. Thomas pushed the fourth-floor button. When he got off, he entered the stairway and ran up one flight just in time to observe, through the glass panel of the fire door, Fritzsche striding down the hallway, taking out a door key as he walked. Thomas got a glimpse of the apartment before the door shut. He memorized the apartment number and returned to the street to wait. The chauffeur was reading a newspaper by the aid of an overhead map light.

Brewer was elated. Pillow talk had brought down empires. He was eager to have Thomas bug the entire apartment. Fritzsche wasn't probably going to be long up there. His chauffeur was waiting and neither had had any dinner. Thomas guessed what kind of a mistress Fritzsche had. Nothing matronly. Fritzsche's flinty face didn't seek companionship. A piece of confection: something young and soft and baby-skinned in furs.

Thomas was reading a newspaper when Brewer nudged him. They had finally come out – Fritzsche and his bird. And Brewer got his first look at her. He took a good long look. Just what he'd expected: whipped cream and sugar and very young – teen-aged. They were going to go to dinner; the call of the belly.

'After nookie, noshing,' Brewer said.

When the limousine disappeared around a corner, Thomas put some tools in his pocket.

'Let's see if this damned thing works,' he said to Brewer.

He plugged a lead from a small black box into the cigarette lighter. Then he clipped a cigar-shaped cylinder to his jacket pocket.

'If they come back before I'm finished,' he told Brewer, 'push that button. It'll ring the buzzer in my pocket. Like so.' The alarm emitted an irritating squeal.

'Don't I get to help you?'

'Play sentry for me,' Thomas said to Brewer. 'I won't be long.'

She had a typical dime lock on her door. Thomas didn't even bother picking it. A flexible strip of plastic popped it in less than ten seconds. He allowed himself an hour for the job, although he expected them to be gone at least twice that long.

The apartment was a combination of boudoir and campus dormitory. The bed was extra large and extra long with a mirror in the ceiling. The sheets were pink with lace edges, and the closet was stuffed with Paris label clothes, boudoir gowns, evening dresses, expensive suits, afternoon frocks, hats and dozens of pairs of shoes and slippers. The drawers were filled with lace underclothes, blouses, scarves. There were boxes of jewels, pendants, bracelets, rings and necklaces. Yet juxtaposed against all this feminine elegance was a student's desk crowded with school papers, chewed pencils, packets of gum, posters of rock stars, sketch pads, layouts, term projects. And cast on the desk chair was a pair of faded blue jeans and a worn pair of striped sneakers.

First, Thomas checked for an escape route. He looked out of the living room windows. It was a straight drop five stories down. The bedroom window was set in the back wall of the building but it, too, looked straight down. There was a drainpipe that ran down the side of the building. If he stood on the sill of the bedroom window, he would just be able to reach it.

It was a long climb down. He wondered how well set the fasteners were in the brick wall. It was too dangerous. Besides he'd be done long before they came back, especially with the pocket alarm system. He returned to the hallways and checked the walls. One bedroom and one living room wall paralleled the corridor. He could run circuits in the hall baseboard molding. He came out of the apartment and down the hallway, searching for a place, secret but accessible, outside her apartment to put the tape deck. At the end of the corridor, he found a small utility room with circuit breakers, telephone junction boxes and valve turnoffs for the water. Perfect.

He returned to the car and got a toolbox and a small metal kit. Brewer looked at him hopefully and Thomas almost invited him in.

'I won't be much longer,' he said to Brewer.

It was a pushover. Thomas attached the tape recorder to the wall of the utility room up above the circuit breaker box where it was almost invisible. Voice-actuated, at a very slow rpm, it could be left for days. It had taken him only fifteen minutes to wire it.

Then he ran the lead from the utility room inside the baseboard molding. He placed the taps in a series every four feet by drilling holes into the wall behind the molding. He looked at his watch. An hour had elapsed. He was running a little behind. Fifteen more minutes would do it.

Thomas went back into her apartment and studied the

interior-wall layout thoughtfully. He needed to place only a few more to completely cover the whole apartment. If Fritzsche had half the cunning Thomas expected him to have, then he would as a matter of course have his little nest swept for taps every week or so. The best Thomas could hope for was two weeks. In fact, it would be smart to remove the taps in twelve days or so and never be discovered at all.

Thomas was in the bedroom, on his knees by the molding, thinking about this when the door opened. They entered talking. Thomas stepped into the closet behind the gowns and waited, furious with his own bush-league lapse in attention.

He was completely trapped. He couldn't get out until they went out and there wasn't a good hiding place in the whole apartment. They stood near the bedroom door. Fritzsche mentioned a bottle of wine.

Thomas looked down and saw his toolbox in the middle of the bedroom floor just as the girl entered. She stood by her bed working the catch on the back of her gown. It wouldn't move and she struggled with it. Her eyes seemed to pass over the toolbox several times. Abruptly she walked out of the room. Thomas unhesitatingly put his foot out of the closet to the box and gave it a slow push under the bed. It just fit. Then he tried to conceal himself behind the clothes. It was a pretty poor cover.

The girl returned with the gown open and, slipping it off her shoulders, stepped out of it. She removed her underclothes and stood by the vanity table and brushed her hair. Fritzsche appeared silently in the doorway with a glass of wine and watched her nude figure sway in tempo with the hairbrush. She smiled at him and stepped over to the closet for a robe. She was the only reason Fritzsche didn't see Thomas.

Thomas tried to crouch down and away from her as her hand reached out.

'No,' said Fritzsche. 'The blue one.'

Saved.

She brought the robe over to him and let him put it on her, wrap it and tie it at her waist. He kissed her under her right ear. 'Wine?' he asked her and led her back to the living room.

Thomas didn't believe in relying on luck. It always set you up then ran out on you at the crucial moment. Waiting meant discovery. Soon, old Fritzsche would lead her back to the bed for some dalliance. So Thomas had his opportunity to leave now while they were sharing the wine. In minutes it might be too late. Without hesitation, Thomas crossed the bedroom, opened the window in front of the desk and stepped out on the brick ledge. He looked down. Cement walkway, five stories down. He looked up. The roof was one story up, above the sixth floor – an eighteen-foot climb. He reached out and gripped the square white drain that ran from the roof to the ground. Made of plastic, it was attached to the wall by means of white plastic straps nailed to the cement. He reached out and squeezed it. It was thin-walled and flexible. The straps that held it were nailed to the wall with thin roofer's nails. He would have to descend by gripping his way down by hand and the slightest extra weight might pull the whole thing away from the wall. It was safer going up.

He had to make a move. He could be seen on the window ledge by any number of other apartment windows. He looked at the frail drain and decided he was getting too old, too breakable, for this game. And with that, he reached out a hand and seized the square drainpiping. Hanging by that one hand, he shut the window and stepped off the ledge and prayed. His weight made the drain squeal in its straps. Pressing his knees against the brick wall, he began to walk himself up the wall. Fear made him move quickly. The drain complained and the straps flexed as he climbed. He was parallel to the sixth-floor windows now.

And he eyed the window speculatively. Safety was just a reach away. But he might find the tenants asleep in bed or the window might be locked. And the lateral reach might put too much stress on the drain. He continued his climb,

150

hand over hand. His arms were tiring and the muscles in his forearms were feeling the terrific strain from his hands. Above him, at the top, the drain bowed out like a square funnel. The whole installation talked and flexed.

He needed to make one last great effort before his arm muscles gave out. As he paused, he felt the strap at belt level pull away from the wall. The drain began to bow. With a furious lunge, he got one hand on the parapet. Another strap yielded and the drain pulled away from the wall and got in his way. For an instant he hung by one hand, waiting for his body to sway the other way. As it came about, he got his other hand on the parapet. His arms weren't going to make it. The upper-arm muscles threatened to cramp.

Bracing both feet against the wall, he pushed, found a new grip and slowly pulled himself up. And up. At last, a knee on the parapet. Another pull and he was on the roof, his legs sticking out over the edge. Like a snake he gave a wriggle and lay facedown on the low parapet. The funnel of the drain swayed loosely by his foot in the wind.

He lay with his face down, smelling the dusty roof tar as his left hand fisted, squeezed into a tight pain-filled cramp, locking the muscles of his wrist and forearm. He knew that the hand could not have supported him for one more attempt to boost himself on to the roof. He would surely be lying six stories down, a smashed body. He rolled over on his back and reached into his pocket, found the pocket alarm and flung it off the roof into the darkness.

Good thing Brewer hadn't come. The two of them would never have made it up that drainpipe. It would have torn off the wall. Then he remembered. Brewer had a paralytic terror of heights. What a scenario that would have been.

The trap door in the roof led down by a metal ladder to a locked closet. It took him a few minutes to pick the lock in the dark. When he got down to the street, he was surprised to see Fritzsche's limousine just pulling away.

'Is he in it?' asked Brewer.

'Yes. Let's see where he goes. It's too early for him to go home.'

Brewer smoothly positioned the car behind the limousine and cruised a safe distance away.

'How'd you make out?' he asked Thomas.

'A piece of cake.' Thomas took several tools out of his pockets and put them in the glove compartment. He'd ruined the knees of his trousers on the brick wall. 'I'll have to go back for the toolbox.'

'Yeah?'

'Damned alarm didn't work.'

'Jesus God. I pushed the bejesus out of the button. What happened?'

'I got trapped in the bedroom. She changed her clothes and nearly took down the gown I was hiding behind. I had to climb a drain to the roof.'

Brewer surprised him with his next question. It had nothing to do with the traps or the dangerous climb to the roof.

'What did she look like?' he asked.

Even in the dark, it looked just like the photograph in the travel folder. When they rolled slowly into the parking lot far behind Fritzsche's limousine, Thomas knew it was the Bismarck Club. A wind had arisen and was buffeting the shrubs around the entrance; the weather was turning sharper.

The Bismarck Club stood on a high rise of land, a vintage 1880 mansion with a spectacular view of the Rhine, which lay, a glittering curve, under the stars. The club was a massive structure, all stone and brick with battlements and towers and spiked ornamental ironwork, the home originally, according to the club brochure, of a hardware manufacturer with fourteen children. The stables and carriage houses and servants' quarters and other structures were all brick with slate roofing and metal window shutters, set in a grove of mature linden trees, leafless now and holding the scribbled black lines of bare branches up to the night sky.

Inside was a huge hallway floored with a striking

black-and-white checkerboard of large marble squares. The entire interior was done in carved woods and panels including a dual curving stairway that rose from the marbled vestibule to the second floor. Club employees in striped blue-and-white vests and black trousers were busy on many errands, passing through the many rooms. The whole building was lit up like a luxury liner. Most of the cars in the parking lot, Brewer noted, were Mercedes. A meeting seemed to be breaking up. There was a sudden crowd of club members near the vestibule, donning overcoats and still talking to each other.

A very attractive woman walked across the parking lot to the entrance and the doorman admitted her with great courtliness. It was Kaethe Dorten. She had been sitting in her parked car, looking at the festive lights of the Bismarck Club. She was bracing herself for a head-on confrontation with Manfred Fritzsche and wondering how she was going to bring it off. For if she didn't find some way to stop him, Fritzsche was well on his way to destroying the conspiracy and everyone concerned with it.

During the afternoon, when the evidence had begun to come into her office, she'd first doubted that it was true. But Fritzsche was clearly behaving like a wild man. Then came the report of Roland's death on the cathedral steps, and she felt depths of anger she'd never known before. Had he become senile?

She knew she should see her father for guidance before acting. This was all too new and unfamiliar to her. But he was too ill; it was out of the question. He had thrown the problem to her like a drowning man. He couldn't handle it. So she had to, alone. Besides, she knew what her father would do if he were well. He would put a bullet through Fritzsche's head without hesitation.

She had to walk out of that meeting with the upper hand tonight. She opened the glove compartment of her car and took out a pistol and put it in her purse. And all the while she didn't believe she was doing what she did. A pistol. Madness.

It seemed absurd, trying to dominate Fritzsche, to intimidate him. A man in his position knew all the tricks. He was one of Germany's most powerful men, arrogant as an emperor, power-proud, fearless, even ruthless, a father figure to the country, a national monument who was deferred to by everyone – a man accustomed to dominating others. But he was also pigheaded, impetuous, heedless of good counsel, not nearly so intelligent as he considered himself, with blustering, battle-ax methods that were going to bring ruination on that small army of the country's leaders who were in the conspiracy with him – and possibly bring on a catastrophic confrontation with the Soviet Union. Through the windows she saw the members moving inside the club. None of them knew of the grave jeopardy Fritzsche had put them in. If she didn't get the ring through Fritzsche's nose in the next hour, it might be all over for the lot of them.

As she crossed the parking lot to the canopied entrance, she felt the double-mindedness that actors and jewel thieves know. There was the great tension and the clawing fear just before one commits oneself, walks onstage or climbs into the window. But there was also the curiosity, the eagerness to work the trick that wins the audience or uncovers the diamonds. It was as though she were both inside her body and outside, calmly observing herself. The mood of recklessness was taking over.

The club was busy. Members sat in small groups in the main club room in wing chairs, on Persian carpets, tête-à-tête with drinks in German crystal, or in the walnut-paneled bar, on the stairway. Many others, she knew, were in the meeting rooms, drinking, smoking, plotting.

In all those years she had visited the clubhouse, she had never known that within these walls the best minds in the country were in a vast conspiracy to destroy another nation. Behind the tuxedos and the expensive cars, the rich trappings of the clubhouse, the red-jacketed attendants hurrying here and there with drinks, cigars, newspapers, behind the pampered tastes, the fine wines and gourmet foods, there was a secret deadly purpose.

Each one of them was responsible for solving one small part of the total problem and deliberately unaware of what problems the others around them were solving. She looked around at the members with a new appreciation.

Her father had conceived the idea of the club as he had conceived of everything else. But it was Fritzsche who had set it up; it was Fritzsche's handpicked men who operated it. To the outside world it was the Bismarck Club but inside it was Festung Fritzsche. She was on his turf, she reminded herself as she mounted the stairs to the meeting room on the third floor, originally the family nursery. She was needling herself into recklessness. She climbed eagerly.

Fritzsche had set the stage with care. The lighting was subdued. There was a cheery fire going in the fireplace, and under the hanging bridge lamp stood a small round table with three chairs, a sideboard cart with bottles of liquor, ice, water and cocktail trappings. Pads and pencils were on the table and in the center, striking under the small circle of light, a small vase with American daisies and ferns. It was almost the setting for a love tryst. Courtly, gentlemanly Manfred Fritzsche, your host. He and Behring were standing by the fireplace in serious low conversation when she entered.

'Ah!' Fritzsche stepped toward her immediately, arms extended, a beaming German-poppa smile on his face. He greeted her like his own daughter. She allowed him to play his part, let him hug her. She saw that flush of love on his forbidding face again – smitten. The same flush she had seen during the air show. He had a new mistress, she realized. And he was being foolish about her. The flush of adolescent romantic love on that willful old face that had long lost innocence was as obscene as lipstick – or as mascara on those small brown eyes. It made him grotesque.

Behring came up to her, the strangely metamorphosed man, in World War II the ferocious Black Hawk of the

German skies, now a deft, compromising politician with mellow manners, politic and discreet in a padded banker's body, the wild fury of his youth long ago burned out. The pupils of his eyes told the story. The false courage of alcohol looked out at her. He had made one compromise too many in his life; he had lost his nerve; there was no road back; he would never fly again as the Black Hawk. He kissed her hand fondly, avuncular and merry. He was hard not to like and hard not to pity: some said his wife had put horns on him. Many, many times.

'Come,' Fritzsche urged. 'Let's sit down. We have a lot to discuss.' He pulled out a chair and held it for Kaethe. She chose another and seated herself.

'Behring,' Fritzsche said. 'Sit over there. Fill up your glass. Kaethe, some wine perhaps.'

'Nothing.'

'Well, then, let us get right to it. Your father tells me you are completely informed and we can all speak plainly to each other. Good. I have been in touch with our Chinese friends. I am to meet with them tomorrow night.' He looked triumphantly at them as he rubbed his hands together, waiting for an overjoyed approval. But he found only a tired smile on Behring's face. 'Forty years,' he said to Behring. 'Imagine, Gustav.'

Behring saluted him silently with his glass and refilled it.

'So,' Fritzsche pursued, 'the plan is simplicity itself. Tomorrow night some of my people will take me to a point of rendezvous. They will make sure I am not followed. You can tell your father to rest easy. Everything is under control.' He tried to pat her arm reassuringly.

'No, Mr Fritzsche,' she said in a low voice. 'Nothing is under control. Everything is in chaos.'

Fritzsche couldn't have been more stunned if she'd slapped his face.

'Chaos? Show me where. We will deal with it immediately.'

'You. You are the chaos. You have almost destroyed everything.'

Fritzsche shut his mouth angrily and drew up in his seat. His face became red. 'Pardon?' He really doubted that he had heard correctly.

'You were told by my father to keep your hands off Thomas. Instead, you have jeopardized every member of this organization with your terrible blunders.'

'What are you talking about?'

Behring had risen, almost upsetting his chair. He stood out of the light, staring at her with gaping mouth. She leaned over the table toward Fritzsche.

'You sent Quist to kill a man named Dancer in London.'

'Of course,' Fritzsche said. 'He knew that Parker had come here that night.'

'But you failed! Then you tried to kill Brewer at the airport and that failed. You tried to kill Thomas again on the steps of the cathedral this morning and that failed. In fact, you killed an American agent. Roland.'

She heard Behring exhaling in shock. 'You must be mistaken, Kaethe,' he protested. 'Manfred, you—'

Fritzsche thrust his chair back from the table. 'Are you finished?'

Kaethe Dorten shook her head. 'No. But maybe you are, Mr Fritzsche. This organization can't stand any more of your bumbling prima donna tactics.'

'How dare you!'

'You didn't tell us that you had hired that man Dancer to go to London because he knew too much. And you didn't tell us you were sending a man to kill him. Or that he botched it. Dancer could have given us valuable information about Parker. Now he's in hiding. And, worst of all, you have Thomas in full cry after us. We are all now in the gravest peril because of you.'

Fritzsche pitched his pencil on the table. It hit the daisies as it fell. 'I do not permit people to talk this way to me.'

'And that's been the problem all along. You should have been told off long ago.'

He looked at her with outrage, then glanced at the handbag in her lap. She held both hands on it. He said, 'Thomas should have been killed the moment he entered Parker's office.'

'No. You should have been killed. The moment Parker was murdered. And then there was that other incredible blunder – grinding up Parker's records. You might as well have painted a sign on the wall with a road map for Thomas.' She heard the trembling bottleneck tapping on Behring's glass as he poured himself another drink – a triple. He was breathing heavily.

'The security of this program,' she said to Fritzsche, 'has never been your province before.'

'Your father was never sick before! Who else is there?'

'Me.'

Fritzsche leaned toward her then paused to look again at her purse. 'Suppose I don't accept you.'

'You haven't been given the choice of accepting me. I am here with a message from my father. He is still in charge and we can't afford one more blunder from you.'

Fritzsche sat with the glass in his fist, away from the table. He finally averted his eyes from hers. Then he stood and placed the glass on the table. All his bluster was gone. His people had botched every move he had ordered and he had no cards to play in this meeting. He rubbed his hands on his trousers uncertainly. 'Would you like to put this to a vote downstairs?' she asked him. 'Right now. We will tell them what you have done – how you have exposed them all to certain ruin.'

'You are your father's daughter,' he said and walked toward the door.

But this time she could leave no doubt in his mind. 'Mr Fritzsche,' she said. 'I will handle your transportation tomorrow night. Also it would be a grave mistake for you to contact my father – except through me.'

He gave her a long look.

'This is your last warning,' she said. 'You have given me an incredible mess to clean up. It'll be a miracle if I save anything.'

Fritzsche banged the door shut when he left. Panting, Behring sat down and slumped in his chair. The liquor almost slopped out of his glass. He stared at her face.

She said, 'You should have stopped him long ago.'

'I had no idea – my God, what has he done?'

'What has he done? He's gotten too old. So have you. So has my father. You should have done it ten years ago. Twenty. Three old men bumping along the edges of senility.'

He seemed not to have heard her devastating remark. 'Listen, Kaethe, I know Fritzsche so well. He will chew on what you said. He will have to decide how he feels about this. If you won his respect, he will be a pussycat, rubbing up against your ankle.'

'I see.' She shook her head at him impatiently. He was close to being drunk.

'Otherwise–' He shrugged. 'Everything depends on how you handle things tomorrow night. Everything.'

After the meeting, Kaethe Dorten went back to her office to think, away from club and home, phone and friends.

She sat looking down at the crowds under the blinking neon lights of Hohe Strasse and told herself angrily that she hadn't gotten the ring through Fritzsche's nose. It would have to wait until the next night.

Her immediate problem was to prevent Thomas and Brewer from following Fritzsche to the Fox meeting. She had decided she would employ the technique her father was using against the Russians: divide and conquer. She would split Thomas and Brewer up. If she could she would make a date with Thomas and keep him preoccupied until after the Fox meeting. At the same time, she would decoy Brewer with a pantomime show.

Then after the Fox meeting, she could get back to the crucial job of finding Parker's tunnel into the cabal before

Thomas did. Her father was right: this wasn't so far removed from the skulduggery of the publicity business.

She picked up the phone and dialed Thomas's hotel. She was going to be bright and amusing, ready to trade witty quips with him.

'This is the competition speaking,' she said.

He surprised her. He didn't make a humorous rejoinder. Instead he said, 'It's nice to hear your voice again.'

For a moment she hesitated. It was nice hearing his voice too, nicer than she'd anticipated. 'Thank you,' she said, still groping for a response.

Thomas said, 'I was going to call you at home tonight. Can I see you again sometime?'

It was as though he'd written the script for her. 'Why, yes, of course. That's exactly why I'm calling. I have to take a quick look at a site for a television commercial tomorrow. It's an old farm. I thought I'd pack a picnic basket. Would you like to come along? Then tomorrow night we could have dinner at the Bismarck Club.'

'Tomorrow?'

Don't say no, she thought. Too much depended on him accepting.

'What time?' he asked.

'How about eleven-thirty tomorrow morning? I could pick you up at your hotel.'

Kaethe heaved a sigh when he accepted. And he hadn't even asked how far away the farm was.

6

Kaethe Dorten picked Thomas up fifteen minutes late the next morning.

When he got into the small car, he seemed bigger than

she remembered. And better-looking. She moved him up to a six and a quarter.

'Have I got a day worked out for you,' she said. 'The weather's perfect for a picnic, the food you'll love and the old farm is right out of a picture book.'

'All three?' he asked. 'I can't believe it.'

'Okay,' she said with a grin. 'I lied about the food.'

She watched him carefully from the corner of her eye as they drove into the airport: she hadn't told him about this and she waited for a protest.

'Are we flying somewhere?'

'Not far,' she said.

'When will we be back?'

'Before two, I should say.' She watched his face with growing doubt, then he nodded.

Good, she thought, no argument. Once she got them airborne, he'd be four or five hours incommunicado with no nearby telephone service. Her plane was all ready, standing on the apron outside the main hangar. 'Ever flown in a Fritzsche?' she asked him.

'Fritzsche? No. Never heard of it.'

'The best business craft in the world. Has two of the most reliable aircraft engines you'll ever meet. My uncle helped develop the engine.'

'Isn't Fritzsche the air freight company?'

'Yes. They have a subsidiary that makes business and military planes.'

Fifteen minutes later, they were airborne, flying south and climbing toward the looming mountains. It was a beautiful day for a picnic. But the meteorologist had warned of a sudden change, a cold front preceded by heavy rain and wind. Squalls at sea. She had to watch for a wind shift to the southeast.

Brewer went to check out Tatzie's apartment. The tape recorder was right where Thomas had said it would be. Brewer took the reel off and replaced it with a fresh one. He also made an interesting discovery. The apartment next to hers was empty. When he had arrived three men were moving the last of the household contents down the elevator. An empty apartment could prove useful.

When he left, he discovered Tatzie was right behind him, in jeans and jacket, carrying schoolbooks in a backpack. Natural, honey-colored hair, big eyes, great body: nothing but the best for Fritzsche.

Brewer took the tape back to his hotel and put it on a deck and set it winding. For safety's sake, he listened through earphones. The conversation was predictable. Brewer had listened to hundreds of bed chats. He felt he could write the scripts for them. No rockets went off, no great lines of poetry spoken; just hard breathing. As usual with most men around their mistresses after sex, Fritzsche had the need to utter profound words. It was always confession time.

'Ah, Tatzie,' he said. 'If I could talk.'

Tatzie didn't answer. She was probably not listening. Mistresses knew that after sex was a good time to tune out the ego-preening that always came.

'Your generation will see a new united Germany, Tatzie. I am going to see to it, personally. Tomorrow night I am having a very important meeting to bring it about. You'll be very proud of me.'

Tatzie didn't answer. Probably asleep. Germany re-united was old talk.

Of all the dialogue on the tape, there was only one significant sentence: 'Tomorrow night I am having a very important meeting...'

He erased the whole tape and went down to get his car. He was going to have to lock onto Fritzsche for the next six to twelve hours. Tonight was the meeting. There was no way to contact Thomas until he got back from his picnic. Brewer drove to the Fritzsche building to look for the limousine.

The view from the air was splendid. The terrain rolled and rose, climbing to the mountains, given over first to vineyards, then to potato farms, and then to thickly grown timberland as they approached the Black Forest.

'Stuttgart's that way.' She pointed northeast. 'And the Saar is that way. I have industrial clients in both places. Making lots of money.'

She kept referring to her map in her lap now and checking for landmarks. At last, she found the farm and flew over it several times. It seemed to be abandoned and the dirt landing strip was in rough condition, reverting to the wild. In another year, it would be unusable by aircraft. She studied it carefully and checked her wind direction. She cleared her throat and gave him a tight grin. 'Could be a bit lumpy. Hang on to your wig.'

She was an excellent pilot and he had enough experience as a windship sailor to appreciate it. She played the updrafts like an Olympic helmsman and they touched down with barely a ripple.

She gave him a broad grin. 'Very good piece of work if I do say so myself. How good are you with a machete?'

'Machete?'

'When we leave, if the wind shifts, we'll have to clear some of the grass and shrubs from that part of the strip.'

He looked down where the forest was encroaching with seedlings. 'I never have this problem when I'm sailing,' he said.

'Okay,' she replied. 'Let's go sailing in Greece.'

'When I get the Spanish contract,' Thomas said. 'We'll celebrate.'

'That's liable to be a long wait, Thomas.'

She glanced at her watch. She had to keep him here until five o'clock and that now seemed a long way away.

The farm was very old. The trees along the edges of the fallow fields were towering and full and the fields were overgrown with wild grasses that had gone to seed. Bushes and saplings were taking over. In one corner of the farm a small arbor of fruit trees had become overgrown. The farmhouse had a long sloping roof with a wide overhang, a reminder of the heavy snows that fell all winter.

'A change in the weather is coming,' she told him. 'They may have their first snowfall up here tonight. We don't usually have such long pretty autumns. Do you ski?'

He nodded. 'Do you?'

'I have to be very careful. I'm addicted to it.'

They walked along the side of the house, glancing through the windows. The broad overhang of the roof made it seem dark inside and Kaethe strolled around, with a severe expression on her face, trying to picture it in the television commercial.

They walked through the barn, breathing the old odors of hay and cattle. A shaft of light fell from a roof hole, illuminating motes of straw dust. The daws had chewed through the roof and swallows had gotten in and soon the roof would be in distress. The heavy crossbeams were already covered with bird lime. In the dark sulked several rusted pieces of farm equipment.

A cat came to greet them, mewing, complaining of her heavy breasts and the insatiable kittens that ran sideways behind her. Kaethe found large patches of autumn flowers growing in the sunlight along the south side of the barn and stood there studying them.

'Here,' she said to Thomas. 'Sit on this blanket.'

He sat and watched her stroll up and down, squinting one-eyed, a human camera. She came back and took out some sausages from the picnic basket and strew them on the blanket. She hummed a commercial jingle.

Then with a few plucked wild flowers, she sat beside him and put one in his hair. 'There,' she said. 'We are the ideal German couple having the finest sausage in all of Germany. Look healthy and handsome for the camera.'

He coughed consumptively and groaned.

'Marvelous,' she said, adjusting the flower. She leaned closely to study his hair. 'Do you know you have blue-black hair? Very Celtic.'

'How do you know I'm Celtic?'

'The Welsh are Celts, along with the Irish, the Scots, the Cornish. And you have a Welsh name. You came from here

164

originally, Thomas. Germany. The Celts once dominated all of Europe. Where did you get that?'

'The scar? An injury.'

She was surprised. She knew very well where he'd gotten it. The dossier detailed it. It was an opportunity for him to make some points, play the hero. And he hadn't.

'It makes you interesting,' she said. 'Like a saber cut. An air of mystery, I think.'

'No mystery to it. It's a memorial to a lot of pain. And not worth talking about.'

Not worth talking about. She tried to decide whether he was modest or secretive.

She began bringing out the food. 'There's beer and there's wine. And for me there's soda water.' She smiled at him. 'I'm flying.'

The sun was warm, the food delicious and she realized she was hungry. She sliced the sausage and fed him some. 'What do you think?'

'It's very hard to smile at the camera when you're chewing.'

When he'd eaten enough, Thomas balled his jacket under his head and lay back.

'Have you spent much time in Prague, Thomas?'

'No. I've never been there.'

She considered that, chewing a piece of blackbread. 'Interesting. Your accent is enviable. Where did you learn German, Thomas?'

'From a neighbor in Connecticut. An old man. Blind. He once taught in Prague. A doctor of literature. He paid me to read to him.'

'In German?'

'No. That came later. He wanted to learn to speak like an American. He had an uncanny ear. He listened to me read, then he would imitate what he'd heard. He developed an authentic American idiom without a trace of a foreign accent. He had a lot of books all in German and he tried to get German-speaking people to read to him. But they

165

always quarreled. He didn't like their pronunciation or the way they read the poetry. So he taught me.'

'How old were you?'

'Eleven. Twelve. Pretty soon, I was reading all the German classics aloud to him and he'd sit, head bowed, listening and correcting as I went along.'

She tried to picture him as a boy, far away in America, learning better German than most Germans. 'Marvelous. He gave you a flawless German accent. You intimidate native Germans with it, do you know that? How long did you read to him?'

'Oh. Years. Until I went off to college.'

She chewed thoughtfully. 'He must have missed his old culture a great deal.'

'He said he would never go back. He was a Jew.'

'Oh. How did he become blind?'

'You don't want me to tell you.'

She put down the bread. 'We always come to that.'

'Always,' he answered. 'He's dead now. He left me all his books.' He sat up and changed the subject. 'How does this farm measure up for your commercial? Will it sell a lot of sausage?'

She nodded. 'A great amount.' She saw him glance at his watch. And she looked up at the sky. The weather vane on the barn still indicated a northwest breeze, but it might be a false reading caused by a mountain updraft. Still there were no clouds yet rolling out of the southeast. When she saw them, she knew she would have to leave quickly. She wondered how far she would have to go to keep him here until five.

'Do you really think you have a chance to get that Spanish contract, Thomas?'

'Do you think there's even a remote chance I won't?'

She laughed. 'You don't have even a small hope. I've wrapped it up.'

She felt his fingers touching her hair. 'It's after three.'

She nodded. 'When I was a little girl, I was madly in love with a stable hand. I was nine, I recall, and he was

166

probably very ancient – at least fifteen. He had a graceful way of walking, like an athlete, which I found irresistible, and he had gray eyes the same color as yours. They were very expressive. He never knew how mad I was about him. And when I first saw you, I saw him instantly – those eyes with little flecks of light and whorls. And now I don't know whether I'm attracted to you or just recalling my first love.' She put her fingertips on his eyelids and shut them. 'There. Now I see that it's just a memory. You mean nothing to me.' She snapped her fingers.

It was confusing. She couldn't decide whether she wanted to kiss him or to challenge him to a footrace. She would love to have him as a business competitor. It would be such a great triumph to beat him. Then she recalled they *were* competitors and in a much more deadly game.

'The girl I first loved didn't have brown eyes,' Thomas said. 'Nor did she have dark-brown lashes to set them off.' He began to unfold his jacket. 'But she would have been even prettier with them.'

'Cows have brown eyes,' she said. 'I hate them.'

She knelt by his side and glanced at his watch. Less than two hours to go.

She considered kissing him. Considered making love overtures. But she had never used sex in her business affairs, never played the wanton. And if she did it now she wouldn't know if she was doing it for personal or business reasons. The difference was significant. She decided to fake engine trouble and to chop some of the shrubs. That would delay them long enough.

They packed the picnic basket and the blanket and when they stood up, he kissed her. 'Thank you. It was a fine day.' Then he slung his jacket over his shoulder, and carrying the basket in the other hand, commenced the stroll back to the plane. The weather vane had shifted to the south.

On an impulse, glad she hadn't cheapened their day, she stepped beside him and helped carry the basket. She felt his hand next to hers on the basket handles. She decided he was higher on the scale. Six and three quarters. Seven even. Not bad. There weren't a great many sevens in the world. 'Thank you,' she said. 'It was a fine day. But I'm still going to take that Spanish contract from you.'

Thomas did exactly what she hoped he would. He stopped and kissed her.

She pressed on the basket handle, forcing him to stoop to put it down. She stepped inside his arms, embraced him and waited. This was the time of her greatest failure – trying to lead, wanting not to submit, but to control. It was her moment of panic – and she felt it rising, the inability to let go, to be dominated.

At thirty her love life was largely a failure. She had always been attracted to strong men who at the crucial moment refused to be passive and submissive to her. It always broke off – two angry people turning love into a tug of wills. 'Jesus,' one man had told her. 'We both can't get on top.'

Thomas fooled her. He didn't take charge. No attack. He stood and waited, relaxed. No recriminations. And at last she recognized the one trait in him she hadn't been able to identify. Complete self-possession. He had no need to prove anything, either to dominate or to submit.

He smiled at her and undid a button on her blouse. She accepted the challenge, grinning, and pulled the tail of his turtleneck shirt out of his pants. She saw a brown muscular belly and black hair. He undid another button, and she unzipped his fly then stood laughing at him. A mock battle, she was matching him stroke for stroke. He smiled at her and kissed her lightly, then stooped, picked up the basket and walked away. He fooled her again.

She hurried up to him and rezipped his fly. He paused, put down the basket and refastened one of her blouse buttons. They laughed together. The war was over.

He enveloped her with his two powerful arms and pulled her up off her toes and kissed her again. And she let him. He pulled the tail of her blouse out and reached up inside and unfastened her brassiere. And she let him. Holding her in his arms he massaged her back and scratched it and kissed her. And she wanted him to.

Later she didn't remember how the blanket got spread there on the old grown-over footpath. She didn't remember how she'd gotten out of her tweed jacket, who had unbuttoned her blouse or removed her tan slacks, pulled off her panties or her shoes.

All she remembered was the onset of passion, the eager demand to be satisfied instantly that he met with a calmness that slowed her down. She kept her eyes tightly shut, her arms wrapped around his neck, feeling the grass through the blanket on her neck, and waited, with her heart pounding, waited for him. Again she sensed his gentleness as she felt his weight on her, then the rising of her passion. She rode it like a wave as it rose higher and higher until it crested. She heard herself panting now as though she had passed a great barrier.

She looked up at the bare branches windswaying against the sky and understood. It *was* submission. By both. To each other. His gentleness wasn't weakness; it was affection. She'd discovered the difference between having sex and making love. He'd gotten past her defenses.

With her eyes open, the world was dazzling with sunlight and life was suddenly incredible. Their clothes were strewn in a circle around them.

She saw the scar on his cheek, saw it continue down his shoulder. She touched the channel of scar tissue on his back.

'Did you get that in the war?' she asked.

He tried to sit up but she held him on her with her arms. 'Tell me.'

'Yes. Vietnam. It's all in the past now.'

'How can you of all people sell weapons?'

He tried to rise again and still she held him and he put his head down beside her.

'That was more than sex, wasn't it, Colin?'

'Yes.'

'For me too.' And holding him still, she kissed him. And that was more than just a kiss.

When she opened her eyes she saw the weather vane on the barn roof. The wind had shifted and was coming out of the southeast. But how long ago? How long had they lain there?

'We have to go,' she said. A great black cloud covered part of the sky and there was a sudden chill in the breeze.

But the fields were still full of sun, the breeze stirred the wild grasses, the sweet odors of fallen fruits came from the arbor, and the kittens were chasing each other through an abandoned pile of cordwood. She felt a flush of exuberance, of boundless joy. Like two children, they held hands as they walked back to the plane.

They put the basket down and she took out the two machetes. 'Chop or walk,' she said.

There were a number of pine seedlings that had grown out from the treeline along the edge of the far end of the landing strip. They were over a foot high. The machetes were very sharp, and the young trees fell at a stroke. It took them more than a half hour to clear the strip to her satisfaction.

She felt a sudden rush of cool air and another shadow covered the field. The wind was increasing. It was her last warning. They would have to run for home, to land before the coming gale made it impossible. She toyed with the idea of faking engine trouble to stay overnight there with him, but knew it was not the right time. She had to get back to Cologne.

Instead of fooling with the engine as she planned, she fooled herself. She walked up to Thomas and kissed him and felt herself wrapped tightly in the crush of his two arms. The earth was still warm where they lay and it smelled of dried grasses.

Brewer had to wait until nearly two-thirty before he got a fix on the limousine. It appeared unexpectedly and stopped near the green-and-white-striped canopy of the entrance to the Fritzsche building.

He had been waiting there for more than two hours. All during that time, German businessmen had greeted each other on the street, raising their hats high and half bowing to each other. They all commented on the beautiful weather.

'We've done something right for a change.'

'Oh, no, my friend, we will pay for this. Forty feet of snow.'

The chauffeur got out of the limousine and waited expectantly. Fritzsche himself stepped through the doorway under the canopy with two well-dressed businessmen. He talked with them briefly, then waved them off as they entered his limousine. Brewer didn't bother following it. Fritzsche was his target. He took a good look at him in the daylight. Today Fritzsche wore a double-breasted nautical jacket with brass buttons and a gold emblem on the breast pocket, a gold-and-red-striped tie, and complementing pearl-gray slacks. On his lapel was the military rosette. He gazed up and down the street with an attitude of proprietorship and reentered the building that bore his name.

Brewer looked at his watch. The limousine undoubtedly had gone to the airport. He had nothing to do but wait. He walked up the street to a telephone and called the Hotel Central. There was no message from Thomas and Brewer hesitated to leave one himself. One of Fritzsche's people could be detailed to hang around the desk, waiting for just such a lead.

'Just tell Mr Thomas that Brewer called.'

That was the third such message he'd left. It was still too early to be concerned.

He called again at three-thirty, then at four. The limousine had returned and was waiting at the entrance. At any moment he could be off following the limousine, and there was then no telling when he would be near a phone again.

When Kaethe Dorten opened her eyes, the clouds directly overhead were mountainous with dark ragged edges. Under them she knew there was a lot of wind, a lot of weather. There was no time to waste. It was a large dangerous storm. They had to leave now or be grounded. And if the storm carried enough snow, they could be grounded until spring.

They quickly stowed the gear including the two machetes and she got the engine started. With complete concentration she did her mental countdown, her eyes going from gauge to gauge on the instrument panel.

The wind was out of the southeast and gusting. The mountainsides and trees made it capricious and abrupt. That was very dangerous, for windshear could pluck the small craft apart. It would fall like a broken bird. She told herself she'd waited too long this time.

She felt on the edge of things again – the excitement of risking everything. It was the parachutist waiting until the last possible second to pull the rip cord – and then waiting one second more. She felt taut and eager.

Kaethe rolled down the strip feeling the wind trying to lift the wings. At the end of the field she turned into the wind and checked her engine and instrument panel for the last time. The next five minutes would tell all. Thomas sat next to her watching with great interest.

'Prayers help,' she said and let the plane roll forward into the wind.

The air was capricious and inconstant, veering almost 180 degrees at times. The two engines quickly brought the craft to airspeed and she lifted off. Almost immediately the wind tried to slue her to the right and Kaethe held the plane's nose until the breeze slackened, then dropped the left wing and went into a long slow bank.

'If we were sailing now, I'd be reefing canvas,' Thomas said.

'It's moments like these when life gets your complete attention.' She smiled at him. It was ten of five. Made it.

So far so good. She'd managed to delay their departure so long that Thomas would have little chance now to find Fritzsche and follow him. And for Brewer she'd prepared a real surprise. She turned her attention to her flight instruments. They were going to have a dirty ride home.

Fritzsche came out of his office at six-fifteen. Warm air was lifting the fringe of the canopy and snapping it lightly. Brewer smelled rain.

The limousine drove to the Bismarck Club. When Fritzsche went in, the chauffeur waited. That meant what?

Brewer went to a telephone and called the hotel. It was quarter to seven. There was no message from Thomas. Brewer knew something was amiss. He decided again not to leave a message for Thomas.

A few minutes later, Fritzsche emerged with a thick zipper case, the kind that catalog salesmen carry, with two leather loop handles. He stood talking to Gustav Behring. Then Behring took his hand as though he were bidding him a farewell. Behring gripped Fritzsche's jaw and shook it. Fritzsche patted Behring's shoulder and got into the limousine.

'Mother of God, we're off to somewhere this time,' Brewer said.

The limousine got back on the Cologne–Bonn motorway and headed north for several miles, turned off and proceeded another few miles to a restaurant, a huge building made to look like a Bavarian chalet. The parking lot was crowded with cars. Fritzsche got out and the limousine left.

Obviously Fritzsche expected to have a long leisurely dinner. Probably the chauffeur was going off to get a meal too. But nonetheless Brewer didn't like the feel of it.

Brewer felt a little more confident when he saw Fritzsche was seated by a large floor-to-ceiling window. He ordered a drink, and a few minutes later he greeted another man who sat down and ordered a drink.

173

Brewer slumped back in his seat. Dear God. A complete German dinner. They would be there for three hours or more. He looked for a telephone. But he didn't see any. Fritzsche's leather case was under the seat. A freshening breeze blew against the car. Could this be the meeting Fritzsche mentioned to Tatzie? There? In full view?

Kaethe had her hands full of airplane.

As they headed northwest toward the airport, the ground dropped more and more toward sea level. The ride became smoother and she had a nearly perfect tail wind. But a following wind can be dangerous, especially when it's the leading edge of a major cold front, and she flew alertly aware of it.

Kaethe felt happy.

Briefly about fifteen minutes before they approached the airport they flew under stars. Then heavy black clouds covered the sky and intensified the darkness. She had a detailed discussion with the radio operator, listened attentively as he gave her the wind readings and the latest weather forecast. Landing conditions had already become dangerous.

'I hope the factory riveted this plane together good and tight,' she said to Thomas. She smiled at him. 'If you're a normal person this is a good time to get damned good and scared.'

'I did that when I saw the first thunderhead back at the farm.'

The wind was picking up fast now and minutes counted. She made one pass over the landing strip, circled and came in for a landing. The wind had gotten so strong it wouldn't have been safe just sitting in a plane on the ground.

The plane rocked. The wind wheezed furiously on the cabin doors; the entire craft was bucking. The landing lights on the ground seemed to be rocking.

The plane's flight was as undulating as a roller coaster. Over the landing strip a sudden downdraft could slam them onto the ground and kill them instantly.

The plane kited, raised the right wing and tried to slice. She fought it, brought the wing down, and then the nose, then got into the wind and dropped her.

She hit the landing strip and bounced, rose, losing airspeed, and began to fishtail. Kaethe was all arms and legs working the controls and she dropped the craft again. An unexpected pause in the wind and she was down with a touch as soft as a kiss. Kaethe rolled her into the lee of the first hangar.

'How about dinner?' she said. 'I'm starved.'

It was nearly seven before he could use the phone at the airport. It had begun to rain mixed with large wet snowflakes.

There were a series of messages that Brewer had called but there was no additional information and Brewer's room phone didn't answer. He wondered briefly where Brewer was. But since he couldn't find Brewer, it was better to have Brewer find him. Thomas left a message that he was dining at the Bismarck Club with Kaethe Dorten.

The driving was treacherous and even though Kaethe Dorten drove her convertible Mercedes with the skill of a racing driver, she proceeded with care. The rain, carried on the blustering southeast wind, fell in great sheets now and at times it was more snow than rain. The road surface became a slurry of slush as the temperature fell. The wind rocked the car.

As Kaethe drove, she'd become curiously pensive, chewing on a knuckle, driving one-handed.

'Well. Do you mind women pilots?' she asked him.

'Only the incompetent ones.'

She glanced at him then burst into laughter. 'Colin. You're all right. You get an extra dessert for dinner.' She glanced at him again slyly. 'Let's see how you like a woman picking up the dinner check.'

At the Bismarck Club, he was requested to sign the guest register. As he did, he asked the steward, 'A friend of mine visited here the other night. Would his name be in the guest register?'

'Yes, sir. All guests and visitors sign the register.'

'It was last Friday night.'

The steward glanced at Kaethe Dorten. Her nod was almost imperceptible.

The steward turned the pages back. 'Sunday, Saturday, Friday. Here we are, sir. What is his name?'

'Parker. Bernard Parker.'

'Parker, Parker, Parker. Hmmm.' The steward ran his fingernail down a column of names. 'Hmmmmm.' He went down another column. 'Hmmmm. I'm afraid, sir – is it Palmer?'

'No. Parker.'

'I'm afraid, sir, it wasn't Friday. Might it have been another night?'

Thomas considered. 'No,' he said. 'Friday night. About eight.'

The steward searched the names again. Two columns. Thomas read the names and, by his side, Kaethe Dorten did. They didn't find it.

'I'm sorry, sir.'

'It's nothing.'

The steward held a necktie out to him. 'Club rules, sir.'

She smiled at him. 'I forgot. I'm sorry.' She took the tie and put it around his neck. 'I promise you you will be the only person in the dining room wearing a tie with a turtleneck.'

'Is this good for the Celts?'

They had a drink first in the bar. There were few women in the building. And none of them received the attention Kaethe did. Men of all ages came up to her and bowed with that strange German stiffness, a cross between Victorian and Prussian etiquette. Several touched her shoulder or arm. 'Kaethe,' they would say softly or 'Miss Dorten.' It was all not far away from a hand-kissing ceremony. She greeted them all by name but they were gone too quickly to be introduced to Thomas.

When they entered the bar, the men at the tables near the windows all stood and smiled at her, eager to vacate their seats. She nodded and selected an empty table. When she sat, everyone else sat.

'Club rules?' he asked her.

'Something very like that.'

'A tribute to the old days, then?'

'You might say.'

It was a splendid old building, flooring of Italian tile or pegged oak, paneled walls, hand-carved inlaid wood chandeliers overhead in the bar with a wood-inlaid hunting lodge fireplace in which a fire was going. Through one doorway Thomas could see the large club room, gleaming oak floors with a number of antique Persian rugs, wing chairs, newspaper racks, hassocks and beside the fireplace, a towering grandfather clock with the calendar and moon phases on the face. The pendulum maintained a stately pace. It was as though someone had deliberately reproduced a wealthy men's club from nineteenth-century Germany. Around the time of Bismarck, he realized.

It was 1890 again, when German was all potential and nothing had been written, before Germany lost World War I, before the nightmare of the Versailles Treaty, the inflation, Hitler and World War II. Back to square one to relive history, correct the errors and play at what might have been.

Through the other doorway, he looked into the dining room, an expanse of white tablecloths and thick carpeting, drapes and well-dressed diners. A string quartet played on the dais. Over the barroom fireplace hung a large portrait of Bismarck. Over the fireplace in the club room, the wall was white with a long jagged line descending, channeled in the plaster and painted a striking red.

'What is that?' he asked her.

'Oh. Just a club symbol.'

'Strange-looking.'

A red-jacketed waiter brought their drinks.

Thomas turned his eyes to the huge windows of the barroom. They overlooked the Rhine River, a spectacular view even in the downpour. Through the outside lights, wet snow swirled down. 'To happy days down on the farm,' he toasted her. She laughed.

Trying not to show it, she glanced again at the dining-room entrance. Had Fritzsche eluded Brewer? Everything depended on it. Everything. Where was the messenger?

Snow – large wet flakes – mixed with the windblown rain and washed down his windshield. It was getting colder, and Brewer would soon have to turn the engine on to get some heat into the car.

Fritzsche was still at it. They'd had three steins of beer and a nice long chat with two front-row seats to the storm. Then they'd ordered food. The waiter brought them rollmop herrings with sour onions, then liver dumpling soup, more beer.

There was an incongruity not lost on Brewer to the tableau before him. Fritzsche was a practising aristocrat, an abstemious one. Although he was sitting in a first-rate restaurant, he was not the type for such a place. Private clubs, expensive small Continental places, away from the crowd, that was his style. And he was a stern controlled person, not given to banqueting. Yet here he was eating his way through a heavy German meal right in the window of a large restaurant like an advertisement.

The waiter next brought smoked Rhine salmon with dark bread and butter. It went with two more steins of beer. Fritzsche and his companion, who looked and ate like an indigent actor, chatted merrily with each other. His companion was apparently addicted to jokes and seemed to tell one after another, all causing Fritzsche to chuckle. There was much touching of each other's arms, poking with fingers, rocking with mirth. And more beer. The salmon must have been delicious; they both praised it to the waiter.

The beer got to them finally and they nipped off to the men's room for a quick comfort call. Then back to the table for the big wurst course. Fritzsche sat fingering the rosette on his lapel waiting to be fed. They both had a different kind of pork with sauerkraut and dumplings and more dark bread.

They rested for a while; then the waiter brought the dessert menu. There was a discussion and the waiter went away and returned with a younger waiter wheeling a dessert cart. It was nearly nine o'clock.

The dessert waiter served two huge slabs from a Black Forest cherry cake topped with whipped cream. A large pot of coffee was put on the table. Brandy was served at the same time. They sat still chatting. The leather case remained untouched under Fritzsche's chair. The companion seemed to be still hungry; he kept wetting his fingertips and wiping up the crumbs on the cake plate. They had another brandy.

At last the waiter brought the bill. It was nine-thirty. They stood. They patted each other's shoulders. Fritzsche picked up his leather case, smiled and walked toward the door. And that's when Brewer realized it wasn't Manfred Fritzsche. It was a look-alike. He'd been watching the wrong man for hours.

Thomas had become somewhat preoccupied. Twice he'd gone to make a phone call and she guessed he couldn't find Brewer. She ordered two brandies and wondered if he would come home with her. She hoped not. She wanted to get off by herself and sort things out. It had been an enormously complex day.

She glanced once more at the entrance to the dining room. Their waiter came with a silver tray. At last. He proffered it to her; on it was a folded phone message. She glanced at it.

The bratwurst was delicious, it said.

She felt a slight flush of victory on her face, and she put the paper in her purse.

She smiled at Thomas: she'd beaten him. Adversary and lover.

She touched his hand and he responded by gripping hers briefly. His hand was as warm as love.

Fritzsche had made the change in the men's room. At seven forty-five, he'd gotten up from the table in the window and walked to the lavatory. The actor Kaethe Dorten had hired entered through the rear door, passed through the kitchen and into the men's room and was waiting for him.

He wore the same double-breasted blue blazer with brass buttons, the same gray flannel trousers, the same regimental tie, even the same rosette in his lapel. It was astonishing how much they resembled each other. Fritzsche took the man's raincoat and wide-brimmed hat, put them on, received the leather case and walked through the kitchen, out the back entrance and into the car parked by the garbage cans, away from Brewer's view.

The actor returned to the table and sat down to eat the monumental meal that Fritzsche had ordered for him. Beside him sat another actor, hired because of his huge appetite. The second actor had told Fritzsche that if he ate too much he lost weight. It was a terrible night for driving. With the darkness the temperature had dropped and the wet snow made the roads dangerous, while the rain made visibility very poor.

There were two men in the car and neither spoke to him. The wheelman was an excellent driver – a professional, no doubt – and the other man looked like a Greco-Roman wrestler with a double roll of muscle on the back of his squat neck.

'How much of a drive is it?' Fritzsche asked.

'Not long,' said the heavy man politely. But that was no answer.

He wanted to ask them more questions about Fox, but

180

he decided that it was indiscreet, and anyway they would give him non-committal answers.

He settled back in his seat and resumed his mental habit of the last few days. He worried. The Doomsday Book weighed heavily on his lap and he let his mind prowl yet again – ever again – over its contents, seeking for a fatal flaw, a misstatement.

It would have been difficult to describe the document. It was a complete study of Germany, Russia and China, history, geography, politics and future prospects. It was also a detailed military plan. It was a terrorist's bible. It represented four years of unremitting toil on the part of over fifty experts on many subjects pertinent to the joint conspiracy.

However it was described, Fritzsche had spent too many years in business to fail to give it its proper label. It was the world's greatest sales document.

At his bleakest moments, Fritzsche had vowed that if the Chinese turned them down, he would shoot himself. After forty years of exhausting labor, he did not have the emotional reserves to survive a turndown.

He looked out of the window and all he saw was sheets of rain and passing headlights. He had no idea in the world where they were.

They drove for nearly two hours. At one point, he glimpsed a road sign and realized that they were driving south toward Switzerland. Under the driver's skillful hands, the car seemed as surefooted as a Mongolian pony, and Fritzsche found himself relaxing more and more. The tension had been wearing and he began to drift. He became completely alert when the car slowed for a turn. It entered a service road off the main road, and Fritzsche squinted to see recognizable landmarks. All he saw was smears of headlights on the wet roadway.

They turned again left and drove for another fifteen minutes. They were in a rural area, few lights, a narrow road and cattle fences, a farmhouse shining its lights through the bare trees here and there. The car slowed, pulled off the road into a picnic grove and stopped. They were parked next to a very long black limousine. His driver opened the door as the chauffeur of the limousine opened his. Fritzsche stepped out, straightened up, stooped and stepped into the limousine. The door shut behind him. He sat back with a sigh.

'Good evening, Mr Fritzsche,' said a voice.

The man was as thin as a girl and smaller, seated cross-legged in the corner of the rear seat, a camel's-hair overcoat draped over his shoulders, a smoking cigarette in his hand. He looked solemnly at Fritzsche through perfectly round eyeglasses. Mr Fox was Chinese, probably sixty or more. 'I regret the long ride. Precautions, you know. I can't offer you many amenities but we do have hot tea and a bar. What is your pleasure?'

'A toilet.'

'Alas. I can offer you only the simplest accommodations.' He pointed through the window at a public toilet.

When Fritzsche returned, Fox poured a cup of hot tea and he drank it gratefully. His mouth had grown quite dry.

'I think it is safest if we drive as we talk. You recall the old axiom about moving targets.' He knocked on the glass panel and Fritzsche felt the car begin to move.

'We have a long night ahead of us, Mr Fritzsche,' said Mr Fox, lighting another cigarette. He was to smoke many during the next hours. 'Suppose you start at the beginning. And please take your time.'

Fritzsche was astonished to see, in the downpour, a flash of a white face and sad eyes. A cow. He opened his case and began what he believed would prove to be the most momentous conversation in the entire twentieth century.

They drove most of the night. They stopped once around two o'clock for fuel. And in all those hours, Fritzsche never once took note where they were. In fact, he was completely unaware of the car's motion.

Fox rarely said a word. He produced a masterpiece of listening. Fritzsche talked for nearly six hours nonstop. He used the Doomsday Book as his guide, turning the pages to chapter and verse as he gave the litany of conspiracy.

He recited the background, briefly, of World War II and the ultimate division of Germany. He explained – masterfully, he felt – the geopolitical incompatibility of Germany and Russia. He stated in simple terms the grave danger the Germans felt vis-à-vis Russian expansionism. He detailed the collision course of the German and Russian drive for hegemony, recalled the ancient German dream, *Drang nach Osten*, then analyzed the characteristics of Russia that made it the natural enemy of both Germany and China.

He next discussed the many years of labor that went into the German proposal. The Germans, he told Mr Fox, felt sure they had discovered a way to destroy Russia without a major war and without a nuclear holocaust. Then he told of the day in Berlin when he and Dorten and Behring had watched the Russians on parade and saw – he didn't credit Dorten with the concept – how it could be fragmentized. Balkanized.

He explained the theory and practice of terrorism and guerrilla fighting, a lengthy discourse, drawing greatly on the bitter experiences of the United States in Vietnam.

He explained the problems they had encountered with that idea, how they had come to see the need for intervention from the outside with a large military force at the right moment. He cited the problems confronting Germany in placing a modern army inside Russia, the many buffer states that would object. At last, ineluctably, he came to the one solution. A Chinese army. A modern Chinese army, armed by Germany, to be ready at the key moment when the German infrastructure of terrorists and guerrillas would pull down the central government of the holy Russias, and bring on chaos.

At length, with a cup of tea to wet his dry mouth, Fritzsche rested his case. It was the most difficult presentation of his life: Fox had made no reaction, absolutely none. He'd sat and smoked and listened with his eyes fixed unwaveringly on Fritzsche's, hearing every word, never lapsing once in attention, but never, not for an instant, presenting the slightest response. Fritzsche was spent. When Fritzsche finished, Fox turned his face away and lit another cigarette.

Do something, Fritzsche silently prayed. The man had had uncounted cups of tea. At least, thought Fritzsche, get out and piss. Show something human. The car went on for at least ten minutes. The only sound was the rhythmical swish swash of the windshield wipers. Fox shifted in his seat, uncrossed his legs, then cleared his throat.

'You feel the initial terrorist program can let you arm China without Russia noticing?'

'Of course. Besides, how did Russia mass troops on the Afghanistan border without the United States noticing? This vaunted satellite system is highly overrated. We have also perfected camouflage techniques that fool satellite cameras.'

Mr Fox asked another question. And another. He asked questions for more than an hour. They were incisive questions, knowledgeable, searching; they suggested doubts about Germany and Germany's ability. They indicated a great respect for Russian power, Russian cunning. The Chinese felt quite weak in relation to their neighbor.

In answering the questions, Fritzsche made every effort to remember them. With a few hours' rest, he faced a massive debriefing at the Bismarck Club, and his memory had to be flawless.

It was nearly 4 a.m. when the limousine returned to the picnic grove.

Fritzsche shook hands with Fox. 'Do you have far to go?'

'To Basel,' Fox said.

'Safe trip,' Fritzsche said and with ceremony, prayerfully, he presented the Doomsday Book to Fox.

'You are wondering how long before I give you an

184

answer.' Fox said. 'It will take months to work out any details that interest us. But I can tell you that you will have a yes or no positive answer in three or four days.'

'What do you think of it?'

'What I think, Mr Fritzsche is of no moment. But what others think you will hear shortly. Good night. Safe trip.'

Fritzsche climbed out of the limousine, stood briefly in the rain, then entered the other car. Before it was a mile away, he had fallen asleep with his chin on his chest. He felt naked without the Doomsday Book.

Gustav Behring didn't even bother to get into his pajamas. He stayed in a hotel in Cologne with a chauffeur and a car waiting in the garage. All through that wet night, he sat and stood, flipped through magazines, watched some television and as the hours passed became more and more gloomy.

The idea was preposterous, he now saw. There was no doubt about that. Only a bunch of fanatics could have even conceived it. And worse, it wouldn't work. It meant concealing enormous activity from the Russians, the nosiest people on earth. It meant orchestrating undisciplined, volatile and unknown groups inside Russia. It required staggeringly precise movement of huge forces. It was predicated on certain things happening in certain ways that could be altered by random factors. It was the frailest military operation in the history of the whole world and the Chinese had to be insane to consider it for more than five minutes.

And yet his hope was like a feather in the wind, always buoyed anew just when it was about to touch down.

The hours wore on and the weariness settled on his shoulders and penetrated his body. In a collapsed sitting position, he fell asleep.

Dorten was wiser than that. He had spent too many days in his career with a worrying mind that would not be shut off. They'd done their best. They had examined their idea endlessly from every angle. And now that Fritzsche was meeting with Fox, there simply wasn't another thing they could do. He took two strong sleeping pills and went to bed.

Others found other ways to pass the longest night of their lives, including Dr Hesse, who put on freshly pressed pajamas, lay neatly on his back on his bed with his pudgy hands clasped over his rotund belly and, without moving for the rest of the night, never slept a wink.

Behring's phone rang at 6 a.m. Fritzsche was back at the Bismarck Club. He would take a two-hour nap and be ready to talk at precisely eight-fifteen.

Behring called Kaethe then Dr Hesse. And Kaethe waited until eight o'clock before calling her father.

'Well,' her father said thoughtfully, 'prepare yourself for the three longest days in the history of Germany.'

At 8:15 a.m. precisely, Manfred Fritzsche entered the small meeting room adjacent to the vault in the basement of the Bismarck Club and gave his report to Behring and Hesse, who made careful notes. Fritzsche talked for an hour and a half before going back to bed in the clubhouse.

Even in his deep fatigue, he yearned for his Tatzie.

7

Thomas had drawn that strange wiggling line from memory on a piece of paper. During most of the evening at the Bismarck Club, the night before, he'd sat gazing at it over the fireplace where it was cut into the plaster wall and painted red. It had looked for all the world like a line done in wet plaster with the tip of a fencing foil dipped in red paint or blood.

Now drawn on a piece of paper it was still utterly

meaningless. Kaethe Dorten had said it was a private symbol, meaningful only to club members. But it was so odd in appearance, not a square or a cross or a triangle. Just a squiggle. He stood by his hotel room window looking out at the rain and wondered what the line represented.

Actually, he was using the jagged line as a mental diversion, a brain twister that kept him from thinking about last night's setback. Fritzsche was their only lead and they'd been decoyed from a great opportunity to eavesdrop. Fritzsche had attended a key meeting with someone and it must have been very important, for he put a lot of effort into deceiving Brewer. If only he hadn't gone to that picnic.

He was in trouble. He admitted that he had no alternatives, no more moves to make. Someone had completely covered over Parker's trail. He could spend days wandering around to no avail while Frank Gorman waited impatiently in London for him to return to work. Parker's death could remain a mystery for a very long time.

He thought of Kaethe Dorten. He could recall the old farm with striking vividness, the grasses leaning in the wind, the high old trees, the farmhouse and barn. And most of all he could see her: he could see her face, that superb skin and those vital brown eyes, saw her nude figure and shapely limbs. He heard her voice again, heard her laugh, inhaled her scent, felt her hair on his face and felt her embrace again. Haunting: he'd never met anyone like her before, never felt passion like that before, and his mind insisted on dwelling on it.

Thomas had to admit he was smitten. Kaethe Dorten could make an event out of opening a door. And the wild glint in her eye made her unpredictably fascinating. And he'd never met a woman before who seemed to become happiest when she was in the gravest danger. There were dozens of moments when they could have been killed in that plane yesterday.

He tried to shrug it all away. He had an overpowering desire to see her again, to make sure that yesterday wasn't just an illusion. He was being drawn to her like a nail to a magnet. Love had overwhelmed his freedom like a wild sea.

Thomas took the piece of paper with the squiggled line he'd drawn on it and carried it down to breakfast with Brewer.

'What do you make of that?' he asked.

'What is it?'

'That's what I want to know, Charlie. What is it?'

Brewer shrugged indifferently. 'I'm fresh out of ideas.' Brewer opened the newspaper and began to read.

After breakfast, Thomas put the piece of paper in his pocket. Then he stopped, shocked. 'Charlie, I'll lay you eight to five I know what that line is. Let's get the car.'

Thomas's car came up the high hill to the Bismarck Club and entered the parking lot. He parked it close to the building and turned off the engine. No longer brightly lit and thronged with people, as it had been the night before, the club looked withdrawn and hostile in the cold rain.

Brewer peered through the windshield, through the windows of the club room to the fireplace. In the dull light, on the white plaster wall, the line stood clearly, chiseled into the plaster and painted a vivid red.

He took up the map and studied it for a few moments, then studied the line on the wall. 'You're right. Can't miss it.' They were identical: the line over the fireplace was the same as the line on the map. It was a replica of the border between West and East Germany, mined and fenced with barbed wire. And it was set into the most visible wall in the club, evident from the vestibule, from the dining room, the barroom, the dual stairway and the corridor that led through the building − a constant reminder to the membership of the dismembered state of their country, the line that divided Germany. The borderline.

Was that line what had drawn Parker to the Bismarck Club? Thomas studied the building thoughtfully. If Parker could find a way in, he could too.

'What next?' Brewer asked.

'We have to get inside.'

'How?'

Thomas rubbed a hand over his cheeks thoughtfully. 'Charlie,' he said at last. 'How would you like to become a traveling soap and cleaner salesman from London?'

The autumn storm was still pouring rain on Cologne the next morning, and there was the usual pressure in Kaethe Dorten's office: new-account presentations, a publicity program for an oil company, several package designs to review and a new corporate symbol for a food store chain.

Yet Kaethe sat at her desk and looked down on the rain-swept Hohe Strasse, doing nothing. All she could think about was Colin Thomas. She had hardly slept. She wanted to talk to him about this incredible sensation she was living through. She wanted to share it with him and experience it again. She didn't care a fig for her business, her employees or her clients.

She tried to tell herself it was the setting that had charmed her – the lovely, windblown fields of grass, the wild flowers in the sun, the old farmhouse, the odors from the fruit orchard, the country odors in the barn and the kittens playing in the woodpile. But she couldn't deceive herself.

She looked down at the Hohe Strasse swept clear of shoppers by the rain. Through the wet pane of her window, the neon lights seemed to run like dye.

Getting to know Colin Thomas had been like opening a marvelous gift. Inside was a bunch of charming packages. His wonderfully pale gray eyes revealed everything that was going on inside his mind. And she loved his face and his curly brown hair. She wanted to have his strong arms around her again. She wanted to say I love you.

She broke out of her reverie and looked down at the pad on her desk. It was urgent that she find Parker's pipeline into the cabal before Colin did. But how could she think about that when all her mind wanted to dwell on was the overwhelming joy of making love to Colin Thomas?

'Later,' she told herself and forced her attention to her pad. She had drawn a line down the center of the page. The left-hand column she had titled 'Known,' the right, 'Unknown.' In the 'Known' column she wrote a summary of all the facts about Parker that she knew. And in the 'Unknown' column she wrote all the unanswered questions about Parker. Where did he find his information about the cabal?

By 10 a.m., she thought she'd found one strong possibility. She called Gustav Behring.

'Have lunch with me at the club,' she said. 'I want to see the vault.'

Behring raised his martini glass to her. 'Here's to your marvelous plan last night. How brilliant – a lookalike. Even Fritzsche had to admire it. But now the suspense is killing me. Three days of waiting.'

She made him think of his wife, who was becoming completely indiscriminate in Sicily. Her antics had been noted by other Germans on holiday there. Maybe all he had to do was wait three days. In the face of a world cataclysm, the sexual escapades of a woman in menopause were insignificant.

If he had been a truly blessed man, it was Dorten's daughter that God would have sent him. She was an even better pilot than he was on his best day over the English Channel. A vibrant woman, audacious, alive, elusive and sensual. Oh to be thirty again – with her.

She let him hold her hand for a moment. 'Tell me about the security system,' she said.

'Suppose,' Behring proposed, 'that I show you the vault, then show you the club's security system – in detail.'

She agreed. In that system somewhere was Parker's tunnel.

The vault, she was told by Behring, as he led her to the

basement, was one of the finest in the country. Indeed there were banks that didn't have such a fine piece of equipment. And why not? After all, bank vaults held only money. He chuckled at his lame joke.

'That's hardly a joke, Gustav,' she chided him.

'Even jokes are hardly jokes these days. Here. Step in.'

She walked into the vault and gazed about. It was a small room with incredibly thick metal walls, a six-foot round metal door with dials and clocks on it and, inside, several metal cabinets.

'The door is timed to open only at certain hours,' Behring told her. 'And then only three of us have the keys necessary to unlock the other locks. It's impregnable.'

Ceremoniously, he closed the door for privacy, then opened a cabinet door. He lifted out a large leather-bound volume.

'The Doomsday Book,' he whispered. 'Our copy.'

Kaethe stepped up and opened it, then slowly began turning the pages. It was filled with charts, maps, diagrams, tables and text.

'Actually, it's a very melodramatic term,' Behring said. 'One of Fritzsche's. But it's apt. Doomsday. Every single study in this book was conceived and written in the various committee rooms of the club and immediately put in here. I can't tell you how many experts have come together in this building to resolve the questions our conspiracy raises. This book will give the Chinese the answers to every conceivable question they can come up with. It took nearly four years and the labor of over fifty of the finest minds in the country to make it. Yet no one knows more than just the part he himself worked on – except for four people. It's a conspiracy in which everyone is willingly ignorant.'

'So the only way anyone could know about the Doomsday Book is to get into this vault.'

'Right.'

'And it's impregnable.'

'Yes.'

'Then how did Parker know about it'?

Brewer sat alone in his car by the delivery entrance to the club and waited. He had watched the produce delivery man arrive and carry crates of fresh vegetables from his van to the kitchen, then sit and drink coffee, talking to everyone, making them laugh.

When he came out Brewer approached him. He said he was a soap and cleaner salesman from London, on the road and wanting to know who inside the club did the buying. The produce man was flattered. Brewer offered to buy a stein of beer, and the produce man led him to a tavern.

'I'm there every day,' he told Brewer over a stein, 'and I can tell you where the bodies are buried. Everyone talks to me. I'm the priest – the father confessor.'

Life, in a moment of mirth, had marked him. He had large pink ears edged with down and a sharp pointed nose. He loved gossip. He loved talk. He loved beer. He told Brewer who in the club would buy his soaps and much more.

'The club steward, Lamprecht, gets into everything. The reason he's so good at his job is Ditmars, the assistant club steward. He wants Lamprecht's job. They watch each other like hawks. Spit and polish and maintenance is under Meiers. Budheimer is his assistant. Mrs Kurtz is the laundress. Now that's a lady who can talk. She could talk a dachshund off a sausage wagon, that Mrs Kurtz.'

'Another stein?' asked Brewer.

Mrs Kurtz, the laundress, finished every day punctually at two. But she lived alone and was never in a hurry. So she always had tea and a parting chat with the staff before she left. When she came out, Brewer approached her. He asked her about selling his soaps and cleaners. It was like opening a fire hydrant. She stood under her large black umbrella, her round face collapsed with age, oblivious to the rain puddle she stood in, eager to talk. After a few moments, Brewer noticed that they were being watched.

'That's Lamprecht,' Mrs Kurtz said. 'He sees everything.' She agreed to go to the tavern for a glass or two. Her preference, it turned out, ran to *Roemers* of fruity white German wines.

Mrs Kurtz had faded-blue eyes that saw everything, a mouth that disapproved, and a marvelous memory for gossip. In all, she had a very poor opinion of the whole world. And she could talk like a brook in springtime. In twenty minutes, the laundress unwittingly told Brewer who on the staff could provide the rabbit hole that would bring Thomas inside the club.

A German beer hall is a fine place to exchange secrets. It's large, crowded, noisy, filled with talk and music, and eavesdropping is impossible.

The one where Brewer met Thomas was no exception. They got two seats against a wall and ordered from the plump waitress two steins of pale Kölsch beer.

It was near the end of the day and the hall was crowded with businessmen and shoppers. Through windows high on the wall, the faint last light of the rainy day fell on the drinkers.

Brewer started his report of the club employees to Thomas with a profile on the club steward, Lamprecht. Reputed to be able to run a first-class hotel, Lamprecht was paid top salary by the Bismarck Club. He was completely dedicated to his job; the club was getting more than its money's worth. Some said the Bismarck Club had, because of Lamprecht, the finest restaurant in the entire Rhine Valley. Lamprecht was forty-five, married, two children, a solid burgher with no problems, no debts.

Brewer went through the other names on his list, pointing to them with a pencil. 'She's in the billing department. Just married. Pregnant and unhappy about it. She wants an abortion.' His pencil touched another name. 'Divorced two years ago. He's just broken up with his mistress. Very despondent about it. Feels he didn't make enough money to hold her. This one is head of the service staff, including the billing department. Very fussy. No one likes him but he gets the job done. There's a rumor his wife is cheating but it's probably just malicious talk. The wife is very plain and timid. This one is pissed off. Lamprecht passed over him and gave someone else the job as head cashier. Everyone says he taps the till.'

Brewer's pencil touched the next name of the list thoughtfully. 'This is the head cashier. Rudy Stott. He's a favorite subject for gossip in the club. They call him Night Life. Makes a good income. Good credentials. An older guy in his forties. Divorced years ago. He's been chasing a rich woman – that's her name – for a couple of years. She's the widow of a man who owned a famous inn up in the snow country. Rumor says that Rudy has cleared all the hurdles and the lady's about to say yes. All he has to do is keep his nose clean for a while longer and he's in clover. But there's also talk that he's deep in debt from wooing her. I have a feeling this is our guy.'

Thomas drank some Kölsch. 'Find out,' he said.

Rudy Stott *was* their guy. In two hours, Brewer found out he was in debt. And not bank debt. As head cashier he couldn't afford to have his debts known to his employers. He had turned to loan sharks.

'Who are these sharks he's been going to?' Thomas asked.

'Local people. They've been bankrolling him. They know what he's up to and they figure to get a big piece of the action once he's married. Only it's taken a long time – longer than anyone expected – and Rudy has spent a lot on caviar and opera tickets, and the boys are beginning to politely muscle him. Nothing serious. They don't want to spoil his face and ruin the wedding. But they're all nervous.'

'And is that what he owes?'

'At least that much. He needs a large lump and soon. Next few weeks. I'd say he's a desperate man.'

Thomas thought about Rudy Stott.

For Rudy Stott, the head cashier, it was a night of slight victories.

The sommelier's wine inventory came out on the first count and that saved hours of recounting. The new assistant cashier was working out well and didn't ask unsettling questions about the books. And tonight he'd gotten word that the outside audit was deferred for two weeks.

He left the club around midnight, and his mind smoothly adjusted to his own affairs. He was glad he didn't have to see Ida tonight. His irritation was showing. For one thing, he had looked into his checkbook and saw that he didn't have enough money to pursue her beyond the next week or so. He had no more sources to borrow from. And she seemed no closer to making a decision. If she finally said no to him, he had a debt that could cost him his life.

He admitted he was baffled. She was very fond of him; she had shown it in a multitude of ways. She told him she loved him. In fact, she was a little too touchy-touchy with her hands. She found him compatible in bed. Heavenly, she said. They shared common interests in opera and museums and wines and classical furniture. Indeed, they had talked often about how they would furnish their home. She had given him presents, eagerly accepted his, taken him proudly among her friends, complimented him on his poise and cultured conversation. There were a thousand intimacies between them that meant he had achieved a special place in her life. He would, he knew, make an ideal mate for her, make her happy. And still maddeningly she hung back.

Somewhere deep in her heart, there was, he was sure, a speck of doubt. There was some one thing about him; was it personal or just excessive caution on her part?

Stott walked to the employees' parking area at the far end of the property. The rain had stopped at last but it was sharply colder, and he pulled his coat collar up against the breeze. Tonight in the Alps, the innkeepers were rubbing their hands over eight to fourteen inches of new snow.

That's where he belonged, in a mountain inn with her money and her knowledge of innkeeping and his drive. They were a perfect pair.

If only he had a fatter bank account to stay in the game, eventually he would win her. If only he didn't owe all that money. The sharks had been patient but lately they had been hostile, insistent. They wanted to see at least earnest money. They had begun to doubt that he would conquer her heart. They were soon going to cut their losses. One evening it would be up against the wall for him, a rough-up, then what? A knife? A bullet?

If only an angel would fly over his head tonight and drop a little white bank envelope fat with money.

Abruptly he was seized from behind, his arms pinned, lifted nearly off the ground and impelled through the archway into the shadows and up against the old garden wall.

'Your time's run out, Rudy,' said Brewer. He put a palm against Stott's chest and leaned his weight on it. It was not painful but the pressure was terrifying for some strange reason. Stott felt the heat of the man's hand penetrate his jacket and shirt. He waited for the first punch, struggling desperately with himself to suppress a whimper.

'I will have the money soon. All of it, I promise.'

'This is your last warning.' Brewer seized him by the lapels and shook him violently, then flung him toward the sidewalk. He stumbled and just managed to catch himself before he fell. When he looked around the man was gone.

Stott's heart was racing violently. He felt panic in every part of his body. He was in far over his head. For just a brief moment, he felt a fury for Ida. He would cheerfully have strangled her. He was hanging by a thread over an abyss. He couldn't go home now. He was too upset. He found himself driving to downtown Cologne. He wanted lights and laughter, a drink perhaps. He parked in a side street. There were a number of people in the streets, hurrying into beer halls and night spots away from the sharp wind.

A man approached him. 'Rudy,' he called cheerfully.

'How good it is to see you.' Stott regarded him with shock. The man had bulky shoulders and a happy, almost mocking smile. He didn't have the hard face of a collector.

'Pardon. Do I know you?'

'Well, you will shortly,' said Colin Thomas. 'You will regard me as your benefactor. Come. A small wine, perhaps, or a coffee if you like – right here in public – in here.' He led the way to a hotel bar. 'I have a suggestion for you, Rudy, that will make you very happy.'

'I – can you tell me what this is about?'

'Listening will cost you nothing, Rudy. Then you are free to go if you wish. No hard feelings.'

Reluctantly, with great doubt, Rudy let himself be led by the elbow to one of the tables. They both sat. It was very dark inside and the evening crowd went to and fro past them along the bar.

'How is she then, your Ida?' Thomas asked.

The man's accent was excellent. It was well educated and his open face invited trust. His eyes were amused by Rudy's confusion. But the shoulders were broad and the face muscular; the man's whole bearing was one of strength and unhesitating force. Rudy felt intimidated.

'How do you know about Ida?'

'Oh, there are ways of knowing these things.' The man ordered a small glass of wine. 'And for you, Rudy?'

'Nothing. Oh, well, the same then.'

'Rudy, you must persevere with your Ida. These women are maddening, I know, but she is the one for you, and just when you are about to despair, she will relent and make you a happy man.'

Rudy studied the face, totally mystified. 'Yes, of course,' he answered lamely.

'I will come right to the point,' said Thomas, almost gaily. 'My, this wine is not very bad at all, my friend. Try yours. See? It is passably good for a house wine, isn't it?'

Rudy watched, hypnotized. The man spoke with the voluble literary style of a university lecturer.

'You must persevere, Rudy. That is my message. In fact, I feel so strongly about this matter that I want to help you. It is painful to me that you struggle under such a debt as you have, so I am prepared to advance you a large sum of money to take care of your debts and even finance your future activities with the lady. You understand?'

'I – no. I don't understand.'

Thomas pulled a fat white envelope from his jacket pocket and placed it before Rudy.

Rudy opened the end flap and almost comically squinted one-eyed into it. He shut the flap with awe.

'What did you see, Rudy?'

'Money. I saw paper money. It was filled with it.'

'Would you like me to tell you how much is in there? Exactly what you owe those blood-drinking sharks. You could pay them off tonight, free and clear, and then you could have more for a long, long pursuit of Ida. Your success would be assured. Your life would be filled with joy. You could leave your employment and spend all your days on a permanent vacation with your Ida.'

Rudy looked fascinated. Deliverance. That's what was in the envelope: deliverance from all his material problems. A renewed life. He wet his lips. He dreaded to hear what was next.

'Rudy. I understand you are an excellent photographer. You even develop your own pictures, is it not so?'

Rudy nodded.

'I would like a small favor from you in return for this money, Rudy. I too am a photographer and I wish to take a few photographs. A half hour's work at the most.'

'Photographs of what?'

'Oh, an inconsequential matter. A few papers.'

'Where?'

'In the Bismarck.'

'Bismarck? All the papers in there together aren't worth this much money.'

'See? My point is made. It is a small matter. I want pictures of only a few pages.'

Rudy sighed wearily. Could it be that simple? He felt such relief, he nearly slipped off the chair. The tension had him shuddering. First the roughing up in the parking lot and now this.

'What papers?' he asked at last.

'Will you do it, Rudy?'

'I – what papers? Are you sure you don't have me mixed up with someone else? Do you know where I work? It is not a very secret place.'

'Yes. You are Rudy Stott, the head cashier at the Bismarck Club. There is no mistake.'

Stott's heart beat in his chest like a running hare. Did he have enough nerve to do that? Would his nerves stand it?

The man seemed to read his mind. 'It is not hard. Not even illegal.'

Rudy sat hunched over, suffering.

'Relax, Rudy. We have plenty of time. Gather your thoughts. You know yourself that there is nothing in the club that you would have any regrets about photographing. It is a simple matter.'

Rudy miserably watched the people walk by, and he envied every single least one of them, even the humblest.

'What papers?' he asked finally.

'Are you saying you will do it?'

'When must I do it?'

'Now. Before dawn.'

'But you have no camera here. I—'

'I do. Right around the corner. A complete kit, camera, special close-up lens, and flash attachments. Everything I need. We could do it now, in minutes, when no one is there.'

The man was as persuasive as the devil himself. He seemed to anticipate every thought, every objection, and he knew exactly what to say to tempt Rudy.

'All that money, Rudy, for ten minutes' work. What do you say? Yes? Nod your head. Bravo.'

'What papers?'

'The membership list. And the steward's ledger for the last six months.'

Rudy frowned. The steward's ledger contained notations about dull matters – what meeting rooms were used, who used them, charges by club members for drinks to be posted to the billing ledger and such housekeeping details. Worthless information.

'But the ledgers are worthless,' he said.

'See?'

'But I can't do that!'

'Oh?' Thomas laid his hand on the white envelope. 'Then I will get someone who can.'

'Wait!'

'If you don't do this small service for me, Rudy, there are many others in the club who will. You can name a few yourself, can't you? Someone is going to take my money and do this job. Why not you, Rudy? The money will fit just as neatly in your wallet as another's.' He whispered the next question. 'Isn't it far better than being found floating face down in the river, Rudy?'

Rudy sat miserably with his hands on the white envelope.

'My advice, Rudy. Do it now. Don't think about it.'

'There are people in the club.'

'Only a few, and they all sleep in the second floor. You have your keys. You know exactly where the ledgers are and the membership list. I can operate my camera with great speed.'

Rudy began to perspire. I am making too much of this, he told himself. Don't think. Do it. 'I'll do it,' he said. Deliverance.

The man picked up the fat little white envelope. 'Follow me,' he said.

Stott followed him several blocks past a group of boisterous drunks to a parked car. And there in the trunk, he saw the carrying case for the camera equipment.

Stott held the flashlight while the man took some money

from the envelope. 'That's half, Rudy. I will give you the other half after we do the job. Fair enough?'

Rudy pushed the money into his raincoat pocket.

Thomas unlocked the car. 'Don't be upset, Rudy, I have brought my assistant along.' As Rudy got into the car he saw another man in the back seat, his face barely discernible in the weak streetlights. Rudy's heart thumped in fear. Two of them.

They drove through Cologne past streets of inexpensive restaurants and shops, the leather carry-all camera case between them on the seat. The man in the back did not speak.

Stott was experiencing the strangest mix of emotions he had ever felt in his life. He felt fear. He felt guilt. He felt joy. Patience, he counseled himself. In a short while, he would be finished with this job and back home with the money. Deliverance. He said that word over and over to himself. Deliverance.

To avoid approaching the clubhouse, the man drove the car up the hill and circled to the back where the employees parked. They sat in the car while the two men studied the building.

There was a floodlight at the back of the building and inside low night lights were burning.

'Any dogs?' Thomas asked.

'No.'

After a few moments, they set out on foot across the parking area.

Stott watched the darkened upper windows apprehensively. They circled around the parking lot through some hemlocks to avoid the floodlight, then walked along the side of the building, under the bedroom windows above. There were only four or five staff members who lived in, and they all seemed to be asleep.

When they reached the back door, the two men looked at Stott expectantly and he gave a start. 'Oh,' he exclaimed and pulled out his key ring.

'Is there any burglar alarm?'

'Yes. The building is heavily protected but this door key will prevent it from going off.' He inserted the key and opened the back door. Now he felt faint. He felt sweat streaming down his armpits and torso. His shirt collar was wet. He tried to remember a prayer but all he recalled was Now I Lay Me Down to Sleep.

Brewer stayed outside near the door, which had been left open a crack.

The interior was filled with shadows and faint pools of light. Rudy led the way through the kitchens, through the dining room, through the barroom to the vestibule and the cashier's office. Here he took out his key ring and unlocked the cashier's cage. Inside, he snapped on a wall light. They crossed to a metal circular stair down to the files. As he went down, turning, he glimpsed the main stairs and nearly fainted. He was sure he'd observed a trouser leg and a shoe through the banister. If his face was seen, he was ruined.

He nearly panicked down in the file room. He could pass through a doorway to the cellar, along a passageway and come up in the kitchens and out the back door. He could flee now before his face was recognized.

'First the membership list,' Thomas said.

'Now I lay me down to sleep,' Stott murmured as he turned to the files.

'What did you say?'

Stott pulled out the manila file with the typewritten master list of members. It was updated once a week and was far more accurate than even the addressing plates in the billing file.

He handed the file to the man.

'Mop your brow,' Thomas said.

The work went quickly. The man had a very good miniature camera and an expensive flash unit. He set the membership list on a table and photographed each page twice. In a few minutes, he handed it back to Stott.

'Now, the ledger.'

Stott went to the large file drawer where he kept the

records of primary entry, the steward's ledger, the chef's daily book and the like. He seized the steward's ledger and riffled the pages.

'It's only for the last three months.'

'Where's the previous one?'

'In the main vault.'

'Do you have access to that?'

'No. It has a timed alarm on it. It can't be opened till nine in the morning and then only by two or three club officers with the right keys.'

'What's in it?'

Stott shrugged. 'Records, I suppose. I've never been in it.'

'Is it big?'

'Two or three people can stand inside it.'

Thomas put the ledger on the top of a file cabinet and held his miniature camera up. With the book open flat, he was able to photograph the left and right pages simultaneously.

He glanced once at Stott, who was panting audibly and mopping his face. 'You're too nervous for a life of crime, Rudy.'

'Yes.' The man's utter calmness astonished him. Was he really as unperturbed as he seemed? He apparently didn't have a nerve in his body. Rudy glanced up the circular stairway, watching fearfully for the trouser leg and shoe.

'Hurry,' he whispered. 'In the name of sweet merciful Jesus, hurry.'

But the man would not be rushed. He calmly shot two pictures of each spread. When he finished he said, 'Are you sure you haven't got access to the vault?'

'Yes. Are we through?'

'We're through, Rudy.'

'This way.' Rudy unlocked the door and led the man into the main cellar under the kitchen. He turned on the overhead lights. There were shelves of tinned foods and kitchen supplies in neat rows, and Rudy walked quickly through them, almost running, to the stairs up to the kitchen. He turned off the light when they mounted the stairs, then quickly led the way to the back door. Soon soon soon, he told himself.

They stepped through the doorway, and Rudy locked it after them. Brewer watched without saying a word. Now they walked along the side of the building past the hemlocks in a circle around the parking lot and across to the car.

Stott remembered with a suppressed gasp that he'd left the light in the cashier's cage on. He turned and glanced back at the club-house. The light was clearly visible, lighting up two different windows near the main stairway. A beacon illuminating vengefully the dark spot of his transgression. They got into the car and drove off. As they reached the road down the hill, Stott glanced again at the forgotten light. Someone inside turned it off.

Back in Cologne, they let him out beside his car. He had no idea what time it was. The driver handed him the white envelope.

'You do nice work, Rudy,' he said and smiled. 'But honesty's the best policy for you. Don't you want to count it?'

Stott shook his head dumbly as he pushed the envelope into his raincoat pocket. When they drove off, he was too spent to feel elation. He went home and, caked with dried perspiration, lay facedown on his bed and slept.

Thomas developed and enlarged and printed the film in Brewer's hotel room. As Brewer flushed the developing chemicals down the toilet, Thomas studied the photographs of the steward's ledger. Brewer found Thomas's eyes on him.

'What is it?'

'I have a sinking feeling in my gut.' He handed some of the photographs to Brewer.

Brewer frowned at them. The entries recorded all sorts of information about the operation of the club as seen from the steward's desk. The ones that Thomas pointed to concerned the use of meeting rooms, who occupied them, when they were occupied and when they were empty, food and liquor charges.

'This man is a manufacturer of garden supplies and flowerpots according to the membership list,' Thomas said.

'That figures,' Brewer replied. 'He was the chairman at this meeting, garden supplies in foreign trade.'

Thomas checked the other names against the membership list, which included title and company affiliation. The garden-supplies meeting consisted of bankers and marketing men and makers of other kinds of garden and farm items. The other meetings were all the same type.

'So?' Brewer asked, still not comprehending.

'I don't believe it. This is a phony. Someone is covering up the real meetings that took place the last three months. I'll bet they talked about a lot more earth-shaking matters than flowerpots. I bet this membership list is phony too.'

The man was a fox.

Kaethe Dorten sat in her apartment and waited for the report to come in. At her elbow was the steward's ledger from the club, the real one. Next to it was the club's membership list, the real one. Thomas had almost found Parker's tunnel. She'd discovered it only hours before Thomas arrived. If she had visited the club even a day later, it would have been too late. Thomas would have uncovered the truth.

She turned the pages of the club's membership list. It read like a Who's Who in the German War Establishment. There were army tank manufacturers, rifle makers, explosives producers, ammunition people, ballistics people, military jet makers and all kinds of experts on Russian affairs – foreign, domestic, military.

Then she thumbed through the steward's ledger. What a narrow escape. Thomas would have understood it at a glance. Even half an idiot could guess what the club members were up to. Here's a meeting attended by an expert on Russian public opinion conferring with two experts on urban guerrilla tactics. Guess what they discussed? In another meeting, an underwater demolitions expert talks with a city-water-supply specialist and another specialist on Russian urban planning. In another meeting, just six weeks ago, an explosives man talked for four hours with an army sabotage training officer and an army specialist on Russian rocket installation. Who could not guess what was taking place in these meetings – what was being discussed, what country was the target?

She made a mental note to recommend to the housekeeping committee of the club that they remove the symbol over the fireplace. It stated the club's purpose too obviously. Thomas had stared at it all evening. And his mind was not the type to rest until he had discovered its meaning. In the future, the ledger and membership list would have to be kept locked in the vault.

Even after she realized how damning those records were, she never expected Thomas to move so quickly. On a hunch, she and Gustav Behring had spent the afternoon and part of the evening forging a new, innocuous steward's ledger. The false membership list was taken largely from Who's Who in German Industry (Nonmilitary). She couldn't help smiling: what would Thomas make of a meeting of flowerpot makers?

Most important, Parker must have seen the ledger too. She'd found the leak.

The apartment buzzer sounded and she admitted the Banker and the Pallbearer. They handed her the false ledger and false list and she handed them the true ledger and list.

'I don't want Stott hurt,' she said. 'Nothing must happen that would make Thomas suspect he got fake records. I don't even want Stott to be made suspicious of anything. In a day or two he will be offered a splendid job in Mr Behring's bank. An irresistible offer. You inform the committee on employment that we are to receive his resignation with reluctance and give him excellent references and a handsome severance payout. If Mr Behring fires Stott in a few weeks for incompetence, it's very sad. Maybe Stott's plump little widow will marry him in the meantime. That's a fate too good for the traitor, but he's not to be touched. Ever. Understood?'

They both nodded.

'Do not muss so much as a hair on his head.'

They nodded again.

'Now, what have you learned about Dancer?'

'He's well hidden.'

'He's a disaster if you don't find him. He's the next battleground.'

'We're diligently seeking.'

'Put more people on it. That Dancer looks more and more like the key piece. We need him alive. Find him. Fast.'

She watched them nod their heads unhappily. They were embarrassed by their failure, in front of her – a nonprofessional. She still hadn't won her spurs with these two yet.

'One more thing,' she said. 'That Brewer knew something the other night; that's why he tried to follow Fritzsche. Either someone talked or he's got a tap on a telephone. I want a sweep made of Fritzsche's phones, at home, in the limousine and at work.'

'The whole Fritzsche building?' asked the Banker with dismay. 'Just Fritzsche's phones – all of them.'

They nodded unhappily again.

'We have to find the leak that Brewer found.'

She waited for their unhappy nods again.

'Last thing. Put a tail on Thomas. He's almost out of moves and he's liable to do something – ah – interesting. He may lead us to Dancer. Whatever you do, don't lose him. He's a fox. Understood?' When they nodded mutely once more and glanced sidewise at each other she said: 'These are exactly the moves my father would have made if he were well. Would you like to discuss this with him?'

They quickly shook their heads.

'Do you have any reservations about my instructions?

No? Suggestions? No? Then I can assume you enthusiastically endorse what I am doing? Yes? Good, you are both nodding your heads.'

'We are trying to do our best for you until your father recovers,' said the Banker. 'It is what he wants us to do.'

The Pallbearer spoke. 'You think very much like your father. You have a cunning mind.'

She nodded and suppressed a smile. If that wasn't a pair of spurs, it was at least one. 'Not cunning enough,' she said. She escorted them to the door.

Dancer was the shadow that fell over her plans. He was the only person who might tell what else Parker had been up to, how he'd gotten his information and how much.

She tried to think as her father had taught her, to get inside the head of her adversary. Thomas was almost more than she could handle. She yearned to see her father for guidance but she knew she wouldn't. He was far too ill.

Anticipate, she told herself. Anticipate what Thomas will do next. Inside his head, she saw that it had to be Dancer. Thomas would have to interrogate him; there was nothing left. It was interrogate Dancer or go home. Go home, she hoped. Go home to safety.

She couldn't be so lucky next time. But still, she had to give herself points. She had seen the danger of the ledger and set the false trap. She had beaten Thomas again.

She felt exhilarated, alive, on the disastrous edge of things. She did her best when she felt overmatched.

How like a fox he was. A beautiful fox. She couldn't wait another minute. She dialed Thomas's hotel room. 'Did I wake you?'

'I was sitting here wishing I had the nerve to call you at three-thirty in the morning.'

'Is that what time it is? What are you doing?' She knew: he was staring at photographs of the ledger pages and wondering at the significance of flowerpot conferences. 'Whatever you're doing, come do it here.'

He arrived a half hour later. And she kissed him eagerly.

'Oh Colin, what have you done to me? You've cast a spell. I can't sleep or eat. I can't concentrate.' She led him by the hand through the apartment, past the glass partitions and the modern furniture to her bedroom.

'It's not the old farm,' she said. 'No breezes or wild flowers or kittens.'

She wanted to make love eagerly, quickly, but again he slowed her down. He smoothed away her sudden qualms of ineptness and feelings of submission. His tenderness was even more irresistible this time and she fell in love, *dove* in love as recklessly as she'd done everything else in her life. She gave herself completely to Colin Thomas, wrapping him in her arms and thighs and wanting to absorb him totally. She kissed him with soaring joy. 'I love you,' she said. 'I love you, Colin.'

He held her and said nothing.

Later they lay on her bed and watched the sunrise light up the Rhine Valley.

Why didn't he say he loved her. 'Were you ever in love?' she asked him.

There was that hesitation again. She'd put her finger on the same spot before. He seemed to draw in within himself like a turtle. She waited for an answer.

'Yes,' he said finally.

'Tell me about it.'

'No. It's an old story.'

'What was her name? At least tell me that.'

'Martha.'

'Was – was she like me?'

'No. Totally different.'

She grabbed a fistful of his hair. 'Tell me, Colin. I want to know everything.'

'She was very pretty. Sweet. Quiet.'

That fierce gleam of competitiveness appeared in her eyes. 'Did you make love to her?'

He suppressed a smile. 'No.'

'Oh?'

'I wanted her badly but—'

'Ah! Someone else—' She kissed him gently. 'She was a fool, Colin.' And with that Martha was dismissed. 'Tell me. Am I good in bed?'

'Fair.'

She pulled his hair again. 'Tell me I'm fantastic. Go on. What do you like about me?'

And there again was the hesitation.

She pressed him. 'Nothing, Colin? Nothing about me you like?'

'Your hair.'

'What about it?'

'It has copper highlights in the sunshine.'

'What else? More. Do you like my figure?'

'It's lovely.'

'And my face.'

'It's a wonderful face. Your eyes – they haunt me.' But he turned his face away.

'Go on, Colin. If you run out of things to say then lie to me.' She was puzzled. It was labor for him to say this. He was saying them as though they were secret treasures he didn't want to share with anyone. But love meant sharing. And he didn't say he loved her.

'Tell me I'm so fantastic that I'm going to get the Spanish contract,' she said. They lay side by side, their noses touching, and laughed together at that.

'I love you, Colin,' she said again. The words seemed to embarrass him. For the moment she ignored the little warning bell in her mind as she kissed him with renewed passion. If he was still in love with Martha, he had to be made to forget her.

'Make love to me again,' she whispered.

8

Thomas was stymied. He was making no progress on the Parker case. And now he'd gotten completely distracted by a love affair.

Worse – he saw that in his relations with Kaethe Dorten he was trying to go in two directions. He should have told her that he loved her. But he was quite content with his arrangement with Lucia in his house in Chelsea. She was an ideal companion – the older and wiser woman with no ulterior motives. They came and went indepedently, were good friends and slept together with no complications. Just a nice selfish hedonistic life. He didn't want to give that up.

But the merest thought of Kaethe made his pulse race. She was inside him, in his head and in his heart. He found himself in long reveries thinking about her. He hadn't told her one tenth of the things about her he loved, the soap-and-water scent of her skin, the way her hair lay, the feel of it in his fingers, the devilish gleam in her eye, the marvelous way she had of smiling, that trusting, irresistible look of love on her face, the flawless skin and its silken sheen, the rich brown color of her eyes and the thick dark lashes, her voice, her laugh. And the thought of embracing her set off a storm of passion in him. He knew he was smitten.

So he struggled between a fear of being captured by love on the one hand and a sudden panic seconds later that he might lose her to another.

He stood before his mirror shaving and felt the dread of loss anew. He reached for the telephone. 'I want to tell you how much I love you – ' he said to himself. 'No – I want you to know how unbelievably happy you have made me. No – I love you. Just say that to her. I love you.' But maybe he should wait: he had to solve the Doomsday problem first. The memory of his dead friend Parker shamed his feeling of love for Kaethe.

When he had finished shaving, he summoned Brewer.

'Dancer,' Thomas said to Brewer. 'Get him here. During the night. Under heavy security. Don't bring him in on a commercial flight. And make sure no one sees him. If he's spotted they'll kill him.'

'He's not going to want to come.'

'He has his problems and we have ours. Bring him here alive. How you do it is up to you.'

Thomas had a hunch. He knew how Parker had worked and he knew Dancer's talents. All of them. Parker never minded breaking into people's homes and offices when he wanted something they might have. And Dancer was a good second-story man. Thomas felt they had teamed up. Many times. Thomas wanted to know what windows, what doors.

They flew Dancer up from Madrid to Paris and held him there in an airport motel for Brewer.

Brewer arrived with a wheelchair, a male nurse and a makeup expert from the London theater named Ronnie. He wanted to bring Dancer to Cologne in a disguise that would make him unrecognizable by the Doomsday people.

'We're going to find out what your mother looks like, Dancer,' Brewer told him. 'Won't hurt a bit.'

When Dancer realized what they were going to do to him, he was outraged. 'Me? In drag? You are out of your bleeding mind, chum. Not this one.' He pointed to the wig. 'The only way you're going to keep that on me is to rivet it to me skull!' He paced up and down in his undershorts, a skinny stringy little man, ribs showing, thin arms, drawn bony face and sparse pale hair.

He took another bottle of beer from the bag they had

212

brought him and drank half of it in his anger. 'That's a crock, mates!' He seethed. 'Not this lad. Not today. No thank you.' He paced and drank and smoked while they all stood about and silently watched him.

Then Brewer opened the door.

'Help yourself, Dançer.'

'What's that mean?'

'Go. You're free. Do as you please.'

Dancer looked at Brewer, then at the male nurse and the makeup man, then at the open door. 'There's a catch in it somewhere.'

'Sure. There's an old Brooklyn proverb, Dancer. It says you could always get free cheese in a mouse trap. Go get your free cheese.'

'They're still looking for me?'

'They want you very dead, Dancer. And the only friends you have in the whole world are standing in this room with you.'

Dancer thought about that. He leaned against the bathroom doorjamb, arms crossed, holding a cigarette in one hand and a beer bottle in the other, and thought about it. He stared at the partly open door.

'Where are we going?' he asked.

'Cologne,' Brewer said.

'Jesus, not there, mate. Are you daft?'

'Cologne it is, Dancer. Where else would you be going?'

'Where's Tommy?'

'In Cologne.'

Dancer looked unhappily at the door again. 'Shut it, mate.'

Dancer made a convincing old woman. He weighed less than 140 pounds and was none too tall. Ronnie built the disguise around the almost pure white wig, using cosmetics and gum and powders, mascara and a touch of lipstick. With metal-rimmed glasses and deep age creases around his mouth, he looked seventy. The eyes were a slight problem: fear and anger and defiance radiated from them. They had too much fire in them for a fading old woman.

'Just stare at the floor,' Ronnie said.

They dressed him in special elasticized stockings for varicose veins and ground-gripper orthopedic shoes and a dark print dress and a navy blue overcoat with a fur collar, and they capped it off with an old lady's fritter with a black feather that sat upon his head like the last shout of defiance at life.

'You could toddle off to mass in the morning, Dancer,' Brewer said.

'Mass! I'm a bleeding proddie, you asshole!'

'Sit,' the male nurse said.

Dancer got another beer and sat in the wheelchair. The nurse put a lap robe over his bony knees. 'You look like the mother of nine,' the nurse said. 'Holy Name Society. Ladies' Sodality. Irish Mothers of War Veterans. Irish Widows League.' They all began to chuckle.

'Up yours,' Dancer said. He looked like the terror of the old folks' home. He blinked when they removed his hat and took his picture with the flash camera.

'What's that for?'

'Your passport, Mrs Grogan.'

So they wheeled him out of the room and put him in a car and drove him to Orly airport nearby and put him on a private chartered plane, where he was introduced to the pilot, who promised him a smooth ride to Germany and not to worry, and they brought him to Cologne, the last hope that they had of finding out what happened to Parker and what was going on in the Bismarck Club. If he would tell them. For Dancer was probably the last one to see Parker alive – may have been actively involved in Parker's affairs in fact.

All because of two words: Doomsday Book.

Mrs Grogan arrived by cab at the Hotel Central in Cologne in midevening, accompanied by a male nurse and a good supply of baggage to occupy a reserved suite.

When she was settled and the bellhops had withdrawn

214

with very poor tips from the frugal old lady, Thomas entered and shut the door behind to study the figure before him.

'How are you, Dancer?' he asked.

'Like a pig in shit. I figured I'd be flying in tons of stuff to Galápagos for you by now. Or am I still on Excalibur's shit list?'

'Patience, Dancer,' Thomas said. 'We haven't started shipping yet.'

'I hope you're still not shirty about that Sahara shipment.'

Thomas smiled at him. 'When you do something, Dancer, you do it better than anyone else. You scattered a fortune in rifles halfway across the Sahara.'

'Jesus, Mary and Joseph, Tommy. I scattered myself even farther.' He held up his right hand to show where parts of two fingers were missing, the stumps and scars still red and fresh. 'And a piece of my leg.' He raised his dress. 'And a rib. A whole rib, Tommy.'

'That's what happens when you run out of fuel.'

'Run out, my royal Irish arse, Tommy. You mean you don't know what they did to me? I had all the fuel I could carry. I was so overloaded I was barely maintaining airspeed with all the spare cans of petrol I had to carry – I mean, didn't I have to fly back out, you know?'

'I understand, Dancer.'

'Oh no you don't. The bastards put water in the cans of petrol. And that was that. Eleven thousand feet and I fell like the bishop's drawers. In the desert. At night. Marvelous things will happen if ever I meet those bastards. They'll rise bodily to heaven.'

'There's a stage career waiting for you, Mother Grogan,' Thomas said. 'Can you act?' He watched Dancer turn away in disgust.

'Suppose we start at the beginning,' Thomas said.

'What beginning?'

Thomas got a chair and placed it in front of Dancer's wheelchair and sat, straddling it, his arms folded on the

215

back, and he put his face close to Dancer's. 'I don't have much time, Dancer.'

Dancer, fighting anger and fright, looked into Thomas's eyes and saw no sympathy there. Those eyes told him how far Thomas would go. 'Got any beer?'

'All you can drink, Dancer.'

The male nurse produced a bottle and also lit his cigarette.

'Start at the beginning, Dancer.'

Dancer sat holding his beer in his old-woman's outfit and sighed. He was trapped. The only security in the whole world he could count on would come from Thomas. A benevolent Thomas. Or else he was on his own, on the dodge, running like a chicken for his life. He started at the beginning.

'It was easy money,' he said. 'And I needed it. There was a time when smuggling was a real profession. But it's on hard times now, you know, Tommy. Governments do most of the smuggling and they're far worse than we ever were. Making big bloody noises when they place an embargo on a country like South Africa, then at night slipping the goodies to them from submarines. So I've been seeing some lean years. In fact I'm just about done up. So Parker and me got together. He fed me jobs and paid real handsome, too, I don't mind telling you. It was mostly easy work, getting papers from office files. Offices are easy to do unless there's some valuables around with alarm systems, which ain't very often the case.' He looked around for another beer. It was incongruous – a little old woman sitting there and enumerating her complaints to her doctor – her arthritic knees, an inconstant bladder, shortness of breath and night visions – all spoiled by the beer bottle and cigarette clutched in bony mechanic's fingers.

'Parker didn't tell me everything. In fact, Parker never told me anything. But you knew him – he was always rooting around. He loved information, business reports, charts, tables, and if you could get him what he wanted, it would be steak and ale every night for dinner. God knows how many windows I went into for him.

'Well, a while back – a few weeks maybe, couple of months at most – he tied into something that had him excited, so he had me nip over from Amsterdam, where my bird was laid up, and I was in and out of a few places here for him and I began having thoughts of a permanent thing until they shot him down in Paris.'

Thomas smiled at him and said in a low voice, 'Stop. You're breaking my heart.'

Dancer's old lady's hat bristled. 'You think I'm playing the fiddle to you!'

'You've just skimmed the surface. I want the whole story. How many windows did you go through? And where? And I particularly want to know about that last night you saw him – and no sad songs about a farewell drink in the pub with the stainedglass pig.'

"S the truth! We were there!'

'Sure. And then the two of you went somewhere from there.'

'Got another beer?'

'Have six,' Thomas said and he leaned closer. 'Just keep talking, Dancer.'

'What do you want to know?' He looked around for another bottle.

Thomas reached a hand out and put a finger tip on his chest. 'Did you finger him, Dancer?'

Dancer tried to back away from the finger. 'Come on, Tommy. It's me. The Dancer himself.'

'Did you finger him?'

Dancer sighed. 'Can I have another beer?'

'After you tell me.'

'Jesus, I will and all. Now give me the bleeding beer!' The male nurse saw Thomas nod once and got another beer. Dancer took a long pull on it, the fluid gurgling in his rising and falling gullet like a chicken. He wiped his mouth with the back of his hand and sighed again. 'It wasn't my fault. He set it up.'

217

'Go on.'

'I went into one window too many – and they killed him for it. And that's the whole story.'

'From the beginning, Dancer.'

'He had me over. Even paid up something on the bird. You don't know what that meant to me. There's this johnny who has an aircraft museum down in the Riviera and he's been after me to sell him the DC-3. Parker's money saved my bird.' He drained the bottle. 'Shit. Oh, well, here comes all of it. He had me into four maybe five places around here. It was a routine. He would give me the name of the mark and the title and all that and drive me to his office and tell me exactly what to look for.'

'Why didn't he go in with you?'

'Too big. Too heavy. Too slow. He was without doubt the worst second-story man you ever met. He just didn't know how to sneak.'

'Go on.'

'Well, I'd go in and sniff around and when I got it I'd bring it out. He'd look at it and then say yes or no. If it was no, back in I'd go. Only once, after I brought half the man's office, did he finally quit. "It's someplace else," he says. On that last night, when he ran for Paris, he and me sat around drinking and eating and waiting for the workday to end, then he drove me to this office and told me what he wanted. So in I went. Only this time' – he looked around for another beer – 'only this time, we bought the farm. They were waiting for me. Four of them. Sitting there in the dark. When I came in, they grabbed me and put a hand over my mouth and talked to me. They told me I was to do what I was told or the party would be over. They gave me a folder and said that it was the material that Parker wanted and to bring it out to him. I wasn't to say nothing to him. Just give it to him. Then I was to go get my plane and fly to London – Heathrow – and do that job for two weeks. And I done it.'

It was a standard move. Thomas saw that they wanted to salt Parker, then follow him to see where the leak was.

Only he took one look in the folder and ran for Washington. To stop him they killed him. Now – who were they?

'Put some clothes on, Dancer.'

'Oh no. This is my disguise and I'm staying in it until I get out of here.'

'You can't climb in and out of windows in that outfit, Dancer.'

Dancer stared curiously at Thomas for a moment. 'Oh. That's what we're going to do, hey. Revisit the scene of the crime.'

'Scenes, Dancer, scenes.'

The first place Dancer led him was a civil engineering firm. It was a contemporary wood-and-glass structure in a woodsy setting on a rise of land that overlooked a shallow valley twenty miles from Cologne. The modern sign on the lawn said: Water System Specialists.

Dancer was very fast. He seemed to touch the door with his lock pick and it opened. Once inside he moved with the speed of a ferret. He was surprised when Thomas accompanied him. 'Going to watch, mate?'

'I'm a little thinner than Parker.'

Dancer moved down a carpeted corridor and into an office. It was barely lit by bounce light from outside streetlamps. Dancer went to the desk, stepped to the left and crouched. There was a sharp click. He had opened the lock. The drawer slid open silently.

His quick fingers riffled the tabs on a drawerful of manila envelopes. He slipped one out and held it under his flashlight. 'That's it. "Bismarck Club."'

'Thomas took it and opened it. There was one sheet of paper in it. 'Did Parker keep the papers?'

'Nah. He would come in a van and he'd photograph all the papers. Then I'd put the folder back.'

'Is this all the paper that was in here?'

Dancer looked at it. 'Dunno. Didn't pay much attention, to tell the truth. I'd say there were more papers than that one.'

The paper had some notations about water systems in city settings. The word 'Permafrost' was written and circled. Thomas gave it back to Dancer. 'Can you relock that desk?'

Next Dancer led him to an office building just outside Cologne. He had a moment of difficulty with the front-door lock, but then he led the way unerringly up the stairs to the second floor and to an office door. Dancer tapped the words 'Telemetry Systems' with his finger. 'This is it.'

He led the way through a secretary's office, through a smaller room with blueprint and copying machines, into a large file room. Without hesitation, he went to one file cabinet and again found it locked.

'It's an advertisement,' he said to Thomas. 'I always go for the file that's locked.' He pushed two probes into the lock and the spring inside released audibly. Dancer riffled the files in the uppermost drawer. 'Took me three tries to find what he wanted.' With his pencil flashlight he squinted at the tabs and pulled one out. 'B.C.'

'What?'

Dancer pointed to the tab. 'B.C. for Bismarck Club. See?'

There were hardly any papers in the folder except for a stapled and mimeographed document, 'The Future of Telemetry in Telephone Systems.'

'Lock it up, Dancer.'

'Export/Import Diversified Marketers' was in the office building behind the Fritzsche Building, and this time the tab on the folder was marked in pencil 'Bismarck Notes.' Again there were only a few sheets of mostly blank ruled paper. On the front page was the notation – 'Three elements. Chair legs. Drinking fountain tubes.'

'There's just one more,' Dancer said. 'Down in Bonn.' He looked anxious.

'Is that where they were waiting for you?'

Dancer nodded.

They drove out of Cologne on the Bonn motorway. It was

a sixteen-mile drive and while Thomas drove, Dancer sat beside him drinking beer and smoking.

He spoke only once to Thomas. 'Parker was okay. I would have helped him if I could. I mean, without him, I haven't got a copper to fart on, do I?'

It was an old college campus.

'I want to go in alone,' Dancer said.

'Just in case, Dancer?'

'Just in case what?'

'Just in case they're in there again, you can stick it to me while I wait out here.' He opened the door. 'Help yourself.'

Dancer slipped out of the car and hurried away in the shadows. Thomas adjusted the pistol in the arm holster and settled back to wait. He planned to follow Dancer after a three-minute interval.

When the minutes had passed, he got out of the car and made his way to the doorway. The door was unlocked and slightly ajar. He stepped inside and listened. Then he mounted a short flight of stairs and listened again.

He heard a sound, a long weary sigh, it seemed, and he hastened down a dark corridor toward it. Now there was a scraping and he glanced into a darkened office. Another sigh. Thomas stepped into the doorway.

It wasn't much: in the faint light, it was just a silhouette, possibly a head and one shoulder. It should have been Dancer bending over a file or a desk. When the figure straightened up though, it was clearly not Dancer, taller, with broad shoulders. Had the man followed them? Or had he been waiting for Dancer? The man turned and moved right at Thomas with a knife.

Thomas's actions were reflexive. He kicked with his right foot at the groin and made solid contact. The figure doubled over and Thomas grabbed the wrist of the knife hand. Quickly he turned it, bent it up behind the man's back, felt the knife fall and kept twisting. It was probably the wrist that broke with a soft pop and the man shouted. They fell. The man rolled away, stood up. Thomas was up and starting after him when something gripped his ankle. He fell down and the man tramped noisily down the dark corridor and away from him.

Thomas turned his attention to his ankle. It was a hand, attached to a thin arm. He pulled it away from his ankle and stood up.

A door slammed distantly somewhere in the building.

Thomas found the light switch and pushed it. At his feet, the hand now unclenched, lay Dancer. He'd been stabbed in the back and died with his fists clenched – one around Thomas's ankle and the other around a crumpled manila folder. A car raced by the window as Thomas examined the folder. It was empty.

The four of them arrived at Kaethe Dorten's apartment late that night.

She still didn't know their names; they didn't volunteer them, and she felt that there was some sort of professional discretion at work. So she continued to identify them with labels: the banker, the pallbearer, the thief and the housewife.

The banker handed her a pile of miscellaneous notes in a brown paper bag about an inch thick. 'You were right,' he told her. 'We went to the offices of the members on this list and found these papers in their files.'

Kaethe took the papers out of the bag. She had selected nineteen names of club members from the Cologne area who had attended secret conferences in the club. And her guess had been right. Some of them had made notes during those secret meetings and carried them back to their own offices and put them in files. Very German. Very meticulous. Very foolish.

'How many kept files?' she asked. She had begun to quickly sort through the papers.

'Twelve. That's all we could find,' the banker said. 'Some of those notes are most revealing.'

Revealing was hardly the word for it. For Parker, these files were a treasure trove of information. Many of them

222

contained detailed diagrams. Dr Hesse's file was the most incriminating. There was a series of psychographs of the Chinese leadership – attitudinal scales, personality graphs, personal and political bents. From these Dr Hesse had predicted how each would respond to the German offer. It wasn't good: Hesse felt their decision would be very close – half for and half against, in fact.

She felt quite elated: she'd discovered how Parker had gotten his information. The steward's ledger had led him to the reports in the club vault. But he couldn't get in there, so he went in search of files in the members' offices.

Parker was a smart man to have figured that out and she gave herself equal credit for having figured Parker out. And Thomas – she gave him the highest rating of all, for he didn't even have the true steward's ledger for a guide. But he did have Dancer.

She put the papers back into the bag. 'Excellent,' she said. Then she realized there was more: the four were standing silently waiting for her to finish examining the papers. She regarded their glum faces. 'Well?'

'Somehow, Thomas slipped Dancer into Cologne,' the banker said.

'Superb!' She almost clapped her hands. Dancer would be a mine of information.

'It was the purest piece of luck that we spotted them leaving the hotel,' the banker said. 'We followed them to one office – that one.'

He pointed to a name on the typewritten list she'd given them. 'But then they eluded us and we found them again finally at Dr Hesse's office in Bonn.'

'Good. Then they uncovered nothing but empty files.' She was overjoyed. She'd beaten Thomas again.

She found their solemn eyes on her. No one spoke. There was still more.

'Well – go on.'

'Quist–'

'Quist. What about Quist?'

'He killed Dancer,' the banker said.

She brought both fists down on her thighs. 'Damn! Damn-damndamn!' She looked at their hangdog faces. 'What about Thomas?'

'They fought. We think he broke Quist's arm.'

Kaethe had never felt anger take her so violently before. Dancer had been the last living person who could have told her how much Parker had learned of the Doomsday cabal. So now she couldn't tell how much Thomas knew. The danger for the cabal was greater than ever. She yearned to put a bullet through Fritzsche's head. That stupid interfering old fool. He'd become an extreme liability.

For the moment she dismissed Fritzsche. She had to keep her mind on Thomas. Think, she urged herself: what will he do now? Thomas the fox.

9

Manfred Fritzsche felt that things were getting out of hand. As he rode in his limousine to Tatzie's apartment that evening, he considered the consequences of Dancer's murder.

This time, the killing was completely justified. Dancer had been caught by Quist in Dr Hesse's office with the incriminating folder right in his hands. Quist had had no choice: he had to kill him; the cabal had been one step away from exposure again. Things were getting out of hand. Kaethe was an admirable woman; truly she was her father's daughter. But she wasn't her father. Otto would have been on top of these things. There would have been no need to double-check on him.

In the next confrontation with Kaethe, Fritzsche planned to go on the attack. His man Quist had just saved the cabal – again. Thomas was too cunning to be toyed with.

Fritzsche would now demand that either Dorten's people kill Thomas or his people would. Period. He would have a meeting with Kaethe Dorten tonight and demand it.

Fritzsche wished that the Dancer affair were his only concern. For his emotions kept whip-sawing him from one extreme to another. But there were other things. While he was still exhilarated from his meeting with Fox, he was also profoundly anxious over what the Chinese response would be. It was so late. Everything depended on it, yet he was not at all convinced they would say yes.

And he was worried about Brewer. Why had that man followed him the night he met with Fox? Even though Brewer had been thwarted, he must have had a tip on the meeting. There had to be a leak somewhere. It was no accident.

As he clambered out of the limousine, he looked up at Tatzie's windows and felt a twinge of doubt. Again. He confessed to himself once more that he had grown foolish over that girl. Could she – he thought the word fearfully – betray him? Was she the leak?

He scanned the upper floors for her window. There seemed to be no light in her apartment. Fifth floor corner. His breath caught in his throat. The window was dark. He hurried into the building and took the elevator. All his dormant fears, like wraiths and phantoms, came flocking around him on the elevator car.

This time, they told him, she's gone. She won't be there. This time someone younger with holes in his jeans and no money, someone her own age, has made off with her. The elevator began its ascent. He vowed, he promised that soon he would release her, a little bird from her cage. Soon. Only let the time of parting be of his choosing.

Yet in spite of his prayer, he knew this time it was over. His sure instinct that helped him build an empire was never wrong. She's gone.

The elevator, mortally slow, reached the third floor. Hurry. If she's not there, I will be strong, he told himself. Already he has been given a measure of love and passion and incredible beauty far beyond that of any other man he knows. No one has been so gifted.

At the fourth floor, his heart begins to pound. Ah, Tatzie, don't leave me. He feels a shortness of breath. Never has his instinct been so overwhelming. He knows – he can't lie – she finally did it.

At the sixth floor, the car comes to a soft rest but the doors don't open quickly enough. He places an impatient fist against his lips to stifle a cry. Hurry.

The doors at last open. He does not feel the familiar psychic vibrations. The nest is empty. The key trembles at the lock. Impatience! He tries to turn it before it is fully inserted and must pause to push it home. No one is there. With a triumphant thrill in his chest he sees her standing in the middle of the living room in her gown, her hair the way he loves it, smiling at him and silently waiting. Ah God. To reach heaven, you must go through hell.

'Tatzie.' His arms enfold her, he holds her and still holds her. 'Tatzie, I love you more than life itself.'

He felt the reassurance of her strong young arms about him, inhaled the joy of her scent and scolded himself for doubting her. What did a sixteen-year-old girl know of international intrigue?

Eagerly Fritzsche thrust his hand into a jacket pocket and brought out a small jeweler's box. He watched her lovely eyes stare as his fingers opened the box on its hinges. In the familiar nest of jeweler's satin, resting in its slot, was an emerald ring. It was flawless and Tatzie inhaled sharply. Her fingers seemed to tremble as he put it on. She held her hand high and smiled at it and then put her arms around his neck and kissed his cheek. He almost giggled with happiness.

'I have a present for you,' she said.

'Me?' He was astonished. The only complaint she had ever made to him was she had no funds to buy him presents.

Tatzie hurried into her room where he watched her reflection in the wall mirror. She removed her clothing then put on a false mustache, a black derby, an unbuttoned vest. She picked up a flexible bamboo cane and skipped into the living room, doing a Charlie Chaplin shuffle. Her glorious buttocks made it uproariously funny. His gale of laughter brought on an encore. Tatzie rolled her eyes, wiggled the mustache, wiggled her buttocks. And Fritzsche laughed to excess, laughed until his sides hurt and the tears flowed. He wept with joy. His Tatzie could never betray him.

Brewer arrived a few minutes after Fritzsche. He saw the limousine at the curb and let himself into the building at the side vestibule, away from the chauffeur's eyes. He had felt the need to know when the girl's apartment was occupied, so that morning when she had gone off to school, he had entered the empty apartment and put two peepholes through the wall and inserted a magnifying unit in each one – one in the living room and one in the bedroom. They were no thicker than a pin, barely visible, yet, with a separate hand-held eyepiece, each provided a clear view of an entire room.

Before collecting the day's tape recording, he went into the empty apartment and checked the living room peephole. Tatzie was putting on a skit. Brewer looked at her animated nude figure. Then he got his first close view of Fritzsche's abandoned laughter. He faintly resembled Brewer's father. Through the wall as though from a great distance, he could barely hear Fritzsche's howls of mirth. On Tatzie's hand, the one holding the bamboo cane, he saw a new emerald ring.

At last she stopped. She stood in the bedroom doorway and bowed. Fritzsche, unknotting his tie and daubing his eyes, followed her to the bed.

The simple pleasures of the poor. Brewer went back to the car to wait until Fritzsche finished, to pick up the tape. He tried not to think about Tatzie.

This time when Fritzsche arrived at the Bismarck Club,

Kaethe Dorten was already there, waiting for him, and this time there were no flowers.

Fritzsche entered talking. 'I called this meeting,' he said as he shut the door behind him, 'so I have the floor first. We have to take care of that Thomas immediately. We almost had an irreversible catastrophe this time.'

'Tell me about it,' Kaethe Dorten said.

Fritzsche looked at her then at Gustav Behring. 'Tell you about it. You already know about it. I'm talking about that Dancer in Dr Hesse's office.'

'How did you know about that?' Kaethe demanded.

'Quist followed your people, who were following Thomas and Dancer.' Fritzsche had promised himself he would not give way to the pleasure of righteous anger, but he felt his face flushing. 'Quist caught Dancer with an incriminating folder in his hands. If he'd gotten that the whole world would have known about our negotiations. Fortunately Quist is a man who can make decisions—'

Gustav Behring was waggling a forefinger at him. 'Manfred. Enough.'

'Enough. Enough!'

'The folder was empty, Manfred. It was planted there.'

Fritzsche's face was surprised, then flushed a dark purple along the jowls. 'You mean you had some monkeyshines going on and you didn't tell me.'

'We were going to capture Dancer and question him,' Behring said. 'We had a trap set and you killed him. Do you have any idea what you have done?'

'I haven't done anything yet.'

'Manfred,' Behring interrupted again, 'Colonel Dudorov arrived an hour ago. He's in the Russian Embassy in Bonn and he's brought some of his men with him.'

Fritzsche slowly sat down. He looked at Kaethe Dorten. 'These things never happened when your father was well.'

Kaethe Dorten watched his face, heard his infuriating words. There wasn't much they could do about him. He was in the midst of the negotiations with the Chinese. He

228

couldn't be removed; he couldn't be handcuffed or muzzled. The biggest challenge for her in this whole affair had been coping with this willful old man who sat across from her.

'I say,' Fritzsche rumbled, 'that Thomas must be killed immediately.'

'While Dudorov is here,' she said to him slowly, 'not a word from you. Not a breath. Not a ripple.'

The empurpled anger faded from Fritzsche's cheeks. At last he'd read the menacing message in her eyes.

After the meeting with Fritzsche, Kaethe went to Thomas's hotel. She was discovering things about herself she never suspected. She felt like the jealous lover: her eyes quickly searched for any flagging in his ardor. And when she read anew the affection in his smile, then his hotel suite was hardly large enough to hold her joy.

That night he told her about Parker. He talked of their friendship and of the night that Parker had saved his life. It was clear that Thomas would not give up easily the chase after Parker's killer. And her anger for Fritzsche came flooding back.

Thoughtfully she cradled Thomas's head and combed her fingers through his curly hair. A growing sense of guilt was claiming her. Here she was holding Thomas in her arms, giving her complete love to him, while at the same time being his secret adversary. Worse was her association with Fritzsche, who pressed constantly for Thomas's murder. And she tried not to think about what would happen if Thomas learned who her father was.

She couldn't go on much longer being both lover and enemy. Something would have to be done.

'I love you, Colin,' she said. 'Don't ever forget that.'

For Kaethe, the next few days became a game of waiting and watching.

The three days had passed and there was no word from the Chinese. And after Dancer's death, Thomas had remained in his hotel. If he had another move he hadn't revealed it. Was he waiting and watching too?

And Colonel Dudorov remained in the Bonn embassy. There had been only a few glimpses of him getting in and out of cars, a thin middle-aged man still pale from his major surgery.

But Dudorov never traveled alone. Undoubtedly Dancer's death, so soon after Parker's, had drawn him to the Cologne area, and he surely had fielded a team of agents to sniff out what was going on.

Almost half of the gun dealers were still in town. Although the auction had a few more days to run, many of the dealers had gotten what they'd come for and departed. Many were probably out selling the German matériel they'd bought – wandering the most remote corners of the world in search of business.

Maybe the Chinese were aware of Dudorov's presence. That could be why they hadn't contacted Fritzsche yet.

One night, she had a dream about Thomas, sitting in the old farmhouse during a snowstorm. In her dream she was overjoyed and ran to him and held him. She woke up irritated with her childish yearning. 'Go home, Thomas,' she said aloud in the dark. 'Go home and stay alive.'

She still hadn't guessed what his next move would be.

Dudorov clambered into the limousine with disgust. Just when he was putting back a few of the forty pounds he'd lost from surgery, he had to come down with a stomach virus. He hadn't eaten in two days. He felt sick as a dog.

Gregov sat beside him looking out at the countryside of the Rhine Valley. There wasn't much to see in the dark.

'This is one of my best men,' Dudorov said. 'I recruited him in East Germany and put him in the Bismarck Club right after it was formed – what is that, fifteen years ago? Dorten and his cronies can't make a move inside that club that I don't know about.'

Gregov nodded without interest. He'd received his orders to clean up his affairs and return to Russia. If he was

230

lucky, he would get a one-room apartment – locked in a one-roomer with his wife. He was in agony. What if Frank Gorman tried to contact him while he was here in Cologne? Gregov considered the risks in calling Colin Thomas, who was staying in the Hotel Central in Cologne.

'You must always double-proof your illegal when you're dealing with Dorten,' Dudorov prated in his paternalistic tone. 'So, just to be sure, I recruited another illegal in East Germany, a woman, and put her in the Bismarck Club also. Neither one knows about the other. Then I compare their reports.'

Gregov wanted the old man to stop talking. He had to think.

The first rendezvous was in a parking lot of an industrial plant between Cologne and Bonn. Gregov thought that it was particularly ill chosen. The Soviet limousine stuck out like a nose boil. When they arrived a parked car blinked its lights three times at them, and their driver replied with three blinks. A moment later a stocky, well-dressed man walked across the lot and leaned in the window. He looked exactly like a German banker.

'What is going on with these two deaths?' Dudorov said without preamble.

'They're related to the arms convention here,' the Banker said. 'Both Parker and Roland are connected with Excalibur Ltd, an arms firm based in London.'

'So?'

'I hear that there's a big battle going on between Excalibur and some of the other arms firms for new business.'

Dudorov shifted in his seat. He felt nausea coming on again and by moving around tried to stave it off. 'Well, what is happening inside the Bismarck Club? Any talk about the two murders?'

'All is quiet,' the Banker said. 'There is no talk about the murders. And Otto Dorten remains bedridden. He is forbidden to discuss business affairs with anyone. They say his health is failing and the winter will probably kill him.'

Dudorov shifted in his seat. So the old ferret was dying. And so was he himself. The two combatants after forty years had fought each other to a standstill, canceled each other out. He felt deep regret that it was over – their four-decade war. The contest had been marked by brilliance on both sides, but secretly Dudorov gave himself higher scores than he did to Dorten. Much higher scores.

The Banker continued talking at the limousine window for another fifteen minutes. Detailed information about the inner workings of the club tumbled from his lips. But nothing sensitive. Dudorov was convinced that the two murders had nothing to do with Dorten. Just a few packs of wild animals squabbling over some gun orders.

But the next meeting would put the stamp on the Banker's report. The limousine drove through Cologne, past the old Roman wall gate of Eigelsteintor, now used as a museum, and into the green belt near the Cologne sports stadium. They parked and waited. Down a long tree-lined promenade came a small old woman carrying a shopping bag, walking from light to light with a firm tread. She was obviously from the old school, and she almost curtseyed as Dudorov opened the window.

'I want to know what is going on with the two recent murders of Parker and Roland,' Dudorov said.

'Trade war,' she said without hesitation. 'The contracts were put out here in Cologne by a consortium of small-arms traders trying to compete against a large firm in London – Excalibur Ltd.'

Dudorov nodded impatiently. 'I have heard that it is connected with the Bismarck Club.'

The woman shook her head. 'That club has become nothing but a debating society. The members complain all through the night. They cannot agree even on the speaker for their annual banquet. Most of the attendance is from the older members. The young men stay away in disgust.'

Dudorov held her in conversation for a few more minutes. Then he felt he had to go. The car ride had agitated his stomach virus. He had to lie down.

Kaethe Dorten was astonished when the Banker reported to her what had happened.

'How did you become Dudorov's agents?' she asked.

'Your father didn't tell you?' the Banker asked. 'When the club was founded, he knew that Dudorov wouldn't rest until he got someone inside. So he fed the two of us to him. More than fifteen years now.'

Kaethe pondered that after the Banker left. Such a move took more than a brilliant mind. It also required a marvelous sense of humor.

Later her father said to her, 'Don't laugh. I have no idea how many doublers he's wrung in on my organization. I could be getting reports right now that were prepared inside the Kremlin.'

The private detective stood on the beautiful Persian rug before Fritzsche's desk and gave his report, wetting a thick thumb with his tongue as he turned the pages of his notebook. The report took some time. He had three days of notes to go through, reciting the hour and the minute that Tatzie entered her classes, whom she spoke to, where she dined for lunch, what shops she browsed in.

Fritzsche sat in his chair, elbows on knees, head bowed, and like a priest in the confessional listened to the list of sins. He heard the events and discounted them as the detective read them out. Nothing. Harmless. Usual. In the bookstore. In the class. In the restaurant with two girls. And so home. And so here. And so there. Innocent. Totally innocent. Fritzsche could have wept.

'What did the phone tap reveal?'

The detective withdrew a spool of tape from his pocket and placed it with a formal bow on the desk, then withdrew one step. 'Nothing. She talks mainly with the two girls she dines with. The conversation is, pardon, banal.'

'Did you check to see if there are other taps on her telephone line?'

'There are none.'

The detective left.

Fritzsche thanked God for his Tatzie and berated himself for his fears. Fate had given him this splendid child and he spoiled it all with his doubts. He went back to his papers.

But the speck of doubt had begun to spread its corruption. Brewer had learned of his movements from somewhere. His home, his limousine, his office, the Bismarck Club, these were all swept for taps regularly by a team of professionals. But obviously it wasn't Tatzie either, was it? There was one way to definitely exonerate the poor child. He left the office in the early evening and went down to his limousine, Othello through the evening streets.

He lay on the bed, watching her. Unhappy. In an agony of doubt. He dared not ask her. He was terrified that she would admit it. But so innocent. He wanted to forget. To forgive. To have his own little Tatzie again in his arms, unblemished, faithful and loving, and he would give her the whole world.

He watched her in her white blouse at the mirror, the emerald flashing as she combed. He cast an arm over his eyes and in the darkness hid his dismay. She approached the bed. She placed her hands on his bare belly and stroked softly. He felt his belly muscles contract. So unhappy: his penis remained shrunken. Incapable.

She massaged it. 'Come on. Wake up,' she crooned. 'Cock-a-doodle-do. Reveille.' He felt her lips kiss it. 'Wake up,' she said with her lips on it. The vibrations of her lips stirred within him. She pretended to play a bugle call, crooning, and his penis felt the vibrations. It stirred. She held it against her throat and hummed. The vibrations were thrilling. 'Come on,' she called. And it rose, phoenix from the ashes.

She is innocent, he was sure. She had done nothing. She

cared too much for him. Near tears of repentance, he opened his eyes and sighed. 'Ah, Tatzie.' He's a monster, an old fool, to doubt her. She's innocent, pure, loving, forgiven. Yes, forgiven.

'Tatzie. The hat.'

And she got the hat from the closet. She loved it: a very old straw sun hat, an authentic antique with cloth flowers and long trailing blue ribbons, some faded, and a cartwheel, floppy brim. She gazed happily at it.

'Put it on,' he said.

She smiled at him and placed it on the back of her head. The effect to him was electrifying: the hat created a halo around her face. Blond ringlets were crushed by it around **her** brows and temples. Her lovely blue eyes were accentuated by the dangling old ribbons. And the delicate smile on her face was almost the look of love. She was an angel with a straw halo.

'Tatzie,' he said, surprised by the hoarseness in his throat. 'Take off.'

She gave him a naughty grin and began to unbutton her blouse. She had surprisingly long slender fingers, beautiful and softly white, and he watched them greedily undo the buttons. When the blouse was off, she turned and let him open her brassiere. He was irritated with himself when he saw how his hands trembled with excitement. He felt as inept as a young groom on a wedding night. She watched his eyes as she pulled away the brassiere.

It was like removing the wrapping on a priceless painting by an old master, watching her disrobe, and with each garment that came off the more of her loveliness was haloed by the old straw hat.

She stepped out of her tweed skirt that he'd bought her, then stepped out of the half-slip. 'Pull,' she said and kissed him as he pulled down her panties. 'Your hands are like ice,' she said, and held them for a moment in hers. Then she stepped out of her panties and stood before him, smiling and radiant in her nudity.

'Shall I put—'

'Yes,' he said eagerly. 'Yes. Now.'

She stepped to the closet and his eyes never left her swaying buttocks and splendid back.

'Ready?' she called.

'Yes,' he whispered.

She stepped back to the bed in a pair of thigh-high black leather boots. He felt a catch in his throat as he gasped at her. 'Lovely, lovely,' he sighed. 'How lovely you are.'

If she knew how much power she had over him, she could have put a ring through his nose and led him through the streets of Bonn. Manfred Fritzsche was completely bewitched.

She strode slowly, languidly about the room in the boots and flop hat, letting the ribbons flutter along her shoulders and back, swaying her buttocks provocatively at him. His eyes took in everything, the creamy skin, the golden ringlets of her pubic hair, the soft down on her arms and the amazing blue eyes that gazed back at him so wantonly.

She beckoned to him with an exaggerated theatrical gesture. 'Come to my arms, my love,' she said.

'Tatzie,' Fritzsche held outstreched arms imploringly, his eyes hungrily roving over every memorized square inch of her flawless beauty. Dancing with swaying ribbons, she approached the bed, got up and, still in the boots, straddled him.

Head raised, slightly panting, he watched transfixed as her hands stroked his penis, then carefully settled her hips over it. He sighed and crooned as he felt penetration. He lay back and watched her now straddling his hips. She hummed something supposed to be Arabic music, stroking his belly, writhing her body over him, her version of a belly dance.

Her hum became intermittent and the rhythm of her body intensified. She was caught up in her own passion, and his eyes, barely slits, watched her incredible beauty, felt the rising of his passion, praised God for his great good fortune, and watched her enraptured face, her eyes closed, her head swaying to one side totally absorbed.

He reached his hands to her hips and stroking the soft flesh, felt himself flowing out of his own body. 'Don't end,' he pleaded, 'Never end.'

When he opened his eyes, she was still straddling him, smiling sweetly. He reached his forgiving arms to her. 'Tatzie. Tatzie.'

She lay upon his chest and he enfolded her in his arms and wondered how his aging heart could hold such monumental love. His passion exhausted him as though some of his very life escaped from him.

But with that overpowering passion spent, insidious doubt returned. She's guilty. He knew.

'Tatzie,' he murmured in her ear. 'Tomorrow night I will be late. I am to meet a man to talk about the reunification of our country.'

'Ummm hummmmm.' She sighed in his ear, half hearing.

'At eight o'clock tomorrow night,' he said. 'At the Bavarian House Restaurant. Can you remember that?'

'Ummmmmm hummmmmm.' Guilty girl.

'I'm hungry,' she said.

The next night, shortly before 8 o'clock at the Bavarian House Restaurant, exactly as he had told Tatzie, Manfred Fritzsche arrived in a rented car, alone, parked and waited. If his suspicions were right, then Thomas and his man, Brewer, would appear in the precincts somewhere.

If he was wrong, then Tatzie of course was innocent, and the leak was elsewhere. His throat was tight and painful and he was very thirsty. It was the closest feeling to panic that Fritzsche had ever known.

'Please, Tatzie, be innocent,' he murmured. 'Be innocent.' And with that he settled down to wait out the most terrible evening of his life.

There was a continuing flow of people entering and leaving the restaurant, a continuing exchange of cars in the parking lot. In the barroom sitting on a stool overlooking the dining room was the private detective. Fritzsche could see his head. Between the two of them, they could see everything that went on inside and outside.

It was demeaning, Fritzsche knew, a man of his age and stature spying on a sixteen-year-old child, but the consequences were so great he felt he had no choice. He had his responsibility to the others. He watched each car door opening with trepidation. His heart raced in his breast with each face he saw, and he developed a headache. Waiting was, for him, agony.

He'd never had patience or subtlety and envied those attributes in Dorten. Yet they were feminine wiles – and they had made Behring grow soft and indecisive.

It was the lack of those two characteristics, the lack of tact and shrewd maneuvering, that had made Fritzsche. Direct, soldierly, stern, unimaginative – those qualities are what helped him. From the beginning life was a cavalry charge, arriving with all guns blazing, frightening everyone, taking charge, grabbing power.

His tank unit had slugged, kicked, battered and slashed its way through eight hundred miles of Russian countryside, days ahead of its supporting infantry, moving faster than any army before in all of history over the worst roads in Europe, encircling vast Russian armies, capturing as many as six hundred thousand troops in a single day, then rushing again toward the biggest prize in Russia, Moscow. And in early December 1941, they drove right up to the gates of the city. From the suburbs, late in the afternoon, he saw sunlight touching the rooftops of the Kremlin itself. It was the high-water mark of Germany's invasion.

The next day in a snowstorm, Siberian troops entered the city from the east and the German troops settled down in their summer clothing to wait out the winter and the spring campaign. Germany's dream of conquest was doomed.

After the war, Fritzsche took stock of himself. It was appalling. He had battle scars and gouges all over his body, and a stubborn thigh wound that wouldn't heal. He was penniless. For his efforts he had a large number of decorations, an unparalleled history of bravery and a legendary war record.

His brother was dead, two uncles were dead, so were eight cousins. The Fritzsche family was almost destroyed. All the extensive land holdings in East Prussia and the family estates were gone, swallowed up by the Russian troops forever.

He was proud, angry, destitute and sick – a walking symbol for Germany itself. As far as he could judge then, Hitler was the greatest calamity of modern times – for Germany and for all of Europe. He had accomplished three things: he'd managed to get Germany severed in two; he'd brought the Russian barbarians into Western Europe; and he'd left Germany with a permanent exposure to another Russian grab through East Germany.

Hitler also left the Germans with a reputation of being monsters and ghouls. 'I never killed one Jew,' Fritzsche told himself.

Fritzsche faced the postwar years with the same attributes that had sustained him in battle. Using bluntness, tactlessness, force, muscle and unhesitating attack, he had blundered, bullied and fought his way into an industrial empire and brought to Otto Dorten the industrial power base needed to mount the secret campaign on Russia.

He would never change his ways. The same techniques would serve him in handling this problem with Tatzie.

Fifteen minutes had passed and he allowed himself the first nibbling of hope. He made himself hold his head up and boldly stare at the faces that entered the restaurant. He glanced at the detective's head through the window in the bar for a signal. Nothing.

She appeared insidiously in his head, strolling about with that slim grace in the leather boots and the flop-brim hat with the trailing baby blue ribbons and the cluster of flowers on the crown. Those pale, pale blue eyes, the color of applewood smoke, and that maddening full lower lip, and the nose, the lovely, delicate, perfectly formed nose. He tried to put it out of his mind. Each arriving car was like a stab in his heart. He would hold his breath until the passengers alighted. Each false alarm was like a narrow miss from an artillery shell.

At eight-thirty-five, he began to seriously hope. He clutched his hands together and bowed his head, begging. How terrible it is to wait, in battle and in love.

Once, he saw the detective turn and glance through the window at him. Fritzsche felt uncontrollable alarm. Had the man seen something? But no, the head turned back to his drink.

By quarter of nine, Fritzsche began to realize he was out of danger. They weren't coming. It was a false alarm. Tatzie had told no one. He vowed he would shower her with presents.

The relief he felt was enormous. His preoccupation with Tatzie had kept him from concentrating on the next meeting with Fox. In the last three days or four or five – he couldn't recall – he had paced the floor agonizing over the next meeting and yet insistently his mind would return to Tatzie. Madness.

Relief.

It was five before the hour. No one was coming. With great joy, he would rush to his Tatzie and spend the entire night with her. He fumbled for the car keys in his pocket, glanced and saw the detective on the restaurant steps. The man dropped his cigarette, stepped on it and descended slowly to walk across the parking lot, across the street and up to Fritzsche's car. He wanted to go off duty, obviously.

Fritzsche rolled down his window.

The detective stooped down. 'Brewer has driven by here three times.'

The last time Kaethe Dorten had cried she was ten years old.

She'd been thrown by a stubborn horse and suffered a bad ankle sprain. Her tears were shed in frustration: the sprain prevented her from remounting and conquering the animal. He had won – temporarily, until her ankle mended.

Tears were not on her mind when she got to her office that morning, for she was drawn into a violent quarrel that gave her combative nature a great lift.

A well-known musical-show master of ceremonies had acquired air time on a German television station for a late-night disco show. He then had sold commercial time to a number of advertisers including one of Kaethe's clients, a maker of several low-priced candy bars.

The client called her personally at midmorning. His voice fit the rest of his physiognomy: coarse and guttural, it went with his fat bullet head, protruding eyes and massive chest and arms.

'I want to get off that disco show,' he told her.

'Oh? Why? It's got very high audience ratings.'

'It's draining too much of my advertising money.'

'You have an ironclad contract with them. I don't think you can break it.'

'Find out.'

Before she had a chance to call the disco show, the show's business manager called her. A coincidence.

'Kaethe. I have to report that the television station is exercising its prerogative and is dumping our disco show.'

'Ah, too bad. What happened? Didn't it work after all?'

'Oh, yes. It was very successful. But the station wants to put on a talk show so we're out in the street.'

'I'm sorry to hear that.'

'You're sorry. You ought to hear the weeping around here. We've lost a fortune. Anyway, tell your candy man that our contract is abrogated.'

She called the candy factory and got her client. 'Well, I have good news for you,' she said.

'Ah, what?'

'You're free from your contract on the disco show.'

'Kaethe, you're a wonder. How did you do it?'

'I didn't do anything. It's just a coincidence. The station is replacing the disco show with a talk show.'

'Oh. Hmmmmm. Well, let me see. You mean you didn't tell him that I wanted to get off the show?'

'Never had a chance to.'

'Then let's sue them for breach of contract and ask for sizable damages.'

'What?'

'Why not? Pull out the contract and see what it says. Call me back.' He hung up.

She called him right back.

'That was quick,' he said. 'What does the contract say?'

'I don't know what the contract says. But Kaethe Dorten says you're no longer her client. I'm resigning your account.'

'What!'

'I said I'm resigning your account. If you'll sue them without just cause, then someday you'll sue me, and I won't have people like you under my roof. I'm sending you formal notice today.' And while he was still in midsentence, she hung up.

She was in the middle of dictating a letter resigning the account when the candy man's lawyer called her.

'My client is demanding that I sue you and some television station for breach of contract.'

'Good. Call my lawyer.'

Twenty minutes later, her lawyer called. He was bewildered and she was furious. 'I've had enough of this bastard,' she said. 'You get out a copy of our standard client contract and read it over. I want you to find some pretext on suing him and I want you to make it stick.'

'How – in the name of heaven!'

'Well for one thing, my contract calls for payment of all bills within thirty days. He's sixty days late on several of them. Put a hold on all his corporate funds, tie up his cash flow, and sue for the money including substantial interest and penalties.'

242

'My God, Kaethe. You'd bring his whole operation to its knees. He could lose a lot of money.'

'Good. The thought gives me great pleasure.'

An hour later, three calls came in simultaneously, from her lawyer, from the other lawyer and from the candy maker.

'He's screaming bloody murder,' her lawyer told her. 'I don't know if I can make it stick, but your countersuit has scared the hell out of him. It turns out he's got all kinds of cash problems right now and he's very vulnerable.'

She let the candy maker dangle on the end of his telephone while she spoke to his lawyer. 'As far as I'm concerned he started it and I'll finish it.'

'Miss Dorten,' the lawyer said soothingly. 'He's just impetuous. I've assured him there's no case for him to sue you. Your contract with him is quite explicit. You are quite within your rights to resign his account. Now he's very contrite. He tells me he needs your services very badly right now. Although his cash flow is very poor at the moment – it's that time of the year, you know, with Christmas coming, and all his capital is tied up in sugar and supplies. However, he's drafting a check right now for the money he owes you. All of it.'

'Good,' she said. 'We'll talk after I get it.'

'He's having a special messenger bring it around. Now why don't you call him and kiss and make up?'

'Let me see his check first.'

She turned to her secretary. 'Is our esteemed client still on the line? Tell him I'm busy. I'll speak to him after the check arrives.'

The check arrived later in the afternoon. The messenger had a breathless quality about him that made her smile and he delivered the check to her personally with great ceremony.

When the messenger left, she sent her secretary to the candy maker's bank to cash the check.

It was another hour before her secretary returned. Meantime, he had called her three times.

With his money on her desk, she called him.

'Ah, Kaethe, dumpling,' he crooned. 'Such a hot temper.'

'Nothing hot about it. You just showed your true colors to me and I'm making my resignation stick. I don't want your account in my shop.'

'What! You must not do that! I need you!'

'There are plenty of other agencies in Germany.'

'But there's only one you. You helped build this company. Kaethe, please. Play nice.'

'I am playing nice. I'm resigning.'

'No you won't. If you do, I'll cancel that check and make you sue me. You won't see your money for years.'

She hung up. 'Send the letter of resignation,' she told her secretary.

It had given her day a real lift. It had cost her the account she was using as a wedge into other food accounts, but the man himself was a small loss and she had saved herself a major headache in the future.

She loved winning.

Kaethe had picked up her father's habit. She paced. When she was a girl she could lie in her bed and hear him many a night stepping back and forth across his den. And now here she was walking to and fro across her apartment. She was thinking obsessively about Colin Thomas.

During the day, while quarreling with her client, she had settled on the solution to her problem: she would resign from the cabal. She should have long ago anyway rather than try to work with that old fool Fritzsche. And once free of the encumbrance, she would feel no guilt about her affair with Thomas. It was a perfect solution – until, that is, she thought of the expression she would see on her father's face. She could hear his voice:

'Forty years, Kaethe. And this may be the last chance for Germany before Russia swallows us whole. What a tempting prize we are for the Russians – one of the most industrialized nations in the world. One snap of the bear's jaws and we're gone – our entire economic miracle crated and shipped to Russia. There'll be little time for your love affair if that happens. Germany needs you, Kaethe.' And he would easily talk her out of resigning.

So the conclusion was inescapable. Since the deceit was unendurable – sleeping in Thomas's arms all night, plotting against him all day – the affair must end.

He arrived at ten that evening and kissed her. She barely responded. Instead, she pulled him by the hand to her sofa.

'Sit,' she said. 'Please.'

He sat, with those quick, pale eyes reading her face. 'What's happened? There's something wrong.'

She sat across from him. 'I've been rehearsing a speech over and over to get it letter-perfect. And now I can't remember a word of it. So I'll say it simply. We can't see each other anymore. It's over.'

He didn't speak. Yet the perplexity in his eyes made her almost lose her resolve.

'I should never have let it get started, Colin. I'm sorry. I didn't realize what I was doing and before it develops any further, I have to stop it.'

He nodded. 'You are going to tell me why, aren't you?'

'You're entitled to an explanation but I can't give you one. I can only say that I'm not free to continue.' She watched him stroll over to the glass balcony door and look out at the nightscape of Cologne. With him in the room, she saw even more tangibly how great her loss would be. She clenched her fists in pain. But there were far sharper pains, she told herself, waiting across the East German border.

'Please sit,' she said. He did. 'I need to convince you of the hopelessness of any further discussion. It's even pointless to ask questions. You've done nothing wrong. None of this is your fault. The cause is on my part – and there's nothing you or I can do about it.'

'It's permanent?'

She hesitated. Would there be a 'someday' – a peaceful

aftermath to Russia's collapse? When? A year? Two? She shook her head. 'Don't hope.'

He gave her a searching look.

'No,' she said, reading his mind. 'It's not another man.'

'Then there is hope.'

'No. There isn't. And don't search for a reason in your mind. You won't find it there.' It was agony to watch him, feeling her love inside her beating in violent protest against her ribs. She wished he would go. She had vowed not to cry – particularly not in front of him. That could be disastrous.

'We can solve this – somehow,' he said. His attitude panicked her. He wasn't accepting her decision. He was still the fox, patiently looking for the way to solve the problem.

'Colin, if you care even the slightest bit for me, you'll just go.'

He stood up and, to her surprise, he began to pace, and he walked along the same path she had followed across her apartment. She almost smiled and resolve failed her. Maybe he could find a solution.

Her heart leaped. They loved each other. They were intelligent people. Together they could find an answer. Her reckless impulsiveness began to loosen her tongue. She would tell him – about the cabal, and the plot against Russia, about the Chinese plan and her father's role. Eager to be rid of her burden, she opened her mouth to tell him.

He saw her expression and stopped pacing. He watched her face expectantly.

She changed her mind. 'Go,' she said. 'Please. Say goodbye and don't look back.'

To her great relief and dismay, he turned and walked out.

The next morning, Kaethe was standing at her office window, looking out at the rain, a slow winter drizzle. What she was feeling was despair mixed with hope: Thomas would burst into her office and present a solution that neatly conquered all obstacles.

The very fact that he hadn't argued was encouraging. He had walked out without a word because he had formulated a plan and hurried off to implement it. Having told herself that, she would recognize its absurdity and plunge into despair again. Through her mind like a snapshot album flashed pictures of him, his face, his smile, his gentle arms – taunting her with images of what might have been.

Her secretary signaled her. There was a telephone call. She answered it.

'Thomas left,' the Banker's voice said.

'Left? When?'

'We're not sure. About four o'clock this morning.'

So he wasn't going to burst into her office with a solution after all. Without a murmur he had gone away. And he had taken hope with him.

10

Normandy, France: Colin Thomas entered the American Military Cemetery above Omaha Beach in the gray light of late afternoon and walked along the main path toward the sea.

On his right stood the massive military cenotaph memorializing the war dead. On his left lay a great army under crosses and six-pointed stars. Ten thousand American troops dead liberating France. In a sea of grass, the precise rows of grave markers seemed to converge in infinity. Salt mist blew across the cemetery, and a few lone figures, one with a black umbrella, wandered among the stones.

At the edge of the cemetery Thomas stood at the top of the steep switchback stairs that led down to the distant beach far below. Many were led to the graves beside him trying to scale that sandy sea wall.

'You've been stopped cold,' General Wynet said.

'You might say that,' Thomas turned to him. 'I don't know any more about Parker's Doomsday than the day I started.'

'Let's walk. Toward that bunker.'

The rising mist softened everything, soaked everything, put details out of focus in the dull light. Soon it would be dusk. Thomas gazed about him. A dour land in the bitter season.

'Whatever made you decide to sell guns, Thomas?' Beyond Wynet, the markers seemed to listen accusingly.

'Did you fly me all the way out here to ask me that?'

Wynet shrugged and walked on. 'Well, then, where are we with this Doomsday affair? You ready to throw in the towel?'

'No.'

'What then?'

'What's happening with Gregov in Amsterdam? Has he defected yet?'

'We're trying to decide what information we can get from him,' Wynet answered. 'I have the dream list from a half dozen people in Washington. But there's nothing Gregov can deliver. He's no catch. He's not in anything sensitive. I mean, there's not much he can bring to the party, is there?'

'That depends, General.'

Wynet paced on toward the bunker. 'See down there? That's where my unit was. Bloodbath. The army that makes the least mistakes wins. That's our plan for Russia.'

'What?'

'To force them to make more mistakes than we do. We're dumb; they're dumber. There's a story going around Washington that we have actually declared war on Russia three times since 1945 and Moscow has declared war on us three times. Trouble is, in each case, the declaration got misrouted and filed away without being delivered. We aren't at war because we can't get each other's attention.'

Thomas smiled at the absurdity. Peace was a clerical error. 'I don't know what to tell you about Gregov,' Wynet went on. 'These Russian defectors all think they're God's gift to the West. They all wear high price tags, and most of them have only stale data that was worthless when it was fresh.' He glanced at Thomas. 'We're thinking of telling Gregov that if he wants to defect, he should simply walk into the nearest US Embassy and he's a free man.'

'But,' Thomas countered, 'he wants to defect in style. He wants his goodies.'

Wynet snorted. 'Of course.'

'Suppose he could bring material on Doomsday.'

Wynet stopped and stared at Thomas. 'Not likely, is it? I mean what would their Amsterdam office – '

'Dudorov.'

'Oh?'

'He was just in Cologne.'

A drizzle began and the breeze drove it into their faces. The land of the sideways rain. Wynet led them into the German bunker, a bomb-battered concrete pill gradually being swallowed by the sand. Inside were small dunes and cigarette butts and some wine bottles, charcoal graffiti here and there, a faint odor of urine. Iron rungs led down several stories into darkness. Outside the wind whistled in the marram grass.

From inside, next to the huge artillery piece, its rusted barrel pointing eternally out to sea, Wynet looked down on Omaha Beach. His eyes were eloquent.

Then he said thoughtfully, 'Let's do this, Thomas. We'll run up to Amsterdam tonight, and you can have a little chat with your Russian dandy. If he has anything to trade, we'll listen.'

'What about Cassle's section in Washington?'

Wynet sighed. 'If we let Cassle's people handle it, they'll

want to interview Gregov at his desk in front of his boss with a standard government questionnaire that he'll have to fill out in triplicate. Then he'll wait three years until the papers are processed. No. You do it. With my blessing. You know the man. And you've handled this type of operation before.' He looked at Thomas solemnly. 'If we don't get some information on Doomsday soon, we'll be out of time. And, God help me, I don't even know what that means.'

'There's one consolation. If it's doomsday for us, it's doomsday for the Russians too.'

Wynet managed a faint grin. 'You think they have more to answer for, eh? Listen. Your partner has been giving me heartburn. He thinks I'm forcing you to stay on this assignment. Am I?'

'He thinks you've hit him in his wallet.'

'What will he do with that fat wallet if doomsday does come?'

Thomas left General Wynet strolling along the curving length of wall containing the multitudinous names of the missing in action. With his hands behind him, forefingers hooked together, he walked, an aging man looking for something he'd lost.

Thomas felt accused by the grave markers. Had Wynet chosen this meeting place to shame him into leaving the arms trade? He could never go back to military intelligence.

After dinner, Wynet's Lear jet flew them to Amsterdam and Gregov.

There was a part of Thomas's mind that was numb. It refused to function. As the aircraft passed over the night lights along the French and Belgian seacoasts, he still had not gotten over the scene with Kaethe.

He had gone to her apartment to tell her he was leaving Cologne on urgent business for a day or so. He had just enough time to get to the airport. But before he could tell her, she made her astonishing speech to him, ending their affair. He'd had no time to discuss it. He had to leave. It was the most difficult thing he had ever done in his life.

Now it would be days before he could get back to Cologne. Then maybe it would be too late. He felt utterly helpless.

From the inside, the little Dutch church seemed more like the inverted hull of an old sailing ship. Entirely of wood, the interior was finished in ship's joinery with braced crossbeams and wooden paneling and teak rails throughout. A shaft of morning sunlight touched the prowlike pulpit.

The front door swung open, and a broad beam of morning sunlight lit the main aisle of the church. A man's shadow lay indecisively on the oak floor. It hesitated for a moment, then the door swung shut. Footsteps came slowly down the aisle past rows of high-backed pews. He stopped at a stall at the front and looked in. 'I think,' he said, 'you are trying to convert me, Tommy.'

'Perish the thought.' Thomas watched Gregov open the half door to the pew, enter and sit down beside him.

'Nice,' Gregov said. 'Very nice.'

'The last place anyone would look for a loyal communist.'

Gregov nodded his head with a smile. 'Your precautions for me are appreciated.' He had left none of his gaiety behind.

Thomas said, 'I am told you would like to visit America.'

'Residence. That is my pleasure. Permanent residence.'

'They want to sample your wares first, Uri.'

'Of course. Naturally. And they must be interested in my terms.' He looked at Thomas for all the world like a child eager to recite his Christmas list. He had rehearsed it in the mirror so many times.

Thomas let him speak.

'My terms,' Gregov said, 'are enormously reasonable for

what I have to exchange. You'll agree when I tell you. I merely want a modest photography shop in an American city in your sun belt.'

'Go on.'

'It must be fully stocked, of course, with modern photographic merchandise. Established, say, five years and providing the owner with a twenty percent return on investment per annum as well as an excellent salary for the owner-operator with a growth potential greater than the current rate of inflation, plus paid-up medical benefits, including maternity, and an IRS-approved retirement program.'

'Is that all?'

'Profit margins in the photographic retailing business are excellent. Oh – I must have both German and Japanese camera franchises – including medical and scientific equipment with protected territories. Of course, it must be in a city of a half million or more, somewhere that your State Department has placed off limits to Soviet personnel. Minimum stock turn of three times and a break-even point no later than July first.'

'Just your little everyday communist camera shop.'

'It's very modest, you'll see.' He was as merry as the sunshine.

'Oh–'

'Your Dutch sweetie.'

'Yes. My new wife.'

'You're already married.'

'Russian marriages don't count in the US. Besides, who's to know?'

'God.'

Gregov turned to share the joke with Thomas, then frowned at his face. There was a time when that scar looked inappropriate on Thomas's guileless face. But in recent times, the guile had faded. Too soon, now, cynicism would put the skeptic's inverted wishbone around Thomas's mouth, and the eyes would lose their sympathy entirely. 'You've been in the business too long, Tommy. You should get out while there's still something human left inside you.'

'Like you?'

'Like me.'

'Let's hear the rest of the package, Uri.'

'This will have Washington dancing the mazurka on their desks, I promise. I can bring out intact, Moscow's new US and Canadian intelligence network. Totally reorganized, names, contacts, everything. It isn't even operational yet.'

'And–'

'And! Why, that is the intelligence coup of this decade. The British would pay enormously well for it.'

'Then why don't you take it to the British?' Thomas watched Gregov's triumphant expression fade.

'You've become hard, Tommy. Very hard.'

'I have to have more than that, Uri.'

'More? What more? There is no more. Do you know how long it took me to get this material? Two years. And it's absolutely accurate. And of course you'll get a gold mine of current information when your interrogators get through sweeping out all the bits and pieces in my mind.' He watched Thomas's face pleadingly. His confidence sagged.

'More, Uri, more.'

Gregov glanced about the church anxiously. The shaft of sunlight had gone behind a cloud and he looked at Thomas with his mouth open.

'I'm astonished, Tommy.' He groped in his pocket for a package of cigarettes, then shoved it back into his pocket.

'Come on, Uri. You're a very low echelon guy. You don't have access to much. You're asking for a retail store and operation that could be worth up to two hundred thousand dollars. Maybe a quarter of a million. You have to offer something incredible for that kind of a deal. What else have you got?'

'How about Russian war plans?'

'You don't have access to that kind of information.'

'Yes I do.'

'You're not offering the Zharkov Corridor plan, are you?' Thomas gave a weary sigh. 'That was moldy when I was still in uniform, Uri. I can get you all the copies you want.'

'You shouldn't laugh at such things.'

'Laugh? It was a clumsy fake the Russians tried to palm off on us years ago. I have to go.' Thomas stood up. 'If you come up with anything–'

'I have access to something about France and Belgium and Germany.' Gregov was desperately groping in his merchant's bag for something to sell – anything. His market day was turning into a disaster.

'Oh, come on, Uri. That's hardly sensitive stuff.'

'What would you like? Help me, Tommy.'

Thomas sat down again. 'Well–' He thought. 'Do you have access to Dudorov's files?'

Gregov became bitter. Sullen. 'He has no files.'

'What do you mean?'

'All of Dudorov's material is tied into a central computer in Russia.'

'Spell that out for me.'

'Your people know about it. America has been very generous to Russian intelligence. We have used American computers to build a global telephone network tied to the files inside Russia. If a mob breaks into any Russian embassy they will find no incriminating papers. There will be no Irans for the Kremlin.'

Thomas studied Gregov's face, concealing his own dismay now. 'Dudorov can't fly to Moscow every time he wants to refer to a file.'

'He telephones the computer in Russia and, voilà, by telephone a computer display shows him whatever he wants to see in the file. Oh, we use only the most modern American techniques. You should use your own products. They are very good, you know.'

'Can you get a look into Dudorov's files?'

'Oh, no. Only he can authorize it.'

Thomas watched Gregov carefully. Only Dudorov? It was time to push harder. He stood up.

'Uri, I think you just struck out. I have to go.'

'But surely, Tommy, there must be – for old times – I mean–' He took out a cigarette and lit it. 'There must be a way.'

'Going back to Russia's not so bad, Uri.'

When he got to the door, Uri Gregov leaned out into the aisle and called after him. 'As I said, Tommy, get out of the business while you're still human. Weeks count.'

Thomas drove back to his hotel in grave doubt. If Washington learned what he had just turned down from Gregov, he'd be summarily shot. It was more than the coup of the decade. When he got back to his hotel, Thomas found a message waiting for him. Mr Katz called. He went back out to his car and drove through Amsterdam to the Zwanenburgwal and parked by a telephone. He dialed a number and watched across the broad canal. At another phone he saw Uri Gregov answer.

'Tommy, if it's that important, I can try to get access to Dudorov's files. It's very dangerous. If they catch me, they'll torture me, then execute me on the spot.'

'Are you sure it's worth it, Uri?'

'Are you?'

The next night, Osip Pavlovich Dudorov had a ticket to the concert.

There were few Western pleasures he allowed his stern Russian soul, but at the top of that short list was chamber music, especially the most decadent from the classic and romantic periods. It was his passion. In his heart, Dudorov believed that one of the main casualties of the cold war was a brilliant young violinist named Dudorov, who had become a gifted intelligence man instead. He would often remind his colleagues what a great sacrifice he had made for Mother Russia.

Dudorov left his offices early to have a brief supper before going to the Concertgebouw on Van Baerlestraat. He

255

didn't feel first-rate and he planned to eat lightly. The music would be his restorative.

After his recent surgery he had developed a severe case of dandruff. It showed like talcum in his hair and showered his neck and shoulders.

'It's the postoperative medicine,' the doctors told him. But he didn't trust them: one lied and the others covered for him. After two months the skin doctor was still unable to arrest it. 'It's nerves.' Dudorov was excruciatingly conscious of it and had managed to get a seat in the last row so no one could sit behind him and stare at it.

From the barred window of the computer room, Uri Gregov watched Dudorov out of sight. It was time to begin, and he rehearsed his moves in his mind for the last time. Gregov had often planned his escape to the West. And always it would be by bicycle.

As a young man he had entertained thoughts briefly of becoming a cycle racer but had to admit early that he was not made of the right components that went into winning. But he had had his great moments on his cycle and when he thought of flight, he thought of pedaling. And Amsterdam was the perfect city for it. There were many footbridges over the canals and many narrow paths and alleys where automobiles could not go and where a pursuer on foot was too slow.

Earlier in the day, he'd rented a bicycle and had ridden over the trickiest part of the route. It was flawless. During the day, also, he'd gotten into the computer room and, quickly, with a jeweler's hacksaw, cut through the hasp of the lock that held the hinged metal grating over the window. He was ready.

He placed a call on the computer telephone and identified himself with Dudorov's number. And he asked for two files: the Starmetz file and the file on Manfred Fritzsche. Both had cross references. The Starmetz file was cross-linked with a file on the Yugoslav committee. And the Fritzsche file was cross-linked with both the Bismarck Club and a list of German industrialists.

The screen went on. The display requested 'Signal when you want transmission to begin.'

In the semidark room, his face bathing in the green glow of the screen, Uri Gregov hesitated.

He surprised himself. He was trembling. He was close to tears. Suddenly, everything in Russia was near and dear to him, faces of people he would never see again. Childhood memories clamored in protest. Schooldays became vivid. He was renouncing all of that. For the rest of his life he would be on the run. For the rest of his life, at any moment, he could be in his shop in America working on a camera when the door opens and in walks a Soviet agent, looking right at him. Traitor.

Run, little Uri, run for the rest of your life.

He glanced about. If they caught him, they would kill him.

He took out his wallet, took out her picture and, by the green light of the screen, looked at her pretty Dutch face, that marvelous hair; he put his arms around her robust figure and thought of her sweet disposition. She will give him children and will help him make a new life in America. Russia would soon be forgotten.

But he couldn't do it. He couldn't renounce it all. He paced before the waiting computer screen.

Then he thought of going back there, to Russia, to the shortages and the hungers and the overcrowded apartments and the long lines and the constricted life and the suspicion and the surveillance and constant scrutiny, the disappearance of friends and family, the distrust everywhere, the cynicism, the lies and, everywhere, the stink of fear.

He knew he couldn't breathe that air anymore. He reached out and pushed the button that was marked 'Transmit.' He crossed his Rubicon.

The camera was a marvel. Thomas had told him it could photograph two lumps of coal inside a box in a dark closet on a moonless night. Smaller than a cigarette package, it clicked off the frames from the screen on microminiature film. He settled down to filming the endless number of pages.

Dudorov was restless. Bitterly, he realized he was unable to concentrate on the music. While he had been recovering from surgery, many matters had passed through the Amsterdam office and he still hadn't familiarized himself with all of them. He was anxious. He had seen their looks back home. How he has aged, they said. His bald spot has grown. His face has aged, he's grown cynical, lost his enthusiasm. He's no longer the man he was. They would trip him up if he weren't careful. They would watch for his corner-cutting, the fatigue at the end of the day, the little lapses of a tired, aging mind.

He sat watching the musicians and heard not a note. He talked himself into dismay and fear. He left the auditorium.

Every key Soviet building in every city in the world outside Russia has guards, including those in Amsterdam. There is one at every central window on every floor of every building, around the clock, around the calendar.

When Dudorov got out of the cab and looked up he saw them looking down at him, one pair of eyes on every floor. He went through the formality of signing in, showing his credentials to a man who had been signing him in day and night over the past few years. The guard barely glanced at his identity card.

'Enter,' he said.

Dudorov went up to his office and picked up the phone and requested computer display time. The evening hours were often the best. Clearance was usually quick.

The woman asked for the file numbers and he read them off to her. 'We can commence broadcasting as soon as you finish your current broadcast.'

Dudorov snatched open his office door. 'Guard! Guard! Quick! The computer room. An unauthorized broadcast!'

The guard's younger legs got down the flight of stairs first and, running with a pistol in hand, he reached the door to the computer room and flung it open, falling prone on his elbows, the pistol held in both hands before him.

The computer room was empty.

Dudorov reached the doorway and saw the open window and the opened metal grating that covered it.

Gregov hardly noticed that he had scraped his knee and torn his trousers, for as he ran he made a grave discovery: he was in terrible physical shape.

His lungs began to burn almost immediately. His feet hurt. He felt hulking and fat. He regretted every cigarette, every martini, every bite of Dutch chocolate dessert he'd had in Amsterdam.

When he got to the corner and turned for a glance back, he felt nausea from the sprint. Meantime four guards had come out of the main entrance and were sprinting after him – all in Olympic condition, all armed.

Gregov had his first doubts about his escape plan. His bicycle was a long block away.

He turned and ran. Time had taken the steel from his cyclist's legs and replaced it with lead – heavy lead. The youngest guard, an officious dedicated bastard named Dmitri, was already within shooting range, and in an instant would pause under a streetlight and fire.

Gregov turned from his path and ran into an apartment door. Miracle of miracles, there was a hallway and a back door. He ran to it prayerfully and found it unlocked. He pulled it open and then leaped under the staircase, amid carriages and tricycles.

The front door burst open. Dmitri the Officious leaped into the hallway brandishing his pistol, saw the back door open and took the bait. He ran down the hall and out through it. God knows where it led.

Gregov hurried back out on the street. They had all run by. He turned and continued his course to his secreted bicycle. He ran under streetlights in a direct line. He'd nearly reached the bicycle when he heard Dmitri's shout. Damn! He opened the door to the bike rack. The damned hall was dark. No light.

He stumbled into a long row of cycles, all chain-locked. He couldn't see enough to find his own. Too late. He ran down the hall and out the back door into an alley. That bastard Dmitri burst into the darkened hallway and paused.

Gregov hurried up the lane and turned. He found a fence and squeezed behind it. He was panting loudly. His legs wouldn't do the job. He had miles to go and not that much time. He glanced at his watch. If he got to the rendezvous place late they'd be gone. And he would have lost it all, new citizenship, new career, new wife. And no place to escape to. He was a dead man.

He had to have that cycle. Dmitri the Officious, Dmitri the Dumb entered the lane and hurried past him, eager to shoot. Gregov stepped out from behind the fence and hurried back to the hallway. In the dark, he began to grope among the bicycles, lifting each from the rack until he felt the pull of a chain around the wheel. He tried six, compelling himself to be stealthy and deliberate.

Seven was lucky. The cycle came away from the rack. No chain. He wheeled it quickly to the front door and opened it. There were people strolling around out there. A couple with murmuring voices strode right by him. He pushed the cycle out on the road and stepped up on it. Softly, silently, he rode away.

Behind he heard a shout. They were shooting at him. Gently, he told himself: frantic pumping would bring on cramps. He headed for the first footbridge over the first canal. Once over that only another cyclist could catch up with him. He approached his first intersection.

As he crossed it, he was caught full in oncoming headlights. A shot was fired and he realized that they had gotten a car. He pumped fast and the bicycle raced off. The car was unable to enter the alley. It stopped, thwarted. Then it turned and raced furiously away.

Gregov reached the footbridge and pedaled over. As he did so he looked down the canal and saw the car racing over another bridge parallel to him. They were going to try to head him off. He rode on, hurrying to the next footbridge over the next canal. The car had already reached the canal but there was no bridge waiting for it and it raced away seeking an auto bridge. Gregov crossed his next footbridge.

He made himself cycle in a slow, measured rhythm that carried him quickly through the night without cramping. Distantly he could hear the car's rubber tires squealing as it twisted and turned through the narrow old streets between canals.

Gregov turned and cycled down a long alley. He had fooled them. The car was racing in the opposite direction, toward the bridge he'd just crossed. He heard the shrieking of tires and the backing and filling as the car turned yet again and raced back the way it had come.

It passed him on the next parallel street and went racing away. Each steady pump now brought him closer to sanctuary, to freedom, to his new life. He followed the map in his head, turned here and there, a quickly moving ghostly shadow making barely any sound, his dark clothing barely visible in the night.

He came out on a road that paralleled a canal. It was glittering with reflected lights and a number of houseboats tied up there glowed with lamps. People were dining, or watching television. Some sat in coats out on the decks. The rows of houses on both sides of the canal were also brightly lit. The tranquillity and warmth of the scenes seemed shockingly indifferent to his plight.

He began to realize that his little escape plan was not so foolproof after all. At night there was little auto traffic on the streets and the congestion that should have slowed the car to a crawl was not there. The vehicle was able to move much faster than he anticipated, and he had to admit that there was a very good chance they would catch him.

The power boat lay snubbed to the floating dock. In the stern the two-man crew sat in low conversation under the stars, while beyond, out on the Nordzee canal, the running lights of larger vessels crept by, powered by gurgling engines.

Thomas looked down from the canal wall at the girl who leaned patiently on the coaming of the cockpit. In the dark, her white face smiled up at him, eager, courageous, worried, a runaway to America with a mad Russian dreamer and just one suitcase.

Gregov had had enough of the hard eyes and stern mouth of his wife back in the muddy Russian village of Pinsky Minsky Dinsky. He was going to wear cowboy hats and live and laugh forever free under the sun of Arizona or Texas with his Dutch miss, a fat capitalist with his own business. No frowns there: a nice girl from a nice home, raised on the values of frugality and hard work combined with cheerfulness and husband-trust.

She looked as though she would quickly learn how to run that photography shop. She would have to. Gregov was as improvident as a grasshopper.

Thomas looked left toward Brewer then out on the large square dock area, a place of cobbled paving and loading platforms. Brewer in turn glanced down at the girl, then at his watch, then shook his head at Thomas. He had no faith in Gregov, no faith in the operation.

'He'll botch it,' he had told Thomas.

Gregov was proving hard to catch. He knew the old streets and the byways by heart and could alter his route as he progressed. The squealing tires told him where Dudorov's car was. Deceiving them again, he rode over another footbridge and headed for the next canal.

He passed pedestrians walking dogs, people chatting, two men unloading a small van. He prayed that his legs would hold up. He crossed the next footbridge without incident and he allowed himself time to coast, listening for the racing tires of the car. It was silent. And that was ominous. Dudorov would never give up. He pedaled on, measuring out his time by streetlights, pumping ever closer to her and to safety. He felt for the camera in the side pocket of his suit jacket.

It was too quiet – too ominous. He kept glancing over his shoulder. Where were they? As long as he could hear them, he could trim his course to suit. In silence, they could be in ambush ahead of him.

Each traffic intersection now was agony. He had two ways to go and didn't know which was the safer. On and on he pedaled, crossed another bridge and entered a long straight walk.

At an intersection, he passed a group of people chatting on a doorstep. Just past them, a Russian guard leaped out, his gun held in two hands, aimed right at Gregov's head.

Gregov swerved and wobbled. The gun went off and completely missed him. One of the women screamed; the guard panicked and ran off.

But where had he come from? How had he gotten there? Gregov pumped frantically away and lost himself in dark lanes and shadows. But the next time he looked back, there was a cyclist on the path riding toward him.

Gregov settled down to a steady fast pace and looked back. The rider was gaining on him, racing at full speed. Gregov realized he was being pursued. Dudorov had put them on cycles.

He pumped harder. Up ahead the path turned, crossed an island and went over another footbridge. He raced toward it. The little bridge loomed. Then he saw another cyclist on the other side coming toward him. If he was another guard, Gregov would be trapped on the bridge.

He was about to turn away from the bridge and try for a difficult path when he saw the running lights of a boat in the dark canal. Quickly he turned back to the bridge and pedaled up on it.

He was right. The two cyclists had him trapped. He stopped in the middle and they stopped at each end. They laid their cycles aside and began to converge on him. Both were armed.

As the canal boat chugged under the bridge, Gregov stepped over the railing, poised himself and dropped. It was a short fall and he landed on the stern, lay down and rolled. He was in the midst of pots of flowers, and the scent was ridiculously pleasant. No shots were fired.

Gregov raised his head. The two guards were racing on foot parallel along the side of the canal toward the next bridge. They would easily reach it first and be waiting on the bridge as he rode under – a perfect target. They could empty their guns into him.

Gregov sat up and looked ahead. The helmsman of the boat was totally unaware of what was going on. Gregov swung his legs over the side and pushed off. He slid into the canal, a scant foot from the throbbing propeller. The water was sharply cold and tasted faintly of motor oil and sourness. The running lights of the boat moved on without him.

Gregov set off paddling softly in the other direction. The brick walls of the canal were completely smooth, and he looked for a ladder or some hand grips to climb up with. Soon the running lights of another boat came slowly down the canal making straight at him. He swam as close to the wall as he could and waited. As it coasted by, he saw a row of rubber tires hanging as fenders along the side. He reached up and put his arm through one.

Abruptly he was in tow, feeling a strong pull of the water. He was making his own wake beside the boat. Struggling, he almost pulled himself up on board. He braced himself once more and was about to lunge when he saw the figures of the two guards on the bridge ahead. They were still searching the water.

Gregov swung his head and shoulder under the tire and hung on. The boat approached the bridge and sailed under it. Gregov, looking up, saw their two heads bent over and scanning the open cargo area of the boat. They were not fifteen feet above him. He was looking right into their eyes.

The boat sailed on. They'd missed him. Gregov clambered aboard. He crouched in the cockpit and got his bearings. He didn't know what canal he was in. It was either the Heren Gracht or the Keizers Gracht moving south and that would take him in either case eventually to the Amstel River. It was the wrong direction.

He checked his jacket pocket. The camera was there. His hand groped over it. Evidently none the worse for wear. He hoped it was waterproof; his passport to sanctuary.

He was freezing. He trembled violently. And panted. He felt as though every muscle in his body had been pummeled with a club.

He knew he should get off. But he was spent and even though the boat was taking him in the wrong direction, it was movement away from his pursuers.

He looked at his watch. And felt panic. Time had passed. He was due at the rendezvous at ten but he wasn't going to make it. He forced himself to sit up and look ahead. At last, the canal approached a cross canal and he saw a series of rungs on the wall.

Gregov slipped over the side into the water. It felt twice as cold. He clenched his teeth to keep them from banging together.

He kicked and wiggled and finally reached the ladder. The weight of his sopping clothes made climbing an ordeal, but rung by rung he mounted the wall and reached the top. It seemed incredible to him that he was having this life-or-death adventure in the midst of throbbing family affairs all around him, and no one was the least aware.

He stood up. What had seemed a mild evening when he set out, fit and dry, was now as cold as an icebox. He needed a bicycle.

He walked along a row of houses by the canal searching for an alley and found one. He turned in, found an apartment door and opened it. There was a row of bicycles. He glanced around, then began trying them. They were all locked. He went to the next apartment. And there he found a loose one, an old veteran of the streets but in good repair.

He got on it. It was a dog, hard as hell to pedal. Still it was willing to go and he rode off in it. He told himself he should have shopped for a better one. But something else inside told him to hurry. He felt his future slipping through his hands. Time was racing. Soon he was counting streetlights again, rolling inexorably toward the rendezvous.

He crossed another bridge, turned onto the main thoroughfare and headed directly toward his goal. He was less than a mile away. Only three more bridges and a long roll to the pier. His legs were trembling with effort, pumping that old cycle.

He crossed the next two bridges without incident. He reached the third bridge and was crossing it, preoccupied. He was late, maybe too late. He pictured himself reaching the pier and finding no one. A chance missed that would never return in all of eternity. Life was outrageous. Why had the fickle gods let him come this far, evading his pursuers, exhausting himself like this if he wasn't to be allowed to reach his haven? It was unspeakably unfair.

He hit the brakes abruptly. A car had pulled in front of him and cut him off. As he collided with it, he knew it was them again. They'd caught him. He and the bike went sliding across the paving, tearing his clothes and scraping the skin off his hand and one cheek.

Reflexes took over. As the doors opened and the shouts began, he was up and running. He was in trouble: his body was just too battered, the muscles too exhausted, the lungs too frail and the human will too weak. He yearned to surrender, to lie down on the paving and rest. Even being shot through the head seemed appealing. Anything to stop the screaming pain of motion.

But he put one foot in front of another and another. Courage, someone once said, is taking one more step. And Gregov took many. He was running.

Thomas looked at his watch and glanced around. Ghostly shadows of barges and deepwater vessels glided by out in the canal. Periodically there was a short burst on a ship's horn. Time was running out.

Brewer had grown restless. The two crewmen kept looking up to Thomas expectantly. The girl's shoulders had begun to sag a bit.

Thomas felt bile. The operation was going to rack up a Maggie's drawers: Gregov had failed. Thomas had been beaten again. He had a lot to answer for. In the hope of finding something in Dudorov's files – an unlikely event at best – he had cost the United States a priceless intelligence coup. He'd bet everything and lost.

He stood up. There was no reason to wait any longer. It was blown. He nodded his head at Brewer, who descended and got the girl's suitcase. She mounted the gangway behind him, being careful not to cry.

'Gregov's very late,' Thomas said to her. 'We have to assume the worst. We'll take you back home. Maybe later if he shows up we can reactivate the plan. Right now I must tell you that things do not look good for him.'

'Is he dead?'

'He may be in trouble. They may send him back to Russia.'

She'd been brave too long and she cared too much. She wept with her hand to her mouth. Thomas waved at the power boat, and the crew started the engine. They prepared to cast off.

For Gregov, serious running was out of the question. They were after him, fresh, angry, adrenalin pumping. There was only one chance. He ran into a church, ran through the benches, crossed the church on pounding feet toward a door to the left of the altar. Dmitri was right behind him, reaching for his collar, his face a fury of determination. As the others spilled into the church behind him, Dmitri staggered against a pew and fell.

Gregov reached the door first and tried to slam it. But Dmitri had his arm through. Gregov put his weight behind it. Dmitri cried and pulled his arm out. Gregov locked the door.

The minister looked up astonished at the filthy, bedraggled, wet, bleeding specter dripping on his rug. His assistant sitting beside him with a pen gaped in wonder. Gregov crossed to the casement window, swung it open and stepped out. He landed on garbage cans, tore open a finger, blackened an eye, stunning himself momentarily and felt terrible pain from his chest. He probably had cracked a rib. Or two. He couldn't breathe. His lungs struggled desperately for air yet every breath was a shocking stab of pain.

He pulled off his belt and almost weeping with agony he got it around his lower chest and drew it tight. The effect was magical. He was able to breathe again. He stood. And turned. And pushed off, breaking into a slow jog.

He saw the pier area dead ahead. A quarter of a mile or so. To be so close. He begged his body to sprint, to run, to lope even. But it was beyond caring. Every muscle cried out, and his left calf was twitching ominously. If it seized in a cramp, down he would go.

As he scurried, he kept his locomotion to the rhythm of her name. Anna Anna An-nah. He felt the camera banging painfully on his hip. Anna Anna Anna.

When he looked back, the church door was open and they were all bursting out of the door and sprinting after him. Dudorov was hurrying back to the car.

He could see the pier ahead of him. Anna, I love you.

He would have traded it all – the camera store, the sanctuary, the sun belt climate – for a few moments' rest – traded it all but Anna; she made him keep running.

He reached the end of the long factory building. He turned and his heart leaped. There they were waiting for him, waving to him. Run. Run. Run!

He took the last thimbleful of strength he had and put it into a sprint. The calf muscle knotted. He hopped on one foot. Then his ankle exploded and as he fell, he knew he'd been shot. He'd failed.

Thomas heard the shouting and signaled the boat to stop. Then into full view came Gregov. He was barely running. Even in the near-darkness under the lights, his gasping mouth was visible. He looked exhausted.

'Run! Brewer shouted. 'Move your butt!'

A Russian guard appeared at the intersection and without hesitation, drew down on Uri and fired. His shot hit the mark and Gregov went down. He lay gasping on the cobbles, his arm outstretched toward the girl, his head up searching for her. She cried his name, 'Uri! Uri!'

Thomas fired first. Then he and Brewer and the others began to run toward Gregov. The Russian guards had reached him and pulled him to his feet. He couldn't walk. He hopped. They dragged him. At a full sprint, Thomas put his head down and dove. He knocked them all down, sent them rolling.

He used his feet. He used his hands. He used his pistol. He slugged and kicked and battered the rolling mass of humans. He took a tremendous blow on the head from a pistol, felt a kick in his armpit. Gregov, panting, managed a kick himself. Thomas was up, still punching. He seized Gregov and slung him over his shoulder. The man cried out with pain.

Thomas ran. With every step, Gregov hooted from the terrible pain in his ribs. The guards stood up and came after Thomas. One ran alongside and Thomas threw a punch, struggled, tripped the man and managed another kick in the head. Brewer arrived, throwing punches. Turning again, Thomas sprinted with Gregov on his back. He had almost reached the pier's edge when Gregov stiffened.

'Ahhh!' he shouted. 'I'm hit.'

Thomas tumbled him down the ladder to the floating dock. The two crewmen dumped him into the cockpit. The girl seized him in her arms and crouched below the coaming. Thomas jumped down. Brewer, firing his last rounds, jumped down with the others and they all stumbled and fell into the boat as it roared away.

The boat sped down the canal at an illegal speed toward the wide Nordzee Canal. The wake made other boats and barges bob in the wake. Protesting voices carried through the dark after them. From behind, their pursuers fired a few despairing shots.

Thomas crouched down to examine Gregov in the girl's arms. The whole side of his face was torn and bleeding down on his collar. He was filthy with oil stains and crusted matted hair and sopping clothes. His right hand and small finger were bleeding, leaving a large bloodstain on his coat. The ankle was in bad shape. It had been hit, bones were broken, and it was swelling fast.

Thomas saw the belt around his ribs, and gently put his finger inside it. Gregov groaned. Cracked ribs. But the principal wound was in his buttock. As Thomas had run with him, he'd taken a shot there. Blood was welling up out of the hole. Thomas moved Gregov's leg up and down. Evidentally the bullet had lodged in the fatty tissue, just missing the hip bone.

Gregov lay like a battered drowned corpse. Then slowly his hand went to his pocket and pulled out the camera.

'Bought with blood,' he said to Thomas.

'You might not be able to open your store for a while, Uri,' he said.

'We'll manage quite nicely,' a voice answered in the dark. It was the girl.

Thomas held the camera clutched in the fist of his left hand.

They'd gone quickly up the main canal to the other side and there transferred Gregov and the young woman into a waiting van. And that was the last that Thomas saw of them, two red taillights diminishing, hurrying Gregov to a doctor. Later that night, the pair would be carried to the United States, where Uri Gregov would talk a camera store's worth.

Thomas looked down at the camera in his hand. In there was Dudorov's file on the Bismarck Club. Good news or bad? The power boat turned and hurried back to Amsterdam.

The building stood near the Oude Schans Canal, the usual solid and scrubbed Dutch house, and, after they'd parked, General Wynet led the way to the side door. There were just three of them, Wynet and Thomas and one of Wynet's people, a Russian-language specialist. The darkroom man was definitely Dutch with that invincibly healthy look and light hair. A man about fifty he was, wearing a darkroom apron, and he received the camera from Thomas without a word.

'It's been in water,' Thomas said.

The man entered his darkroom and shut the door. A red light went on over the doorway.

There were shelves of strange-looking photographic equipment and jars and bottles of chemicals, all neatly labeled and arranged. The small sign on the wall identified him as a photographic consultant, whatever that was.

Wynet sat wearily in a chair in a corner beside a shelf loaded with new cameras in their shipping containers. He looked sourly at Thomas but said nothing. The Russian specialist stood reading labels on the bottles of chemicals. He yawned several times. Thomas sat in another chair and folded his arms with reluctant patience. They all waited.

It was such a long shot. They had to have incredible luck to find anything significant in Dudorov's file. Now that the chase was over, Thomas felt ashamed for having exposed Gregov to so much danger. The man should never have survived that ordeal.

Finally Thomas could stand it no longer. He stepped out of the door and onto the street and paced. There is something mysterious and romantic about the multitudinous waterways of Amsterdam after dark, and even this late at night there were still many windows lit up.

Thomas paced up and down beside the canal and

271

thought about Gregov. He envied him. Gregov had beaten the rap – no more suffering Russia for him – and he'd gotten a marvelous girl. Thomas had almost made a widow out of her before she'd become a bride. And that made him think of Hilda, Bernie Parker's widow before she'd become his bride.

It had grown chilly. The season of North Atlantic storms was at hand. Absentmindedly he buttoned his raincoat.

It had been a long road since that night in Wynet's office in Washington – a long road with no turning. What a welter of events and people: the ruin of Parker's office, a foot deep in confetti, Hilda, Roland's murder, Dancer's murder, the chase through the files in the Bismarck Club, Fritzsche and Tatzie – a kaleidoscope of fragments that wouldn't fit together. He had to admit he had a brilliant adversary.

He wondered what his next move would be if the Dudorov file turned up empty. He suspected Wynet would make it. The door opened and the translator beckoned Thomas. He returned indoors with relief. His mind had begun to focus on Kaethe Dorten again.

The man stood in the doorway of his darkroom. The red light was out, and he held up a long thin strip of film that curled in air. When they followed him into the darkroom, he put the strip into a backlighted viewer. They stood around him and looked down at the magnified frames.

'All the frames developed,' he said. 'No water damage.' He handed the camera back to Thomas.

The Russian interpreter glanced at the frames and fed them quickly through the magnifier. 'This is material from the Starmetz file.'

'Skip that. What about the Fritzsche file?' Wynet said.

The interpreter quickly turned the feeder nob. 'Here,' he said at last. 'A biography on Fritzsche. It's three years old. Not very complimentary. Not too bright. Impulsive. And this – this is a list of names. Let me see. These are names of members of a club. The Bismarck Club. Three – four months old. And this is a situation report, also, let me see, four years old, on the Bismarck Club. Hmmm. He concludes it by saying the correct name should be the Complainers' Club. Disgruntled businessmen and harmless intellectuals, and here's a status report three days old. Unchanged, it says.' Then Dudorov hadn't found anything either.

'What else is in that file?' Thomas demanded.

'Nothing.'

'That's it?'

'That's it.'

Wynet gave Thomas a long look. 'I'll wait in the car.' Pointedly, he took the miniature camera from Thomas. 'I want to see you at noon tomorrow, Thomas,' he said over his shoulder.

Thomas leaned wearily against a wall.

'I can give you prints of the membership list right now,' the interpreter said. 'The other written material I can translate – ah – how about noon tomorrow in the general's hotel suite?'

Thomas shrugged indifferently. Gregov had almost died for nothing. The Dudorov file was useless.

Thomas had failed.

And now General Wynet was going to set up a major operation in Germany – an office and an army of agents with lots of visibility. And the German Government was going to want to know why. A European operation was just what Wynet didn't want.

The reason why he wanted Thomas at his suite at noon was obvious – to push him out of the case. Thomas supposed that Wynet expected an argument; Parker had been a close friend of his. Thomas was also nursing a bruised ego. He'd been aced by an expert.

Thomas went at noon.

The Dudorov file on Fritzsche had been a disaster but the Starmetz material on Yugoslavia that Wynet requested was evidently a treasure trove. When Thomas got to Wynet's suite, three of the agents were sitting in chairs in a circle close to each other, the blown-up photographic prints on the floor at their feet. They sat elbows on knees, bending over the material and talking in low, excited voices. Starmetz was murmured several times.

That material plus the Russian intelligence network in the United States had earned Uri Gregov a dozen camera stores.

Wynet pointed unhappily to a large manila envelope on the bed. 'That's the Fritzsche material.'

Thomas opened the envelope indifferently and glanced at the translation of the Fritzsche biography. The material was dated. For Fritzsche's mistress it gave the name of a woman economist, aged twenty-six, who worked for the government in Bonn. But there had been another woman since then, aged twenty-one, the one before Tatzie.

Dudorov wrote for his audience back in Russia. He mixed shrewd insights into Fritzsche's character with carping moralizing about capitalist businessmen.

Wynet handed him a scotch and got right to the point. 'Go home, Tommy. Back to your guns and revolutions.'

Thomas nodded. 'Soon.'

'No. Now. Pack it in.'

'All right. Fine.'

'There's no reason for you to go back to Cologne.'

'I have to close out the arms auction stuff with my German rep.'

'And that's it?'

'I suppose.' Thomas evasively turned the pages of the Bismarck membership list.

'Thomas.'

'I hear you, General.'

'You did a fantastic job.'

'Someone did a better job. On me. And I can't believe it was Fritzsche.'

'How would you like your old job back – with me?'

'Never.' Thomas's eyes roved over the list of names. He pointed at one. 'Know him?'

Wynet took the page and put on his bifocals. 'Jesus. Is

he a member?' He took up another page and studied it. 'Be damned. Dudorov is getting senile. He's calling these people disgruntled businessmen and harmless intellectuals? His professional contempt has blinded him.'

Thomas spread the prints over the bed and bent over them. 'What do you think the subject of conversation would be if this guy and this guy and this guy had a meeting in the Bismarck Club?'

General Wynet nodded thoughtfully. 'I'd say they'd discuss the sabotaging of the city water supply somewhere inside Russia. Jesus. Here's an expert on explosives and this guy is an army specialist on terrorist tactics. And there's Hesse. Dr Hesse himself.' Wynet tapped other names with his fingertips. 'The subject would always be Russia.'

'How did the Russians miss the significance of these names?' Thomas asked.

'Because the Russians are as dumb as we are.'

Thomas looked again at the list. 'The list I got was a fake. I'll bet the steward's ledger was too.' He smiled. 'I was set up.'

Wynet nodded. 'Seems that way.'

'These people could manufacture it for you.'

'Manufacture what?'

'Doomsday,' Thomas answered.

Thomas thought that distance would help. Distance, he expected, would make him free. But it hadn't. The first thought that occurred to him when he boarded Wynet's Lear jet for Cologne was that he'd be near Kaethe Dorten again.

Distance hadn't worked. She haunted him. He was obsessed with her, obsessed with her lively brown eyes, the devilishness in them, the cocky smile and the combative competitiveness. She was explosive with life.

He'd always enjoyed women, enjoyed their company, their shrewd insights, their essential gaiety. He liked being in love, the flowers and the wine and the wiggles and the giggles, and the bittersweet farewells at parting, those fragile moments that could not be prolonged. There was always a sales trip or a distant war to end things.

But this time parting hadn't worked. Distance hadn't healed. Even though the bond between them had been firmly, adamantly cut, it wasn't over for him.

But for him hope still fluttered – like the last match.

'What are we going to do in Cologne?' Brewer asked as he buckled his seat belt.

'Focus on Fritzsche. The full treatment.'

'What about the club?'

'Right now all we have is a bunch of experts in that club playing war games against Russia. There's got to be a lot more to it than that. And Fritzsche's the outside contact man.'

'Sounds like we might settle in for a long stay,' Brewer said as he shut his eyes.

'Sounds that way.'

But as it turned out, Thomas didn't stay twenty-four hours.

Anton Boxx had gone to Dartmouth with Thomas, and they had started together in the Federal Reserve in Boston. Now Boxx was based in Paris as vice-president, export/import division of the Rosetree International Bank. He had helped guide Excalibur through its first years of international arms trading and, in turn, through Excalibur, had picked up several large accounts for his bank.

But Boxx's voice was hesitant on the phone, distant. 'How can I help you?'

How can I help you? Strange stilted greeting. Bernie Parker's phone bill recorded twenty-six phone conversations with Boxx in the last month before he died and Thomas wanted to know why. He made an educated guess. 'I need a financial report, Anton,' Thomas said.

'Financial report,' Boxx echoed. 'I'm a little disoriented. I just got back from Bogotá. Let me get a pencil. Okay. What's the name?'

'Fritzsche.'

Thomas could hear Boxx drawing breath through clenched teeth.

'Anton. Is everything okay?'

'Where are you calling from, Tommy?'

'Cologne.'

'I see.' Boxx cleared his throat. 'Would – can you come to Paris?'

'Sure.'

'When you arrive at the airport, call me. Okay?'

'Sure.'

'Good night.'

Thomas stared at the phone. Curiouser and curiouser, said Alice in Wonderland.

If anything, Boxx was even more alarmed the next morning when Thomas called him from the de Gaulle Airport in Paris.

'You know the Pompidou Cultural Center, Tommy?'

'Yes, of course.'

'Take a cab and meet me there. On the top deck at the entrance to the Modern Art Museum. Okay? And listen, make sure you're not followed. You're good at that sort of thing. I mean take *extra* precautions.'

When he came out through the door to the cab stand, the cab drivers were standing in a group chatting. The first two cabs were loading passengers and he walked up to the third. The driver threw down his cigarette and hurried to open the door.

As the cab swung into the traffic lane, Thomas noted one of the first bilingual signs he'd ever seen in Paris. The no-smoking sign on the dashboard was in both French and English.

'What hotel?' asked the driver.

'Tronchet on Rue Tronchet. You know where it is?'

The driver nodded. He drove past the Louvre to the Place de la Concord and turned and rolled past the Madeleine church, past the steps of the Madeleine Métro stop, where Parker had been shot, and pulled up at the Tronchet, a small quiet hotel favored by businessmen. Thomas glanced into the lobby and through it to the back entrance on the next street. Then he looked back at the traffic for a tail.

'Driver. I'm going to walk through the lobby of the hotel and out the back entrance. You drive around the block and pick me up there.'

The driver turned and looked at Thomas as though it were an everyday request. 'By those back doors?'

Thomas paid him. 'Yes.' He stepped out of the cab and entered the lobby. There were several people at the registration desk, and Thomas paused there to give the cab time to get around the block. When the cab appeared at the curb at the back, he turned and quickly strode out of the lobby and reentered the cab. He looked now to see if anyone had followed him into the lobby.

The cab drove off. 'Where to now?'

Something had been nagging Thomas about the driver subconsciously, and he finally understood what it was. The driver had thrown down a cigarette at the airport. And yet the cab sign requested no smoking. It could have meant nothing – more than one driver shared a cab – but then what better way to shadow somebody than to be his cab driver?

'Turn left. See the Métro steps? Let me out there. I'm going to go down the steps and come up on the other side. You make a U turn and pick me up. Okay?'

The driver gave a slightly irritated shrug and let Thomas pay him again and watched him step out and down the stairs. When Thomas got down the steps he didn't cross to the other side. Instead he bought a Métro ticket and hastened down to the platform just before the automatic platform doors shut. A train was coming.

A man came jumping and skipping down the stairs, clambered over the steel doors and ran out on the platform. He was too late. He watched the train pull away, then ran all the way up the stairs to the street and jumped into a car.

Thomas got off at the Rambuteau stop and waited on the platform. The train left; the disembarked passengers wandered in a loose band along the platform and went up the stairs. Except for some people on the platform across the tracks, he was alone.

He ascended to the street and began walking toward the most improbable building in all of Paris. The Pompidou Center for Art and Culture was born in controversy and continued to exist as the center of bitter quarreling over the future appearance of Paris.

The Pompidou, said the critics, looked like a boiler room turned inside out, as though it had disgorged all its network of pipes and tubes. It was a glassed-in, skeletal steel structure with giant tubes all over it, color-coded by function – air intake, air exhaust, electrical circuitry, water system, heating system – blues, oranges and greens and reds.

Others said it was colorful and refreshing contrast to the somber buildings around it.

He walked along Rue Rambuteau to the other long side of the building. Here were the escalators that carried the visitors up and down the outside of the building in a diagonal glass tube like the transparent digestive processes of a gigantic worm. Up he rode the stairs, higher and higher above the city, and soon he was looking down on the Cathedral of Notre-Dame, the Seine, the Etoile and the Eiffel Tower – Paris spread out around him, and to the north on its hill was Sacré-Coeur.

Paris was vivid in autumn sunlight. Below in the square, crowds of people stood in rings observing musicians and magicians. Periodically the faint sound of applause or cheering came through the glass dome around him. At his back was the entrance to the National Museum of Modern Art.

'Tommy. Don't laugh.'

Thomas turned and almost did laugh. Boxx stood at his

elbow in a cheap blond wig and sunglasses. What wasn't amusing was the gaunt expression on Boxx's face. Around his forehead at the edge of the wig was a faint beading of sweat.

'Were you followed?' Boxx asked.

'I don't think so. I took several precautious. Were you?'

Boxx opened his mouth to speak, then shut it. It was evident he had not thought about that. 'I doubt it. I mean with my disguise and all.'

This was not an ideal place for a secret meeting. Crowds of people came up and went down on the escalators. There were throngs of them on every floor, in the library, in the art gallery, in the restaurant and the exhibition halls, out on the square. A trained shadow would have a field day: follow one, find the other. He shrugged. Boxx had done the best he could. Thomas led Boxx over to the glass windows so he could look down on the square.

'Tommy, this is the last time I want to see you. Okay? I'm in over my head already and I want out.'

Thomas nodded and waited. His eyes were scanning the square.

'Parker told you about Fritzsche, right?' Boxx expected immediate corroboration.

'Anton. Suppose you tell me what you know.' A car appeared at the far side of the square and four men got out. The car drove off and the four men began strolling through the crowds in the square, scanning faces.

Boxx adjusted his wig. 'Well, it started off easy enough. I kind of enjoyed it. It was like being in espionage. Parker would bring me numbers – manifests, bills of lading. I don't know where he got them but my bank is tied into a humongous international computer network and I could get readouts for him on all kinds of shipping activity. You know, sources, destinations, cargo descriptions. Then he would go away and a while later he'd feed me more numbers and I'd run them through the idiot box. I didn't come up with a winner every time. A lot of numbers were not in the readouts. That was no surprise. But one day, I looked at the numbers and the cargo description and I realized what was up and I asked Bernie about it. He said it would be a good idea if I didn't know anything but it was too late. I knew. Bernie was on the track of smuggled merchandise and now I'm in the middle.'

The four men progressed steadily through the crowds and they converged near the entrance to the escalators, where two tumblers had drawn a crowd. They scanned the faces there, then turned to the escalators.

'Wait, Anton. Slow down. What was the smuggling operation?'

'Arms. Weapons. Like rifles. Disassembled parts.'

'Who was smuggling them? Where were they going?'

'Oh, Jesus.' Boxx wiped his brow with a handkerchief. 'See. The manifest would be for table legs, containerized, and bound for Greece. Okay? Another was for, say, pump activator parts. Then there was one for drinking fountain tube parts. They all came from various parts of Germany, and they all went to different places in the Mideast. Syria and Greece and Turkey. Then they would be transshipped. I thought I was pretty clever but I was getting in deeper and deeper. You see, all these shipments were ending up in the same place up in northern Turkey, near the Soviet border next to Iran. You figured it out yet, Tommy?'

'You're doing fine, Anton. Keep going.'

The four men were on the escalators.

'When I saw the ultimate destinations of those shipments, my old ulcer started to rumble. So the next time Bernie was in Paris, I met him at the usual place – a café up on Avenue Wagram – and I asked him point-blank, what's it all mean? He didn't want to tell me but I'd already guessed. They were rifle parts. Somebody was shipping rifles disassembled. The chair legs were really rifle stocks, and the pump activators were the firing mechanisms or the triggers or such and the drinking fountain water tubes – now you see it, right? – they were gun barrels. He admitted they were. He admitted they were all Russian caliber seven point six two. You know what was going on? People are walking across the border from Turkey into Russia with rifle parts in their pockets or down their pants legs. Every month there's thousands more rifles in Russia. And that was only part of it. There were other shipments through Iran and Afghanistan and Pakistan and still more up through India and the Baroghil Pass. All kinds of small arms, and parts for radios and explosive devices. People are walking a revolution into Russia.'

The four had finished searching the first floor and were on the escalators again. They were very quick.

'See, Tommy, I don't want to know this. I could have killed Parker for involving me. It was all plenty scary and then the other day they shot him right out there on the street by the Place de la Concorde. And I've been wetting my pants ever since. I think I'm marked.'

'Take it easy. There's no reason they should know about you—'

'Jesus Christ. I'm so scared my hands tremble all the time. Every morning when I leave my apartment I look at Greta and the two kids and wonder if I'll ever see them again. Maybe they'll be hurt. I'm out of my mind. All I do all day is look out of my window. You should see the work pile up. I haven't done a lick of work since he was killed.'

Boxx took several paces, wringing his hands, a frown of deep pain on his face. The cheap blond wig looked festive, cosmetic, like a queen cruising for the evening. From under the sunglasses a tear flowed down his right cheek. 'Tommy. Get me out of this. You have to.'

'Easy does it, Anton. What else?'

Boxx took a deep breath then exhaled sharply. 'He said this would be the last job. He promised.' His hand started to reach into his inside coat pocket several times then stopped.

'It's okay, Anton. It's your last job. What have you got?'

The four were on the escalator to the third floor when

Boxx pulled out a folded paper. 'It's a readout on the boards he serves on.'

'Who?'

'Fritzsche. I doubt if this is all of them. But I identified twenty-one German corporations.'

'He serves on the boards of twenty-one German companies?'

'Yes. You can read it later. I can tell you right now, almost all of them are in the defense industries – arms, military metallurgy, jet components, electronic wiring harnesses – the lot. He's also on a number of German Government advisory commissions. All military. Your friend Fritzsche is the secret spider in the middle of the arms web in Germany. Fritzsche is a warlord.'

Boxx paced again, wiped his brow, wiped his tears, blew his nose. 'Look, I'm a banker. I love it. Jesus, shot dead on the steps. Me? With two kids. I want out.'

'Okay, Anton. You're out. Mum's the word. If they were going to move against you, they would have done it days ago. Go home and relax. You won't hear from me again.'

'Tommy, the whole world's gone crazy. You know how much the human race is spending on arms each year? A half a trillion dollars. There's never been an arms race that even faintly resembled this one. The whole world is going to explode. The pressure is unbearable. Listen. The Third World nations alone have an annual debt service on their arms loans of eight billion dollars. That's just the interest on their loans. Each year. Eight billion. Can you imagine what the debt is? What are they doing with so many guns? That money is desperately needed for tools, and seeds and irrigation systems and small manufacturing and hospitals and schools. It's criminal. And what are Russia and the US and the European countries doing selling that much armament to them? Tommy, we're going to die in our beds. My two kids will never grow up.'

'Okay, Anton. I understand.'

'No you don't. You people in the arms business have a

lot to answer for. You're going to wipe out the human race!'

The four were scanning the floor below them, looking at faces, peering through glass panes, stepping through doorways.

'Anton, do you know what the Doomsday plan is?'

'I – Jesus Christ, it sounds terrible. What is it?' He didn't wait for an answer. There was more he wanted to say – a need to babble. Thomas looked down and saw the four now moving toward the escalator.

'Look, Tommy, I want to help. But I know the most terrifying secret in the world. Someone's trying to start a revolution inside Russia. It could be the beginning of the end of the world. And I'm just a physical coward.'

'Anton. Go home. I'll stay here until you've safely gone.' Go and sin no more.

Anton Boxx hesitated. There was still more he wanted to say. Thomas looked down and saw the four now moving toward the escalator.

'Anton. Turn around and start down the stairs. Now.'

Boxx saw something urgent in Thomas's face, shut his mouth, and stepped over the moving stairs. He slowly sank from view. At the last possible moment just as his brassy wig disappeared, he turned and glanced at Thomas. Then he was gone. Just as another head appeared on the up escalator.

Thomas turned and strolled into the museum. The art was exhibited on movable walls like a labyrinth and he strolled slowly, openly, along the priceless treasures. Glancing sidewise, he saw one of the four stepping along a few feet behind him, gazing at the paintings. The other three had already taken up their stations.

Thomas continued his stroll for another half hour, giving Boxx plenty of time to get away. Then he made a show of looking at his watch, turned and walked out. Three of them were strung out behind him on the stairs. The fourth he could see down in the square watching the entrance. Four professionals.

Thomas took a cab to the Printemps department store. As he got out and paid the driver, he saw the four getting out of a car a half block away.

He entered the store, walked through the cosmetics department to the escalator, went up one flight, continued through the map department around back to the downstairs. As he expected, they followed him. Two had gone up the escalator after him. Descending, he saw them hastily searching for him farther and farther into the second floor. A third was trotting up the rising stairs.

When he reached street level again, Thomas saw the fourth man outside at the corner entrance. Thomas turned and crossed the store on a diagonal to an exit, quickly walked down the street to the American Express and got a cab. 'Orly,' he said.

Thomas waited nearly an hour at the airport cab stand. At last the cab with no smoking sign on the dashboard appeared in line. The driver remained in his cab with the motor running. Passengers were coming out in numbers and there was a brisk call for cabs.

Thomas went over the driver's window, holding a wad of money in his hand. 'I would like to know about the man who rented your cab from you this morning.'

'Rented?' The driver looked at the note in his lap. 'But that is illegal.'

Thomas dropped another note through the window. 'You remember him. He picked me up and took me to Paris. What did he tell you?'

The driver pursed his lips and looked mutely at his lap. Thomas dropped another forty-franc note.

'Eh, well,' the driver said. 'He got us in a group by the door and said he would hire the cab that you got into – whatever one it was. You got into mine so he paid me.'

'Was there another car?'

'Oh yes, it followed you. With four or five men.'

'What did he tell you when he hired your cab?'

The driver looked down at his lap again. Thomas dropped another note.

'He said very little, monsieur. He said it was a special secret case for the government, and we weren't to ask any questions. Later he brought it back to me and slammed the door. He was very angry. Then he made a telephone call inside there by the entrance and I could see he was waving his hands as he talked.'

'Was he French?'

'He spoke with a Parisian accent. I think he is a local person, yes.'

'Where did he go?'

'There. Toward the parking lots.'

Thomas had first seen communism at work as a young officer in Vietnam. It was far from the glossy conference tables and flannel suits of polite Boston banking. It was brutal, direct, ruthless and bent on winning at any cost: a mountain of skulls was a low price. Later he found himself confronting it in other parts of Asia, in the Mideast, in Africa and in Central and South America.

Now as he flew back to Cologne, he was confronted with it again; but this time communism would be on the receiving end, trying to cope, on its own turf, with the very techniques of subversion and mass conspiracy it had used against others elsewhere in the world.

And he wondered why he should oppose Fritzsche's assault on the Soviet Union. The simplest thing he could do would be to quietly pack his bags, round up Brewer and head back to London to watch the headlines for the inner convulsions of the Soviet Union.

It was enormously tempting. Even more tempting was the idea of knocking on Fritzsche's door and volunteering.

11

The Banker called Kaethe Dorten late in the evening from the airport. He'd just arrived from Paris. 'I am ashamed to report,' he said, 'we lost Thomas at the Place de la Concorde. We found him again but he had a meeting with someone in the meantime.'

'Where is he now?'

'He's back in the Central.'

So he'd returned. That beset her with different emotions. Dread filled her heart, for Fritzsche was quite capable of trying to kill Thomas again. Also she felt a twinge of fear that Thomas might have learned something about the cabal during his two days' absence. But the strongest emotion was happiness. She had been sure he had gone for good. And now, he was near her again. She almost hummed – until the old weight of despair pressed down once more. The affair was over. She made herself say it aloud. 'Over.'

She realized she needed expert guidance. So with considerable reluctance, she went to see her father.

She knew she'd made a mistake the moment she walked in the door. His appearance was shocking. He had failed visibly since her last visit. He lay in his library under two blankets with a hot fire blazing in the fireplace. The room was very warm.

It was a chilly day with great chunks of cloud blowing across a late-autumn sky. On the library rug, sunlight and cloudshadow alternated like semaphor signals.

The only vitality she saw was in the intensity of his eyes. He smiled wanly at her and raised himself a little higher on the chaise.

'Well, I do have a daughter after all. Your reports have been masterpieces of brevity.'

'I'm sorry,' she said. 'I didn't want to bother you with them.'

'But now he's got you on the run.'

'How did you know?'

'I know Thomas.' He struggled up a little higher. 'Still no word from the Chinese?'

'No.'

'That's very bad. It's five days now.'

She began her report. He was delighted when she told him how her series of moves had outsmarted Thomas.

'Clever girl,' he said.

'Lucky girl,' she answered.

But when she tried to edit the more unpleasant details, especially concerning Fritzsche, he seemed to read her mind, and guessed what she omitted.

'Fritzsche's been playing cavalry again,' he guessed. 'Tell me all of it.'

She did, reluctantly, and as she expected, rage placed two purple spots on his face. 'He should be shot.'

She stood up. 'That's enough. I've told you too much and it's not the reason I've come. I have a problem.'

'I want to hear the rest.'

'We'll have some tea first.'

He sighed. Impotent frustration: he couldn't flog another mile out of his exhausted body.

They drank tea in the library with Kaethe's mother and chatted about the weather and the coming winter. Her mother wanted to take Dorten to Italy. Dorten stared out of the library window, his tea grown cold at his elbow. After a while the purple spots on his cheeks subsided.

'I will hear the rest now,' he said. 'We'll talk about Fritzsche another time. That heedless blitzskreiger.'

When her mother had carried the tea things away, Kaethe sat again beside his chaise and told him about Thomas's absence and about his later trip to Paris.

He smiled. 'You outfoxed him and got overconfident. I

warned you that he was clever. Ahhhh! If only I were well. I would love a match with Thomas.' He sat and stared at his fire for a while.

'Well,' he said after a long silence. 'If I were Thomas and I was bricked by a clever adversary like you, what would I do? I'd probably look elsewhere for information. Maybe I would try to peek in the Russian files. He went to a lot of trouble to hide his destination from you. Try to get a copy of his hotel phone bill and also try to check out the Excalibur phone in London. He might have called there from wherever he went. Kolb can do that job for you.'

'Who's Kolb?'

Her father was astonished. 'Kolb,' he said again. 'Kolb. He's one of the four people I sent you.'

'Oh, that's his name.'

'What do you call him?'

'Nothing. I identify them by labels. I call one the Banker.'

For the first time that day, he laughed outright.

She laughed too. 'I call the other the pallbearer, the third one the thief and the woman the housewife.'

At last his laughter died and he became thoughtful again. 'If he went peeking into Russian files, he probably went to Dudorov's offices in Amsterdam. I doubt if he found anything, but you might check and see if any Russians defected lately. The trip to Paris is more difficult. That might be connected with the Russians too. But then Parker had so many sources of information. Tell Kolb to get a copy of Parker's phone bills for the last two months or so. Let's see who he was talking to in Paris.'

'Do you think Thomas had checked into them?' she asked.

'The worst mistake you can make is to underestimate him.'

He seemed to grow thinner and weaker and colder. He drew the blankets up around his throat and seemed to wind down like a child's toy. 'I think I'll sleep now,' he said and in a moment was deep in slumber.

She sat in the kitchen with her mother for a few minutes, watching the maid preparing food. She regretted having disturbed her father – his rage over Fritzsche had weakened him visibly – and she wondered if this Bismarck conspiracy was worth it after all. They were setting a forest fire that none of them could extinguish.

When she crept back into the library to get her purse, her father opened one eye. 'If Thomas feels the need to, he will kill without hesitation.'

Then his eye shut.

That night back in Cologne, Thomas and Brewer held a quick conference in Thomas's room. Three times they had seen Fritzsche with Gustav Behring. Before going to Paris, Thomas had put Brewer on to Behring.

Now Brewer was giving his report. 'Mark him down as a possibility,' he said. 'Behring, it turns out, is one of the key men in the Bismarck Club. Right up there with Fritzsche.'

Thomas sat on his hotel bed, listening, still remembering the sad, silly picture of Anton Boxx in the brassy blond wig.

'Behring's a banker,' Brewer pressed on. 'Controls a lot of banking power. He's also politically active, a can-do type that brings people to the negotiating table. And he's very, very close to Fritzsche.'

'See what he does,' Thomas said. 'Tag along for a day or two.'

Brewer left.

Thomas still wondered half seriously why he should interfere with a plan to destroy Russia. A few minutes later, he left to go get the twenty-four-hour tape from Tatzie's apartment.

Manfred Fritzsche knew he looked terrible. His wife had told him so. Behring had told him so. His secretary cast sidelong glances after him, filled with alarm. For the first time, his chauffeur of twenty years had taken his elbow to help him into his car.

He was being torn apart. First of all, there was no word from Fox. He had placed four or five phone calls to the contact in the last two days and there was as yet no reply.

Both he and Behring agreed, for a change. They both felt that the silence was ominous. After all, all the cabal was asking for at this point was a nod of interest. No commitment.

Second was Tatzie. Last was Tatzie. The end was Tatzie. Fritzsche had barely slept five minutes in the last two nights and his sleeping pattern before that had been fitful and intermittent. He'd barely eaten anything in a week.

There was only one term to describe his condition. He was grief-stricken. He'd lost his Tatzie. For the last two days he hadn't gone to see her, nor had he called her. And just an hour ago, she'd called him on the private line. It was to be used, he'd instructed her, only for emergencies.

Her voice sounded so childlike and innocent and – yes – lonely, he nearly wept. 'Please,' she said. 'I miss you so much. It's very quiet here. Come. Tonight?'

'Yes.' His voice was hoarse with emotion. 'Tonight. I shall be there.'

He arrived at seven. With champagne. She was as joyous as a puppy. She couldn't do enough for him.

'How did your meeting go the other night?' she asked.

'Excellent. It was a great success.' He took up one of the bottles of champagne. 'In fact, we are going to toast a victory.'

'Then let's go eat,' she said. 'I'm starved.'

She ran to get two glasses.

Thomas entered the empty apartment next to Tatzie's before checking the tape and peered through the peepholes. They were in the living room, fussing over a champagne bottle. She was laughing and holding a flop hat with

291

ribbons to the crown of her head, pointing with the free hand and laughing. It was like watching a silent film.

Fritzsche looked terrible. He had purple patches under his eyes and his whole face had an apoplectic hue. He looked like a dying man. The girl by contrast was lovely. It was only Thomas's second good look at her and he was struck anew by her beauty. It wasn't beauty alone. It was the childish innocence that blended so wickedly with her mature femininity. She brought out the love of corruption in a man.

At last, silently, the cork shot off and, also silently, they laughed as she held a glass to catch some of the foaming contents. Bacchus and a wood nymph celebrating the new wine.

Thomas left the apartment and went down the hall to the tape deck. He plugged in his pocket hearing piece and listened. She was shrieking with laughter. 'Wait!' she cried. 'I'll get another glass. You cracked it.'

Thomas disconnected the old tape and pushed the rewind button.

'Here,' her voice said. 'Ah. One for you. Now. *Prosit*.'

She giggled. 'Bubbly. Makes my nose itch. More. Ohhhhhhhh.'

The tape was rewound and he removed it. They would probably go out shortly. He decided to check the tape twice a day now. Fritzsche had to make another move soon. But in his ear came the sound of weeping. Deep racking sobs. Terrible sobs.

Thomas slipped the tape into his pocket, then went down the hall to the empty apartment. He fumbled with the lock picks. 'Damn.' He got it open finally and stepped up to the peephole and fitted the eyepiece to it. The front door was just closing. A small table was upset. The champagne bottle was tipped over and had made a broad stain on the rug. The glasses had fallen on the rug and the flop hat was upside down on an upholstered chair. They were both gone. They must have gone to dinner. Maybe he was wrong. They weren't sobs he'd heard; they were giggles.

But he didn't believe it. He hurried out of the apartment and down the hall.

He rang for both the passenger elevator and the freight elevator. The passenger elevator arrived first. But it was a mistake to have taken it. It stopped at the fourth floor to pick up a passenger; and at the third, a man wheeled on a woman in a wheelchair, a slow process.

Down in the lobby, Thomas hastened to the street. He glanced up and down the street and got a glimpse of the taillight of the limousine. It went around a corner like a ruby and disappeared.

He ran for his car and drove after the limousine with squealing tires.

'Crazy!' someone shouted at him from the sidewalk.

He guessed that the limousine had gone back to the Cologne motorway and hurried toward it. When he reached it, he saw the limousine, driving south toward Bonn. Thomas drove up behind it and peered through the back window. He could see the chauffeur's capped head and after a moment he located Fritzsche's bowed head in the back. But the girl was not in view.

Thomas pulled abreast of the vehicle. The chauffeur was driving in a stiff manner and casting glances over his shoulder at Fritzsche. His figure was in shadow. He seemed to be sitting with his arms folded, staring pensively ahead at the road. The chauffeur hardly noticed Thomas.

Dropping back about a quarter of a mile, Thomas followed them. It was a long ride. The chauffeur drove erratically, fast in bursts, then long periods of crawling. The car turned off the motorway and entered a secondary road and followed it for quite a distance. It turned again on to an old country road, then slowed. They were driving along the edge of an estate. A long high wrought-iron picket fence was set well back from the road. With a flashing turn signal the limousine passed through high old wrought-iron gates and proceeded along a roadway into the estate.

Thomas pulled off on to the shoulder and got out. He hurried after the car on foot. It was a cool and starry night but Thomas barely glanced up through the bare branches of the trees. Ahead of him, starkly, in the dark, were the outlines of ancient hemlocks. The limousine's taillights had gone through them down the drive and disappeared. He hurried after it.

At length he saw the house – a mansion almost concealed behind the towering hemlocks and shrubs. The building seemed wan and distant – only a few lights were on – and gave the feeling of life at low ebb. It loomed larger as he approached but there was no car in front of it. He hurried along the road past the house. There was no car in the back.

He continued along the road behind the house. The grounds were extensive and probably noteworthy in daylight. There seemed to be an extraordinary number and variety of growths. He continued for a considerable distance and began to suspect that he had overshot the mark. The chauffeur must have parked in a garage. He halted and looked back at the distant house.

He heard a noise. It sounded fearfully familiar. He hurried down the road again, toward it. He passed a thick stand of evergreen shrubs and there saw the limousine. And beyond it through the trees the glow of a lantern. He saw Fritzsche's bowed form, sitting, it seemed, on the ground. When he got closer, Thomas saw that he was sitting on the edge of a large hole in the ground. It was a gravesite that must have been dug sometime earlier. The chauffeur was in the grave itself, straightening a wall with his shovel.

Beside Fritzsche was something wrapped in a dark-gray blanket. A moment later, the chauffeur scrambled out of the pit and stood up. He stood over the blanket while Fritzsche pulled it back. He lifted up Tatzie to a sitting position and held her in his arms. Thomas heard wretching sobs again, grief-stricken, inconsolable.

The chauffeur took the body and carefully wrapped it in the blanket to step down into the grave. Just before he stepped, Tatzie's left hand waved out from the blanket as though in farewell. A ruby ring glinted in the lantern light.

It was her favorite, favored over many pieces that cost far more. It was the first thing he had given her.

Fritzsche directed the arrangement of the body, then filled the air with great cries as the chauffeur filled the grave with a shovel. Fritzsche rolled on the edge of the grave and pulled his hair.

Thomas drove back to Cologne at a crawl. After all the years of seeing death, whole villages in Vietnam, Vietcong mass executions done as casually as shooting beer bottles, even after the body count of young boys in Galápagos, he should have been inured to it. But there was an unspeakable horror to this murder – of a vivacious, and trusting girl in the middle of a musical laugh. No doubt Fritzsche had used cyanide in the champagne. She died in seconds.

And Thomas felt he knew why she was murdered. That night they had followed Fritzsche to the restaurant – the eight o'clock meeting that he never showed up for. That was a trap. The old fool had decided she was the traitor without even checking for taps. While he was killing her the taps were in place a few feet away from him, recording the entire act.

The reports on Fritzsche were all too accurate. A bull in a china shop. A heedless plunger, on the move before he had all the facts.

And those tears. The great wracking sobs. Fritzsche had killed the thing he loved and then wept. The man could no longer tell right from wrong. Nothing must get in the way of what he wants, when he wants it, not even love.

The sobbing would always ring in Thomas's ears. And for the rest of his days he would react with a smoldering rage.

Inside the mind of every Fritzsche, away in a bottom drawer of that mind, was a pair of highly burnished jackboots.

And it was the same old game whatever the names. The communists, the Fascists, the Vietcong, Vietnam, the Sindicalistas, the Benevolent Protector, the rightists, the leftists, the Purple Gang of Detroit, the Cologne cabal. Him versus him. Two power hungry forces going at each other, leaving uncounted bodies of the weak and innocent in their wake, the bystanders unable to get out of the way.

Thomas stopped at the American Bar of the Hotel Central for a double brandy. He gazed around at the faces in the bar. He knew most of them – arms dealers after a busy day in the dismal trade. He looked out at the lobby. It, too, was packed and very active. As the crowd moved to and fro past the glass doors of the bar, it all resembled an aquarium of feeding fish.

Abruptly he was sick of them – this army of relentless grief merchants covering the earth, stirring up strife and fear, feeding the lust for weapons, all for the sale, the quota, the bonus.

Machines spewing guns like sausage links, day and night, each destined for a dirty, hate-filled hand with broken fingernails.

But it was Manfred Fritzsche, the world's biggest arms dealer, that he hated most of all.

Thomas did the one thing that Kaethe feared he would do. He sent Brewer out to check into her background. Somewhere in there would be the explanation for their breakup. His years of business experience had long ago taught Thomas the futility of speculating without at least a few facts, so he refused to make a single guess while he tried to wait with patience for Brewer's report.

With the narrow suspicion of the cynical, Brewer began with Kaethe's love life, but that led him in circles. She'd dated many men, most for business reasons, others for their interest in flying or car racing. There was no obvious romantic attachment, and Brewer knew that to check out all the men she associated with would take months. So he switched tactics.

He next did a thorough profile of her business. It was sound and very profitable. He came away impressed with her business ability and net worth but he'd learned nothing personal. He looked next into her education, and her flying and car racing background. He found out a great deal about her uncle, who was a famous aerialist. Still nothing. She had no secrets. The only blanks in her background were her parents' identities and histories.

So Brewer did the obvious and most time-consuming thing. He followed her. He let the business hours take care of themselves and tailed her at the end of her office day. But often her night hours were spent with clients. She kept her car, a two-seat Mercedes, in the large public garage around the corner from her office. Brewer would wait in the lobby of her building. If she went out the front door and hailed a cab, he would hail one too. If she went out the rear door to the garage, he had his car parked by the exit, ready to follow her. But his problem didn't end there.

She was a very nimble professional driver who had spent her adult life driving in the narrow streets and alleys of the old section of Cologne, and several times Brewer lost her. Then patiently he would wait for the next time. One night he followed her into the country under a beautiful chilly sunset.

That evening he hunted Thomas up in a café and took him out on the street. 'For Christ's sake, Tommy,' he said. 'Her father is Otto Dorten.'

Thomas stared at him. Otto Dorten. It was clear then: he was Kaethe Dorten's assignment. She was probably the one who was manipulating him from behind the scenes. She was his adversary whose job was to fake him out. Even her love was fake.

Without a word to Brewer he returned to the café.

Thomas had a serious problem now.

With the death of Tatzie, the wall taps in the apartment were useless: he now had no source of information at all. Their surveillance of Fritzsche was fruitless: he was dispirited, lackluster, leaving the office early to go home. He rode one of his horses in aimless wandering over his estate and the horse trails beyond. But he never rode near the grave of Tatzie.

Behring was morose. He stayed often by himself and drank in solitude.

'They're waiting for something,' Thomas said. 'Something's up.'

'How do we find out what it is?' Brewer asked.

They sat in the American Bar of their hotel and Thomas sifted through the phone messages from the hotel desk. Gorman had called twice. There was no need to guess what that was about: When in hell are you coming back to London?

'How about some more taps?' Brewer suggested.

'We may have to. What a job that'll be – his home phone, his car, his office, and that'll be the biggest trick of all, that office building. There must be something better.'

Thomas sat thinking about Fritzsche. They didn't have the time they needed to do a thorough job of tapping all of Fritzsche's communications facilities. 'You know the old Roman tale called "Belling the Cat"?'

'No. What about it?'

'That's how we're going to find out what's going on.'

The haberdasher two blocks from the hotel had exactly what Thomas needed in stock. In slanting afternoon sunlight, he lifted the top off a small jeweler's box.

'I have them in tie stick pins or in lapel pins.'

'Lapel pins,' Thomas said. 'Six of them.'

'You'll pardon me, sir, for observing that you are very young for such a military decoration.'

'They're for my granduncle. In Prague.'

'Ah yes. Prague.' The haberdasher set the case on the counter and selected six lapel pins. 'You'll pardon me again, sir, but your granduncle should exercise great care wearing this in Prague. The communist authorities –'

'They're for his funeral.'

'Alas. He must have been a great war hero.'

The rosettes, all six of them, were identical to the military rosette that Fritzsche unfailingly wore in his lapel. As

Thomas carried them back to his hotel room, he mentally underlined the word 'unfailingly.'

Brewer was busy with the portable snooping unit. 'Works up to two hundred yards,' he said, removing the earpiece. 'Not bad.'

Thomas sat down at the table and took out the rosettes. Then he picked up the remote, cordless microphone. It was the size and shape of a needle with a small round head like a bead set at a right angle to the shaft.

Thomas used a pair of pincers to remove the rosette from its pin, then replaced it on the shaft of the cordless microphone. The beadlike head was buried in the ribbon button, making the shaft look like an ordinary straight pin.

He fitted it to his lapel and examined himself in the mirror. It looked exactly like Fritzsche's. The microminiature speaker in it was so powerful it would pick up everything said within six feet of it and broadcast it nearly an eighth of a mile to the remote receiving unit that Brewer had. And that unit, complete with a miniature tape deck that could record up to one hour, was no larger than a paperback book.

Brewer sat watching Thomas fingering the rosette.

'Now all we have to do is get it into Fritzsche's lapel,' he said.

Thomas nodded. 'That's known as belling the cat.'

They made a list that night, wandering from bar to bar and nightspot to nightspot.

'His barber,' Brewer said. 'Fritzsche must take his jacket off when he gets his hair cut.'

Thomas noted it on the back on an envelope. 'More than likely he gets his hair cut in his office.'

'How about his bedroom?'

'Yes. I've thought of that. It's too risky. He's probably got every burglar alarm in the world in that house. And we don't need a breaking-and-entering rap. Save that as a desperation measure. There has to be a better way.'

'How about his dentist? He probably takes his coat off

there.' It had seemed like such a small problem at first. In his mind Thomas went through Fritzsche's day, trying to find those moments when the man parted from his suit jacket long enough for them to substitute rosettes. Were she still alive, Tatzie's apartment might have been a good place, but he remembered his misadventure with the drainpipe climbing from the room.

'How about Danny the Dip?' he asked Brewer.

Brewer nodded and smirked. 'I don't know if he's ever picked a lapel before.'

'He picked impossible pockets in his time. He even smouched the watch from the wrist of a policeman who was arresting him.'

They finished their drinks and went on to the next place. It seemed absurd to Thomas that monumental affairs affecting the fates of great nations could be shaped by such trivia as two men planning the switching of a boutonniere on another man's lapel. It was in the category of the wanted horseshoe nail.

The arms auction was over. The gun hustlers and their clients had all wandered off to the next watering station, the next sale, the next customer. A new convention was in town, with different products, different bunting, different sales projections, but in the bars the new group looked like the previous group, the same haircuts, the same wives, the same drinks, the same food, the same hotel beds, and they wore the same badges. 'Hello there. My name is–'

The badges gave Thomas an idea and by midnight he had solved the problem. 'I'll fix the old bastard,' he said. 'I know just what to do.'

'I'm all ears,' Brewer answered.

The next morning, Thomas sent Brewer off to a job printer with the drawing he'd made, while he himself went off shopping for two hats. He went from store to store asking for it but it was the wrong time of the year.

He was sent at last to a milliner. She did a brisk business with the theatrical crowd, making up special items for new plays. She also had a vast storehouse of old headgear, including stage helmets.

When Thomas told her what he wanted she nodded immediately. 'Very easy,' she said.

She got two shells, as she called them, then proceeded to make them up according to Thomas's specifications. He walked out with them in a large hatbox. He and Brewer then spent an hour going through books of photographs in an acting and modeling agency.

They found what they were looking for; she was about twenty-five actually, but she had acting experience and most important she was available that afternoon. At the same time they also selected an older woman to work with her.

The blond young woman arrived after four with her hair done as Thomas described it to the agency operator. The other woman arrived minutes later. The operator was skeptical but the two models were willing. In fact they regarded it as a lark and off they went with Thomas and Brewer.

Shortly before five, they arrived at Fritzsche's office building. Thomas got the younger woman to walk with him while he explained the strategy to her. He didn't want the older woman to hear it.

'What I want you to do is go up to this man when he comes out of that office building,' he told her. 'That's his limousine and that's his chauffeur. A very distinguished man in appearance. I want you to say "Hospital Day" and pin this Hospital Day badge on his lapel and let him put some money in this contribution can. So far so good?'

'Yes. Is there more?' She was quick and shrewd.

'He'll be wearing a rosette like this. Switch them.'

'Oh.'

She thought about that, pacing by his side. She waited to hear the jingle of more coin and Thomas jingled it.

'There's more in it for you,' he said.

'Oh. How interesting.'

He held up a packet of money and she took it. 'Count it.'

She riffled it quickly.

'If you succeed, I'll give you the same amount afterward.'

She nodded happily at him. 'Done,' she said.

He led her back to the car.

'If you have any other requirements,' she said to him, 'I'm always available.'

He smiled at her and she smiled at him. They understood each other perfectly.

Thomas got the two hats out of the box – flop-brimmed straw hats with trailing blue ribbons and a round crown. When the younger woman put on hers, the resemblance to Tatzie was almost too close. They got out of the car, carrying a supply of lapel badges in shallow baskets and holding a can for money.

They strolled up and down near the Fritzsche building, soliciting contributions for Hospital Day. A few minutes later the chauffeur got out of the limousine and waited by the front door. The young woman got into position.

When she saw Fritzsche she walked up to him extending her tin can.

Fritzsche's reaction was almost violent. He drew up his hands and leaned back and staggered.

The woman waited while he recovered his composure, then stepped up to him and pinned on a badge. He stared at her unable to move. He made no effort to resist the badge. She pinned it on the lapel to the side of his rosette and smiled at him, then held up the contribution can.

Fritzsche stared at her hat and at her face. At last he understood what she wanted and reached into his breast pocket and brought forth his wallet. He extracted a number of bills.

She refused. Too much, she protested. The chauffeur had moved behind Fritzsche now and was holding a hand on his back. Fritzsche tried to put the money in the slot in the can but his hand was trembling violently and she put her hand over his and guided it to the slot. Her touch seemed to overwhelm him. Her smile made him gasp. Speechless, he patted her hand as though she were a child. Then hesitantly, he touched her hair.

Fritzsche turned away and shuffled like an old man toward his car. The chauffeur was as upset as Fritzsche, and he glanced several times at the young woman and at the other woman nearby. He put Fritzsche into the limousine carefully and drove off in haste.

The two women put their hats in the car along with the baskets and the cans. Thomas handed them each an envelope and thanked them. The young woman palmed the rosette to him. 'No problem,' she said. 'Call me.'

Brewer quickly drove after Fritzsche's car. The chauffeur followed his usual route and it took Brewer only a few minutes to find the car.

'He damned near came apart,' Brewer said.

'I almost went too far,' Thomas rejoined. 'He's a mess.'

Brewer glanced at the Snooper receiving unit and at the earphones. 'You hear anything?'

'Yes. Weeping.'

Otto Dorten actually seemed a little stronger but Kaethe could see that her father would never fully recover his health. He seemed to know it, too, and had turned to his old pastime of reading. Maybe he didn't look better; he looked resigned.

She sat beside him in his den and reluctantly reported what she'd learned about Thomas. 'You're a very smart man,' she said to her father.

'I take after my daughter. What did you find out?'

'There was a defection in Amsterdam. A Russian travel agent. He was chased and nearly killed. The Dutch Government has lodged a strong protest with the Kremlin. And Dudorov has been called back to Russia for consultation.'

303

'That's the end of him. He should have retired. He's no more fit than I am. What else?'

'Parker's phone bill. It's difficult to discover what is significant. He used the phone a great deal; his phone bills were enormous and he called certain numbers in different cities every day, sometimes two or three times a day. There was one number in Paris he called twenty-six times in the last month. It was to the office of a man named Anton Boxx. He's an export/import world trade specialist with the Rosetree Bank.'

'He knows.'

'Who? Boxx?'

'No. Thomas.' He smiled weakly at her. 'The cunning bastard.'

'I don't understand.'

'Parker was undoubtedly matching up manifest numbers, cargo shipments. Through a computer. It's easy. And Thomas tracked it down.'

'There's more. Boxx has been transferred to the New York office. He practically resigned. Apparently they value him and gave him an offer.'

Dorten nodded. 'I'm right.'

'Guess who he went to school with?'

'Thomas? What else? Well—' Dorten sighed. 'They know about our little smuggling operation. I can't imagine what they learned in Amsterdam. Dudorov never paid that much attention to us. He regarded the club with a certain amount of scorn.'

Dorten shifted in his chaise and thought for a while. 'Well – we have to assume that Thomas knows some things and doesn't know others. That Fritzsche's ruined us. Kaethe, we can't play games anymore. An ordinary agent would have been completely stopped by your moves and go on to some other assignment. This Thomas is a bull. He won't stop until he's learned everything. We have to kill him.'

She knew, without looking in the mirror, that her face

304

had become pale. Her fingertips had become cold. The hot room now seemed chilly.

'People like Thomas are exceedingly difficult to kill. Ask Fritzsche.' He almost chuckled.

She found her tongue, glued to her mouth top, and moistened her lips. 'How?' she said almost inaudibly.

'What?'

'How are we to kill Thomas?'

'Let Dr Hesse do it. Before the next Fox meeting.'

'Hesse?'

'Yes. We discussed it once. He'll know what to do. See him.'

12

They took turns following Fritzsche.

He went to bed early, often at nine. He slept badly and frequently read through the night after a nap of an hour or two. But he conducted no business and made no phone calls at night so Thomas and Brewer concentrated on the daylight hours.

At breakfast, Fritzsche received a phone call.

The caller's voice carried clearly over the lapel microphone. 'Meet me,' he said.

Thomas was in the car when Fritzsche's limousine rolled through the ornate iron gates and turned toward Cologne. It followed the usual route for about three miles, then turned and drove along the Rhine River into a stand of trees.

Thomas parked on the other side of the road and checked the tuning on the Snooper. Fritzsche got out of his car and walked off through the trees. It was a breezy cold overcast day and Fritzsche wore heavy gloves and a hat with his overcoat. He turned up the collar as he walked.

'Good morning,' Thomas heard him say.

Another voice answered, 'Mr Fox is ready to meet with you.'

'It's been a long time. Six days. Why didn't you answer my phone messages? My associates were beginning to despair.'

'Well, these things can't be helped. Tomorrow night. Same time, the same arrangements.'

Thomas decided to follow the other car. Fritzsche's limousine came out from the trees first and turned again toward Cologne. A few moments later, the other car emerged. It was clearly a rental vehicle, and after a few miles it was obvious he was driving directly toward the Bonn/Cologne airport.

Thomas was right. The man turned the vehicle in to the rental office and went into the terminal. He took a shuttle flight to Zurich.

When Fritzsche arrived at his office, the first person he called was Dr Hesse.

'I have news,' he said. 'Can we meet for lunch?'

'Of course,' Dr Hesse agreed. 'Did they contact you?'

'Yes.'

The next person Fritzsche called was Kaethe Dorten. 'I have news,' he said. 'Can you meet for lunch?'

'Yes. Where?'

'Why – at the club, of course.'

Before noon Fritzsche appeared at street level and got into his limousine, which went directly to the club.

The three of them had a drink at the club bar, which was crowded with noontime diners. The air was filled with the convivial self-praising voices of the privileged and with the blithe tinkle of glasses.

By contrast, Kaethe Dorten's voice was low, careful and all business. Dr Hesse, conversely, liked food very much and when they were seated at a dining-room table, his

306

resonant lecturer's voice discussed the luncheon menu with the waiter almost caressingly. He ordered soup first – cabbage soup, a club specialty. Fritzsche ordered another drink. Kaethe Dorten ordered nothing.

When Dr Hesse began an elaborate discussion of personality malformations, she interrupted him. 'How are we to accomplish this business tomorrow?' she demanded.

Dr Hesse cleared his throat and spoke in his most didactic tone. 'These phobias are like landmines, my dear. One never knows when one will set one off. They happen most often from childhood experiences. But they can happen in adult life, too, and in his case this is exactly what happened. A mortar shell buried him alive in Vietnam and left Thomas with claustrophobia. And through it we can destroy him.' He'd heavily buttered a piece of roll and put it into his mouth. He chewed hugely, then took a mouthful of wine as a chaser.

'Often one phobia can trigger others,' his voice went on with clinical precision. 'Fear of heights or fear of flying, for example, can engender agoraphobia, fear of being outside, in the streets, in the marketplace. To avoid heights, the patient avoids the world, and when the patient has two or three phobias, then he is truly in hell. He is pursued by the Furies themselves. Avoiding phobic situations becomes a full-time job and the patient's day-to-day functioning is so severely impaired that he becomes almost incapacitated.'

'What is this all leading to?' Kaethe Dorten impatiently demanded.

'Well, my dear, given a severe enough shock, the patient can become catatonic. He cracks. He has to be institutionalized. I would say one more severe phobic situation could make Colin Thomas crack – a sudden power blackout in a Métro, deep underground, or being locked in the trunk of a car, or becoming trapped in an elevator. He'll come out a giggling idiot.' He chewed the delicious crust of the roll with a champing mouth.

Fritzsche sighed. 'I don't put any store in these games.

I think we need the direct route here. Kill him. I have the people to do the job.'

'You have a bunch of bunglers,' Kaethe said. 'You tried four times to kill him against express orders and you nearly ruined this whole affair. You've made your last mistake. And you've had your last warning.'

There was a long silence. If ever a tone of voice could convey a deadly threat, Kaethe Dorten's voice had. There was no mistaking her meaning.

Fritzsche cleared his throat as the apoplectic hue covered his face. He was stunned. Dr Hesse's silence registered acute embarassment. His eyes avoided Fritzsche's.

'Now, Dr Hesse,' Kaethe went on. 'Is it possible that Thomas would have no reaction whatever to being locked up in a closet or in a dark elevator?'

Dr Hesse blew air through his cheeks thoughtfully. 'No,' he said at last. 'There has been a case or two where the patient overcomes his phobia during a moment of very great stress. The phobia literally burns itself out. But it takes special psychological circumstances that are not present in Thomas's case. I have done a psychograph on him. He will crack. In fact, he must be very careful or he could end up doing himself in. His back pains are a clear, serious warning to him. Just five or ten minutes in a closet. He will crack.'

'What you are proposing is a living death,' she said. 'He becomes permanently institutionalized.'

'Well, not entirely. He could function after a fashion but not in a responsible job. You see, one of the principal casualties of a phobic crisis is the patient's self-confidence. He no longer believes he can cope and he retreats within himself.'

'He may live in society but he won't be worth a pig's whistle,' she insisted. 'Is that it?'

'Yes. I suppose that covers it. Given Thomas's case history, even if his mind doesn't crack, the tension and stress on his back could permanently cripple his spine. In either case he'd never bother the cabal again.'

'Enough,' Fritzsche broke in. 'The key problem is tomorrow night. I need absolute and maximum security when I meet Fox. How will that be handled? Thomas must be dead by then.'

Dr Hesse sighed. 'Otto Dorten was very clear on that, Manfred. He wants Thomas taken care of without drawing a crowd of American agents. Do you realize that in the next day or two, the first phase of our campaign in Russia could be launched? The first convulsion. The Russians will go mad trying to find the outside source for their problems. The last place we want them to look is here, in Germany. And a band of American agents will surely draw Russia's attention, especially with a new replacement for that sick old Dudorov.'

Fritzsche disagreed again. 'Arranging an accident to fool the American agents is a waste of time. Kill him, I say. If Thomas discovers what we're up to it will be far worse than a crowd of American agents bumping into each other chasing false leads to nowhere.'

Dr Hesse said, 'I'll take care of Thomas. Agreed? All I need is three or four of your people.'

'Done,' Fritzsche said. He turned his gaze to Kaethe Dorten. 'Remember, there will be no meeting with Fox until Thomas is safely disposed of. If you fail, I'll cancel the meeting. I must be absolutely assured of this.'

'Of course.' Dr Hesse began to happily consume his soup.

Kaethe Dorten said nothing.

Thomas pulled out the earpiece and stepped from his car. He paced up and down the parking area under the trees and glanced periodically at the clubhouse. Through the large dining-room windows he could see the club members inside, supping up their gourmet meals, toasting each other with their wines.

His whole body trembled with rage. His back locked in a series of crushing cramps. She was participating in a plot to destroy him. And yet the sound of her voice still charmed him. Madness.

Kaethe Dorten was in a turmoil.

The three assignments were simple enough. Fritzsche was to meet Fox for the crucial conference. She was to deliver him to Fox's messengers. And Hesse was to turn Colin Thomas into a living corpse.

She sat on her sofa, asking herself incredibly stupid questions. Did she love Germany more than Thomas? Would Thomas condone killing her if he were a part of the cabal and she were an American agent? Logic said that to save Germany, Thomas must die. Emotion told her the opposite. Logic told her that her personal feelings were insignificant in face of the destiny of millions of her countrymen. Emotion told her she came first. She would have given anything to go on another picnic with him.

Unable to stand the clamor in her head, she left her apartment and got into her car. You could always find an insane driver on the autobahns to challenge to a suicidal race. Invariably he would be very amateurish, more ego than brains, and soon enough you could both be killed.

She drove with abandon. Mad Kaethe Dorten. Up and down the nighttime roadways, in and out of traffic. It was some of the most brilliant driving she'd ever done. She picked up a challenge very soon, a beefy-faced man, an executive in a very expensive car. He had had some lessons somewhere and tried to take her on the inside of a curve. She pinched him and he burned off a lot of rubber from his tires. He came up fast behind her again, cut off by a woman, in a fury, eager to teach her. She anticipated him. This time she was inside. He tried to cut her. But she wouldn't flinch and at the last second he straightened his wheels. Mustn't crumple the new toy. On the next curve she let him get inside. She squeezed him again. He refused to flinch and she drew closer and closer, pushing him closer on the inside. And still he refused to budge. Then at over 100 miles an hour she tapped him, fender edge on fender edge. Just enough to crack an egg, as the drivers say. He panicked and rode his brakes violently. He fishtailed, lost control, and slewed sideways. Only at the last minute, he straightened out. He dropped back and she didn't see him again. He wasn't suicidal. He would never tell a soul what happened.

She had discovered she was no longer suicidal. And she had worked out another foolproof delivery system for Fritzsche. He would have no tail tomorrow night.

At home, Kaethe summoned the four – the banker and the pallbearer and the housewife and the thief. They sat deferentially on her sofas and upholstered chairs on the seat edges, straight-backed, hands in lap, and listened solemnly to her as she outlined her plan, went over the road map and dealt out their parts.

'Make sure the car we use is carefully screened for sound devices that can be followed by direction finders. Any questions?'

They shook their heads in agreement. They understood the plan clearly.

'One last thing. I do not under any circumstances want Mr Fritzsche to know what the plan is. He is a very unreasonable person and will do everything possible to find out.' She studied their faces. 'Tell him at the last second and not a moment sooner. If he insists, refer him to me.'

When they left she sat and stared up at the ceiling. What was she going to do about Thomas?

It was a long night for others.

Otto Dorten sat by his study window for hours and watched the winter stars wester. He was firmly convinced that the Chinese would accept the German offer. Then he would become equally convinced they wouldn't. The thought of rejection filled him with despair: every single day of the last forty years paraded before his mind.

Of all his efforts, he felt the most significant was the smuggling of five printing presses into Russia. They had been carried across the border, thousands of pieces, one at

311

a time, passed from hand to hand over a period of years, and now lay buried, waiting to be assembled and started up.

Dorten believed that the presses were worth a hundred divisions of armed men. The Kremlin might survive the guerrilla war in the streets of Russia but never the truth.

As daylight approached, he thought of the long day of waiting still ahead. They would not know the Chinese decision until late that night. He prayed that his heart would continue to beat until nightfall and even longer – long enough to hear the first reports of convulsions inside Russia. He could die smiling then.

Fritzsche tried to read. He failed.

Grief was gradually eating away his entire body, leaving him a hollow, meaningless man. He tried to read repeatedly, murmuring the words aloud, trying to fill up that awful silence that pursued him. Several times, memory wrung a single word from his lips: Tatzie. And he asked himself each time if the entire plan was worth her life.

By sunup, he had convinced himself anew that nothing was more important than destroying Russia, no, not even Tatzie. Her betrayal was unforgivable. Full of resolve, he rose and went through the stations of his morning toilet, reciting again the errors of the Eastern Front.

He still had many hours before he learned the Chinese decision and that filled him with great weariness. What would they say? Yes or no?

Gustav Behring longed for the new Russian revolution. Even without the Chinese; even if it failed. For in the long run it would bring worldwide changes, and sooner or later, Russia must crack.

He wondered, though, would the collapse of Russia – would German reunification – improve the ordinary lot of people? Would it help him? Would it help the suffering flesh of his desperate wife?

He saw her nude figure cavorting among young Italian

boys with large erect penises, a woodland bacchanal, and for the first time in his marriage he felt pity for her.

What good would reunification do for him or her after all? He drank himself to sleep.

Quist finally found Fritzsche in the men's lavatory of the Bismarck Club.

'I'm here,' Quist said.

Fritzsche nodded as he lathered his hands. 'I have your next assignment. I want Thomas taken care of. Rain or shine, Quist. They think he is going to have a mental breakdown. If you have to, follow him into the insane asylum. I don't care if they lock him in solitary confinement with a straitjacket. You find him and do your job.'

Quist nodded.

'If you miss,' Fritzsche said, rinsing his hands, 'run for your life.'

Fritzsche dried his hands. When he looked around again, Quist was gone.

First, Quist cleaned his pistol. In the converted carriage house at the back of the Bismarck Club in the garage under his apartment, Quist glanced at the different wooden gun cases on the shelf, then took down the Walther P-38. It was his favorite.

At the workbench in the bright sunlight, he stripped the pistol, spread the parts on a rubber mat and put out his trays of gun oil and solvents, his tools and brushes and rags. Then he methodically cleaned all the parts, including the locking block. He examined the loaded-chamber indicator in the slide. Critically and with care, he cleaned the long barrel of the silencer. Then he reassembled the pistol, taking special care to seat the locking block. Finished, he pushed home the eight-round magazine. Then he returned the pistol and the silencer to their plush bed and closed the wooden lid and locked the two brass latches.

Next, he took out a whetstone, poured a teaspoon of gun oil on it and took out his throwing knife from a drawer. He sniffed the leather scabbard, which immediately evoked his childhood.

Quist stood and looked at the old hewn beam that stood upright twelve feet away. His eye found the penny-size red circle. He made a quick whipping motion with his forearm and wrist. The knife tumbled through the air and stabbed into the beam in the center of the red circle. Quist made a few more practice throws with it to loosen his wrist. Each time he hit the circle dead center.

He sat at the bench in the slanting sunlight and drew first one edge of the blade, then the other, across the whetstone. The razor edges whispered on the stone, a peaceful sunlit sound. The light touched his angelic, golden hair and illuminated his guileless blue eyes. As he returned the blade to its scabbard, he said audibly, 'Thomas.'

When Quist emerged from the garage and mounted the wooden stairs to his apartment, he glanced out back and saw her car still there. He shrugged indifferently. She was sitting in his upholstered chair, wearing his dressing robe, a bare leg over the arm. She was smoking a cigarette. Her eyes watched him cross the room.

She still reminded him of a Viking, following her berserker mate into battle with ax and flensing knife, sword, mace and spear. The terror of Europe as far as the boot of Italy. Quist stripped off his shirt, then his trousers and shoes, his shorts and socks. Naked, he commenced his exercises.

He was indifferent to her eyes watching him. Gradually, he fell into the rhythm of his exercises, situps, pushups, chins, stretching exercises, until a faint damp film of perspiration covered his golden skin.

When he was through he lay on the mat facedown, feeling the magic glow of his superbly conditioned body. Her two hands touched his shoulders and firmly kneaded the muscles there. Quist turned on his back and watched her lips kiss his belly. He let her have what she wanted.

*

Brewer sat on a chair in Thomas's room and watched him do his back exercises on the floor.

'We don't know when they're going to hit,' he said. 'They could throw you into a closet or lock you in an elevator or put you in a steamer trunk and mail you to Hong Kong.'

He watched Thomas's back muscles ripple, then watched the arm and shoulder muscles respond. 'You could do all that a lot faster if you used weights,' he said.

Thomas nodded. 'I do. In London.'

'You have to do that for the rest of your life?'

'That's what they say, Charlie.' Thomas sat up. 'Look. They're probably going to try to split us up and then go to work on me. It's now or never for us – last chance before they light the fuse. Whatever happens, forget me and follow Fritzsche.'

'If I don't get to you, you could spend a long time in the dark.' He watched Thomas's face attentively. 'How do you feel about that?'

'Lousy,' Thomas stood up. 'Got a better idea?'

'Can you handle it?'

'I have to.' Thomas went into the shower.

Later they went down to an early supper.

When Brewer had drunk the last of his coffee he glanced at his watch. 'I'll get the car.'

'I'll meet you out front after I get the Snooper,' Thomas replied.

Brewer never really saw his assailants. He was in the car-park building, walking along a dark row of vehicles. A man had his car trunk open, taking out a spare tire. When Brewer got abreast of him two men behind a thick post pushed him and tumbled him. Before Brewer could turn, the trunk lid banged shut, locking him inside. The car doors slammed, and the car sped out of the garage. The trunk was so shallow that Brewer couldn't get enough purchase to kick at the trunk lock. He was helpless.

Thomas got on the elevator with two men who were discussing an automobile accident. He got off at his floor and walked toward his room. When they got off behind him, still engrossed in their conversation, he became alert. They walked along the corridor behind him.

His door swung inward just as he reached out with his key. Two men stood inside his room looking at him. They put their hands out for him as the two other men pushed him from behind.

Thomas entered swinging. He broke one man's nose with his elbow, struck backward with his foot and nearly damaged someone's kneecap, then, bending, he threw another man over his shoulder and onto the bed. He was borne to the floor by the sheer weight of them.

'God!' cried the man with the broken nose. Blood was running through his fingers. The others ignored him. Quickly they bound Thomas's wrists behind him with adhesive tape, then taped his ankles together. One of them seized Thomas by the hair of his head to lift his head up, put a cloth bag under his face and dropped his head. The cloth bag was pulled over Thomas's head. He was in pitch darkness.

He was half lifted, half dragged across the room to the closet and thrown in facedown. In the confined darkness, the panic was rising like a launched rocket, going higher and higher. The man with the broken nose drew his foot back and kicked Thomas's head. Next he was covered with blankets, one on top of the other. They felt uncannily like the smothering moist earth of the mortar burst. He felt he couldn't breathe.

The two sliding doors of the closet were slammed shut and two large suction cups on a steel bar – a tool used for carrying plate glass – were affixed to the doors so Thomas couldn't slide them open. A moment later, the hall door shut and Thomas was alone.

Brewer lay in the darkness of the car trunk and felt the vehicle racing through the streets. The rocking motion lasted some time until abruptly the car slowed and halted.

316

He thought it was stopped for a red light until the lid of the trunk opened and blinding light flooded in. He was seized by the arms, pulled from the trunk and flung across a soft shoulder and down an embankment.

By the time he rolled to the bottom, the car had gone. Brewer was up and scrambling. He reached the top of the embankment again and gazed around. He was on the Bonn motorway, some miles south of Cologne. Too far away to help Thomas.

He ran out on the roadway waving his arms. There was a squealing of brakes and angry faces as cars darted around him. He feinted at the traffic repeatedly, causing drivers to hit their brakes. He was nearly struck and killed several times. Soon he'd caused a snarl and he ran to a halted car and around to the driver's door.

Without a moment's hesitation, he opened the door and seized the driver by the arm and pulled. The man struggled. Brewer pulled harder, placed a foot on the doorsill, gave a mighty tug and the man came sliding out. Brewer flung him aside and jumped in. In a moment he was racing up on the shoulder around the jam-up and on toward Cologne.

With horn blowing and gas pedal to the floor, he soon came upon a knot of slow-moving traffic. He challenged the driver on the inside lane, blowing his horn and flashing his high beams. A tough case. Brewer drove up tight and bumped him, and bumped him harder and then rammed him. The car accelerated and finally moved over. Brewer thundered past a violently shouting face.

The traffic got worse as he got closer to the downtown. The crosswalks were thronged with pedestrians and the traffic lights backed up traffic four ways at each intersection. With one foot on the brake and the other on the gas pedal, blowing his horn, Brewer drove wildly in and out, going around traffic backups, darting through red lights, narrowly missing pedestrians and leaving in his wake shouting, fist-waving people.

He struck a car sidewise, sideswiped another's rear

fender, drove up on a curb briefly, sending pedestrians leaping in every direction, spun around completely at another intersection. The crowds were too great. He left the car and ran toward the hotel.

It was a study in surrealism for Thomas. His conscious, rational mind was trying to calmly coordinate an irrational panic-stricken body through a series of difficult movements. He knew how to free himself but the principal obstacle was his own struggling body.

The cloying weight of the heavy blankets added greatly to his terror and made him try to move too fast. The more he tried to shrug off the blankets the more entangled in them he became and in seconds he was streaming with sweat. There he lay in the pitch darkness of the black cloth bag, smothering and struggling to control an insane animal. Himself.

At all times, he and his body were fighting for control of his muscles. He heard himself grunting and panting and sighing and bumping and blowing violent air.

He began to hallucinate. The mortars went off, shaking the earth, deafening his ears with their concussions, showering him with earth. Just one second ahead was the opening grave of earth, he was sure. And this time there would be no Parker to save him. Burial meant madness.

Sirens went off. Blood ran down walls. Contorted evil faces screamed at him. All the terrors of the dark from childhood swarmed after him. He was so preoccupied with them that only a small corner of his mind kept reason in hand.

A key rattled in his door. Someone entered the room. Thomas remained quiet. Soon the suction cups on the doors sighed and the steel bar came away. It was thrown quickly on the bed, and the sliding closet doors were opened. The blankets were pulled out. And the bag was pulled off his head. And then there was a long pause. Hanging down from a hand was a long knife blade.

The bathroom light went on. Thomas had never seen the

man before. He was tall and very thin, pale as death with flat black lifeless eyes. He moved one step closer to Thomas, saw the taped wrists and ankles, then looked into Thomas's eyes. There was not a glimmer of human feeling or communication in them.

The man squatted and, holding the knife at the ready, pushed Thomas over and thrust with the knife. A moment later, Thomas felt the blade cutting the adhesive tape off his wrists. When he'd sat up, the man was gone. The hotel door shut softly and the key turned the lock again. Kaethe Dorten had sent him a message after all.

He'd gotten to his feet, trying to calm himself, when the door-knob rattled and then was kicked open. Brewer lunged into the room. He nodded at Thomas and glanced at the closet, at the blankets, at the black cloth bag and the suction cups. Then he looked again at Thomas's sweat-soaked head.

'I'll say one thing, Thomas. You've got more guts than I do.'

13

When Quist came down from his living quarters, Max was waiting with the car. A black Mercedes, it had just been washed and waxed.

'Hotel Central,' Quist said. 'We have to improvise, Max. Catch him where we can.'

Max shrugged indifferently.

At the hotel, Max parked and Quist went into the garage. He found Thomas's car. If the session in the closet had done its work, Thomas would be an easy victory. Like shooting a rabbit in a cloth sack.

Quist squatted at the rear of Thomas's car and stretched

a strip of adhesive fluorescent tape the full length of the bumper. He put another strip on the front bumper, another on the rocker panel below the doors on each side. Thomas's car would now be visible for great distances in the dark even with the faintest illumination.

Quist returned to the car and waited in the back seat. Max read a magazine, yawning periodically and scratching himself.

At dusk, Thomas's car came rolling out of the garage.

'There he is,' Quist said. The genie got out of the bottle, he thought. 'On him quick, Max. Don't lose him.'

'How could I lose him?' Max asked. The florescent tape glowed like a neon sign as Thomas's car moved in and out of the night traffic.

Quist slumped low in the back seat, his head barely above the window line, waiting for Thomas to make a move. In an alley, on the road: it was all one to Quist. The excitement of the chase was everything.

At the rendezvous point, Manfred Fritzsche had become difficult. He wanted the exact details of the delivery operation explained to him. Kaethe Dorten and four men stood at the far end of the parking area of the Bismarck Club, listening to Fritzsche's furious harangue. Beside him was the open door of the transport car.

'This is a cat in a bag,' he said to her. 'You want me to just get into this car and leave everything to you. And I won't do it. Not until I know every step of the plan.'

'If I tell you, you'll start to change things. And that's not going to happen. I'm responsible for getting you there. And I assume full responsibility.'

'Then I'm not budging.'

'Bring the unit,' Kaethe Dorten said to her aide.

'What's that?'

'It's an electronic sweep. I want to check to see if you have any bugs on you.'

320

'Me?' Fritzsche raised his chin even higher. 'Are you out of your mind? Me? I refuse.'

Kaethe Dorten sighed. 'It will take a few seconds. We've already swept the car.'

'No! It's the principle of the thing. I refuse.'

'Fine. Just get into the car then.'

'No.'

She smiled at him. Her father's smile. 'It will give me the greatest pleasure of my life if you refuse to get in that car.'

Fritzsche glanced at the group around him. Her people: Dorten's people. And they were all looking at him. He turned his eyes once more to hers. She wasn't bluffing. Abruptly, Fritzsche turned and crouched into the car. He slammed the door.

'What if Thomas got out of that closet?' he asked her.

'It doesn't matter,' she said. 'It was never my plan. We have a foolproof escape route. He'll never follow you.'

'We'll see,' Fritzsche said.

She stepped back. 'Go,' she said to the driver.

Fritzsche's car moved out on the Bonn motorway south from Cologne, then branched off and hurried southeast on a dual highway. There was a median separator wall three feet high. Thomas's car moved into the inside lane next to it and increased its speed.

'Perfect,' Quist said and patted his gun case. 'My favorite accident. A blown tire.' A racing enthusiast, Quist had seen many times what happens when a tire blows at high speed on a curve.

This time, unlike the courier in London, Thomas didn't need to be prodded into high speed. He was following Fritzsche's car about a quarter of a mile behind, and driving well over eighty miles an hour.

'Find me a curve, Max,' Quist said. 'Even a mild curve.'

The speed picked up, touching almost ninety. 'Curve ahead,' Max said.

Quist lay on his back on the back seat and fitted the silencer to the barrel of the pistol. The slightest tilting pressure on a tire at ninety miles an hour and bang! – the car would roll for a week.

'Is he alone, Max?'

'Yes.'

A piece of cake.

'Now,' Max said.

Quist sat up and reached for the window button. Not fifteen feet ahead and in the left lane, Thomas's car was flying. Max had timed it perfectly. They would be just abreast of Thomas's car when they reached the curve. The window rolled down and Quist rested the silencer barrel on the window frame.

Thomas blew his horn three times.

'What the hell was that, Max?' Quist asked.

'I don't know.'

Abruptly, Thomas's trunk lid popped up and Brewer sat up with an over-and-under shotgun at the ready. A jack-in-the-box.

At less than six feet, he drew down on Quist's face, which filled the window like a portrait in a frame. The shotgun made a low boom and Quist's face was literally blown away, leaving the window an empty frame.

Max dropped back, yawed and veered wildly toward the soft shoulder cutting in front of several cars. With Quist dead, he didn't know what to do next.

Brewer pulled the trunk lid shut and crawled through the hole to the back seat and clambered into the front next to Thomas.

'I almost didn't hear the horn blow,' he said to Thomas.

'Next time, I'll use a bugle.' They were driving at ninety-five miles an hour.

'Hang on,' Thomas shouted.

Fritzsche's car was braking sharply and the cars behind were making panic stops.

'Beautiful,' Thomas said. 'Great move.'

Fritzsche's car stopped dead and Fritzsche was thrust out of the rear door into a two-foot break in the medial wall just as an oncoming car on the other side of the wall also braked to a stop. The back door opened and Fritzsche was yanked inside. The car raced away in the opposite direction right by Thomas's car.

Brewer picked up the Snooper and turned the directional loop. 'He's already out of range.'

Thomas drove nearly two miles before he found a turnoff, spun the car and got on the northbound lane. He put the gas pedal to the floor. He said, 'My odd's-maker's soul tells me that that car got off at the very first exit.'

Brewer shook his head at the silent Snooper. 'Nothing,' he said. 'That broad's got some beautiful moves.'

They passed the break in the wall where the transfer was made and watched for the next exit. The Quist car was gone. Thomas slowed the car at the exit and raced up to an intersection.

'You getting any kind of a reading at all, Charlie?'

'Go that way,' Brewer said, pointing left. 'It may be just a false reading.'

Thomas raced left toward the east. It was an old uneven high-crowned road, and the car bounced up and down like a power boat in a bow wave.

'Anything yet?'

'No,' Brewer said.

They drove as fast as the road would permit. Several times the car almost turned over.

'Anything yet, Charlie?'

'Forget it. We lost them.'

Thomas set his jaw and increased his speed.

'Easy, Thomas, easy. Go back.'

'What did you get?'

'Very weak signal.'

Thomas turned and at the intersection went south. Another uneven old road. The car plunged like a rocking horse.

Brewer said, 'I'm getting a signal.'

It got stronger, a faint whistle that increased in volume.

Thomas smiled at Brewer. 'If that old fool had let her find that rosette, we'd be out of the action right now.'

'You hear her voice when she ordered him into the car? That's one tough broad. If she ever finds out that he was bugged, she'll wipe up all of Germany with him.'

They saw the taillights of the car a little more than a half mile ahead and Thomas settled back to a matching speed. He put off their headlights and drove by the weak light of the moon.

'Can you see?' Brewer demanded.

'No.'

Brewer cleared his throat and rode with both hands braced against the dashboard. The cars drove for over two hours due south toward Switzerland.

Following the bobbing red taillights at a distance of a half mile was hypnotic and Thomas and Brewer fell into a long silence.

They were both taken by surprise when the Fritzsche car began to slow down. Thomas slowed, then crawled, then stopped dead in the roadway. Fritzsche's car had pulled off the road and into a grove of trees. Thomas backed up to a gate in a pasture and drove the car in and behind a hedgerow.

With Brewer following, he carried the Snooper and walked hastily along the hedgerow toward Fritzsche's car. One of the men had gotten out and was strolling back and forth beyond an old picnic table. Fritzsche had remained inside.

'Now what?' Brewer whispered.

'They're waiting for someone. When he gets here, we can tape the whole meeting.'

They sat down behind the hedgerow about fifty yards from the grove and waited. Under the clear and starry night, a night damp flowed across the land with a penetrating chill.

At first it was just a twinkling, like a distant star through the trees. Then the headlamps became stronger and it was clear another car was approaching. It moved along the road toward them rapidly, then slowed and swung into the grove.

'Damn!' Thomas said. 'Fritzsche's going to get into that other car.' He got up and in a crouch hurried toward the grove. Fritzsche stood between the cars momentarily, stretched his back and then, bowing, stepped into the other limousine. The door shut behind him.

'I have to get this Snooper onto that car chassis,' Thomas whispered to Brewer.

'Not with that other car still there.'

As if on cue, the other car started up. Its tires crackled on the mast and leaves as it slowly moved, turned and drove back toward Cologne.

Thomas broke into a run. The other car rolled forward a few feet, paused then began to pull out of the grove. Thomas, running in a crouch, came up behind the vehicle and tried to put the Snooper on the chassis frame under the trunk. He stumbled and the car began to roll faster. He wasn't going to make it.

Thomas gathered himself, sprinted and dove with the Snooper held out in his two hands. He slid under the rear of the vehicle and thrust. The Snooper's four magnets seized the chassis. As the car drove off, Thomas saw, between the taillights, a Swiss license plate.

Thomas and Brewer ran back to their car and drove out of the pasture and after the other car.

'I don't see that car ahead of us anywhere,' Brewer said. 'You think they turned off?'

Thomas picked up his speed. The car seemed to have simply disappeared.

Brewer tapped his arm. 'Is that it? They look like taillights.'

Thomas turned sharply at an intersection and raced after the lights.

'That's it,' Brewer said. 'Couldn't miss that long black boat even in the dark.'

Thomas settled back and followed the car at a great distance. Once again he drove without headlights. All he was concerned about now was recovering the Snooper when the meeting ended. He tried to remember pushing the tape-record button. If he didn't the Snooper was useless.

'Who do you think is in that car with Fritzsche?' Brewer asked.

'Guessing doesn't count,' Thomas said.

The limousine drove aimlessly for two hours and then unexpectedly began to slow down and turned into a lane.

'It's an airport,' Thomas said, noting the sign they were passing. The limousine had driven up to a small airplane and Thomas recognized it immediately. He'd flown in it himself. It was Kaethe Dorten's.

Fritzsche got out of the limousine, shook hands with someone inside, said a few more words and turned to walk over to the aircraft. His manner was noncommittal, neither elated nor cast down. Kaethe Dorten spoke to him and his answer was a shrug. He wasn't talking to her. Then he climbed into her plane and waited to be flown back to Cologne, his rosette still in his lapel.

The limousine with the unidentified man in it turned and headed south toward Switzerland.

'Don't lose him now,' Brewer said.

'Wash your mouth out with soap for saying that.'

It was a long ride. The limousine stopped for gasoline once, then drove for hours at very high speed. The road climbed higher and it got colder. The night sky gathered huge clouds and several times snow flurries blew across the headlights.

It was still dark when they crossed the border into Switzerland. The limousine headed straight for Basel.

It led them through the downtown section of Basel, drove into an area of old and large residences, then turned into an archway of a brick building.

Thomas drove slowly around the block and past the house. Two wrought-iron gates were now shut. The limousine was locked in.

'How do we get in?' Brewer asked.

'I don't know.'

It was still more than an hour before dawn. Thomas parked the car around the corner from the house, and he and Brewer walked toward the gates and the car. It felt sharply colder and they pulled up the collars of their coats.

The house was built flush against the sidewalk, a high four-story brick structure.

The limousine was parked in an open court, twenty feet beyond the wrought-iron gates.

Thomas squinted at the brass plate on the wall. 'Sino-European Trading Company,' it read. 'Chinese?' He frowned at it.

Brewer was peering through the gates, trying to see the underside of the limousine.

'Look at the size of the lock on this gate,' he whispered to Thomas. 'We haven't got anything that'll turn it.'

They were stopped: the gates fitted flush into the brick wall above and the iron bars were too thick to cut. The limousine sat there in the dark beyond reach like the torment of Tantalus.

They looked up and to the sides of the building, searching for a way to scale the walls. As Thomas backed across the street to study the building better, a light in a window on the third floor went out; someone had just climbed wearily into bed. Thomas envied him. He walked up and down the sidewalk studying both sides of the building and the rear. A Chinese puzzle with no way in. It was hopeless.

In the middle of the street, he looked down and saw that he was standing on a sewer cover. He crossed to the gate again.

'You see anything under that car?'

'Shadow,' Brewer answered. He squinted. 'An oil spot. A drain maybe. It's hard to see.'

'Is it a drain?'

'Yes. I suppose so.' He turned and looked out on the street.

'Oh, I see. Let's find out.'

He walked back to the car and returned a few moments later with some tools protruding from his coat pocket. 'Damn, it's cold.' Squatting in the middle of the street, he tried to lift the sewer cover with a pair of pliers. He failed. He blew on his hands and tried again with a claw hammer and a screw driver. It moved, lifted and the lip came up. Then it fell back with a loud clang. 'Hot damn!'

They hurried into the shadows of the brick wall and waited a few minutes. After a while, they went back to the sewer cover again. This time, working together, they got the cover up and slid it to one side. Brewer knelt down and put his head into the opening. He sat up.

'There's the main sewer down about six feet, maybe more. And then about three feet down there's a takeoff that runs under the driveway. It must come out by that sewer cover under the car. Probably some kind of storm drain.'

Thomas nodded and hesitated. Then he asked it. 'How big around is it?'

'You mean is it big enough to crawl into?'

'Yes.'

'I don't know,' Brewer said and sat on his haunches. He was gauging the distance the storm pipe ran under the street to the car. 'Must be a thirty-foot run. Maybe more.' He looked up at the houses around them, all dark save for a distant streetlight. The first morning light in the east faintly silhouetted the roof of one house. Dawn was not far.

'We don't have much time,' Thomas said.

Brewer looked once more at the car, then down into the sewer. He pulled off his overcoat and suit coat. He knelt over the sewer opening, put his head in, then his shoulders. Soon only his legs were sticking out. Thomas watched for oncoming cars. One of Brewer's legs went down. It seemed as though he was in. Then the leg came back up and Brewer lifted himself out. His shirt-sleeve fluttered in the predawn air. 'It's my gut. I'm too thick in the waist to bend into it. You follow?'

Thomas nodded. All that free beer. 'Can you see any light at the other end?'

'No. There's about a quarter inch of water at the bottom of it. My back's wet.' He seemed to read Thomas's mind. 'Forget it. You can't handle it. Even if your gut bends enough. I'm not sure that even I could stand it.'

Brewer started to slide the cover back into its rim. He felt Thomas's hand on his arm.

'Wait!' Thomas whispered.

Thomas stood up and walked back to the gate. What he was thinking made his hands tremble. The memory of the hotel closet was still vivid in his memory – that terrifying sensation of going insane. He told himself it was hopeless anyway. There was no assurance that the Snooper was still clinging to the chassis or that the tape had worked. Also the sewer cover under the car might be smaller in circumference. If he couldn't turn around how would he crawl back out?

He looked back at Brewer kneeling patiently by the sewer opening. The thought of going insane inside that pipe three feet under him filled him with unreasoning terror. He decided to accept defeat. For the rest of his life he was going to have to live with his phobia. There would always be a blind side to him – things he would not be able to do because of it. Find another way or – he stepped out into the street. Kneeling he helped Brewer softly slide the cover toward its rim.

'Wait,' Thomas said again.

'Easy, Tommy. Don't try it.'

'I can't let this haunt me for the rest of my life.'

'You can't handle it, I tell you. It's bitter cold down there, just barely enough room to wiggle in. It's wet and blind dark. You could get stuck and there's no way I can

329

get you out. And if you ever panicked you'd go off your chump in there. They'd have to dig up the street to get you out.' He felt Thomas's overcoat land on his knees, then his suit coat, then his shirt. Before he could utter another word, Thomas was squatting and lowering his head into the dark opening.

'Tommy.'

'What?'

'I have to warn you. I have to put the cover in place in case any cars come.'

'I understand.'

'Good luck.'

'So long, Charlie.'

The chill was numbing. The first touch of the metal on his back took his breath. The sour odor of old drainpipes cloyed at his nostrils. He wondered if there were any rats in the pipe. He got his head down to the lateral drainpipe and pushed it in upside down. A wave of panic seized him. He had to fight his hands to stay in position. He waited a moment. There was a soft sighing in the pipe, the air passing over the grate at the other end. It sounded like the breath of a creature waiting for him inside there.

He couldn't do it. He pulled his head out and pulled himself up on the street on his knees. He was panting already and the sweat was running. The memory of the closet was too vivid and he felt he was sharing his body with another creature, a mad terrified creature.

'Enough?' Brewer began to work the sewer cover into position once again. Thomas reached for his shirt. His flesh was crawling with cold.

The cover moved with a faint metallic scraping. Then Thomas put his foot in the way. His shirt fell to the street once more. 'Move it, Charlie.'

Reluctantly, Brewer slid it back out of the way. And Thomas knelt once again and put his head back down into the opening. Upside down he thrust his head into the lateral drainpipe, and felt his shoulders clear the opening. It was a very tight fit. He bent his torso and felt himself bending, then bending some more. The cold was astonishing but his belly cleared, and then his legs, guided by Brewer, swung down. He was inside the pipe on his back.

He started to crawl out again. Then paused and waited. In the confined space, he could feel his heart pounding. He heard the menacing sigh of the wind, smelled the sour odor and now felt the sharply cold water soaking his back and buttocks. It was totally dark in there and almost as confining as a straitjacket. As his fright increased, his panting grew louder. He clenched his jaw and pushed off.

He could just wiggle forward, pushing with his heels and his palms. He wanted, more than anything in the world, to crawl out of that bitterly cold dark pipe. He crawled on. A heavy noise sounded, followed by a clank, and it took him a moment to identify it. Brewer had put the cover in place. Thomas was entombed three feet under the earth and alone.

Now all he had for company was the sound of his panting. He told himself he was mad and tried to recall the mental exercises he had been taught to cope with his fear. He began with the multiplication table. At two times thirteen he couldn't go on. The fears were swarming. The sound of mortars filled the air. And the mad faces began to cluster around his head, screaming.

There was no turning around now. He had to go forward. He had no idea how much progress he was making, how far he had to go. He tried to recite the names of the fifty states, starting with Alabama. He couldn't get past Alaska. He tried to remember happy days as a child with his sister and brother. But he couldn't even remember their faces. He couldn't remember his mother's face or his father's.

'Two times thirteen is twenty-six,' he said aloud. 'Now two times what?'

But it was no good. Panic was seizing him again. The mortars would have their way. They went off, the faces drew closer, the blood ran, the flames exploded and that gaping grave in the embankment waited to receive him again. He shouted in terror.

To escape his panic he commenced a hysterical squirming inside the pipe and rammed his head repeatedly against the pipe. He began to tear the flesh on his back. His knees were cut and bleeding. His hands began to grow sore. In the flooding sweat that streamed through his hair, he felt blood flowing. There were giant rats ahead of him with burning red eyes and flashing teeth, he imagined.

'Alabama,' he cried through clenched teeth. 'Two times what? Two times what?' His head rammed against an obstacle.

He was looking up through a grating at the outline of the limousine bumper. It had grown lighter. And just beyond it, he could see the Snooper.

He lay spent and panting, looking through the grate feeling like a man in his coffin. And now, inexplicably the panic was worse than ever. He wanted to get out, to wake the house and surrender – anything to get out. But he was afraid to reach up and push against the grate. Maybe it was screwed down. Maybe it was too small.

'Two times Alabama.'

He reached up with his left hand and pushed. The grate resisted him. He pushed again. It still didn't move. Absolute fright gave him superhuman strength and he pushed a third time. It lifted straight up. That's when the light went on. Up above him in the drive, an electric light flooded the area. Thomas let the sewer cover settle back into position. But it settled on an angle. It was lapped over the rim. He heard a footstep. A man was standing beside the car. He could see a pajama leg and a slipper tip.

Thomas's panting seemed loud enough to be heard a block away. He tried to silence it, taking longer, quieter breaths. The sweat was freezing cold on his body and the draft was drying it. His teeth were chattering. Surely the idiot standing there could hear him.

He suppressed a cry for help. It was as though someone else were in charge of his voice, someone with a demoniacal will to make him shout out the word 'Help!' He shut his lips and clenched his jaw. The slipper moved. The man walked toward the twin gates. He must have been scanning the street, looking and listening.

The slippers walked back and stood again by the car. He must have been staring at the cockeyed sewer cover. He must see it. A slipper reached out and pressed against the side of the cover. It pushed and the cover clanked into place. Thomas nearly shouted. Abruptly the light went out and a door shut firmly.

Thomas pushed the sewer cover aside and reached up for the Snooper. He got it, and pushed it down into his pants on the lower part of his belly. He sat up and thrust his head out of the sewer line. It was getting lighter by the minute. He would have to hurry.

But he couldn't face it again, that long cold frightening sewer pipe. He crawled out and lay under the automobile, shivering and ready to surrender. He could simply stand up and knock on the door. And that would relieve him of responsibility. He would never have to enter a sewer pipe again. He took a deep breath, turned, rolled and put his head back into the sewer line.

'Two times two,' he told himself. The capitals of the states would be next. But the only capital he could think of was Boston. Arizona came after Alabama.

He couldn't get the sewer cover back in place with his feet and decided to leave it. Now, fatigue added to his other problems. Each time he crawled too vigorously, his bleeding knees complained. His palms shot pain up his arms every time he pressed on them. He had a thumping headache and now his muscles were too tired to push effectively. A fluttering of the muscles of his back warned him. The cold and the fatigue were getting to them and they were on the verge of cramping. He would never be able to sit up and stretch and work them out if that happened. His back could be thrown out. They could paralyse him in the pipe.

The mortars exploded in his head. The screaming faces returned. Sirens sounded. It was so bitterly cold. His teeth chattered uncontrollably. He was in a race now with his incipient back cramps. It seemed twice as long. There was no end. Each thrust should have brought him to the end. But all it brought was more disappointment. He shouted in terror again.

Now it was too late: his back muscles seized. 'Oh my God,' he sighed. He had to sit up. He tried to bend his head upward and found it had more play. He thrust higher. He was free. A moment later the sewer cover slid aside, and he was looking up at the concerned face of Charlie Brewer. In the dawn light, he noted irrelevantly that Brewer needed a shave. And he realized that his phobia was gone.

Brewer reached down and helped pull him out of the pipe. A moment later, with the cover in place, they were stumbling and jogging toward the car while Thomas struggled into his overcoat. All he could think of was turning on the heater in the car.

He'd almost forgotten about the Snooper.

Brewer got the car started, and they drove through the morning streets of Basel while Thomas worked the controls on the Snooper. His bleeding palms were caked with cracked scabs.

He pushed the play button.

'Nothing?' asked Brewer. 'Hot damn.' It hadn't recorded anything.

'Good evening, Mr Fox,' Manfred Fritzsche's voice said abruptly.

Mr Fox replied in an unmistakable Chinese accent.

'Chinese,' Thomas observed. 'Why Chinese?'

Mr Fox served a cup of tea, then immediately addressed himself to the business at hand.

'Mr Fritzsche, my government has had a very difficult time with your proposal and I'm afraid I bear unhappy news for you. We reviewed all the terms of your offer which include...' Mr Fox then recited, very knowledgeably the major features of the German proposal, twenty-six in all.

'It took us much longer than I expected,' Mr Fox said, 'to reach a decision and I must tell you now that we can

334

accept it only if you accelerate your timetable. Your proposal takes too long.'

There was a long sigh, obviously Fritzsche's. His voice asked uncertainly, 'You mean you accept if we increase the timetable? Is that what you are saying?'

'Precisely.'

'You accept? Those are the two most fateful words of the twentieth century, Mr Fox.'

'I think so too, Mr Fritzsche,' Mr Fox replied.

Thomas looked with wonder at Brewer. 'Great God on the Mountain. Germany and China against Russia with a subversive army already inside and in place. Round three.'

They took turns napping and driving. By nine o'clock in the morning they were in a steady downpour again.

'In Germany in the winter all it does is rain,' Brewer said.

'Except when it's snowing.'

They covered the miles with a weary determination, heading for the one telephone that could handle the Snooper tape.

Sheets of driving rain were falling when they reached Bernie Parker's office. It was just as they'd left it days before, still ankle-deep in confetti. It looked all the more dismal in the gray light and falling rain.

Thomas struggled through the confetti to Bernie's office and opened the desk drawer. There was a telephone unit with a separate tape deck. And there he stopped. And considered.

The moment Wynet got the tape transcript, he'd work it up through channels to the Joint Chiefs of Staff. Thomas could picture them all sitting around one of those gargantuan conference tables they were so partial to, all of them awed, listening to the voice of 'Mr Fox' and Manfred Fritzsche. The JCS would then slump back in their chairs and solemnly agree that the President must hear the tape.

And then the voice traffic between Washington and Bonn would reach a din. And no doubt the timid souls on both sides would overrule and Russia would be saved. But if he withheld the tape, a terrible war might break out. Thomas sat down and looked at the sea of confetti. Brewer stood in the doorway waiting.

'What are you going to do?' Brewer asked.

14

There was a festive air in the barroom of the Bismarck Club.

The few, the very few, who knew about the Doomsday Book and about the Chinese response, stood with Fritzsche at the bar, periodically chuckling over silly jokes and patting each other on the shoulders.

'A great day for Germany, Manfred,' Dr Hesse said.

'Too bad Otto isn't here,' Fritzsche replied. He glanced over at Gustav Behring, unconscious at a table, his head on his arms. The three of them had done it.

Fritzsche stared into the clubroom at the jagged line over the fireplace. The Borderline. Soon it would be just a bad memory. Something avenged.

Now – right now in Russia – he knew, they were digging up the printing presses and laboriously, a piece at a time, assembling them. Soon clandestine broadsides in several dozen tongues would be exhorting ethnic groups to dream of freedom and self-destiny, incendiary words, read aloud to men assembling rifles and other weapons by candlelight. The fuse had been lit and the Russian bully would at last be getting his.

The doors would truly blow off the Kremlin. No one wanted to leave. They stayed in the small knot all afternoon, joking, laughing and periodically whispering solemn words to each other.

At five that afternoon, in the still heavy rain, a special messenger in peaked cap and glistening raincoat drove up to the entrance of the Bismarck Club in a van and stood dripping on the black-and-white chessboard tiles of the lobby. He refused to deliver his package to anyone but Fritzsche himself.

'Top secret,' he kept saying. 'For Mr Manfred Fritzsche only. No one else.'

Eventually persistence won. He was led to the bar where Fritzsche stood.

'Well,' Fritzsche said, holding out his hand. The others, in silence, watched the messenger.

The messenger glanced at them and waited.

'We are all friends here,' Fritzsche said. Someone chuckled. Fritzsche held out his hand again.

The messenger still held back.

Fritzsche frowned thoughtfully and stood up. 'Very well. Follow me.' He led the messenger to a small meeting room and sat behind a desk. 'Now,' he said. He gave the messenger a tolerant avuncular smile as a fresh salvo of laughter carried from the bar.

The messenger put a small box on the desk as though it were a gift of inestimable value. It was wrapped in ordinary brown paper and tied with office string. Fritzsche, wondering if it was from Otto Dorten, pulled the string away, opened the wrapping and found a small box inside. He lifted the cover.

Something was wrapped in white tissue paper inside. He opened it. A button-sized microphone tumbled out and rolled on the desk – a wall tap. He frowned at the messenger.

In a second piece of tissue lay a rosette identical to the one on his lapel. The pin was loose and when he examined it he saw it was a miniature microphone. Fritzsche removed the rosette from his lapel and pulled out the pin. It too was a miniature microphone. Everywhere he went, every word he uttered, was broadcast to secret listeners. And in bed he babbled his love into a wall tap.

There was still another small package in the box. He opened the white tissue paper and into his hand fell a small ruby ring. He gasped. It was the ring Tatzie was wearing the night he buried her.

From the bottom of the shallow box, three words in black ink stared up at him. 'She was innocent.'

Fritzsche was too shocked to move. The tiny ring lay in his palm, reminding him how small her hand had been – that lovely hand that had so often held his. The ring stone winked in the light like a smirking coconspirator: you and me.

Innocent: a permanent torture chamber made up of eight letters. He stood up. He had to be alone. 'Innocent,' he murmured as he fled down the hall, past the laughter in the barroom, away from his great victory, pursued into the rain by the word. Innocent.

Kaethe Dorten had left the club before Fritzsche.

She probably should have gone to her parents' home to be with her father. After all, it was the greatest day of his life. But he had become so excited when he heard the news of the Chinese decision that he had to be heavily sedated and put to bed.

She could have stayed at the club and represented her father at the festivities. Gustav Behring had made quite a fuss over her. But he'd seemed unaccountably sad and drank too much, then had passed out with his head on his arms. He would have to be sobered up by club personnel so that he could meet his wife's flight from Italy in the evening.

And she found Manfred Fritzsche's crowing all over the bar too much to bear. He didn't deserve the accolades he was receiving.

At dusk, in the rain she emerged from the Bismarck Club and paused by the entrance, arrested by the sound of the muffled laughter inside. It was different from the usual, civilized chortle. This laughter had something angry in it, the guttural back-of-the-throat laugh one heard at boxing matches and bullfights. It was a tribal, bloodstained laugh of triumph.

She wanted to get away from it yet she wondered what to do with herself. She couldn't simply go home and go to bed. And in the morning she couldn't go back to the publicity business and worry about a campaign to sell a new soup cracker while an awesome future was unfolding in Russian cellars.

Had she really held Colin Thomas in her arms? Had she really felt the walls of her heart ready to burst with the flood of love for him? She wanted to negotiate with someone in charge of the universe – strike a bargain – to get Colin back if for only a week or even one night.

Good dutiful Kaethe, she called herself. For the sake of a mad plot, she had turned away the man she'd been seeking all her life, in every near-crash of her plane, every hairpin turn of her car. She would never meet his like again. Life had sent him to her and she had sent him away. Life never gave second chances.

Ever after Colin's memory would call to her like a sea bird's cry at dawn that woke one with an ache of regret: and the mind would be tossed up on the shores of consciousness for another solitary day. Would she feel a catch in her throat now every time she saw someone who reminded her of him – by the tilt of his head, the set of his shoulders, the mirth in his eye? And what would happen if ever she should see Colin himself – at an unexpected turning of a stair, in an airport or in a dark empty parking lot?

A club member got out of his car, pulled up the collar of his raincoat and strode toward the entrance door beside her. And for a fleeting instant, in shadow, Colin was before her. Hope rose. But the trick always failed in the end and the man was not Colin.

She felt mocked by the terrible laughter behind her as she watched the man step quickly through the rain.

'Colin?'

The man stepped closer.

'Colin, is that you?'

Then he put his arms around her and when she hugged him, she felt the scar on his back through his wet coat.

She didn't want to reason anymore. She'd gotten him back and she was content to stand and hold him and hear her heart pounding in her ears. No other emotion could equal her love.

He took her face in his hands and he kissed her. 'Oh, Colin. How fortunate I am.' Then slowly, she knew. She drew her head back.

'You found him?'

He nodded.

'I mean Fox,' she said.

He nodded again. 'Fox. In Basel.'

She glanced anxiously back toward the noise in the bar. 'What did you do? Colin, tell me.'

He took the reel from his pocket and put it in her hand. She stared at it.

'I transmitted it by phone to Wynet in Washington,' said Thomas. 'The whole thing.'

'Oh. What have you done?'

'I don't know. I truly don't. I just felt that the rest of the world had to be told.'

She didn't know if she was going to weep or clap her hands for the joy of love. 'I don't know either, Colin. I only know that we love each other and that's the most important thing in the world.'

And then he said it. 'I love you, Kaethe.'

General Claude Wynet was struggling through the most difficult hours of his life.

He played the tape of the Fox meeting over and over. He walked around his office, stared for long minutes at the large map of the world on his wall, in particular at the Sino-Russian border and at Germany. It was an awesome idea. If the German plan got rolling, no one on God's earth

340

was going to be able to control it. No one could tell how it would turn out.

But it also presented an unparalleled opportunity. Russian nuclear capability could be destroyed, Russian war plans aborted.

General Wynet poured himself a double scotch, neat, and sat down at his desk. He swallowed a mouthful, then slowly, deliberately, his right index finger reached out and pressed the erase button. In seconds the tape was a blank.

EPILOGUE

Winter was on its way to Central Russia. Already they'd had their first sharp frost and the earth was becoming hard. There was the smell of snow in the night air.

Calloused hands dug a spade into the ground and, in digging, turned up a small lump, wrapped in cracked oilcloth. Inside were five small pieces of cast metal, molded into convoluted shapes with screw holes at either end. They were the end pieces for a paper bail on a vertical printing press. The digger glanced over his shoulders, panting a plume of vapor. He dug now for the next wrapped lump. All about him in various parts of the country, other men were digging in the snow-heavy darkness.

The Doomsday Campaign had begun.

keeper of the children

BY WILLIAM H. HALLAHAN

NOTHING CAN PREPARE YOU FOR
THE NERVE-WRENCHING FRENZY OF . . .
KEEPER OF THE CHILDREN

Alone in a child's bedroom in a suburban Philadelphia home,
Eddie Benson listens for footsteps on the stairs.

The footfall Eddie is waiting for will not be human.
It could be someone's pet cat, or a stuffed teddy bear,
or even a smiling marionette doll.

But whatever it is that comes creeping up the stairs it will
have two horrifying qualities: it will be propelled by a
diabolic force and it will have only one intention – murder.

If Eddie Benson wants his daughter back, he will have to
fight a battle no human has ever fought before. And he
must win. For only the victor can return with his life –
and soul – from the realms of such dark, unnatural evil.

**'Eerie, scary . . . utterly fascinating . . .
this is not going to be what you think'**
Publishers Weekly

HORROR   0 7221 4246 3   £1.00

CLIVE CUSSLER

NIGHT PROBE!

May 1914. Two top diplomats hurry home by sea and rail, each carrying a document of world-changing importance. Then the liner *Empress of Ireland* is sunk in a collision, and the 'Manhattan-Line' express plunges from a shattered bridge – both dragging their VIP passengers to watery oblivion. *Tragic coincidence – or conspiracy*?

Three-quarters of a century later a chance revelation re-opens the question. In the energy-starved, fear-torn 1980s, those long-lost papers could destroy whole nations – and Dirk Pitt, the man who raised the *Titanic*, confronts his biggest challenge yet. Racing against time, against the hired killers of enemies and allies alike – and the horrors of the sea bed – he launches his revolutionary deep-sea search craft in the hunt for the documents. 'Night Probe' has begun . . .

ADVENTURE/THRILLER   0 7221 2746 4   £1.95

A SELECTION OF TITLES FROM SPHERE

FICTION

STILL MISSING	Beth Gutcheon	£1.75 ☐
INHERITORS OF THE STORM	Victor Sondheim	£4.95 ☐
NIGHT PROBE!	Clive Cussler	£1.95 ☐
CHIMERA	Stephen Gallagher	£1.75 ☐
PALOMINO	Danielle Steel	£1.75 ☐

FILM & TV TIE-INS

ON THE LINE	Anthony Minghella	£1.25 ☐
FAME	Leonore Fleischer	£1.50 ☐
FIREFOX	Craig Thomas	£1.75 ☐
GREASE II	William Rotsler	£1.25 ☐
CONAN THE BARBARIAN	L. Sprague de Camp & Lin Carter	£1.25 ☐

NON-FICTION

BEFORE I FORGET	James Mason	£2.25 ☐
TOM PILGRIM: AUTOBIOGRAPHY OF A SPIRITUALIST HEALER	Tom Pilgrim	£1.50 ☐
YOUR CHILD AND THE ZODIAC	Teri King	£1.50 ☐
THE SURVIVOR	Jack Eisner	£1.75 ☐

All Sphere books are available at your local bookshop or newsagent, or can be ordered direct from the publisher. Just tick the titles you want and fill in the form below.

Name _____

Address _____

_____

Write to Sphere Books, Cash Sales Department, P.O. Box 11, Falmouth, Cornwall TR10 9EN

Please enclose a cheque or postal order to the value of the cover price plus:

UK: 45p for the first book, 20p for the second book and 14p for each additional book ordered to a maximum charge of £1.63.

OVERSEAS: 75p for the first book plus 21p per copy for each additional book.

BFPO & EIRE: 45p for the first book, 20p for the second book plus 14p per copy for the next 7 books, thereafter 8p per book.

Sphere Books reserve the right to show new retail prices on covers which may differ from those previously advertised in the text or elsewhere, and to increase postal rates in accordance with the PO.